FLAMES OF LETHE

LETHE CHRONICLES I

LEXIE TALIONIS

CETERIS PARIBUS
PUBLISHING

WARNING

Flames of Lethe is an erotic dark-fantasy / horror romance containing very disturbing situations, non-consent, strong language, and graphic violence.

It is a wild ride, but buried within the fantastical situations and erotic encounters is a deeper discussion and reflection on the nature of consent, on what it means to be good/bad, and who gets to decide to forgive.

Welcome to Hell.

Give me the waters of Lethe that numb the heart, if they exist. I will still not have the power to forget you.

— PUBLIUS OVIDIUS NASO

1

HARD GRAINS of sand bit into the tender flesh of her breasts, the unforgiving bed beneath her demanding she wake. Stifling a groan, she shifted her body and opened one eye. Paused. Both eyes. The briefest breath escaped her lungs as she scrunched her eyes closed once more. Pushing to her knees with a shake of her head, she rubbed her face and tried again.

The night blazed in a chaos of color. Twinkling golden sand stretched out to the horizon, emitting a soft glow that sparkled in random hues. Streaks of blue and violet raced across the sky to lose themselves in the depths of a starless void. And rising up into the violet ocean of night, above the warm blanket of golden light, was a massive moon that filled the sky, swirling in shades of red.

Blood pounded in her veins as her gaze locked on the sphere above her. *What the hell...* A nightmare? It didn't feel like a nightmare. Her breathing felt too real. Her hands buried in the sand. The crisp air hardening her nipples. She shivered, dropping her eyes.

Particles of sand clung to her flesh, illuminating the smooth, pale skin beneath. Firm, full breasts swelled above a slender waist and well rounded thighs, while a small patch of brown curls provided her only cover.

A shiver coursed through her, and she leaned forward, crossing her arms and shaking her head, waiting for her hair to provide cover. Nothing happened.

A sick sensation swirled in her gut as her hand crept up to find baby soft hair no more than an inch or so in length all over. Who would have done this? And why? Tears stung her eyes. Stop it. It was just hair. It would grow back. But her fingers clung to it as her gaze drifted to her right—to find a pair of sharp blue eyes watching her intently.

Christopher. Her mind went blank. Until he spoke.

"Josephine." The quiet, controlled tones drifted across the space between them.

A blood red glow filled her vision, the air around her growing thick and cloying. She heard nothing except the pounding of her heart and her rapid breathing, while a current coursed through her body. But as quickly as the sensations began, they vanished, leaving her quaking and struggling to focus.

Josephine. No, that was wrong. *Jo.* Her name was Jo. Exhaling slowly, she steadied herself and studied him.

He was naked as well, kneeling on one knee with an arm draped discreetly in front of him. His body was strong and lean with a light amount of golden hair on his gently muscled limbs and chest. Like her, his skin revealed no tan lines or other discolorations.

Her eyes began to wander lower, and she dragged them back up to settle more safely on the hair on his head. It was the same length as hers, but it curled into soft blonde ringlets that danced about in tousled abandon atop a face unlined by age. It lent a somewhat boyish air to his otherwise sophisticated, sober appearance. A golden angel with a sharp jaw and soft, tender lips. Lips currently set in a grim line.

She met his eyes once more—and stopped breathing. They were narrowed and calculating. Her arms tightened around her, and the sensation of skin gliding on skin reminded her of just how much he could see.

Falling back in the sand, she pulled her knees to her chest, doing her best to cover herself. Not quite knowing where to look, she pretended to rub her forehead, hiding her eyes.

"Do you know...what happened to our clothes?" she mumbled, looking down to the left and right. She peeked back at him between her fingers when he didn't respond.

He stared at her a moment more.

"That isn't the most pressing concern right now," he said, turning his eyes away.

A shiver went through her. She didn't want to turn and look. *Stop being a baby.* Her head turned to follow his gaze.

The moon was impossibly large. And the color... A sickness rose inside her, and she unconsciously leaned closer to Christopher. He turned to her with a frown, and she stopped.

"Who are you?" he demanded.

She took a breath to answer. And nothing came out. It's a simple question, Jo. Answer him.

"Jo...I'm Jo..." she said, thinking furiously. He narrowed his eyes.

"I'm aware of your name." His voice was colder now.

"If you know my name, shouldn't you know who I am?" She wasn't doing anything wrong. Why did she feel guilty? Maybe because she was so stupid she couldn't remember the most basic information about herself. Come on, think!

"If I knew who you were, I wouldn't have asked the question." Okay. His voice was definitely veering toward hostile now. Her knuckles covered her eyes, rubbing. Stall stall stall!

"Well who are you?" Brilliant. Sit and hide behind her fists forever.

She could feel him staring at her.

"You don't remember me?" he asked.

"Your name is Christopher," she said tentatively, dropping her hands and giving him a questioning look. He stared a bit longer.

"Yes." He was very still, assessing her, before rising to his feet.

Jo quickly looked away, the blood rushing to her face—he seemed completely unconcerned with his state of undress. She couldn't very well keep sitting *now*, so she stood as well, trying to stay out of his field of vision and figure out how to cover herself. God this was awkward. She forced herself to breathe steadily, wanting desperately to match his composure and sure she was failing miserably.

She settled for wrapping her arms around her upper body to hide her breasts and pretending she wasn't entirely naked on her lower half. If she didn't look down, she could almost manage it. Thankfully he was about half a foot taller, so she could just keep looking up at him. She did so now, and followed his gaze to look around the horizon.

There was nothing but flat, oddly glowing sand everywhere. No plants. No rock outcroppings. No footprints or tire treads. Not even a sand dune.

"Please tell me you have some idea of what to do," she whispered. She may not remember who she was, but she was reasonably sure she had absolutely no survival skills. She only hoped he did.

He was silent a long while.

"Find water," he said. He looked at her once more, his eyes dropping down her body and back up in a single glance.

Her lips parted, and the heat climbed to her face as their eyes locked. She hadn't realized how close she'd been standing to him. His eyes grew dark, but she couldn't move. Couldn't breathe. The heat from his skin bled into her as she stared.

When he turned away at last, she closed her eyes weakly, drawing in ragged breaths as quietly as possible. Who was he? A shudder went through her, and her eyes opened once again to see he had started walking. She would just keep a nice comfortable distance between them. For all she knew, he had brought her here.

She looked around at the barren landscape. Okay, maybe that didn't make much sense. And she did remember him, at least. Enough to know his name. That was something, right?

Taking a deep breath, she stepped up her pace to walk close enough to talk. But not too close.

"Do you know where we are?" she asked.

"No." His voice was curt. She hesitated a moment but pressed on.

"Do you have any idea how we got here?

"No."

"Do you..."

She bit her lip. Did he remember anything? She couldn't very well ask him that without revealing herself. Oh well. If he thought she was stupid, so be it.

"I can't remember anything." Her voice sounded so small. It got him to look at her for a few seconds though.

When he turned back to walking without a word, she frowned.

"Do *you* remember anything?"

"No." His answer was so fast, she stopped, staring at his retreating back.

"But you knew my name," she pointed out, hurrying forward again.

"Yes."

Her lips pressed together.

"So you remembered something."

"And you remembered mine," he responded testily.

She exhaled.

"Do you remember anything *else*?"

"No." His pace never faltered. She rubbed her forehead and lapsed into silence.

They walked on and on, the only change the movement of the red moon drifting high above their heads. Jo tried an occasional question, but it always met with the same monosyllabic responses. Always the same—just like the sand. It was level everywhere, as if the wind never stirred. They saw no landmarks of any kind, and the sky was a deep emptiness, terrifying in its implications. She hoped that it was only the excessive light from the twinkling grains that prevented her from seeing the stars.

Don't think like that. She picked up a handful of sand as they walked, separating the glowing grains and tossing the seemingly normal grains of sand back on the ground. Eventually her hand was full of nothing but the luminescent sand, and she could see that individual pieces emitted slightly different shades. Together, they created a soft, warm light, like a weak incandescent bulb. So weird. But pretty.

"Do you think we're getting radiation poisoning?" she asked.

He glanced at her over his shoulder.

"Possibly."

The sand fell from her hands, and her arms wrapped about her once more.

So much for distracting herself. And her feet were really starting to hurt. Rubbing them with sandpaper all night couldn't have been any worse.

She stole a glance at Christopher.

"Are you thirsty?"

"No." To the point as usual.

"Don't you think that's…weird? We've been walking a long time," she pointed out.

"Yes." She stared dejectedly at his back.

"Would it kill you to make conversation?" she sighed.

"It might. Every time you open your mouth, your rate of dehydration increases." He didn't even bother looking at her. But her eyes lit up at the full sentence, and she stepped up her pace to walk beside him, covering her breasts with her arms.

"Okay," she acknowledged, "except I don't feel like I'm dehydrating. *At all*. I know I should be thirsty by now. I should be hungry. I should be at least *tired* by now. But I'm not. The only thing that lets me know that I've been walking all night is that my feet are raw."

He didn't bother acknowledging her.

"Are you tired?" she asked in exasperation.

"Yes, I'm tired of your questions," he snapped.

She groaned and dropped her head in her hands, coming to a halt. He was impossible. And she was in pain. She stood there for a few moments with her eyes closed, rubbing her temples. When she opened them again, he was a good ways in front of her. Her eyes fell to her feet glumly, wanting nothing more than to sit down and give them some relief, but Christopher wasn't slowing down. And the last thing she wanted was to be stuck out there alone.

Steeling herself against the pain, she caught back up and walked behind him in silence.

The night felt abnormally long. She hadn't counted the number of steps she had taken, but it had to be far more than what one could normally manage in a single night, even considering the somewhat rapid pace Christopher had set. And the moon that had risen in the sky now seemed to be moving back toward the horizon near where it had begun. Well that didn't make sense.

"Could we be walking in a circle...?" she decided to risk the question.

"Our tracks are straight."

Jo looked behind them. He was right. She could see back a considerable distance, and their trail was a clean straight line. The perfectly level sand was good for one thing at least.

"How can a moon move that way?" she wondered aloud.

"I don't think that's the moon."

She frowned. What was it then? Another planet? But it was so huge in the sky—and to be that close to them at that size, wouldn't two planets just run into each other? Unless…

"Wait—are *we* the moon?"

"So it would seem."

She mulled this over in silence as she walked.

The night stretched on and on as the moon, as she'd decided to continue calling it, slowly disappeared below the horizon. Its absence left the sky completely blank, and fear crept over her. Although the entire desert floor was well lit from the sands, the soft illumination disappeared into the empty darkness above, a darkness so deep it threatened to swallow them. She shuddered and walked closer to Christopher, no longer wanting to stop, regardless of the pain.

But when the first glow of dawn began peeking over the horizon hours later, she breathed a sigh of relief. Darkness or no, she was ready to begin crawling rather than walk another step. The night had been impossibly long. Yet she wasn't tired—she was just sure her feet had lost a layer of skin. And she still wasn't thirsty.

She looked over at Christopher in desperate hope. "Can we sit down now? Just for a few minutes?"

Christopher considered the question, looking toward the horizon blooming softly with pink tendrils. But he stopped at last, and she groaned in relief as she threw herself to the ground, lying on her back and hugging her knees to her chest to keep her feet off the abrasive sand.

She couldn't walk another step—she would just lie here and die instead. Tightening her arms around her legs and tucking her head into her knees, she rocked back and forth, whimpering and whining and laughing at herself. Christopher's movement beside her drew her attention, and she glanced up to see him lower himself to the ground and sedately brush the sand from his feet.

"You're so respectable," she groaned at him, all her worries eclipsed by the sheer relief of being off her feet. "I bet you always wore a suit and tie."

His irritated glance only made her groan more. She rolled over on her side facing him, her knees still tight against her chest. How could he be so unaffected? A sigh escaped her as she stared at him, but he ignored her, stretching out his legs in front of him and leaning back with his hands in the sand. She couldn't help envying his consistent composure. How on earth did they know each other? Something told her they didn't move in the same circles. Her eyes began drifting over his body.

God, he was appealing, despite his complete unwillingness to have any sort of discussion with her at all. He still seemed intimidating, but with the dawn peeking over the horizon, that had faded a bit. She wanted to lean up on an elbow to watch him, but…she wasn't completely crazy. Instead, she would just enjoy the ability to stare at him since he seemed so uninterested in her. Her lips rested against her knee as her eyes glided over him, down the muscles of his chest, across the soft ripples of his abs, and finally…

Christopher put his knee up and glared at her. She blinked rapidly, feeling like a child who'd been caught with her hand in the cookie jar. The heat flamed in her cheeks as she cringed into her legs as far as she could, her eyes peeking out over her knees.

"Sorry," she said in a tiny voice.

His face was stony, but his eyes blazed. He tore his gaze away angrily and sat staring in front of him.

Fuck. What was the proper decorum when walking around naked with a relative stranger? Squeezing her eyes shut, she rolled back over onto her back, keeping her knees tight against her chest. Whatever it was, it probably didn't include ogling someone. She wanted to groan again but restrained herself. Maybe if she just stayed in the sand with her eyes closed, it would all go away, and when she opened them again, she'd be back home in bed.

The light grew brighter behind her closed lids, and she opened them with a sigh as the sun finally broke over the horizon. And all her thoughts evaporated.

———

Searing heat hit her all at once, blinding, tearing into her, through her, ripping into her flesh and burning the very screams erupting from her lungs. The flames devoured her, eating through her skin, her muscle, through her very bones. Dragging her into the earth, pulsating and relentless, ravaging even the air around her until screaming was no longer possible. And still it went on.

There was no escape. No moment of peace. Death withheld its comfort. Impossible agony. Torment. An eternity of anguish in every moment, savage and merciless.

And the day went on. Hour after hour, without pause. There was nothing else. No thoughts. No feelings. There was only pain. Endless pain.

———

Jo lay trembling violently in the sand, barely registering her restored body around her. Emptiness surrounded her. A coldness as deep as the heat of the flames that had torn her apart. She curled into a ball on her side, wrapping her arms around her knees, gripping her shaking body with all her strength.

She wanted to cry. To scream. To break down into terrified tears. Everything was gone. Everything was over. Whatever this was… She choked back the tears. No. If she started, she might never stop. And she didn't want Christopher to think even worse of her.

Christopher.

She jerked up to her knees and her heart pounded in an odd rhythm when she saw he was lying beside her, whole and perfect again. He was on his stomach, his face in his arms, and very still. Too still… Her heart stopped.

She reached out her hand tentatively, touching his shoulder. He tensed immediately, and she pulled back, releasing the breath she had been holding.

"Christopher…" she whispered. He didn't move. "Hey… it's…it's over now. We're…" she glanced at his short blonde curls and down at her own body. "We're back to…normal." Whatever that was. He still lay unmoving.

She knelt beside him, uncertain what to do. Finally, she reached her hand out once more, ignoring when he tensed, and began slowly stroking his back.

Soothing. Soft. Gentle. And with every touch, she felt her own tension melt away, moment by moment. She hummed softly, a melody from another time coming to her, and she kept stroking. Bit by bit she felt him relax under her hand, his breathing returning to normal. Her eyes closed, the touch of her hand on his skin lulling her into a cocoon of warmth and safety until she wanted nothing more than to stretch her body out beside his and press herself against him. Tears stung behind her lids. She shook her head and drew a shuddering breath. No crying. Just drift away.

She focused on the feeling of her hand against his skin, tracing the line of his muscles up to his neck and back down the center of his back. Her fingers splayed as she moved back up, gliding across the contours, feeling them ripple beneath her fingers. His breathing seemed to stagger, and her nipples grew hard, the night air around her feeling empty. She shivered.

"You can take your hand off me." His voice was acid.

Her eyes flew open, and she snatched her hand away.

The muscles tensed in his back as he pushed himself up, not

looking at her. He kept his back to her and sat for some time, still and silent.

Jo gripped her hands in her lap and looked down at them with wide unseeing eyes, trying to get her breathing back under control. She felt...she didn't know. It was confusing. Her body began shaking again, and she dug her fingernails into her palms, trying to control it. But the shaking didn't stop.

She looked over at Christopher, still sitting as before, his body turned completely away from her.

"Do you..." *Do you feel what I'm feeling?* She couldn't ask that. "Do you think...this is Hell?" she whispered.

His head moved slightly, but he didn't answer.

"Please talk to me." Her voice was husky. "I'm...I feel like... like I know you. But..." her throat was getting blocked by tears, and she focused on breathing for a moment.

"What is it you want me to say," he asked bitterly. "I don't know anything more than you do."

She heard his disgust at being reduced to her level. But also hopelessness.

"Then..." Then what? What should they do? She drew in a deep breath. Actually, figuring out what to do wasn't the challenge. "We should run," she urged.

He turned his head slightly towards her but didn't look back.

"Run." Contempt laced his voice. "Run where."

She started to crawl around to face him, but he turned his body from her, so she stopped. Releasing a breath, she sat on her knees beside him. He had his knee up, an arm draped across it, and he turned further away from her. She ran her hands through her hair.

"Run as far as we can tonight and hope we finally find some shelter," she said in a single exhale. When he didn't acknowledge her, she continued. "So that we aren't out here when the sun comes up again," she explained awkwardly. He again refused to respond.

She wanted to both cry and shake him in frustration. Instead, she grabbed his shoulder and before he could react, slid around in front to face him.

His hand flew to her wrist to pull it off of him, his jaw clenched, his eyes burning into hers. He held her firmly, and they stared at one another, breathing heavily. And she didn't need to look down to suddenly realize why he'd been so intent on turning away.

She blinked rapidly, swallowing. But neither of them moved. She could feel the heat of his hand on her wrist, gripping her tightly, almost painfully.

"I...we—we're all we've got out here," she said, her voice a bit hoarse as she tried to keep her eyes on his. "Can't you just... talk to me?" His grip seemed to grow even tighter, and his eyes grew dark.

"Why would I want to talk," he whispered viciously, "to *you*."

She jerked as if he'd slapped her.

She didn't even realize she was crying until he shook her.

"Stop it!" He was furious. But she couldn't. She was still staring at him but his image was blurred now. Silent sobs shook her shoulders as she struggled with herself. She wanted to be strong. She was trying so hard to be strong.

Christopher pushed her away from him roughly and stood up, walking away a few steps and turning his back to her again, his muscles rippling with tension. Jo put a hand to her mouth, nausea threatening to choke her, as her body trembled from the effort to control her tears.

They stayed that way for a long time. Until her tears were no longer flowing and she sat staring numbly at the sand between her knees.

"We should go." Christopher's voice was low and calm as he turned to face her again. Jo couldn't bring herself to respond.

She climbed to her feet, wiping the sand from her body, and wrapped her arms around herself, waiting with her head down until he finally turned to go. Then she waited a bit longer before following. He looked over his shoulder at her impatiently.

"Are you trying to keep us from finding shelter as long as possible?"

She just stared at him.

He didn't move, his eyes narrowing, and she looked down again. But she walked forward until she was beside him, keeping her arms around herself.

He turned to walk again, not looking at her. And they walked in silence.

Who was he? The burning seemed to have jarred her mind just enough to bring a single memory of him to the surface. Only one. It was so small—the briefest image. She remembered his eyes. He was looking at her, and it was different. He had been… alarmed. Worried. No, it wasn't quite worry. It was too strong for worry. There was deep pain there. Grief.

She pushed at the memory, trying to see beyond it—anything. But nothing more came to her. And she couldn't reconcile it with how she'd felt when he first spoke. Or the way he seemed to feel about her now. Had she done something to him? Nothing made sense.

He suddenly exhaled in a short burst.

"You shouldn't touch me."

Her eyes jerked to his as the heat rushed to her face. He didn't look over.

"Sorry," she said, her voice small.

"You don't know who I am."

She glanced at him again.

"Do you?"

He didn't respond, and her eyes fell back to the sand in front of her.

"I do have memories." His voice was so quiet, she wasn't sure she was hearing him correctly. "Just pieces. Nothing that makes any sense."

She hesitated.

"It's the same for me," she said at last. "It's like trying to remember a dream. I just can't seem to hold on to anything." Her arms wrapped around her more tightly. "But...I know that I know you. More than just your name although...nothing very clear. But it feels...I...I don't know..."

"I remember you, too." His voice was dark.

"What...what do you remember?" she asked, looking over when he didn't answer. His closed expression revealed nothing.

"I told you: nothing that makes any sense."

Irritation laced his voice again, and she lapsed into silence.

They walked a good distance before he glanced at her, his eyes a bit wary.

"You were right about running. If there is any shelter to be found, we're just prolonging our pain if we walk."

She blinked at him but nodded.

His eyes dropped down her body, but he turned forward again quickly.

"Go ahead," he said.

She hesitated. In front? Feeling his eyes on her the whole time?

"No, you can go first."

He rubbed his brow.

"I can't keep an eye on you if you're behind me."

She frowned. He wanted to keep an eye on her?

"That's okay. I'll be fine."

He shot her a frustrated glance.

"I'm not going first."

"Well neither am I!"

He looked away, his jaw twitching, and she stared at him uneasily.

"If I have to run ahead, I will be turning around to check on you. Frequently. Do you really want me seeing your body. Running." He didn't look at her.

Jo's face filled with heat. She glanced down. Her breasts were new, firm, and not exactly small. And probably really...bouncy.

She swallowed and reached a hand back to feel behind her. How bouncy would that be? He jerked his head further away from her.

"Have you heard of peripheral vision," he snapped.

The heat in her cheeks increased, and she snatched her hand away. She looked down again. Maybe if she... She put a hand over each breast. Yes. That would be supportive. And it would hide her. She could run this way.

"I'll just run like this," she said looking up.

He turned his head toward her again irritably and froze. Her eyes flew down at his expression, worried she'd missed a nipple. No. They were hidden. Her hands seemed a little small against her breasts though.

"It's the best I can do," she said, starting to look up at him again only to freeze as well, her eyes locked on the now rigid length between his legs.

They stood that way for some time before Christopher finally raised his eyes to hers. Then he reached out without expression and wrapped his hand around her upper arm before turning and pulling her into a run alongside him. He let her go once he'd established the pace, never once turning back to her. And she kept her eyes on the ground.

The night flew by as they flew over the sparkling sands, and the red moon rose and set. But still they found nothing.

2

MOON DAY 2

Jo's FEET had specks of blood this time, but the pain paled in comparison with the pain of burning. It had been worth it to push as hard as possible in the hopes of finding shelter, but to have run so hard all night, in a night that was so long, and still see nothing…

"We can try burying ourselves in the sand," Christopher said as they looked around. "Maybe it will block the sun. I tested whether we need to breathe. We don't."

They didn't need to breathe? She realized she hadn't ever been out of breath, no matter how fast they ran. She hadn't realized she didn't even need to be drawing in air at all.

"Do you really think it will work?" she asked, starting to hold her breath to test it.

"No." He didn't even hesitate. Well. She'd asked. "But it's all we've got."

She looked up at him. Not breathing. She didn't feel blue or anything. But it felt weird.

He got to his knees and began digging, and she joined him.

It was a tedious task, as the sand slipped back almost as

quickly as they moved it. They discovered a solid sheet of smooth stone seemed to stretch beneath the sand all around them. It was no more than four feet down, so they pushed the sand aside until they had adequate space for each of them to lie down. *Digging our own graves.* She shivered at the thought and prayed it would work.

Jo limped a few feet away and sat down, the relief of being off her feet only serving to remind her of the torture that was yet to come if the sand didn't work. Dawn hadn't begun yet, and there would be plenty of time to get buried once the sky started getting lighter. For now the night sky was completely black, with the gentle light of the sands a golden anchor in the void.

She looked up in surprise when Christopher sat beside her, resting his forearms on his knees and staring in front of them. The heat from his skin flowed into her, and she shivered. He glanced over.

"Are you cold?"

Shaking her head, she looked down to brush the sand from her feet. He was silent, studying her.

"If this is Hell," he mused, "why would you have been sent here."

He must be thinking about what she'd asked him before. She blinked down at her toes. It didn't sound as if he expected a response, but she considered his question. Was she a bad person? She didn't know. She didn't *feel* bad but…she didn't feel exactly good either. Not that she knew what those things really meant anyway. Who decided? She guessed whoever or whatever had sent them here.

She looked up, meeting his eyes. He didn't turn away but continued examining her in silence, his expression contemplative.

"Why do you think you would have been sent here?" she asked.

He studied her a while longer before answering.

"It would have to be based on the same underlying rule or rules that caused you to be sent here as well. So what do we have in common…" Again, his question seemed more to himself than to her.

In common? Them? She almost snorted. Could there be anything at all?

He was cold. Reserved. Harsh. Jo might not be the life of the party, but she was fairly sure she was none of those things. He was also clearly very intelligent and competent, far beyond her own abilities, but she couldn't see how those things could be deserving of burning in everlasting torment anyway.

What were the stories she'd heard about Hell? She remembered the concept and that there were many different ideas of what could get you to heaven or not. And if this really were Hell…did that mean heaven existed, too? That was too depressing to think about given her current circumstances so she shook it off.

"What do you think we have in common?" she decided to ask him.

He stared at her a moment longer.

"Nothing."

She frowned. She'd just thought the same thing, but he was so absolute that it irked her.

"We're both humans," she said.

He narrowed his eyes.

"For example, you interpret things literally, like a child, rather than considering the context."

Jo opened her mouth and closed it again as she stared at him. Her eyes fell to her knees.

Christopher exhaled in a sharp burst, and he turned back to look at the horizon. It was just beginning to lighten.

"We should get ready." His voice was rough, and Jo kept her eyes averted as he stood.

She looked over at her shallow grave, letting fear seep in and replace the hurt. She dreaded both the idea of being buried all day and the idea of burning. But of the two…

She got up to walk over and step into the cleared space. The sand threatened to shift and fill the hole back up with every movement, but she eventually managed to climb in and began filling the sand in over her legs, wondering how she was going to bury her upper body. She jumped when Christopher knelt swiftly beside her.

"Lie back," he ordered. She blinked but wasn't about to reject his help. Lying down, she covered her face with her hands as he began pushing the sand on top of her. Fear washed over her, the reality of being buried all day long beginning to sink in. At least the getting buried part was suddenly resolved. For her, at least. How was Christopher going to handle burying himself?

She didn't open her mouth to ask as he pushed the remaining sand on top of her. The sand poured into every crevice, and she pinched her nose closed just in time, lying very still while the loose grains settled in her ears, the valleys of her eyes, the crevice between her lips. She couldn't hear Christopher, but she felt slight vibrations from his movements around her.

Her eye was itching. Grains of sand mingled with her lashes. They tickled her ears as well, little granules falling every now and then as she shifted almost imperceptibly. And once she started thinking about it, the itching became unbearable. She needed to move. To adjust. To scratch.

No. The fire was unbearable. This was just an itch.

She calmed down. Just breathe—no! She couldn't breathe. Her chest suddenly felt horribly constricted. Like she needed to clear her throat. To clear her lungs with fresh air. Like she needed to *breathe*.

But she didn't need to breathe. She was alive, or whatever she was, and she didn't need to breathe. Steady. Stay steady.

How long had it been? Had the sun even come up yet?

Her heart began racing, the fear growing with her uncertainty. This had to work. She hoped Christopher had been okay burying himself. But he seemed to think things through carefully. He'd have been prepared with a plan.

She could see light from behind her eyelids as the small flecks of luminescent sand sent gentle waves that were oddly comforting. She imagined little figures dancing to distract herself, as if a hundred fairies were holding court. Their little forms sparkled gaily, swirling into a grand mist, their light growing and growing and—

The light was growing. Her heart pounded. This must be sunrise. It was getting brighter. And brighter. The grains of sand around her shifted with every beat of her heart. And still the light grew. And she wondered if it would work all the way until the moment the searing heat penetrated the sand and ignited her flesh. And when she opened her mouth to scream, the burning sand poured in, and there was no more thought again until nightfall.

———

When evening came at last, Jo pulled herself out of the sand, coughing out grains and wanting to die with each breath she took and expelled. Her throat was being ripped apart from the inside. Her eyes had been scratched so deeply she couldn't see, and she wondered if the tears she felt were blood.

She knelt on all fours, coughing helplessly. Each time she tried to stop breathing to gain some relief, the sand inside her triggered another round. She coughed until she felt moisture rising up with it, and she knew she was coughing up blood. But she could see nothing. She coughed until not a single grain remained inside her throat. And then she coughed until the bleeding stopped.

At last she lay on the sand, tears and blood mingling as she felt the moisture falling down her cheeks. Each breath was painful, but the urge to breathe now was too strong to deny. She lay still, spent, listening for Christopher. She heard nothing.

"Christopher." Her voice was raspy, barely audible. She tried again, but it sounded the same.

"Here." Simple and to the point. And as raspy as her own voice. But he was there.

She let the relief wash over her, and she lay unmoving throughout the night as they waited for the next dawn to put them back together.

Shards of memory swirled in her mind. Cars on a highway. Dark images that could only have come from nightmares. A cursor on a computer screen. Deep laughter that tore at her heart. A flat piece of wood that left her nervous and sick. Her past. A jumbled collection of jagged puzzle pieces that cut her as she reached for them.

And nothing more about Christopher.

The day came, tearing them apart with fire, but when the evening arrived again, Jo wasted no time and sat up immediately to look around. Christopher was still lying down, but he looked healed and she breathed a sigh of relief. Her lungs were okay again, it seemed. And her eyes worked perfectly. Her body was back to normal.

She gave him a few minutes before crawling over once she saw him starting to move. He sat up and glanced at her before resting his arms on his knees and dropping his head.

"Hey," she said softly. She racked her brain for what she could say. "Let's…not do that again."

He looked up at her, and there was so much frustration in his eyes that hers softened. His blond curls were falling on his forehead and she longed to brush them back, but he didn't want her to touch him. So she didn't.

Instead, she sat beside him, her knees pulled up to her chest, half facing him. She put her chin on her knees as they stared at each other.

"Well, at least now we know it could be worse." Her gallows humor didn't amuse him. His eyes were heavy.

"There's nothing we can do." His voice was empty. Helpless.

Oh, fuck it. This was ridiculous. Please please please don't let this be a wrong move. She carefully reached out her hand to his. He tensed, but she just moved slowly to curl her fingertips around his own. Nothing more. Then she put her head on her knees and closed her eyes, their fingertips gently locked.

They sat that way for a long time.

"How." His voice was low but firm, and she froze at the intensity in his eyes when she raised her head to meet his gaze. "How do you get over it so quickly. How do you just get up and move."

"I..." She stared back at him with her lips slightly parted. "I don't think I get over it quickly. But I get up because...I want to see how you are and..."

"How are you not paralyzed?" He gritted his jaw while he waited for her to respond.

"Well...it's all terrifying but—"

Christopher closed his eyes and pinched the bridge of his nose with his free hand. Jo halted.

"For once, you can be literal," he said, looking at her with barely restrained impatience.

Jo stared at him in shock.

"You mean *literally* paralyzed? You've been paralyzed this whole time? I mean, after we burn? That's why you keep lying there?"

"I'm not in the habit of inwardly collapsing to the point of immobilization," he said, narrowing his eyes.

She had thought he was upset. Scared. She'd tried soothing him. She'd wanted to comfort him.

She was an idiot.

"Oh." She stared at him blankly. "Well *I* don't know!" she blurted out as he seemed to be waiting for an answer.

Christopher drew his brows together and looked away, frustration in his eyes.

Jo was reeling. Every moment she had spent touching him, stroking his back, feeling him while he was lying there in the sand before… Oh god.

The hand she'd placed in his suddenly felt extremely conspicuous. She bit her lip and lowered her lashes as she tried as subtly as possible to pull it back, breathing an inner sigh of relief as it fell away. He didn't react. She wrapped her arms around her knees more comfortably and looked far off in the distance, turning her face away as much as she could.

"Come on," he said, getting to his feet. Jo was already halfway up before she noticed he'd extended a hand to her. She finished standing on her own as it fell back to his side, and they stared at each other for a moment.

Something flickered in Christopher's eyes, but it was gone before she could figure out what she was seeing. He inclined his head, and she began walking, keeping her eyes on him as they fell into step. They walked for some time that way before they faced forward once more and broke into a run. And away they flew, side by side, searching for some way out of the hell awaiting them in the morning.

But again they found nothing.

———

Another day burning. Another night spent running, hoping for some sign of shelter only to be disappointed. Over and over. There were no clouds. No rain. No wind. Nothing but the endless certainty of a starless desert night and the torment of flames in the day.

3

MOON DAY 40

Jo PUSHED herself up from the sand. Just another day. Another night. It had been weeks of the impossibly long nights—and days that felt much, much longer. She crawled over to Christopher.

She wanted so badly to reach for him. To stroke his head. To comfort him. To comfort herself. The extreme trauma they endured each day had built up a desperation in her for human touch. But he kept such distance between them that she didn't dare. So she just sat beside him and waited, humming to pass the time.

Eventually he pushed himself to his knees, his back to her. She sighed. Some nights he was like this. As if he wanted to shut her out completely. She fell silent. He might want to shut her out, but all she wanted was to lean into him. She was on the verge of tears nearly all the time now, but her need to curl into him didn't seem to be shared. So she focused on staying strong and trying to be as pleasant as possible—but it was getting more and more difficult not to cling to him and just cry.

She got up and walked a few feet away before giving into temptation.

Brushing off the sand while waiting, her hands glided across her body, feeling for every little stray grain. She raked her fingers through her hair, shaking it softly, her fingertips following the few grains that fell down her body, skimming ever so lightly over her skin, over her breasts, down her hips, her thighs.

Her eyes wandered up to find Christopher's on her, deep and dark. She froze, blinking, and he tore his gaze away to glare at the horizon. Heat rushed to her face as she straightened back up, but he kept his eyes turned away and stayed seated for quite some time. When he finally got to his feet, they set out running without a word.

As usual, they ran without any breaks. They never tired or worked up a sweat no matter how hard they pushed themselves, and Jo thought she could have run at her maximum speed indefinitely if it weren't for the abrasion damage on her feet. Damage that increased substantially the harder they ran—and tonight Christopher seemed determined to push them particularly hard. Great.

Hours passed. Jo could feel her skin beginning to get rubbed away, although the night was still young. If she kept going at this pace, she'd spend the remainder of the night in agony. Was it worth it? Was there even anything out there to find? If she knew for certain there was shelter out there, she wouldn't slow down for a second.

But she didn't know. The only thing she knew for sure was that the day brought unimaginable pain, and she kept taking on additional pain at night in the effort to escape it. Was existence to be nothing more than a never ending cycle of torment? She'd asked herself this question every night and thus far, she had accepted it. But tonight she was just so tired of it all.

She came to an abrupt halt. Christopher quickly stopped as well but frowned as he walked back to her. She kept her eyes on his as she fell to her knees, sitting between her feet and tucking her hands between her legs to keep the sand away.

"I know it was my idea, but we might as well be rubbing our feet with sand paper all night long. And the faster we go, the worse it is," she said looking up at him.

"A small price to pay if it saves us from burning a day or two earlier." His voice was quiet.

Jo sighed. "I *know*. I agree. I do. But…what if…" What if there was no shelter out there. Anywhere. She exhaled slowly.

"Maybe we could consider managing our running in a way that might allow some recovery time? I don't know how much time would be needed, or if it would even help, but couldn't we try?"

Christopher frowned, and she frowned back at him.

"You know, I think I read once that men have thicker skin. Literally," she said.

That seemed to give him pause. He hesitated a moment but then knelt slightly behind her to her side, looking down at her foot nearest him. She tried to keep her breathing steady at the sudden closeness but failed when he reached out his hand to gently brush the sand away to reveal the bright red inflamed skin of her soles. His brow drew together.

"I didn't realize it was affecting you this quickly." He sounded displeased.

"I'm sorry if my fragile body inconveniences you," she scowled, looking over her shoulder at him.

His eyes lifted to hers, and her breath caught in her throat. He was far too close.

"I should have realized," he said. His hands had settled in the sand beside her foot, his fingers grazing the sides as he sat staring at her.

Jo was having trouble breathing. He was just so close. Inches away. Motionless. Serious.

She turned her head forward again before she did something stupid, holding herself very still until she felt Christopher pull away. A quick look revealed he had turned to sit with his back to her, his arms on his knees.

She hesitated only an instant before moving her legs out from under her to get more comfortable and then one instant longer before tentatively moving to sit with her back on his. He tensed immediately as their skin touched.

"It's like...a chair," she said over her shoulder, her voice hopeful. "Is it okay?"

When he didn't move away or answer, she positioned herself more fully and carefully leaned into him, her heart pounding a little too hard. She hoped he wouldn't notice but thought she could feel his pounding as well. Gradually he seemed to relax and she did the same, melting into him more with every moment. God, this was so much better than anything else in the last few weeks. She wanted to cry but leaned her head back on his shoulder instead, looking up at the sky.

"Where are the stars," she murmured. She felt him sigh.

"I don't know. Maybe we're in an alternate universe. A very small one..."

Jo was quiet for a while.

"Why us. Why would we be put here together."

Christopher didn't answer. They'd asked this question multiple times now.

"You said you remembered me," she continued softly. "Why won't you tell me what you remember?" She'd asked this as well, to no avail, but she kept trying.

He shifted, his body tense again.

"Please don't pull away," she whispered, her voice thick. She was tired of hiding. "It's just...I'm just...scared. This is all just really fucking scary. And...I don't know what happened before. But I'm so glad you are here with me. I know that's horribly selfish, but I don't know how I would endure this without you."

He stilled.

"I think you were right," he spat out at last. "I think this is

Hell. My hell. And I think you are here to punish me. I don't even know if you're real."

Jo blinked at the bitterness in his voice. She was his idea of Hell? She sat forward, the air cool against her back as she pulled her skin from his. Was she really so awful to be around? She felt sick.

"What am I doing that is so terrible," she whispered, her eyes wide with unshed tears. At least he couldn't see them.

He made a sound of frustration and stood to walk a few feet away. She stood and turned to look at him. He had his back to her, his hands buried in his hair. Why did she keep trying? Nothing worked.

She walked over to stand just behind him.

"Okay, we can go now."

He dropped his hands and turned his head to the side.

"Is your skin magically healed," he bit out.

She decided to take the question seriously. She knew how much he enjoyed that.

"No. I don't think we heal any faster here."

He looked at her over his shoulder and narrowed his eyes.

"Then sit back down so that this delay serves some purpose."

His autocratic tone was the last nudge she needed.

"Is it so impossible for you to just be nice!" she exploded. "I think you have it completely backwards, and *you* are the one making this hell!"

Christopher turned to face her at last, and her eyes widened at his lower half as he grabbed her upper arms.

"Yes," he said furiously. "Yes, it is impossible. I don't want to be nice to you. Nothing," he said the word with a small shake to her body, "about what I want is nice."

Jo's heart battered against her as she stared into his raging eyes. He was standing so close that if she breathed too deeply, her chest would touch his. His grip on her arms tightened further, and she swallowed, her lips parting, but she was unable to tear her eyes from his. She was tired of being cautious.

Her hand rose slowly, her arms half trapped by the way he was holding her, and her fingertips touched the sides of his waist. He flinched, digging into her even more. But her touch was light on his skin. So very light. She swallowed again and began trailing the tips of her fingers across his abdomen. He grabbed her wrists and twisted both her arms behind her back immediately, the move pulling her body flat against his, as he dropped his forehead onto hers.

"I told you not to touch me," he whispered. He was so hard against her stomach it hurt. She shivered and her eyes fluttered closed. She leaned into him more, her breasts flattening against his chest and his fingers bit into her wrists. She tilted her head back and forth, rubbing her forehead against his softly.

He made a sound of frustration and whipped her body around in his arms so quickly it took her breath away, locking her forearms in front of her and pulling her back against him. He buried his face in her neck and kept his arms wrapped around her firmly, immobilizing her.

Jo was shaking. Every nerve in her body was screaming at her, and she could have cried from the confusion. He had his hands locked on her wrists, holding her arms against her body. She couldn't touch him. She couldn't even move her head against him. But she could feel the hard length of him trapped between their bodies. She wanted to cry. To lean back into him. To get away. She wanted…

She dropped her head forward in frustration but pressed herself back into him, feeling as conflicted as he seemed to be. But at least one part of him wanted to be close to her, and this was a war she had to win. She was too lonely. Too scared. Too exhausted trying to keep up her spirits. She needed him to touch her. She didn't care how. She stepped up on her toes and felt his sharp intake of breath as she slid up his body until he was poised between her legs…and then she began sliding back down.

One moment he was about to slip into her and the next she was face down in the sand, her hands trapped beneath her. Her cheek was cradled in his hand while he buried his other hand in her hair. He pressed his lips against her temple, and Jo started trembling violently. She couldn't seem to control it. She wanted him inside her—she did. But she couldn't stop shaking.

"Shh…I'm not going to hurt you…" he whispered, stroking her hair. Her trembling grew stronger as he kissed her cheek tenderly and pulled his hand from her hair to move it down her body, gliding his fingertips down her hip as his lips brushed her skin. And then he moved his hand between them, positioning himself against her—too high.

Jo froze.

"Relax…" he whispered, rubbing the already wet head against her, slipping easily back and forth between her cheeks.

"Wait," she said in alarm, trying to shift away.

He groaned and trapped her more firmly beneath him, continuing to rub back and forth, lubricating her. Then he was pressing down hard, pushing into her.

"Christopher!" she cried.

He stilled immediately. She could hear his ragged breathing in her ear. Neither of them moved.

Slowly, very slowly, he pulled himself back, pushing himself up until he was kneeling over her, his hand still trapped beneath her cheek. She held her breath as she lifted her head, and he slid out from underneath her carefully, his breathing shaky as he stood. Keeping her face averted, she pushed herself to her knees, sitting back on her heels and wrapping her arms across her chest.

He didn't move. She didn't turn around.

The night was so silent around them. There was nothing out there. Nothing. And for the first time, Jo considered what it could mean to be alone with someone stronger—with someone who could hurt her if he wanted. There would be no one to stop him. No consequences. Ever.

But Christopher had stopped himself. And he had stopped when she asked for a break earlier, even though he knew it could mean an extra day of burning. He didn't want to hurt her. She didn't believe he wanted to hurt her.

Tears stung her eyes when she finally turned in the sand to find dark, bitter eyes staring down at her. She repressed a shudder.

"Christopher…" Her voice was gentle, and she watched him clench his fists. "I…I trust you."

She said it simply, her expression clearing at last, and released her breath.

"Then you're stupid." His voice dripped with venom.

"God damn it!" She had reached the end of her patience and stood to face him. "Is there some reason you want me to be afraid of you on top of everything else in this fucking hell world to be afraid of!"

"I want you to be sensible!" He snapped.

"And do what! Walk around on eggshells? You know what— why not? I tear the skin off my feet for most the night and then burn all day. Why not torture myself the rest of the time by living in fear of you every second, too!"

"At least you might manage to stop torturing me," he ground out.

"If you're so miserable around me, then why are you still here? Why not go off on your own?"

"Do you think I haven't been asking myself that every day?" he fired back, his eyes blazing.

Her anger left as quickly as it had come.

"You have?" she whispered.

He ran a hand through his hair. "This is getting us nowhere," he said, his jaw clenched. "We need to go."

Jo stared at him, her eyes wide. She couldn't seem to move.

He released a quick breath.

"Look, until we know if there is anything else out here, it's foolish to separate. Another person might prove useful and it's worth putting up with a few annoyances in the meantime."

Jo didn't answer.

"What is it you want to hear?" he said, his eyes narrowed on hers. "That I stay because…" His voice lowered. "Because I would miss your incessant questions? The fact that you won't just listen and keep your distance? That I need you crawling over to bother me every single night after we burn, singing your nonsense?"

Jo blinked rapidly, but he didn't stop.

"Do you think I want to constantly hear how you are feeling? Or need your ridiculous attempts to be cheerful?"

His eyes were glistening, and she stepped back, staring at him with wide, dry eyes.

"This is how you see me?" she whispered.

Christopher's breathing was uneven, but when he spoke, his voice was steady.

"We have wasted too much time. Let's go."

He turned to go, and she watched him walk a few feet away before he looked back. He frowned when she didn't follow.

"We can walk if your feet still hurt."

Her eyes fell to the sand below her. She stared down blankly.

"I'm not going with you."

————

Christopher held himself very still as he looked at her.

"Don't be childish."

She didn't move.

He turned away irritably before looking back to speak, but she cut him off.

"I can't do this anymore," she whispered. "Maybe we really

are each other's hell. It's just making the nightmare of being here even worse. And I...I am tired of spending nearly every single moment in pain."

"I said we could walk."

She looked up in slight disbelief.

"Are you really that blind?"

He tore his gaze away, his eyes still burning, while she stared at him. Everything she was doing was ugly to him. He simply wanted her to leave him alone—and that should be easy. But she couldn't. She couldn't look over at him after a day of agony more intense than anything she could possibly have experienced before and then just sit alone. She couldn't spend night after night with him and never speak. She couldn't accept being a potentially useful tool, walking along just in case some day he might need to use her.

So this was it. He would want to keep going the way he'd been going, 'west' toward the sunset. So she could go 'north' maybe. That's where the moon rose and set for the most part. Well, planet. Whatever.

"I'll head toward the moon. I hope you find shelter. And I apprec—" No. He wasn't interested in what she felt. "Well...goodbye."

The decision was made. It was time to go.

Jo turned toward the moon, the red swirls of clouds over its surface reminding her of a blanket. She wished she had one she could curl up in and lie down. Was it possible to sleep? She hadn't felt tired physically at all, but she hadn't tried sleeping. Something for her to try later.

Christopher didn't say anything or look at her as she walked past him. He just reached out his hand and grabbed her arm.

She frowned down at it.

"Let me go."

"You're not going off alone."

She frowned up at him.

"That's not your decision."

His eyes turned to hers.

"It looks like it is."

Heat surged beneath her skin, and she tried jerking her arm away. He just narrowed his eyes and gripped her harder.

"What are you going to do? Drag me around in case you find a use for me?"

"If I have to."

She jerked harder, pressure growing in her chest.

"Let me go!"

"Stop being a child!"

She pushed at his arm, trying to tear herself away, but he held fast.

Her eyes flew back to his.

"Fine. I'll stay. You can let go now."

The look in his eyes set her to struggling once more. He just waited.

"Are you finished?" he snapped when she stilled at last. She looked away.

His hand relaxed. And she ripped her arm from his grasp and took off, only to be jerked off her feet by his arm going around her body, yanking her back to him.

"This is absurd," he ground out, struggling to keep her in his arms. "Would you be still!"

When she tried kicking him with her heels, he wrestled her to the ground and flattened himself on her back once more.

"I am trying not to hurt you!" His voice was hoarse, and his body throbbed between them.

"Well you suck at it!" She thrashed about, fighting to get out from underneath him.

He groaned and dropped his head into her neck, his hard length pressing into her, twitching with every move she made.

"Please stop moving," he said, his voice thick.

"Please get off of me!" she huffed, continuing to try to push him off.

A shudder went through him, but he didn't move.

Jo tried everything she could think of. Kicking only to have him trap her legs with his. Pushing only to have him hold her wrists above her head. Trying to throw her head back only to find his head buried so deeply in her neck, she could barely move.

She could have screamed in frustration. He wanted her to keep her distance? She would put a million miles between them. He was tired of her being cheerful? Perfect. Because the last thing she felt like doing was being friendly now.

Hours must have gone by. Questions? Singing? Her feelings? Every time she considered stopping, his words would come back to her. They'd just see how desperate he was to keep an extra pair of hands around for whatever. He'd have to pin her down all night and then the sun would be up and then—

She stilled. Then they would burn. And he would be paralyzed.

When she remained motionless, she felt him begin to relax. But the rigid length between them didn't soften.

"Will you…be reasonable now?"

She didn't know why he sounded so out of breath. It's not like they needed to breathe.

"Yes."

He hesitated before pulling them to their feet, his eyes wary. His hand remained locked on her upper arm while she brushed off the sand. But it didn't matter. She could wait.

The moon had disappeared again. It wouldn't be long now.

Christopher's pull on her arm was gentle. Cautious. Whatever.

She followed along, not looking at him.

And the sun came up again.

———

Jo sprang to her feet the moment the sun was down and took off. The bright horizon where the sun had set was behind her. If she just veered slightly to the left of where she was standing, that should have her heading toward the moon again, right? Oh, whatever. She'd end up wherever she ended up and figure it out from there.

She ran. Fast. She didn't bother trying to keep track of where she was—as if she could. She just ran and ran until the moon eventually rose to her left. Drat. She was almost headed back to where they'd started. Oh well. Any slight turn would reduce the speed, and if Christopher were chasing her, she would need every single moment to have any hope of staying ahead of him for the entire night. She couldn't look behind her. It would slow her down.

So she ran, the sands beneath her a blur of light, the grains digging into her with every stride.

Her feet had just started getting flayed when Christopher caught up, and her heart jolted inside. He yelled something, but she ignored him, unable to hear with the wind in her ears. She wasn't stopping.

When she didn't slow down, he reached for her and she jerked away. But the movement pulled her off center, causing her to stumble. She barely registered Christopher's arms going about her, protecting her face in his neck, as they fell hard, barreling through the sand, the grains ripping their skin everywhere it touched them.

When they stopped rolling at last, Christopher lay on top of her, cradling her head. She groaned in pain and looked up.

His eyes were roaming all over her face, her body—touching sometimes, brushing away sand and drawing small whimpers from her when he connected with a spot that had evidently gotten the worst of it.

"I'm sorry," he whispered. His brow kept pulling together with each spot he brushed.

She swallowed. Her arms were trapped between them on his chest, and she vaguely remembered pushing at him. A trickle of blood marred his cheek, and she reached up to smooth it away. His eyes met hers, and she paused, watching him.

He said nothing at first, but stroked her temple with his thumb, his eyes tortured.

"Don't go." The words sounded torn from him.

The breath left her lungs in a huff.

"Why? Why do you want me with you? What does it matter? I'm never going to be useful—I can't do anything out here." She hated the hurt in her voice.

He groaned and dropped his forehead to hers, his fingers still stroking her cheeks, her hair.

"Because," he whispered, "I…" His fingers clenched her hair. Then he shuddered and hid his face in her neck, his body trembling.

Jo wanted to hit him. Would he never just talk to her? She released an exasperated sigh but tentatively began wrapping her arms around him, stopping when she felt blood.

"How badly are you hurt?" she asked, trying to lean up and look over his shoulder. He didn't move.

"I'm fine. I shouldn't have grabbed you. I didn't mean to hurt you." His voice trailed off.

Jo hesitated but lay back in the sand and carefully put her arms around him, trying to avoid hurting him. One arm settled around his waist while her hand held the back of his neck. She stroked softly, her fingers brushing the sand from his curls.

He was lying between her legs, but he wasn't hard. He seemed…exhausted. Lost.

"I don't…" she paused, unsure what to say. "You keep telling me—" No. Not that either. She shifted in frustration, and he tangled his hands more deeply in her hair. Her breath escaped her slowly and she stroked his skin, her movements soft and slow as he relaxed into her.

She closed her eyes. She could finally breathe.

Christopher moved far too soon, pushing himself up on his forearms and avoiding her eyes. But he stayed between her thighs.

"Hey," she whispered, her hand moving from his neck to his cheek. He didn't look up. His cheek was still bleeding, and her fingertips brushed around the cut carefully. "Does it hurt?"

He shook his head, his eyes falling to her wounds again.

Her voice was soft as she spoke.

"This was my fault for pulling away. Not yours."

"No," he said, looking up at last. "I never should have grabbed you at that speed. I knew better. I just…wasn't thinking." His eyes drifted to her injuries again. There was a tone in his voice that disturbed her.

"You don't have to anticipate every outcome, all the time," she murmured, her fingers stroking his brow. He jerked his gaze back to hers.

"I do." His tone was flat. Harsh. She froze, and he quickly closed his eyes and turned his face toward her arm, pressing his lips to her wrist. She felt him begin to grow between her legs.

Her body responded.

"Do I really need to be afraid of you?" she whispered, her voice revealing how much she didn't want to believe it.

Christopher stilled, his lips unmoving on her skin. He held his upper body above her while he continued growing against her. She watched his brow pulling together repeatedly. Finally he brushed his lips once more in a gentle sweep along her wrist, now fully hard, and looked down to meet her eyes.

"No. You don't."

And he pulled himself off her completely, kneeling in the sand to take stock of their wounds.

4

MOON DAY 70

A BLACK ABYSS stretched out before them.

It had been weeks since they changed course. Jo's run had put them far afield of the path they had been on before, but Christopher hadn't seemed to think it mattered. So they had continued heading into the moon, this time at a walk. Although they didn't say it aloud, they had lost hope of finding anything. Nothing ever changed.

Until tonight.

Jo stood with Christopher at the edge of the glittering sands. The moon had yet to rise, and behind them the sands bathed the desert floor in warm light. But before them lay a vast sea of emptiness, as if the world had simply ended. She had fought against instinctive terror when she first saw it—the complete blackness a giant wall of darkness. A void that could suck them into an even worse fate.

But the world had not ended. The gentle light from the glowing sand behind them allowed them to see at least a few feet into the emptiness in front, revealing nothing but normal sand.

Earth level normal. There wasn't the faintest trace of luminescence.

"Do you think it's all just…sand out there?" she whispered. In spite of the hope she felt at finally finding something *different*, all her forgotten nightmares from childhood were clawing at her mind. So she whispered because if there were anything out there, she wanted to hear it coming—and she didn't want it hearing her.

Christopher crouched down, taking a closer look at the grains, and she crouched with him. Yes, staying low seemed like a good idea. They were poised against the backdrop of light. Perfect targets. She stared out in front of her, trying desperately to see into the darkness. It was impossible.

Gathering a handful of the glowing sand, Christopher tossed it in an arc in front of them. The grains of light scattered across the dark sands, the tiny particles offering a small amount of illumination as they came to rest. Nothing happened. He looked over at her.

"We could take handfuls of the light sand with us as flashlights."

And walk out into the middle of that darkness with the moon still hidden? Jo suppressed a shudder.

"Maybe wait for the moon to rise first?" she suggested.

He gave a short nod and began separating glowing grains into a pile. Always so efficient. She sighed as she joined in.

He had been very careful with her since that night. Checking in with her—making sure she wasn't in pain. He wasn't exactly warm and friendly, but he hadn't gotten angry with her again.

Of course, she'd been careful as well and kept her distance for the most part. She still couldn't help crawling near him after the sun went down, but she'd stopped singing. And although she couldn't keep quiet the entire night as they walked, she felt like she did a pretty good job of just drifting off with her own thoughts. Though she would catch him looking at her with what she could have sworn was a touch of sadness on occasion.

Eventually they had two piles of more glowing grains than they would be able to carry. Jo sat back on her heels and stared out into the darkness. What would they find in it? Anything? Something even…worse? She shivered, wrapping her arms around herself, and Christopher glanced over.

"We could walk the perimeter first and get a sense of how big this is rather than going straight in. There are risks either way."

She knew he was offering the idea for her sake. She could feel his impatience to explore—to find some way, any way, out of the burning. And he was already willing to wait for the moon. Jo looked at the blackness in front of her and above. Was she really going to let childhood fears hold them back? What could possibly be worse than what they faced every day?

"I'm ready to go in," she sighed. She gave him a wry smile when he hesitated. "I was just letting my imagination run away with me." She began scooping up her pile of light, trying to keep as much in her hands as possible. *This little light of mine.* An echo from the past sang in her mind, for once with words.

"I just remembered something," she said, looking over at Christopher.

He was still staring at her and hadn't picked up his sands yet.

"What was it?"

"Just a child's song. Something I sang in church, I think." She looked at the light in her hands and stood, careful not to drop any. "Basically it says not to let the devil blow out your light."

A sharp line appeared between Christopher's brow, and he reached out to gather his sand before standing as well. She stepped close to touch the tips of his fingers with hers, the golden grains in their hands shining brightly between them. "At least nothing can put these out."

He avoided her gaze and turned toward the darkness. She

shook her head but stepped closer to join him at his side. She would have loved to have just asked what he was thinking but knew he would never tell her.

Okay. This was it. They were going to step forward into the dark sand. The *normal* sand, she corrected herself. It was the most normal thing here. And the absence of glowing grains was *not* because there was some creature underneath eating the light pellets. So there was no chance it was going to come after them as soon as they started walking across it. Everything would be fine.

"Stay here for a moment," Christopher said, stepping forward. She frowned at him for an instant before rushing into the dark sand to walk at his side. He narrowed his eyes at her, and she rushed to explain.

"I'm not waiting behind. What if you get snapped up by something?"

"Entirely my point in checking," he said, his jaw a bit tense.

"Well I am not going to be stuck here watching you get devoured so I can wander the burning desert alone forever!"

He released a frustrated breath and scanned the area, walking slowly. She inched closer to him until their arms were touching and waited for him to pull away or tell her to move—but he didn't.

They walked along in silence for perhaps a couple hours, the lights in their hands creating a small bubble of illumination around them. Everything beyond it was absolute darkness now, the light of the golden shore no longer visible on the horizon behind them. Jo hoped the moon would rise soon.

"What I said before…I didn't mean it. Not the way I said it." His voice was low, and she looked over at him.

"When?"

He didn't answer immediately.

"A few weeks ago."

Well that cleared everything up.

"You couldn't be more specific, could you?"

"I don't want you to stop being...you."

Jo hesitated. Was he referring to the litany of complaints he'd said about her that night?

"But I bother you."

Christopher looked at her.

"Yes," he said softly. "You do."

Jo stopped, and Christopher stopped with her. The night was perfectly still, as it had always been. She could hear nothing but the gentle sounds of their breathing, and underneath the faintest hint of their heartbeats. Blackness surrounded them on every side. Nothing else existed.

And for one moment, she allowed herself to imagine letting the sand fall to her feet and reaching out for him. What would he do? Would he push her away? Or would he push her down again...

"We should go," he whispered. His body had grown hard. What would he do if she dropped to her knees? Their eyes were still locked together, and she couldn't seem to make herself move. "Jo..." He was hoarse.

"I can make it better," she whispered. He shook his head, growing pale in the light. "You can't hurt me if you're holding the sand. Just keep holding it," she whispered as she dropped to her knees in front of him, her own hands still cupping the sands carefully.

Christopher quickly stepped back out of reach, and she groaned.

"Why won't you let me touch you?" she looked up at him, pleading.

"Don't you think I want you to?" His voice shook.

"Then stop fighting me!"

He exhaled in frustration. "You don't know what you're asking."

"No, I don't! I don't know why you fight this so hard! Please just…let me be close to you." Her voice dropped back to a whisper. She watched the expressions flit across his face, and she looked at the glowing sands in her hands…and then carefully placed them in a pile in front of her.

"What are you doing?" His voice was alarmed, and she stood to carefully walk towards him. He stepped back with every step she took, still carefully balancing the sands in his hands. She pressed her lips together and darted forward too quickly for him to move, grabbing his waist and preventing him from moving without her.

"Jo, you need to stop." His voice was stern now, almost angry again, but his eyes looked panicked. She ignored him and dropped to her knees, sliding her hands down to his hips and holding him firmly. Then she carefully leaned forward with slightly parted lips and softly pressed them against the smooth, rounded head that was pressed so hard against his stomach.

She felt a tremor go through his body as her tongue crept out to lick lightly at the tip before flattening against the shaft and sucking him just enough to pull him into her mouth. And the sands came scattering down. Christopher grabbed her hair and dropped to his knees, pulling her close to crush her lips with his. He held her there, his lips apart, sliding back and forth across her own, feeling her, breathing her in. She reached out her tongue, searching for his, and he let out a pained cry and hid his face in her neck.

"Jo, you have to stop now." His voice was ragged.

"Then you have to explain," she whispered, her hands sliding down his body in long, slow strokes. He shuddered against her, and she pressed herself into him more fully.

"The way I want to take you," he began thickly, "isn't something you would enjoy."

Jo's body tightened.

"Is that...the only way you would want me?" Her voice was almost shy. He gripped her harder.

"Yes," he said, his tone harsh.

Jo didn't move for a moment.

"Would you...be gentle?" she asked quietly.

"*Why can't you just accept this!*" he exploded, pulling back. He began furiously gathering the particles of sand.

Jo watched him, the muscles rippling in his back, his arms, his stomach...

"Do you really think I'm so fragile? After everything we've been through here?"

Christopher stabbed the sand harder as he gathered the lights. Jo reached out her hand to his arm, gently stopping him. His eyes burned as they turned back to her.

"I think," he bit out, "that we are in the middle of complete darkness with no idea what might be in it. And the last thing we should be doing is getting so distracted that we can't hear something sneaking up on us." Jo blinked at the harshness in his voice. "Not to mention that this is the first sign we've had of anything different—something that might allow us to avoid the sun. This is hardly the time to be giving into physical urges."

All her courage fled and Jo felt as small and insignificant as she had the first night they'd woken up in this place. His words made perfect sense. She couldn't argue. How could she have forgotten everything around them? Her skin felt clammy, and she slowly let her hand fall from his arm and back to her side, her lashes falling at last to cover her eyes.

Christopher went back to gathering the glowing grains of sand with steady, controlled movements. Jo didn't move. She couldn't. If she tried, she might start crying, and she was humiliated enough as it was without bursting into tears like a child. How could she keep being so stupid...

She finally regained enough composure to begin collecting the glowing grains alongside him, but her hands shook a bit. She saw Christopher glance at her out of the corner of her eye, but she kept her eyes down. Breathe. She focused on gathering the sand, waiting for him to turn his attention back to the ground. The moment stretched unbearably, the sound of their breathing heavy between them. Jo froze.

The breathing wasn't just between them.

———

"Steady..." Christopher's voice was barely audible as he turned to stare out into the darkness. Jo lifted her head slowly to follow his gaze.

The faintest hint of light reflected off a pair of eyes just a few feet away.

Her heart hammered against her chest, but she didn't move. Damn her stupidity. They were sitting ducks out here. With the glowing shore well behind the horizon and the moon yet to rise, the sands they had brought with them held the only light in the entire universe at the moment. If she hadn't distracted them both so thoroughly, they would have had time to run. Time to drop the light and disappear in the night perhaps. And hide from whatever was watching them.

Jo didn't know whether to be relieved or terrified as a very large, very muscular man stepped into the light. He was at least a head taller than Christopher, although he walked slightly hunched over with his arms somewhat stiff at his sides. He had a large forehead with a heavy brow that hung over small eyes—eyes darting back and forth between the two of them. Unlike Christopher's light facial hair, this man had a thick short beard, almost as long as the inch or so of brown hair on his head, while a coarse mat of hair covered the rest of his body. And from what was jutting out from the hair between his legs, he'd been watching them...

He stopped a few feet away, still seemingly unsure exactly

which one of them he should be looking at. He squinted at Christopher finally and snorted before turning his attention fully to Jo.

"You put on a nice show," he said, his eyes roving over her body with raised brows. "Almost made me forget where I was."

His tone was blunt. Loud. And filled with dislike.

Did all men hate her at first sight?

Christopher stood, pulling her to her feet with him and pushing her behind him. The man raised his brows further and snorted again.

"It's a little late for that, boy."

Boy. It seemed a strange term for him to use. He didn't look any older than Christopher.

"How did you get here." Christopher's question sounded more like an order. The man scoffed.

"I don't answer to you, pretty boy. Now why don't you let the little lady go. I'm havin' a real bad night, and I could use what she's offering."

The man stepped forward, his eyes moving back to Jo as he reached out to push Christopher aside. Christopher pulled Jo behind him farther as he stepped away.

"Get back." He was looking at the man, but he pushed Jo away as he said it. Shit. The first sign of life—actual human life —and it didn't look like he was the sort to rationally exchange information.

"Sir, I'm sure it's been rough out here on your own." She might as well try intervening before this went from bad to worse. Christopher tensed at her words, but the man gave a slow smile.

"Now that's more like it. I'm going to enjoy you calling me sir."

"Please," she continued, desperately trying to find some hint of civility in him as she moved backwards. "How long have you been here? Do you remember anything?"

"We can talk all about it later, sweetheart," he promised, as he looked at Christopher standing in his way. He lowered his voice. "You have about five seconds to move, boy, or you won't be moving ever again. I haven't felt this strong in years. You don't want to fuck with me."

Jo's heart was racing. This guy was huge. There was no way Christopher would have a chance against him. And even though it didn't seem like they could die, she knew he could be hurt. Horribly. And he could at least be stopped for the night. What if this guy dragged her off and she and Christopher couldn't find each other again? Panic was clawing at her mind. She had to calm down. Think. Could she throw sand in his eyes?

She was struggling to come up with some way of helping when everything happened at once. The guy pulled back his arm, and his fist went flying toward Christopher's jaw. But Christopher turned to the side, pulling the advancing arm forward while tripping him. She saw the surprise in the man's eyes as he stumbled and fell face first into the sand. Christopher was on him immediately, jamming his knee into his back and reaching around to stab his fingers into the man's eyes, gouging them deeply and tearing a violent scream from him. He leapt back up, evading the man's wild swings, and quickly ran to her to pull her away with him, holding a bloody finger near his lips as she looked at him in shock.

He pulled her quickly into the darkness, abandoning the light as they raced away from the raging man shouting obscenities while he stumbled around trying to find them. But the noise he was making disguised the sound of their feet hitting the sand, and eventually the sound of his fury was far behind. Christopher continued pulling them in a run a while longer, the night complete blackness now. They might as well be running with their eyes closed. Thank goodness everything was consistently flat. Even so, Jo was a little surprised she managed not to trip.

When they could no longer hear the man's screams, they stopped and looked behind them. The glow from where they'd dropped the sand was still visible but only because nothing else was out there. It would be behind the horizon shortly if they kept going.

Christopher turned back around, never letting go of her even for a moment. It was impossible to see each other, and they needed to keep silent to hear if anyone, or anything, else was out there.

They walked on in silence until the moon began to cast a rosy glow over the horizon. It seemed brighter than before, and Jo supposed that must be due to the light of the sands no longer competing with it. Everything around them was well lit, even if it was all rather pink and red. A quick scan of the horizon revealed nothing but sand now. Well that was a relief. Sort of.

Jo sent Christopher a hesitant look. Was he mad? He hadn't let go of her hand yet, so that was a good sign. But she'd almost gotten him—gotten both of them—in very big trouble. And he didn't exactly look pleased…he wouldn't even look at her.

"I'm sorry," she said in a small voice.

He gave her a quick glance but didn't answer, his eyes falling to his hand in hers. He pulled it from her grasp and tried wiping the blood away.

Jo started to cross her arms awkwardly but stopped at the sight of the blood on her hand. It had to have been over an hour, and yet it still hadn't dried. She stared down, turning her hand slowly in the light, the glistening redness deep and dark in the rich red glow of the moon. The sight felt strangely familiar.

Her breathing grew shallow. Rapid. She couldn't seem to get enough air. She knew she didn't need to breathe, but still it went on. Heat coursed through her body followed by a chill that left her shaking. Her breath was coming in small gasps.

Then Christopher was wiping her hand off, rubbing it

between his own. He was saying something. She could see his lips moving, but she couldn't hear. The blood was rushing through her ears, and she felt sick. Her vision seemed to narrow into a dark tunnel until all she could see was the blood.

The next thing she knew they were on their knees and she was leaning against him as he held her close, his chest vibrating in low tones. He was saying something. Her hearing started to return.

"—wasn't you. I did it. Jo… It wasn't you."

And then she was crying. And once she started, she couldn't stop. Her body wouldn't stop shaking. Christopher wrapped his arms around her more tightly, and she turned her face into his neck, trying to stay silent. To control herself.

"I'm sorry," she whispered in tears. "I'm sorry. I'm sorry. I'm sorry." Over and over. She barely knew she was speaking.

"Don't." His voice was hoarse. His hand tangled in her hair, holding her head in his neck as he rested his forehead on hers, stroking her tears away.

Her whispers faded into nothing, but her lips kept forming the same words. Until he stopped them with his own.

At first, it was the barest touch. He held very still, and each word she formed brushed against him. She forgot what she was saying. Her lips stopped moving, slightly apart, feeling his every breath. Breathing him in.

His lips curved around her upper lip, her lower lip, the tip of his tongue teasing the edges. Then he settled his mouth against hers fully and began sliding his tongue inside her, a small groan escaping him as she sucked lightly in response.

Jo moaned in frustration when he drew back to kiss away the last of her tears. She clung to him, trembling, as he held her head into his neck once more and stroked her back.

Her lashes fluttered open, brushing against his skin, and she stared at her hand on his chest. His arms tightened around her, his body hard between them, but she knew better than to try anything further at this point. But she so desperately wanted more.

"Can you walk now?" He said softly, and Jo thought she heard a slight tremor in his voice. She closed her eyes and breathed him in one more time.

"Yes." Leaning back, her arms still on his chest, she looked up for a moment. His eyes were full of…uncertainty? Wariness? She gave him a small smile before pulling away and getting to her feet, brushing the sand away as she stood.

"So…we aren't alone out here after all," she said. "What do you think it means?" She looked over as he stood, watching him scan the horizon before reaching for her hand to begin walking again. She tried to ignore the heat it sent through her.

"I don't think he had burned yet—he didn't seem to realize we regenerate. So he either just got here or…" he looked around again, but then shook his head. "We were the only point of light out here, so he followed us."

Yes. And he would have gotten quite an eye full. Thank goodness he hadn't attacked them while they were…occupied. When she considered the damage he could have done if Christopher had been caught off guard…

She squeezed his hand slightly but avoided his gaze when he looked over.

"Do you feel up to running?" she asked, watching him out of the corner of her eye. She heard him exhale in a short breath before releasing her hand.

"Do you want to see how far we can get before morning?" He meant was she willing to sacrifice the skin on her feet for a chance to find something that would protect them.

"Definitely." It would put more space between them and the psycho behind them. His eyes would be healed once they burned, and she didn't think he was the forgiving type.

So they started running. Christopher seemed to be trying not to push her too hard, but she wasn't worried about being in pain from her feet tonight. There were far more important concerns now. So she pulled ahead, putting everything she had into it.

But not for long—just long enough for what was over the horizon to come into view.

5

MOON DAY 70

Welcome to The City

Jo and Christopher stared at the iron—or what looked like iron —sign above the locked gates. Jo could see a well lit tunnel through the bars, where glowing grains of sand had somehow been pressed into the hard rock, creating a warm cocoon of light. Scattered particles of loose dark sand lay strewn across the floor, tracked in presumably from feet that had left deep marks in the sand behind them. Someone had been through the gates this night.

Jo reached out trembling hands to wrap around the metal bars, closing her eyes and leaning weakly against them when they were solid to the touch. She'd half expected it was some type of mirage.

They'd seen the light of the tunnel as soon as they had made it far enough over the horizon, though it had been impossible to tell what they were seeing at that distance. But the closer they got, the more hope became almost unbearable. She had been almost more terrified of believing than she was of burning.

Yet here they stood, at the entrance to some type of underground system. There was very little to see on the surface. The dark sands began sloping downward in a path perhaps six feet wide, the rock underneath exposed more and more until she could see what she'd thought was a solid slab under the sand was far more solid than she could have imagined. It appeared to extend deep into the earth but had somehow been cut through to create an incline that continued until they were standing far below the normal sand level, facing the tall gates. Metal gates. Forged gates. There was life here. There was actual life.

Jo looked over at Christopher to see him testing the locks, looking for some way to get inside.

"Any idea how we can get in?" she asked. She was grateful her voice didn't shake.

He was frowning.

"The lock isn't a complicated one, but without some smaller thin piece of metal or rock, I can't get it open." He rubbed his brow. "We might have to wait for someone to let us in."

Jo restrained a groan of frustration. How often were the gates opened? What if they had missed their chance tonight? She swept her eyes around her. The positioning of the tunnel entrance would provide shade from direct light during the day if they were unlucky enough to still be waiting around, but the entire surface probably turned into a furnace with the sun. Shade would be irrelevant.

But there was shelter. They had found it.

She looked at Christopher with a little laugh.

"I can't even be worried about it. I don't want to burn again, but even if we do, it won't be forever!"

He leaned against the bars, staring at her, before exhaling and turning around to slump down with his back to the gates.

"Shouldn't we yell for someone though?" she asked. "Maybe

that's what most people do—and how they know to come get them."

Christopher looked up at her with one brow raised.

"It seems a little undignified."

She stared at him for two beats before turning and yelling through the bars.

"HELLO! IS ANYONE THERE? WE WOULD REALLY LOVE FOR YOU TO OPEN THE GATES, PLEASE! HELLOOOOO!"

She yelled for a while before looking back down at Christopher. His expression hadn't changed. She clapped her hand over her mouth when a giggle escaped.

"I think I'm a little slap happy," she managed to get out, stifling further giggles. "Possibly borderline hysterical."

She turned around and sank to the ground beside him, both hands over her mouth. She was shaking. This was ridiculous. Get it together, Jo. So much had happened tonight.

Her knees were up to her chest, and Christopher reached out to slide his hand underneath to hold her ankle. His forearm pressed against her thigh as he stroked her with his thumb, his touch sending warmth through her body. Her eyes closed.

Gradually the weird shakiness subsided. She took a shuddering breath and dropped her hands down to hold onto his, relaxing her head against the bars behind her.

"How do you stay so calm," she whispered. "So perfectly in control all the time."

She felt him look at her, so she opened her eyes and turned to meet his gaze. His expression was as serious as ever.

"I haven't been either of those things since we woke up in this place," he said.

Her lips parted.

"Well you do a really, really good impression of it."

He stared at her a long moment, his thumb still stroking her skin.

"Good," he said. And he smiled. A real smile. The first one she had seen on him. The corners of his eyes crinkled and both sides of his mouth were tilted up. And she suddenly wanted to laugh again, but this time in delight. She settled for smiling helplessly in return.

Leaning back against the bars, she closed her eyes again before she did anything crazy. But she held on to Christopher's hand on her leg.

They sat that way for the remainder of the night. Periodically she would try calling out, but they never heard anything and no one ever showed up. And then dawn was upon them again.

In spite of what she'd said earlier, the idea of burning now was so much worse. She'd previously been able to manage the hours before the sun came up with—if not exactly poise—at least a measure of self-respect. But now…now she was ready to start sobbing and screaming at the gate. The bars were far too narrow for her head to slide through, otherwise she would have willingly lost some skin or even some bone to evade hours upon hours of burning.

But Christopher was beside her. And if he could stay in control, so would she.

"Come here."

He stood, pulling her into a corner that would be protected from direct light. He hesitated after she was in position, and she thought he was planning on turning so his back would be against her. She pulled him to her, throwing her arms around his neck. He tensed for only a moment before wrapping his arms around her as well. And they held on tightly, each second an eternity as they waited to see what would happen when the sun broke over the horizon.

One moment they were clinging to each other so hard it was painful, and in the next a wave of exhaustion hit her—so intense it took her breath away. Christopher slid down her body, completely unconscious. She tried catching him, stumbling to her knees with him in her arms as dizziness engulfed her. She was drowning, her head a fog pulling her to the ground, and wave after wave pummeled her, dragging her down.

It took everything she had to carefully lower his head to the ground, to fight the desperate urge to give in to the weight crushing her. But she forced her eyes to stay open. The world around them was painfully bright, and while she saw no fire, the sands were vibrating, shifting and settling into the smooth familiar blanket they found each night.

They were in the shadows. She could barely think. The shadows. She looked at Christopher lying beside her. The shadows…would move. He was in danger. She leaned over to pull at him, trying to get him out of the way. Wait. She was in the way. Move. She stumbled back to her feet, moving around him, and her fingertips grazed the non-shaded area.

She screamed, jerking back as the pain pierced through the fog immediately and cleared her thoughts. Her skin was black. It wasn't repairing itself. But before she could even begin to question why, the exhaustion returned, crippling her mind. She had to make sure they were as far to the edge as possible—where the sun would never hit.

But trying to figure out the edges…how the sun would move…trying to move Christopher's lifeless body…trying not to succumb to the strange sensation sapping her strength… Focus, Jo!

She slapped her face, and it snapped her out of the fog long enough to think straight. But not long enough to act. She slapped herself again. Harder. She found she could move Christopher for just a couple seconds before she needed to hurt herself enough to keep going. Over and over, inch by inch. She made sure he was in the safe zone.

There wasn't room for her. The sun would hit her unless… Could she lie on top of him?

She stretched her body out against his slowly, holding herself above him on her arms while she tried positioning herself. Be careful. Stay in the shade. Don't hurt him. But the sustained weight was too much. She had nothing left and collapsed on his chest, the fog overtaking her and sucking her into a dreamless slumber.

————

Jo awoke groaning. Fuck. She felt like she'd been hit by a truck.

Her eyes popped open, and she lifted her head. Christopher's blue eyes were open as well, staring up at her, and she caught her breath.

"Can you move?" she whispered. When he didn't answer—or move—she assumed no.

She looked around, adjusting her body to make sure she wasn't hurting him. And felt another part stir against her. Her eyes fell to find him watching her, the light from the setting sun and the tunnel behind them providing ample illumination. His lips looked so soft…

"Sorry—I'll move." Her hands shifted to the ground to push herself up—and she gasped, jerking them back and looking at the hand hit by the light.

Her fingers weren't just black. The flesh had been burned through, with red muscle and sinew exposed. Jo closed her eyes to stop herself from getting sick and fell down on Christopher's chest weakly, moving her hand up above their heads so he couldn't see it.

Just a minute. She just needed a minute and she'd move. She was trembling lightly, fighting back the nausea. That's all she needed now. To get sick on Christopher. Just when he'd finally started to almost seem to like her. Maybe.

"Show me."

She twitched at the sternness in his voice. She must have taken longer than she thought.

"I caught the edge of the light," she muttered weakly. She still couldn't bring herself to move.

Christopher slid his hand up her body from her sides slowly, drawing a small whimper from her. It was just such a welcome distraction from the pain. He paused and moved even more slowly until he reached her wrist, wrapping his hand around it to pull it to him. She whimpered again, this time because she didn't want him seeing it. It was ugly. And she didn't want to be ugly to him. But he must have thought he'd hurt her because he stopped.

She almost choked when he moved his hands back down to her legs and spread them apart to straddle him. But he quickly held her upper body to his chest and sat up, leaning back to look at her hand.

Jo let her head drop to his shoulder. The quick movement to sit up had almost pushed her over the edge. But since they didn't eat, maybe they couldn't get sick? She didn't intend to find out while sitting on his lap.

She felt his hands, warm and gentle on her wrist, turning it back and forth slowly as he looked. He released a breath.

"I'm sorry." His voice was angry. "I should have already had us in position."

"Christopher," she breathed, sitting up just enough to rest her forehead against his. She felt too dizzy to be overly worried about what she was doing. "You can't anticipate everything…"

"I should have anticipated this." His self-disgust was evident. "I knew the sun paralyzed me."

She stroked his curls with her good hand.

"Stop trying to be God," she whispered. Her head was spinning. She didn't know how much was from her hand and how much was from straddling him and having her lips so very close to his. She rubbed her head against his softly, instinct alone guiding her now, and she felt him move between her legs. "I feel really, really sick."

That was not what she meant to say at all.

"I need to lie down," she muttered, trying to lean over on the ground.

Christopher caught her, quickly moving and helping her lie flat on her back. Everything was spinning.

She heard his sharp intake of breath.

"What happened to your face?"

Her eyes popped open. Had she burned her face? *Did it look like her fingers?* She brought her good hand up to her cheek swiftly to feel.

"Ow…" Oh yeah. She'd punched herself a few times. She whimpered again. Was she all splotchy and bruised? She wanted to cry from embarrassment.

He was gliding his fingers across her skin so lightly it was like the air.

"What happened," he repeated. This time it was an order. She groaned.

"It was almost impossible to stay awake. I had to do something to keep my brain working. When I burned my fingers, that woke me up. For about 5 seconds. So I had to keep doing things so I could get us into the shade. I don't know why my skin didn't regenerate this time."

It came out as so much more of a whine than she'd intended. She knew she was being such a baby, but she still felt like sobbing at the idea of how she must look.

"Stop looking at me." She didn't care how petulant she sounded. She was sick. Her skin was gone on her hand. And she was bruised all over her face. "Just push me out in the sand and let me burn in the morning," she muttered, trying to turn away, but he buried his hand in her hair, trapping her.

"Ow," she glared at him.

He relaxed his grip slightly but otherwise ignored her, his eyes still moving over her skin. Finally he met her eyes again, his own filled with anger. And when he spoke at last, his voice was as cutting as she had ever heard it.

"You don't ever damage yourself to help me. Ever. Do you understand?"

She stared at him.

"Fuck you." She was incensed. "How about, 'thank you for helping me, Jo! Wow, that was awfully nice of you, Jo! That must have been such a struggle for you today, Jo, but you did it! We didn't burn!'"

"You burned." His voice was cold, but his eyes were still on fire.

"Yeah, and you're supposed to say thank you!"

"I didn't ask you to do that!"

Jo stared at him for one second more and then began pushing at him with her good hand.

"Get. Off! I want to sit up! This has been a *miserable. Fucking. Day.* And you are making it *worse.*" He finally removed his hand from her hair and let her push him back, his expression still dark. She slowed as she sat up, another wave of dizziness hitting her.

She jerked away when he reached out to help, scooting over to lean back against the gates and close her eyes, blocking him out. But footsteps sounded behind her, and her eyes flew open again immediately.

"Back away from the gates."

The voice was curt, perfunctory, and Jo could detect a faint accent that felt very familiar but she couldn't quite place.

She looked back over her shoulder to see two young, well muscled men approaching. They each wore thick, tailored leather armor and carried sheathed metal swords at their sides. Both men were clean shaven and had short hair, much shorter than hers, cut in a traditional military style.

Holding her injured hand to her chest, she scurried back from the bars. Christopher pulled her to her feet along with him, shielding her from the guards' eyes, and she completely forgot she was angry. She cringed behind him and peeked out over his shoulder.

The guards opened the gates, securing each side against a wall and positioning themselves on either side of the doorway.

Christopher studied them before speaking.

"What is this place?"

"You can ask questions once you're processed. Just follow the tunnel to the waiting room and have a seat until they open the doors."

Jo looked up at Christopher. He didn't appear any happier about that than she was. He tried again.

"What does processing involve?"

This time the guards didn't answer. Christopher looked over his shoulder and met her eyes. What else could they do? Stay where they were?

He reached for her uninjured hand before turning back to the open gates, keeping her close behind him as he stepped forward.

"Wait." One of the guards stopped them as they started to pass, looking down between their bodies. Jo huddled more closely to Christopher's back. "Let me see."

Jo sputtered a bit, not moving. She most certainly would not!

"Your hand, Jo," Christopher said.

Oh. She held her hand out awkwardly for the guard.

"You can't go in like that. You'll have to burn again. You can enter tomorrow."

Jo's heart jumped into overdrive. No. No, she was done burning. There was shade. There was an underground. She was *done burning*.

She swallowed, the sickness she'd felt earlier returning full force.

"Back away from the gates, ma'am." The guards placed their hands on their swords. She blinked, stepping back from Christopher and tugging at the hand he was still holding.

He didn't let go.

"Go on. I'll…catch up tomorrow."

He turned, giving her a repressive look, and guided her a distance away from the gates, out of the guards' sight.

Jo gave her knees the freedom to give out at last and sat down in the sand, pulling her legs to her chest as usual. Her head fell forward weakly.

"I thought it was finally over." A shiver went through her, and Christopher hesitated only a moment before kneeling down beside her and pulling her to him. She turned her face into his neck, trying to absorb his heat. His calm.

He rubbed her back in long, slow strokes, his palm flat against her skin. His lips moved against her forehead, his body growing hard.

"If you're trying to distract me," she said. "It's…working."

She felt him smile against her forehead. But he didn't stop.

The crunch of feet on the sand in the distance caused them both to tense.

———

Jo felt panic creeping up on her. Why had they walked so far from the guards? What if it was that man?

Christopher must have had similar thoughts as he pulled her to her feet slowly.

"My god! People!" The harsh rasp preceded the appearance of yet another naked man, slightly smaller than the one they had seen before. He stumbled toward them and dropped to his knees a few feet away, his body shaking.

"I thought I was the only one," he choked out. And then he began crying. Blubbering really.

Jo glanced at Christopher and then took a step toward the man. Or tried to. Christopher kept his arms locked around her and didn't move. Which on second thought was a good thing. She'd totally forgotten she was naked. Pressing back into him, she tried to hide in his arms.

Still, the poor guy was clearly distraught.

"How long have you been here?" she asked hesitantly.

The man shook his head.

"I don't even know! I don't even know..." His sobs shook him, and he bent further into himself.

"There's a gate behind us. If you hurry, the guards should let you in before the sun hits again," Christopher said coolly.

The man jerked his head up, and looked around to lock his gaze on the sloped area behind them. He gave a pained cry and stumbled to his feet.

"Thank you—thank you," he gasped, no longer looking at them as he hurried forward.

Christopher stood unmoving until they heard the guards let him in. Then he pulled Jo a bit closer to the gates, back in view of the guards. He didn't sit this time but kept his arms around her, his eyes scanning the horizon. And the moon rose. And the guards left. And the moon set.

When the first glow of the sun warmed the horizon, Jo swallowed. This was it. Just one more time.

"You should get in the shade," she whispered.

Christopher shifted in the sand, his arms still around her, but he didn't let go.

She nudged him.

"Go on. I feel...like I need to be in position. To prepare myself."

He exhaled sharply but released her. She nudged him again when he didn't move, and he started walking away, a muscle flexing in his jaw.

Jo sat down where she was, trembling. One more time. *One more time.* Then never again. She pulled her knees to her chest, still babying her injured hand. Hilarious. As if this pain were anything.

She looked behind her at Christopher. He was sitting in the shade against the wall, his eyes on her. She tried to give him a reassuring smile, but based on his darkening expression, she must have failed.

She turned back to face the oncoming light.

Breathe in through your nose, out through your mouth. In… out…in….out… She shuddered. She could do this. What was one more day? She could do this.

She jumped when Christopher's arms went around her.

"What are you doing!" she practically yelled. The sun would be up any moment.

"Be quiet!" He was harsh. Furious.

She pulled at his arms, but they were like a vice around her. She stopped worrying about her injury and used both hands. He wouldn't budge.

"This is stupid!" She was definitely yelling now. "Get back in the shade!"

"Stop talking!" He lashed out, tightening his arms further.

Her body began trembling out of control, and she beat her fists on his hands.

"Dammit—I didn't go through all that trouble last night just for you to burn again!"

He just squeezed her even harder and hid his face in her neck.

She was still hitting him, her screams having given way to sobs, when the sun hit, burning away the tears and the intense comfort of his arms.

When night fell again, she was lying on her side, Christopher's arm around her from behind. She froze in shock when he pulled her close, his body shaking.

"How are you able to move?" she whispered.

He went completely still, and she could feel his lashes move against her skin.

"I don't know."

She heard the frown in his voice and pushed herself around to face him.

"Why would you do that?" she breathed.

He avoided her eyes.

"I don't know," he mumbled.

Her eyes felt soft. Heavy. It was all she could do to not lean into him and feel him with her lips. Taste him. Touch him.

"Come on," he muttered, pulling her up as he stood but keeping his eyes averted. He kept her hand in his as they walked to the gates.

When the guards showed up, they let them through immediately. And this time, there was no hesitation as they stepped through.

The tunnel sparkled around them. Familiar grains of glowing sand had been pressed throughout the stone surface, enveloping them in a gentle light, and the air was somehow as pleasant and crisp as on the surface. It left little room above their heads, extending only seven feet or so from the floor, but the light kept it from feeling claustrophobic.

They followed as it led them in a downward slope deep below, eventually spilling out into a massive hall with soaring ceilings many stories high and sparkling marble-like tiles covering almost every surface. Two giant stone archways at the far end beckoned them with a message engraved above that said "Welcome to the City," but heavy iron gates blocked the paths.

City? This was a metropolis.

Jo shuffled close to Christopher as they stood half hidden in the tunnel entrance. About twenty men waited in the hall in front of them, including the man they had seen the night before. They were far enough back that no one had noticed them, but she still inched closer to Christopher. Some of those men looked...creepy.

He seemed to approve of her moving behind him, so she risked standing against his back and peeking out over his shoulder. He stiffened when her breasts touched him, and her eyes darted up to his face. Stillness. His lashes swept down and he turned his head toward her slightly, but he said nothing. And he didn't move away. She waited, watching him. Finally his eyes lifted to the scene in front of them once more, and she released her breath.

They observed in silence for a while before he reached back for her hand and began stepping forward, only to turn his head in surprise when she didn't budge. Uh, no. No way. She was not going out there naked in front of twenty or so scary looking guys. When he tried pulling harder, she stepped close again and wrapped her free arm around his waist, flattening herself against him completely.

Tension gripped his body, but she held on. His hand released her to massage his forehead, before looking at her over his shoulder.

"We can't just stand here."

"Why not?" she murmured against his skin, her eyes looking up into his. Right now, this seemed the most perfect possible place to be. Or possibly back a few feet. Or more.

Irritation flashed in his eyes, and he reached down to pull her arm off him. She quickly threaded her other arm under his, grabbing her wrist and locking him to her. Her body was plastered against his, her forehead against the center of his back, and he exhaled in a short burst.

"This is childish." He snapped. She didn't care. No way was she letting go. He was either going to leave her there or pull her into that throng, and neither of those options worked for her. He could be as angry with her as he liked. He began pulling her hands apart with one hand on each of her wrists, and her body wiggled against his as they struggled.

"Can you calm down," he choked out, trying to pry her hands apart. Her fingers slipped, and she tried to get a better grip…until the edge of her right hand grazed him and they both froze. She stood very still, their hearts pounding between them so hard their bodies shook with each beat.

She breathed into the center of his back, her face against his skin, her lashes blinking. Neither of them moved. For a moment. Then she let her hand drift lower.

Her fingers slid down the hard muscles of his abdomen until her palm flowed over the warm, smooth hardness pressed firmly against his stomach. Her lips parted against his back, and he gripped her wrists more tightly, his breathing ragged. She paused with her hand at the top of his shaft and stroked the tip ever so lightly with her thumb, feeling the moisture grow.

It was beautifully rounded and so soft to the touch for something so impossibly hard. She moved her thumb along the head in a slow circle as her hand enveloped him, feeling his fingers biting into her wrists. Brushing her lips against his back, back and forth against his skin, she skimmed the length of his shaft with her fingertips. God she wanted him in her mouth again. Her tongue reached out to touch his skin as her fingers at last wrapped firmly around him, pressing him into her grip at the tip and letting him slide through.

"Enough." His voice was hoarse, and he dragged her hand away, forcing both her arms to their sides. She groaned into him and pressed her body close, unable to move her arms.

"Why will you never let me touch you," she whispered. His grip on her wrists tightened.

"There are more important things to think about right now," he said, his voice angry.

Jo grew still. How many times was he going to use that excuse? She pulled back, tugging out of his grip behind him, and stepped over to the side of the tunnel to stare at the men across the room who had yet to notice them.

"Fine." She crossed her arms.

He fell back against the wall, hiding from the view of the hall, and shot her a furious look.

"Do you ever bother to think through things, or do you follow your primitive brain exclusively," he ground out. His hand had a death grip on his cock, clearly trying to subdue it.

"I think it's *your* primitive brain that's the problem. You're just upset you can't control it!"

"The only thing out of control is you!" he hissed.

"Really?" Her eyes narrowed. She was done letting him make her feel ashamed. "Let's test that theory."

She saw the alarm in his eyes the instant before she flattened her chest against his, her hands reaching down between them.

He released himself to grab her wrists, and she leaned into him, the rigid warmth between them digging into her stomach. He pushed her away and yanked her around to press her against the wall until she couldn't move. "Enough!"

She glared at him, vibrating with anger. With frustration. With need. Her chest heaved against his, and she tried not to notice how it dragged her nipples across his skin.

Raging eyes stared back at her, but with each breath, his brow pulled together. Three breaths. Four. He looked down. And the sound he made seemed to come from deep inside. He dropped his forehead to hers, his fingers biting into her wrists. And then his touch softened.

His hands rubbed her arms in long, slow caresses, massaging and soothing them. Knuckles floated across her skin, sliding up her shoulders, her neck, and back down, his eyes watching their path as they moved across the swell of her breasts to the hard pink tips pressing into him. He captured each nipple between his knuckles, pinching and rolling them beneath his thumbs.

The feeling was so intense it was painful, and she released a small cry, pushing him away with one hand while pulling on him with the other. He groaned and leaned down to capture one with his lips, sucking it into the warmth of his mouth and sending sharp pangs into her core. She started to wrap her arms around him but he grabbed both her wrists, imprisoning them behind her while he sucked her more deeply into his mouth, lifting her body.

Her forehead fell toward his as she tried getting closer, but he pulled himself away to drop to his knees, brushing his lips, his cheek, against the skin of her stomach, before resting for a moment against her. She struggled with her hands, wanting them free, and he released her. His hands slid up the backs of her knees, her thighs, as she finally buried her fingers in the soft curls on his head…and he buried his tongue between the soft folds of her lips.

Her thighs came forward against his cheeks as her body convulsed helplessly around him. He held her steady, forcing her thighs apart with his hands as his tongue pushed hard against her, alternately pressing and sucking as wave after wave hit her.

Her legs trembled, but he held her steady, pulling one leg over his shoulder and groaning into her, his tongue and lips continuing to torture her. Sliding his tongue along her slit, his lips caressing every fold, before gliding back to slip into her, his thumb brushing her small curls softly. She stared down with wet eyes, her hands stroking his head the way she'd longed to for so long, watching as he kissed her, his expression pained. She wanted him there forever. And she wanted him inside of her.

She pulled on his shoulders, and at last he stood, sliding his body up hers as he did, trailing his tongue on her skin. She needed to feel him. But he wrapped his arms around her firmly, keeping his body, hard and throbbing, pressed so tightly to her that she couldn't reach him.

Jo pulled back to look at him, but he kept his eyes averted and kissed her shoulder.

"Why?" she whispered. She tried to touch him again, but again he kept her so tightly against him that she couldn't. And still he kissed her body.

Her hand reached for his face, but he captured it, kissing her fingertips, her palm, the inside of her wrist. She leaned her head toward him but he pressed his lips to her neck, sucking softly. No matter what she tried to do, he evaded her again and again.

"Christopher..." she breathed, pleading. He simply groaned into her, pressing her to him. She ground her fists into his back when he didn't answer, hitting him as she said his name, but he just grew still and pressed closer, stroking her cheek. And then she was crying. She didn't even know why. Her arms embraced him tightly, the tears shaking her body. And he held her close, stroking her back, leaving whispers of kisses on her neck, her shoulder. His hands were flat against her skin, holding her to him.

He held her until her shuddering breaths returned to normal. Until she leaned weakly against him. He just held her. And she was afraid to let go.

But somehow she felt more alone than before.

———

After a while, Christopher put his hands on the wall and pushed himself back to look at her. His lower body was still pressed against hers and still fairly hard. She let her hands fall from his neck and crossed her arms in front of her before looking up unsmiling.

"Do you want to wait here while I go find out what we need to do?"

His eyes were clear and steady. She gave a brief nod.

He inclined his head toward the opposite wall.

"Will you wait over where I can see you?"

She nodded again, and he hesitated only a moment before moving back. She stepped around him and slid down against the opposite wall, pulling her knees to her chest. He didn't turn immediately, and she looked out at the hall while she waited. Eventually his shoulders relaxed, and he started to walk out, his body back to normal.

"You won't move?" He paused, sounding unsure. Was he afraid she'd dart back up the tunnel? She shook her head.

The sound of the gates opening drew their attention. Multiple guards appeared from under the stone archways, lining up all along the front. They each wore thick, well tailored leather armor and stood with their feet comfortably apart, holding long, unsheathed metal swords they balanced comfortably on the ground in front of them. She stood as more and more filled in the area.

"Men line up at the gate on your right, women at the gate on your left," one of the guards announced loudly. Women? She was the only woman she saw.

Jo looked up at Christopher, her heart pounding. He didn't react, his eyes scanning the guards and the growing line of men. He watched as the line moved forward, his eyes narrowed. Finally he looked over at her.

"When you go through the gate, just follow their rules. Whatever they are. Don't be reckless."

She blinked at his abrupt tone.

"Just like that? Just…go?"

He released a quick breath.

"They have guards, armor, and weapons. They have created massive structures," he gestured around them. "They have a system, and I know how to work with systems. I'll figure it out. Just…stay out of trouble until I do." His eyes were piercing.

"I'm not a child. I can take care of myself."

"You are careless with your safety," he said flatly.

"It's not careless to care about somebody!"

He looked away, frustration in his eyes. When he looked back, his eyes were heated.

"I am trying to explain the flaws that might put you in danger."

Jo's lips parted, and she gave a humorless laugh.

"Very helpful, I'm sure. Shall I tell you *your* flaws now?"

His eyes narrowed. "This is unproductive."

Jo clenched her jaw. Just breathe.

"Okay then," she said at last, her voice clipped. "Through the gates. After you." She gestured for him to proceed, and the line between his brow twitched.

"You first," he bit out.

She glared at him a moment more and then brushed past him without another glance. If he was fine with them parting, so be it.

She walked over to the left side of the room, trying to breathe evenly, but stopped just before she reached the guards, staring into the empty tunnel. What would be waiting on the other side? The guards and people she'd seen were all men. But they had a separate gate for women so there must be women inside.

What kind of system was she stepping into? Should she even go in? Or just hide out in the tunnel? Or maybe stay in the huge hall? If she did, she was sure to run into some crazy man eventually when the guards weren't around…and she'd be all alone. A little dog in a big dog world. Or a world full of wolves.

She closed her eyes for a moment. There really weren't any better options. She drew in a deep breath, opened her eyes, and took a step forward.

Arms went around her from behind, one hand pulling her waist back and the other reaching up to her neck. Melting with relief, she leaned back.

"Be careful," Christopher whispered.

She shuddered but didn't answer, gripping his arms and pushing back into him to absorb the warmth of his skin. His arms tightened around her almost painfully as he held her close. She couldn't stop shaking. Couldn't get warm enough. But she could feel his heart pounding against her. His fingers biting into her skin. His breath hot on her neck. And a calm came over her, tingling and teasing her flesh, chasing away the fear until she at last could breathe again. Until his grip eased and she could feel his heart beating in time with hers.

Then they were stepping apart and the cool air surrounded her. She stepped toward the tunnel without looking back, her eyes stinging. It would all be okay. This was safety. Everything would be okay now.

She walked through the gate.

6

MOON DAY 92

Jo was back in school. Beside her were three other girls seated in metal chairs with leather cushions, the seats placed in a half circle around a rather stuffy male elocution instructor who was droning on and on. Every few minutes he would have one of the girls stand up and given an impromptu speech in order to critique their pronunciation, word choice, inflection, and even their stance.

This really was Hell.

Jo peeked over at Missy to her left, trying not to laugh out loud at her disgusted look. Missy was the first girl she'd met after entering the gate. Evidently women were extremely rare here, with men outnumbering them almost ten to one. Before they would be allowed to mingle in society, they were required to assimilate into the culture. For women, this consisted of classes like City Safety, Posture and Poise, Minding Your Manners, and —of course—Elocution.

Madison was on the other side of Jo, sitting straight up in her seat and watching the teacher intently. Madison had arrived almost a week after Jo. By that time, Jo and Missy had developed a definite friendship, so Jo had worried Madison might feel like a third wheel. But no matter how much they had tried to include her, Madison just seemed to want to smile thinly at them, her disapproval of nearly everything almost palpable. This is, until Amber arrived.

Amber sat on the other side of Madison, watching the instructor with heavy lidded eyes. She would occasionally cross or uncross her long legs depending on whether he was looking her way, and a touch of a smile would curve the corner of her mouth when he stumbled over his words. Amber was a goddess, and Madison worshipped her. Everyone here seemed to worship her, in fact, and not only the men. The matron held her up constantly as the supreme example of what the City valued.

The matron ran the school. Although the title suggested a woman of far greater years, she—like everyone else here— appeared to be in her late teens or early twenties. Jo had been shocked to discover she'd been running the place for well over fifty years and hadn't burned once in that time. There truly was no aging here.

"And now we come to sentence stress. It's really very important, because stressing a particular word in a sentence can change the meaning—"

"I'm feeling tons of sentence stress! Can I be excused?" Missy's voice was loud and brash. Her signature style.

The instructor looked down his nose at her, frowning in distaste, and Madison mimicked him perfectly as she looked over. Amber looked at her nails.

"Melissa—"

"I told you it's Missy."

"Melissa," he continued, pulling himself up to his full height. It wasn't very far, but Jo had to give him credit for trying. "You have been disruptive multiple times now. I am trying to improve you, but if you continue to reject my training, I will have no choice but to have you removed."

Missy's eyes perked up.

"You mean all I have to do is keep interrupting you and I don't have to take your stupid classes anymore? Sweet!"

He walked over to stand directly in front of her, but Missy stood up with her hands on her hips, towering over him by at least three inches. She was bigger than most the girls—very fit, of course, as was everyone. But her build was naturally larger, and if things escalated between her and the teacher, Jo would bet on Missy.

"You need to listen to the teacher, Missy," Madison piped up. "He's just trying to do his job."

"Well it's not a job *I* ever wanted him to do. I didn't sign up for any of this."

"Would you prefer going back to the surface?" Amber asked casually, not bothering to look at her.

Missy glared in her direction.

"Maybe I would. I don't fall apart in terror and scream all day afterwards."

That got her attention, and Amber stared back at her in fury.

Amber hadn't handled the burning very well. They'd heard her screaming over and over the entire first day—well, technically night—she'd arrived. Amber swore it was someone else, but Madison was the only one who believed her. There were no other women who had arrived after the screaming except Amber.

The days and nights were reversed underground. When the sun came up, everyone fell asleep. They just passed out completely, as Christopher had. Jo seemed to be the only one who resisted the sensation. She had come very close to revealing this to Missy the first week, but Christopher's voice kept lecturing her in her head, so she stayed silent. Besides, it didn't seem very relevant. They had comfortable beds, and the entire city evidently had a curfew in place. Everyone was in bed before the sun came up.

But once the sun went down, their days began. The

Sanctuary was brightly lit with well appointed shades of light from the sands. She'd heard the city itself made you feel like you were outside, with the cavern ceiling soaring high above embedded with lights that mimicked a beautiful summer's day. But she hadn't been able to see it yet. Perhaps Christopher had been allowed to see the city by now, but she was still stuck in the Sanctuary.

Christopher... Her stomach tightened into knots every time she let herself think about him. She hadn't heard a word from him in the three weeks since they arrived. She wanted to ask someone, but she was afraid it might reveal something she shouldn't. He'd been so insistent about not revealing anything that wasn't absolutely necessary. But the longer time went by, the more she felt like she was being incredibly paranoid, and the more desperate she was to know if he was okay.

"Josephine. Are we interrupting you?"

Jo jerked to attention in her seat, and Missy snickered. When did she sit back down?

"Um—"

"We do *not* say *um!*" he said, affronted.

"Yeah, Jo, the proper response is *yes, kind sir, you are fucking interrupting me,*" Missy said.

"That's it!" The instructor was livid. "Leave this room immediately and return to your quarters!"

Missy threw her hands up in victory as she got to her feet, winking at Jo before turning and exiting through leather curtained doorway.

Jo watched her leave wistfully. But when the instructor began hounding her once more, she played along. This all so ridiculous, but Christopher said to follow the rules. So she sighed and got to work.

———

"Did you see his face? I thought he was going to have an aneurysm!" Missy and Jo were sitting on Missy's bed as she relived her mini-rebellion. Missy was trying to give Jo cornrows, but it wasn't going well. Her hair kept slipping out of the small braids, even though it was the longest it had been since she'd been here.

"What did the matron say?" Jo asked.

Missy hesitated, her fingers stalling on Jo's hair. But she was tugging at the hairs again almost immediately.

"Meh. Who cares. What can they do to me that's worse than burning alive all day? The worst they can do is kick me out of this douchey place."

"Oh, that's not true," Amber said from her bed across the room. "I bet they could do a lot worse. For example, they could force you to stare at your reflection. You don't know how painful it is for everyone else who has to look at you…"

"Missy is lovely," Jo snapped.

"Of course you would think so," Amber smiled, her eyelids low. "You're as grotesque as she is. Two pitiful examples of poor genes and poor breeding."

"Breeding is for bitches, so it suits you well," Missy said sweetly.

"There is no call for language like that, Melissa," Madison chimed in. Her bed was beside Amber's, and she was sitting primly on its edge. "Being well bred has to do with upbringing, education, class, and language. Crass language shows poor breeding."

"So you don't have a problem with someone being a cunt," Missy fired back before Jo could figure out how to voice her own outrage at what she was hearing. "So long as they use the proper terminology, right Maddy?"

Madison bristled while Amber's slow smile stretched more widely.

"Don't bother with them, Madison. It's to be expected of people who were raised in a trailer park."

"I'll show you what a trailer park girl can do," Missy ground out as she abandoned Jo's hair entirely and pushed herself off the bed. Amber stood up in alarm.

"This is not how civilized people are to behave!" she said, her eyes wide. Missy lunged for her, and Amber quickly climbed over Madison's bed to rush for the door. Madison darted back out of the way as Missy stomped over it as well.

"Matron! Matron!" Amber screamed as Missy grabbed the back of her clothes. The fine leather ripped out of her hands as Amber made a desperate dive, grabbing the leather curtains in the doorway and tearing them from the wall to land in a heap of torn material.

Missy doubled over, howling with laughter, while Amber scrambled to get out of the now open doorway. She made it just as the matron came into view.

She was a small woman, barely over five feet in height, with delicate features and almost bird like bones. She glanced down at Amber.

"She—she attacked me!" Amber was pointing at Missy, her voice trembling with some combination of fear and anger.

The matron eyed her with the first hint of disapproval Jo had seen her show toward Amber.

"A lady does not crawl across the floor like a dog," she said coldly. "I thought you might be tier one. Perhaps I was mistaken."

Amber blanched and got to her feet quickly. She took a deep breath and opened her mouth, but she froze and closed it again at the matron's look.

The matron turned away from her and stepped into the room with her hands held calmly in front of her, looking around slowly. Her eyes stopped once they fell on Missy.

"Melissa, my dear, what did we talk about," she smiled. But the smile didn't reach her eyes.

Jo was surprised when Missy looked down and didn't move.

She wanted to defend her. Missy had tried being friendly with Amber, but Amber had informed her the first day that she didn't associate with trash. Since then, it always seemed to be war between the two, a war Missy had been forced into, as far as Jo was concerned. She supposed Missy could have ignored Amber's taunts, but that somehow seemed so much worse than defending herself the way she did. And even if physically attacking her might have gone just a little too far, Jo couldn't help feeling like she'd deserved it.

So she wanted to defend her. But she didn't. Because she was supposed to be careful. So she remained silent.

"Come with me." The matron turned sedately toward the door, and Missy paused for only a moment before following behind.

"Clean up this mess, girls. Ladies are always tidy."

Then she continued down the hall. Missy gave Jo a quick glance before she disappeared with her.

———

It was almost bedtime when Missy returned. She didn't say anything until she reached Amber's bed. Then she stopped.

She seemed to be struggling with something and stood with various expressions flitting across her face. Finally she turned to Amber who was lying on her bed, flipping through a large leather bound book of the latest fashions.

"Please forgive me," she bit out. Amber looked up with wide, delighted eyes.

"I'm glad to see you've learned your place. Now move along before I become ill from looking at you," she said, dropping her eyes back to her book.

Jo could see Missy's hands clinch at her sides, but she turned around and walked to their side of the room to climb into bed.

Jo looked at the clock on the wall. They had about half an hour before everyone passed out. She hesitated but got out of bed to go to Missy.

"Hey," she whispered, sitting down on the edge. Missy kept her back to her. Jo grimaced. This felt familiar. "Are you okay?"

Silence.

Jo sighed. "I'm so sorry, Missy. You should never have had to apologize to her. This was total bullshit."

"Then why didn't you say anything!" she hissed as she turned over to look at her. Jo looked back helplessly.

"Because..." *Because there is someone I care about outside these walls. And I have no idea if he's okay. And I don't know what will happen if I get in trouble before I can get out of here and find him.*

But she hadn't told anyone about Christopher, and she needed to keep it that way. She didn't even know why. But he'd said not to be reckless, so she was being extra careful.

"You have every right to be angry," she whispered. "None of this is fair."

Missy snorted.

"Fair. You have no fucking idea how unfair it gets. But you will."

She turned back over, the bitterness in her voice leaving Jo feeling cold. She wanted to ask her what she meant. And she wanted to apologize again. But what use was an apology when she wasn't going to do anything differently?

She stood up and walked back to her bed, troubled. Was she making the right decisions? She laid down and turned away from Missy's bed, pulling the leather covers around her. The covers weren't very warm, but they were good for emotional comfort. It's not like they ever felt truly hot or cold.

She was confused when she felt the covers pulling back, and she looked up to find Missy crawling into bed beside her. Her eyes were wet and Jo scooted over, turning to face her. She reached for Missy's hands, which were clutched together at her chest like she was a little girl.

"I'm scared." Missy's voice was hoarse. "I'm so fucking scared I can't see straight."

Jo squeezed her hands tightly.

"What happened today?"

She shook her head, opening her mouth and closing it again before finally speaking.

"They won't let us go, Jo. Ever."

Jo grew very still.

"You mean…we have to stay in the Sanctuary?"

Missy laughed, a humorless sound, and closed her eyes a moment before looking at Jo once more.

"There aren't enough women to go around." Her voice was steadier now. "So they have rules. The *men* have rules. About how to share. How to share *us*."

Jo could hear their breathing in the silence of the room. Amber and Madison weren't making a sound. And the clock on the wall ticked out each second of the approaching sun.

"What rules, Missy," she whispered.

Missy exhaled in another humorless laugh.

"For Amber, tier one rules. They're probably exactly what she's used to," Missy said scathingly. "But for you and me…?" She threaded her fingers through Jo's and looked at her with bleak eyes. "The best we can hope for is to be some type of…time share." She spat out the words. "And the worst… Our bodies are disposable, Jo. If the men damage us, they will just throw us in the sun so we'll be fresh the next night."

Jo's heart hammered in her chest. She felt Missy squeezing her hands hard.

"I might have already ruined any chance I had of getting into a higher tier. The matron says she is ready to assign me to tier five—that's the bottom." Missy's face was pale but her tone was matter-of-fact. "The top tier gets sold to the richest guys, and the buyer treats his property well. It's a huge status symbol to have the exclusive use of a woman. She won't be shared.

"But all other tiers have multiple owners or, if you're tier five, the city keeps ownership and charges per use. And..." Here she faltered. "They get used a lot."

Jo felt ill.

Missy squeezed her hands again.

"But *you* won't be in tier five! You've been doing what they said. And you're pretty! Some group will want to buy you for sure!"

They stared at each other for a moment, the clock ticking in the background. Then they burst out laughing. Quietly. Their bodies shook as they tried to contain the sounds, and tears streamed from the corners of their eyes. They were squeezing each others' hands so tightly that Jo could barely feel her fingers anymore.

"Fuck. I used to protest this shit!" Missy wiped her eyes, drawing in a breath. "I only have one memory, but it's pretty fucking glorious. I had "rage against the patriarchy" in paint across my tits and ran at some pig who was trying to keep me behind a barrier." She frowned. "I think I might have been fat. And drunk. God I miss alcohol..." she sighed.

They were both shaking a little and Jo pulled the cover up around them. She didn't know how to process this. Or what she could do. Could they try running away? There were guards everywhere, keeping the four of them isolated to the second floor until their first round of training finished. Then it would be the same thing again on the third floor. They were constantly watched except when in their windowless room, and then they had Amber and Madison to contend with.

But more importantly...Jo could never leave without Christopher. Never. She would endure whatever she had to until she found him again. No matter the cost.

The clock chimed, their final warning to be in bed. And then she was falling, her mind dragged down into a dreamless slumber that she no longer fought. It was the only escape she had.

————

It had been almost two months since she had seen Christopher.

Second floor classes were drawing to a close, and they were about to graduate to the third and final floor. Each of them would be given a final grade upon completion that would determine their tier—and the misery of their existence.

"Amber, this is the rumba. Not a rumble. You do *not* come at me when I am walking toward you. You follow *me*. Slow, quick quick, slow…"

Their dance instructor was the only man who had been permitted to touch them. Probably because the last thing he would ever be interested in was a female. Jo had hoped he might be sympathetic to their plight since he didn't benefit from it, but if he'd ever had any compassion, the years in this place had long since erased it. But at least his insults were pretty evenly distributed to each of them. Amber didn't like him.

Missy had managed to bite her tongue for the most part since the big incident with Amber, but Jo could see the restraint was getting to her. And not just to her. Jo's anxiety grew with each day that passed by with no sign of Christopher. Was he okay? Or had he just abandoned her? Men enjoyed a basic democracy, where they voted on the laws they lived under. Laws that gave them absolute power over women. Why should Christopher concern himself with her now? He could live comfortably, safe from the sun. And even if he didn't want to abandon her, what could he possibly do? The city was a giant prison.

"Madison, take the stick out of your backside! Do you want to end up in tier four?" The instructor's harassed voice had no discernible effect on her dancing, although Jo thought she grew a touch more pale.

The instructors no longer hid the realities they faced in this society. It had quickly become clear that Amber had known for some time. Perhaps they had told her to calm her down that first night. Or perhaps the matron had revealed it to her during one of their many private discussions. Either way, Amber seemed quite content to be a valuable work of art, highly sought after by the richest and most powerful men in society. Amber's life would be pampered and luxurious.

But the rest of them were not so lucky. Missy was trying to fight against being put into tier five, but even tier four was pretty horrific. She would be sold to a private company that would rent her out. They had various rental categories, ranging from the lower end to the luxury market and catering to a variety of tastes. But the private companies at least cared to maintain their property, and so the women weren't used as often or as severely as what would happen in tier five.

That left tiers two and three. Madison thus far was likely to be tier three. She would become what Missy called a timeshare, owned by twelve men who would each own her for a month, rotating throughout the year, and occasionally selling their share in her to someone else. However, tier three had better protections because the men were all required to vote on any new member, as they all wished to protect their investment from being damaged.

It was looking to Jo like she would most likely be placed in tier three as well. However, if she couldn't figure out how to get out of this nightmare, she hoped there might be a way to get into tier two, as she would then be owned by only two or three men. It was a long shot as in many ways, tier two was as good as tier one, and Jo wondered if it might not be even better. By having at least two men, each one would act as a type of monitor for the other, providing some checks and balances with how they treated her. At least, this is what she hoped.

The thought drew her up short, and she nearly stumbled.

This was her life now. Hoping to be bought by men who wouldn't torture her. Much. At least it was better than burning, wasn't it?

"You follow well, Josephine, but must you turn into a lurching robot each time I let you go? You must *own* the floor—command the attention of the room."

As if. That sounded like more nightmare material. But this class thus far offered her the best chance to pull ahead with her grades, so she tried swaying on her own the way he'd taught her. God, this was awkward.

Missy's turn was next. The instructor didn't even bother critiquing her. He just limped away after a very short session.

Amber snickered as Missy went back to sit on the floor where they were stretching in between learning the steps. Missy didn't react, but Jo wanted to slam Amber's face into the floor. This was all such bullshit.

"As you know, today the Office of the Director of City Intelligence is sending someone to interview each of you. Normally this would have been done earlier, but," his voice dropped to a mutter, "they always have a problem holding onto the Assistant Director." He cleared his throat and smoothed the leather vest he was wearing. "But the new one was here for the girls upstairs yesterday, so you four are next.

"You will want to be extra respectful, especially if you are going to be in tier five." His eyes shifted to Missy for a moment. "Their directors hold city passes for all city services. They are not under the same...constraints as the normal clientele."

Jo didn't look at Missy. She didn't want to look as if she assumed that's where she'd be going. Missy had been on her best behavior. She wasn't going to be in tier five. Jo was sure of it.

The instructor dismissed them and two guards ushered them down the hall, one leading and one following. The guards never spoke to them, and Jo never caught them looking, either. She wondered if perhaps they, too, weren't interested in women.

The guards led them to a seating area at the top of the stairs.

The one room on this floor with an actual door rather than leather drapes was located just to the left of the stairs. Jo wasn't sure what the door was for, but it was large and heavy looking, requiring the guards to open and close it.

Right now it was open and the girls were called in alphabetical order. Amber went first, sauntering in like a cat. Jo wanted to roll her eyes at Missy, but she was trying to be supportive of her efforts to behave. She shook her head at herself. Behave. *Like a good girl.* Jo shifted in her seat, the phrase reverberating through her mind and calling up sensations from a past that felt more distant every day.

She drifted into her thoughts as the time dragged on, wondering if the interviewer was taking extra time with Amber because she was—well, what she was. A fucking succubus. If this was Hell, why would someone like her get rewarded? Wasn't Hell supposed to provide some justice?

The door opened with a grating sound. Amber walked out of the room, snapping at Madison to move over so she could have her seat back. It looked like Amber's visit hadn't gone so well. Score one for the assistant director. Although if he didn't like Amber, Jo couldn't imagine she herself would fare very well, either.

She kept her head down, as she'd been taught. The dance instructor said to be extra respectful, and if this was going to get reported to the matron, she wanted to look more and more like a fit for Tier Two. She was almost halfway in the room before she looked up to see the man sitting behind a stone desk. He was pulling out a fresh piece of parchment. She froze.

He looked up and dismissed the guards with a casual wave, gesturing for her to sit down across from him. She heard the door closing behind her as she fell weakly into the seat. The door clicked into place. And there was silence.

7

MOON DAY 125

Jo couldn't hear anything beyond her own breathing. If she made a sound, she feared it would be a cry. If she moved, she wouldn't be able to keep from throwing herself into his arms.

So she sat very still. Very silent. And they simply stared.

"Did anyone hurt you?"

Jo shook her head. She didn't trust herself to speak.

Christopher relaxed his grip on the parchment he was holding.

"I found a way to get you out of here."

Jo blinked rapidly. The air felt hot around her skin.

Breathe. Listen. She controlled the shaking starting in her body.

"But I need you to get assigned to Tier Five."

She stopped breathing.

"Why?" her voice was barely a whisper, but she was proud she managed anything intelligible.

"Because that's the only tier I am allowed to take."

When she just stared at him, he exhaled in a short burst and ran a quick hand through his hair. It had grown out on top since she'd seen him, and his soft golden curls fell onto his forehead. His jaw, held taut with tension, was cleanly shaved. He had never looked more charmingly boyish and yet… She wondered what his true age was.

He was wearing a well tailored dark suede shirt, open at the neck. Whatever they did to treat the leather here made it exceptionally thin and supple, and it draped his form comfortably. Unlike the monstrosity she was forced to wear.

Although her clothing was supple as well, it didn't drape. It clung. Her bodice was cropped and laced up the front, exposing both her midriff and cleavage. It was combined with a matching set of leather pants that rode low on her hips and laced all the way up the sides from her ankles to tie at her hip.

She was sure it was the sluttiest thing she had ever worn in her life and a pain in the ass to get on and off, but at least the leather was soft and comfortable and she didn't have to walk around naked. And her hair was growing out. It was long enough now to tuck the sides behind her ears, which she had a tendency to do without thinking.

"How..." How had he accomplished any of this? The question was too big. "How are you...the assistant director?"

"Men go through a series of tests, and recruiters come from all around the city. The tests were elementary," his tone was dismissive, "but the population appears to be largely intellectually stunted. With a few notable exceptions in charge of everything. Getting a good job was a simple task. But getting a job that would give me access to you…"

His eyes were turbulent.

"I just need to buy time, Jo. Get in Tier Five. I can keep you with me until I figure out a way to buy you."

Jo reached up and toyed with the hair at the nape of her neck. It felt familiar—being able to play with her hair. It was comforting.

"You're talking about buying me like it's nothing," she murmured. "Like I'm nothing more than property…"

He made a sound of impatience.

"That's the society. It's senseless not to face it."

"You think…I haven't faced it?"

He narrowed his eyes.

"Do you want to argue over semantics or discuss how to get you out?"

Jo stared at him for a moment before turning toward the window beside them. She still couldn't see the city—just a small stone courtyard stretching up from the first floor below them to a well lit ceiling high above. It gave the illusion of a warm summer sun overhead. She supposed it wasn't so bad. Being able to sit and look at something pretty on occasion. And not burning all day. She needed to keep reminding herself how great that was.

"What happens…if I get in tier five. And you…change your mind?" She didn't look at him.

"I won't." His voice was flat. Final.

She wanted to trust him. She wanted to so badly. But what if she was wrong? He was here now, and he'd helped her in the desert. But people didn't die here. They just went on and on. How long would he hold onto this sense of…loyalty? Obligation? Whatever it was. A few months? A year? All she would need to do is anger him one time. Anger him enough for him to no longer feel concerned. Then he'd be free to do as he liked. And she'd be in tier five.

She thought about what she'd said to him before. More than three months ago now. Was it still true? She turned back slowly to face him.

"I told you I trusted you." Her voice was musing. Thoughtful. Christopher's body grew tense. She stared at him for a while. "And I do," she sighed at last, leaning back.

Then she smiled. She couldn't help it. He was here. And in the middle of all the chaos, she felt weirdly…safe.

Christopher hadn't moved, and she could feel the tension radiating from him. He looked away for a long moment. When he turned back, his voice was low and grim.

"You will need to walk a very fine line, Jo. You have to make enough mistakes to get into tier five. But you can't be obvious. If anyone realizes we're trying to manipulate the system, the consequences would be…" he paused a moment before finishing. "Severe."

Jo frowned.

"What would they do?"

Christopher hesitated, his eyes falling to her chest. Jo looked down and her cheeks grew red at her exposed cleavage. Ridiculous. She'd walked around naked with him for weeks. But she had to fight not to cross her arms again.

The clock on the wall chimed the hour. Christopher met her eyes again, and for a moment, she could have sworn he looked desperate. But it was gone in an instant, and she heard the door behind them being opened. He nodded in dismissal, not looking at her.

Jo felt panic rising up inside. She hadn't had enough time with him! Her thoughts were in chaos. *Think. Get up!* She stood on shaky legs, keeping her eyes down as she walked to the door.

"Josephine, was it?" Christopher's voice was cool. Detached. Jo stopped but didn't turn around. She was too afraid she would cry. "When I return next month I'll expect you to be more forthcoming."

She could have melted. He'd be back next month. She held onto her composure and walked out of the room as Madison walked in and the door closed behind her.

Amber gave a delicate snort.

"Poor little mouse. You can't be timid with a man like that. He will eat you for breakfast."

Jo closed her eyes as she collapsed in her seat, trying not to tremble visibly. She hoped he wouldn't scare Missy too much, but it was a relief to know her own reaction didn't seem out of place.

So now she only had one problem. How was she going to get into tier five?

————

A week later and she wasn't any closer to answering that question. She couldn't suddenly change after Christopher's visit, but she was running out of time.

They were in third floor classes now, which would only last another month. After that, tier fives would be put to work immediately, and the other tiers would be sold to businesses in the city who put them through their own training programs before putting them on the market.

Christopher's position in his job meant that he needed to personally sign off on each woman before she would be allowed to move out of the Sanctuary, so he would be back as soon as third floor classes were complete...expecting her to be in tier five.

"Are you blind or simply stupid? There is a difference between tan and brown, Madison! Learn it. I want the *tan* dress today."

Amber's voice lashed out across the room, and Madison scrambled to put the darker dress back in the closet before bringing the lighter color to Amber.

Amber was usually gracious with Madison's "expected deficiencies," which Jo took to refer to her tier three status, but she was being bitchier than usual this morning. And Madison was making more mistakes. She had already bumped into Amber's bed while Amber was trying to apply makeup, and she'd almost dropped the mirror she was holding for her.

And Jo wasn't immune either. Missy had smacked her hand more than once because she was picking at the edge of her clothes. The matron wouldn't be happy with her for damaging the leather, which actually worked well for Jo now, but she couldn't explain that to Missy.

Missy was the only one who seemed unaffected by their upcoming class. She'd just shrugged and told Jo that compared to what she would have to face if she didn't get out of tier five, a *Sexual Services* class should be a walk in the park.

They walked down the hall together at the appointed time, Amber leading with Madison close beside her. Jo was happy to hang back and Missy stayed with her, although Jo knew she'd have preferred to march ahead. That was Missy—always itching to rush in and get the thing done.

As they sat in the leather cushions that had been placed on the floor for them, Jo breathed an inner sigh of relief. She didn't see anything odd in the classroom. Maybe this would just be a rather dry information session. She hoped.

The matron walked in and closed the door. Jo looked around. Wait. Was she going to be teaching them? Jo felt her skin grow alternately hot and cold. This could be it. This could be where she convinced her. Maybe if she looked extremely uncomfortable with sex. Or maybe extremely resistant. What would work best? She fought down the panic. She *had* to get this right.

"Ladies, over the next few weeks, this class will give you a light introduction to some of the duties you will be expected to know how to perform. The companies that purchase you will expect you to at least have a base level of sufficiency before they take on the task of enhancing your abilities. And if you are tier five, you will learn on the job." Her lips flattened into a thin line with the last comment, but she didn't look at Missy when she said it.

"The first thing you will need to have is comfort with your own bodies. You need to be able to do whatever the man wants you to do. Sometimes he wants shyness, and we will go over some techniques for feigning this. But it is paramount that you obey quickly sometimes, with some of the most extreme demands. To that end, take off your clothing and place it by the door before we begin."

Jo, Amber, and Madison all seemed to be paralyzed. But Missy was already standing up and stripping her things off. The matron raised her brows.

"Very good, Melissa. The rest of you…" Her look jolted the other two into action and Jo had to clench her fists to remind herself that she *needed* to get on the matron's bad side. But it was harder than she'd expected to resist doing what she was told. The matron had a way of making you feel like a child.

"Josephine." The warning was heavy in her tone.

"Well…is this really necessary?" She might have laughed at the shocked look on all their faces if she weren't so scared. "I mean, we walked around in the desert naked already. Isn't everyone already comfortable?"

The matron smiled, and Jo had to suppress a shudder. If snakes could smile, she imagined that is just how they would look.

"You have been given an instruction. I will not repeat myself." The matron stood perfectly still.

"Oh, come on, she's just a little nervous." No, Missy, what are you doing! The matron turned, her eyes beginning to narrow hatefully on her most frequent target.

"Okay! Okay! I'm undressing!" Jo quickly pulled everything off, breathing in rapid bursts. Shit. How was she going to stop Missy from defending her? Missy had only just gotten the matron's approval and now…

Jo joined the other girls, sitting down naked on her cushion. She'd have to try talking to her outside of class. But what could she say? She trusted Missy. She was her friend. But did she really know her well enough? If she were only risking herself, that would be one thing. But if she was wrong, Christopher would also be in trouble. She didn't know what that meant for a man. Maybe he'd just have to pay a fine? Or be banned from having a woman? He'd said the consequences would be severe. For both of them or had he just meant her?

Jo listened during the remainder of the class glumly, following along with whatever she was told with the smallest amount of enthusiasm possible. At least the matron looked at her poisonously at the end of class. This might be the best she could do.

But Missy wasn't having it.

"Jo, you can't be like that with the matron! You were like a slug the entire class! What were you thinking?" she hissed at her as they walked down the hall after class, fully dressed once more.

Jo couldn't look at her. She felt too guilty.

"Missy… Just let me figure this out on my own, okay? I know you have the best intentions but…" She took a deep breath, sick at what she was about to do. "But you're so overbearing! You can't let anyone else be their own person! You think you're some great crusader of justice, but you are just…an attention whore! Just leave me alone."

Missy stopped in the hall but Jo kept going on shaky legs until she got to their next class. Amber arched a brow at her, but she ignored it. And when Missy came in a few seconds later, neither of them looked at the other.

This sucked.

When they went to bed that night, Missy turned her back to her and Jo didn't apologize. God, she wished she could just explain. But if she had to keep it from her, she could at least try protecting Missy from herself.

But she was sick at the coldness between them now.

Over the next few weeks, Jo increased how difficult she was being in the matron's class. Missy didn't try to interfere again, so Jo grew more and more bold. She wasn't even worried about it looking suspicious because absolutely every time she objected it came from a place of genuine shock. The class was absolutely insane.

Missy was the clear winner in the class. She really had turned things around with the matron, and of all the girls, she had the most approval. She wasn't the least bit shy, and she could masturbate in front of all of them without batting an eyelash.

Amber didn't like being second to Missy, but she just couldn't relax the way Missy could. She wasn't a bad actress, but she had certain tells, so you knew she was acting. Missy made it all feel real.

Madison was painful to watch. She was so clearly uncomfortable and awkward, but she was so adamant about following the rules that she did everything without question. But Jo had to close her eyes more than once, which was also not following the rules, as the matron was quick to bark out.

And Jo...Jo had gotten to the point where she would just laugh. She just laughed incredulously at some of the instructions, and the matron honestly looked as if she would try to kill her. But she didn't do anything to her, and when Jo sat idly by and refused to participate in certain activities, she was true to her word: she didn't repeat herself. But Jo knew there would be a reckoning, and she desperately hoped it would mean being placed in tier five.

Finally their last day of classes arrived. Tomorrow the corporate buyers would arrive, and tiers one through four would be auctioned off. Tier five girls wouldn't even go to the auction. They were city property, and after Christopher approved their release, they would go to one of the city's many properties that catered to men's entertainment.

Christopher. He would be here tomorrow. And she would find out if she'd done enough to get into tier five. Today was her last opportunity, and she had to make the most of it.

It didn't take long after getting into the classroom to discover she would have all the opportunity she could possibly want.

"Amber. Melissa. To the front." They were already naked, as that was the first thing required each day when they walked in, and to Amber's credit, she didn't hesitate but walked directly to Missy. But Jo could see the alarm flicker in her eyes.

"You have one minute to convince me that you want each other. If you fail, the final tier I assign you will be one lower. Go." The matron stood a few paces away, her hands folded in front of her.

Amber's face drained of color. She must have thought her admission into tier one was secured. Either that or the idea of making out with someone with inferior breeding was just too much for her. But Missy didn't hesitate.

She slid one hand around Amber's waist slowly, her eyelids low as she watched the expressions flit across Amber's face. Amber's breathing quickened, but she stood still as Missy slid her other hand up her body to cup her small breast, her thumb teasing the nipple. Amber's lips parted and she was visibly trembling, her eyes locked on Missy's. She finally reached her hands out to glide them up Missy's body, causing both of them to catch their breath as they passed smoothly over her breasts, up to cup her neck and draw her close. Their eyes closed and their brows pulled together as their lips met.

"Well done. Madison, Josephine, your turn."

The matron's voice cut through the fog that had permeated the room, and Amber and Missy stood blinking at one another for a brief second before Amber pushed her away with disgust. But her breathing was still erratic once she sat down, and she kept her eyes locked on Madison, who had walked to the front as required.

Missy had a small smile on her face, but it disappeared when she saw Jo still sitting down.

"As before, you have one minute. If you fail, your final tier assignment will be one tier lower."

Jo was worried. She'd been a solid tier three, maybe even verging on tier two, up until Christopher's visit. Was the matron only threatening to demote her to tier four?

"I'm fine with that," Jo shrugged. Oh god, please let this work.

The matron was very still. When she spoke, Jo had to strain to hear her.

"In your case, Josephine, you will not drop a tier."

Jo's stomach sank. The blood drained from her face. *No.* Was there some other punishment? Something other than ranking her lower? Sickness flowed through her, but not for the unknown penalty—for having failed. She had been so sure…so sure she was doing what she needed to do. She wanted to weep. To scream.

"Because you cannot drop lower than tier five."

The matron's words were like a bomb. Of pure joy and Jo would have fallen to her knees had she not still been sitting. She had to look upset! Don't reveal anything!

"No…" she whispered, and her heart leapt at the devastation she heard in it. She could have jumped up and down, and the effort of restraining herself was helping her play the part of being horrified perfectly.

"That is BULLSHIT." Missy's face was raging.

"Missy—" Jo's voice was choked with horror.

"You have done well, Melissa. Do not make me rethink your tier," the matron said, narrowing her eyes.

"FUCK your tiers, you psychotic old bitch!"

Jo scrambled to her feet and ran to throw her arms around Missy.

"She doesn't mean it! She's just very loyal! It's a really good trait!" Jo was almost crying as she looked over her shoulder at the matron whose body seemed to be vibrating.

"Then you will both be delighted to share the same tier. You are now the permanent property of the city. You may return to your rooms. The city no longer needs to train you. The men will do that."

Missy tried launching herself at the matron, but Jo held on

fast. "Stop stop stop..." She was crying. This was her fault. She should have trusted her. "Please, Missy, please tell her you're sorry. Beg her forgiveness," she whispered.

"Fuck that," Missy said, her voice low and hoarse. She grabbed Jo's wrist and yanked her toward the door, stopping to grab their clothes but not bothering to get dressed before ducking through the leather drapes. She handed Jo her clothes once they were on the other side and they dressed while the guards stood on either side of the doorway, their eyes straight ahead as always.

Jo was shaking so hard she couldn't seem to do the laces on the pants. She wanted to puke. She'd been so close...so very close to having everything work out. And she'd failed...and it was going to cost someone who didn't deserve it.

They walked back to the room in silence.

How could she do it? How could she possibly abandon Missy to that place after she was the one who put her there?

They sat down on their beds when they got to the room, facing each other. Neither of them moved. Missy's face was pale, and Jo almost broke inside. But there was no hope for it now.

How was she going to tell Christopher...that she couldn't go?

8

MOON DAY 160

"HE'S ONLY BEEN the corporate handler for a few months, but they've already promised him a contract if his next girl places as well as the previous two he trained. I'll have him wrapped around my finger in no time," Amber told Madison smugly.

"But he's so big and…big," Madison said, her eyes wide.

They had just finished with the auction and sat across from Jo and Missy as they waited for Christopher and the matron to finish talking. Their final paperwork, or parchment work, Jo supposed, was being approved. Amber had been bragging about her buyer for the last few minutes, gushing about his superiority to all the others at the auction. Of course anything that reflected on her would have to be superior, Jo thought, whether it was or not.

"Oh, Madison, you're so simple. Men like that want women like me. Of course, he can't have me personally, since he's only the handler. But he's not too bad on the eyes, so spending the next few weeks with him while he finds someone truly superior for me won't be the most miserable experience in the world." Her smile was all feline.

The office door opened and the matron swept by, not bothering to glance at Jo or Missy, and Amber got up for her final meeting with Christopher.

It had been a long day. She and Missy didn't have anything to do except wait around and worry about their futures. They had spoken very little. Jo had been consumed with fighting her own desire to be free. Free to run into someone's arms because she *could*. Because she wanted to. Needed to. She needed him. How could she bear it?

But then she would look at Missy, her only friend. Someone brash but brave and ready to fight for her. How could she just turn her back on her and let her go to that dark place alone? At least if they went together, they'd have each other.

She dug her fingers into her palms. She couldn't collapse now. She just had to make it through today. Do what she needed to do today. She'd worry about tomorrow when it arrived.

Amber's smile was a little more brittle when she at last walked out of her meeting with Christopher, but she shook her hair back and took her seat again, a parchment in her hand.

Jo stood, a giant weight in her stomach as she walked toward the open heavy door, with the guards waiting on either side. She stopped just over the threshold, the vibrations of the door closing behind her shredding every nerve.

Christopher waited until the door clicked in his place before getting to his feet slowly, his eyes on hers. And then they were both moving, and Jo could feel herself breaking as his arms went around her. He crushed her to him so tightly she couldn't breathe, and she held on just as much.

"You did it," his voice was hoarse, and Jo wasn't sure if the shaking she felt was her own trembling or his.

She pressed her lips to his neck, parting them as she drew a breath at last, the tears choking her. *Please understand.* Her kiss was only a whisper on his skin before she pulled back in his arms, leaning on his chest and looking for strength.

"I can't go with you." The words sounded hollow. Empty. She felt him stop breathing.

"Why." The harshness cut into her, and she swallowed.

"Someone else here…I didn't tell her anything. I was trying to be smart." She could hear the bleakness in her own voice. "And I got her in trouble. She was put in tier five. I can't let her go alone."

She felt the tension flow out of his body, and he dropped his lips to her head.

"Jo," he murmured against her hair. "Do you really think I would ever let you be put there."

She pushed back immediately in his arms.

"You can't make this decision for me." Her voice was firm.

His expression never changed. His eyes were soft, and he stroked her cheek.

"I can."

She pushed on his chest, drawing her brow together sharply.

"You *shouldn't*."

"But I will," he whispered.

Jo felt panic rising up along with something else. Something she didn't want to admit. Relief.

Her head shook back and forth.

"She doesn't deserve it! She's been good to me—the only one who has here! I can't just let her go to that place after she defended me. Please don't let me be that person, Christopher." Her voice was thick with tears and frustration. And guilt.

"Tell me what she did." He continued stroking her cheek, his eyes wandering over her face.

She made a sound of frustration and balled her hands into fists on his chest.

"She didn't do anything! It wasn't her fault! She has been a friend to me from the very beg—" Christopher's lips stopped her, pressing against hers lightly as he held her cheek and stunning her into silence.

"I'm not blaming your friend," he murmured against her lips, watching her through heavy lidded eyes. "I'm trying to see what can be done."

She stared back at him, her breathing shallow, distracted by the feel of his lips.

"You'll help?"

He didn't make a sound, but she felt his answer against her lips.

For the longest time she could only stare, her lips parted beneath his, her eyes as soft as she could remember feeling them. And then she pulled back to smile—and told him everything.

He wrapped his hands around her lower back and leaned back on the desk as he listened, pulling her between his legs. His hands gripped her a little more tightly at some parts of her story, but he mostly stayed very still.

Jo struggled to keep her thoughts focused. Her mind seemed determined to paint pictures of how she might wrap herself around him or what was going to happen when they were living together under the same roof…no more burning…no people walking by. She mentally shook off the images. She had to make sure Missy would be okay first.

Christopher was frowning when she finished. "I can delay her release for another month without rousing any suspicion. It's fairly common for the men who had this role before me to be excessively cautious."

Jo stilled, a memory pulling at her.

"I think I overheard something about the assistant directors not lasting long. Is your job…dangerous?"

Christopher made a dismissive sound.

"They were stupid. I'm not." He was so absolute about it, Jo couldn't help but smile. And believe him.

"So what will happen after the month?"

"I have a month to figure that out. Don't worry."

She stared at him. She really wasn't worried at all. He could do anything.

And right now, she really, desperately wanted him to pull her on his lap. She was trying to think of a way to get him to do it when the door began opening.

Her eyes widened in alarm, and she tried to move away. But he didn't let her go, and she sent him a questioning—if panicked—glance.

"I already gave the matron my card. You're mine now."

His voice was hushed, and for a fleeting moment, Jo thought she saw a darkness in his eyes. But his lashes fell as he kissed her neck before standing to move back around the desk.

"Just have a seat outside, and I'll get you when I'm done."

She was dismissed.

Jo turned to walk out, a line between her brow, barely noticing Madison's shocked look as she walked by. He had to keep up appearances, right? He couldn't very well look like he cared about her here.

But she still felt a bit unsettled.

Amber was fanning herself with her parchment and glanced up as Jo walked out.

"I suppose tier five's don't get to touch their own paperwork. How humiliating for you," she murmured.

The City must be keeping hers since she would really just be on loan to Christopher indefinitely. It was a reminder of how absolute his control over her would be. If he ever changed his mind… But no. He said he wouldn't. And she believed him.

She went to sit beside Missy again, trying to ignore Amber's victorious smirk.

Missy looked miserable. Jo wanted to tell her she was going to be safe, or safer at least, but she'd held her tongue this long. A little longer and Missy would find out without it looking like Jo had anything to do with it. Or at least without stepping in whatever plans Christopher was making. So instead she just reached down and squeezed her hand.

"My handler is back!" Amber's voice was breathless. She must have forgotten Madison wasn't there, as she certainly wouldn't talk to Jo or Missy with that voice. She was staring down the hall with barely repressed excitement. So much for her wrapping the guy around her finger. It looked like the other way around. Jo turned to follow her gaze.

He was walking beside the matron, his brows slightly raised and one side of his mouth pulling upward in amusement as he looked down at her. His hair was dark brown, almost black, cut just long enough to allow the rather wild mane to curve at the ends. He wasn't clean shaven. Instead, he had a well groomed and closely trimmed beard, if one could call it that. It just barely darkened his jaw, adding to his rather dangerous appearance.

And he was huge, dwarfing the diminutive matron by well over a foot. His chest was broad and well muscled, with strong arms and hands placed casually in his pockets. Jo heard him chuckle, and the deep rumble flowed through the air and curled around her. She didn't know she was standing. She didn't know anything except that heat was pouring through her, warming every last part of her soul.

"Adam…" Her voice was just a breath. No one could have heard it. But he froze where he was, his shoulders suddenly rigid, the humor leaving his face. And he slowly turned his head to meet her eyes.

Everything fell silent. Everything fell away.

Her vision blurred as he approached. Slowly. Too slowly. And then he was standing there. Right in front of her. All she had to do was reach out her hand. He was here. He wasn't gone. He was here.

Far off in the distance Jo could hear a door opening. Voices somewhere, somewhere so far away, and then silence. The heat from Adam's skin flowed over her, through her, as she looked up at him.

His face was pale. He reached up a hand to brush a tear from her cheek, every movement so slow, as if it might shatter her. She was falling. And he was here. Her lashes drifted down, and she turned her cheek into his palm.

"Why did you not show me this one." His rough voice was little more than a whisper, and Jo shivered. Then her eyes popped open as the meaning of his words sank in. She blinked and looked around.

The matron was standing at his side, looking nervous for once. Amber appeared to be having some sort of silent seizure. Madison's eyebrows had almost disappeared into her hair, and Christopher…

Jo's heart plunged into her stomach. Christopher was standing in the doorway, staring at Adam. And his eyes were deadly.

"She is just a tier five," the matron said, a quaver her voice.

"She's tier one," Adam said, his voice steady and deep and his eyes alight with…Jo didn't want to know. She was shaking her head in growing horror.

"I'm not—"

"Silence!" The matron's tone was sharp. "Tier fives do not speak to their betters unless spoken to!"

Adam kept his hand on Jo's cheek but turned his head toward the matron, his eyes narrowing. She seemed to catch herself, gripping her hands tightly in front of her.

"If she needs corrected paperwork, I'll be happy to wait," he smiled. Like a wolf about to enjoy a meal.

"You…you don't understand," the matron tried explaining with a little laugh. "She isn't fit. She can't do even the most simple sexual service."

Adam looked back at Jo, and she swallowed at the glint in his eye.

"Don't worry," he said, his voice deep and smooth. "I'll train her."

"You most certainly will not!" Jo glared at him and smacked his hand away, forgetting herself just long enough to hear the matron's outraged intake of breath. She blanched.

But Adam was laughing silently, watching her. He bit the inside of his cheek and put a fist to his lips before speaking again.

"It looks like I'll have my work cut out for me," he sighed, the corner of his mouth twitching at Jo's efforts to control herself.

"Exactly," the matron rushed to respond. "She's no tier one!"

Adam looked at the matron with a raised brow.

"Now I know you've had a long, good relationship with our company. And we respect your scoring abilities. But you also know that since they hired me, I am the voice of the company on this matter. Which means I am the only one who can decide what qualifies as tier one." His voice was deceptively quiet. "The City will be more than compensated, as you know."

The matron looked as if she wanted to stomp her foot, and for once Jo's feelings were aligned with hers. How could she get out of this?

"No more arguments." Adam's voice was fully authoritative now, deep and brusque. "Fix the paperwork. Who does it?"

He looked around—and froze when his eyes met Christopher's. They stared at one another a long time.

"As I said," Adam said quietly. "I don't mind waiting."

Christopher didn't move.

"The assistant director has already submitted his card in exchange for the tier five," the matron explained, still trying to dissuade him.

"Has he now," Adam said, a strange light in his eyes. He kept his eyes on Christopher but reached for Jo, his hand sliding around her waist effortlessly and leaving her a bit breathless. She glanced up at him as he guided her toward Christopher, but he didn't look down. He stopped a few feet away.

The tension in the air was heavy, chaining Jo to the floor. She could only stare at the men in front of her as wisps of memory teased her mind.

A few of Christopher's soft golden curls had escaped his carefully groomed style and spilled onto his forehead in charming abandon, a marked contrast from the chilling blue eyes below. A cold fire. He stood with deceptive ease, but his eyes never once left Adam's.

Adam stood only two or three inches taller than Christopher, but his muscled frame made him seem much larger. He kept his hand on Jo as he studied Christopher, his deep brown eyes alive. Assessing.

"I think the three of us should have a talk," Adam said.

Christopher didn't move. Jo stopped breathing, but Adam waited. Calm. Finally Christopher stepped back and turned to walk inside, and Adam gently pushed Jo forward to follow.

The door closed behind them.

———

The three of them stood in the middle of the room. Jo started to step away from Adam, but she felt a strange urge to throw her arms around him instead when he glanced at her with a hint of outrage in his eyes. So she did nothing. The clock on the wall ticked out each second.

"It's been a while," Adam began, looking at Christopher thoughtfully. His voice was calm, but Jo could hear a thread of something else underneath. Loneliness?

She noticed Christopher looking at her out of the corner of her eye, and she quickly looked down, alarmed. How had she been looking at Adam? She pulled away from him without looking up this time and wrapped her arms around herself. She couldn't look at either of them.

"What do you remember." Christopher's voice was clipped. Jo looked up for Adam's reaction.

Adam raised a brow, seemingly amused by Christopher's tone, but he looked over at Jo as if contemplating the question.

"Oh, just a few images...very pleasant images," he said, his eyes warm as they traveled the length of her. She could feel her face flaming.

"What else," Christopher bit out.

Adam sighed and gave Jo one more lingering look before turning back to Christopher.

"I remember how much you needed a vacation." His voice was brusque now as he cocked his jaw and raised his brows sightly.

"We worked together..." Christopher frowned, a line between his brow.

"Why don't you tell me what you remember, goldilocks," Adam said, crossing his arms and widening his stance.

Christopher narrowed his eyes. He didn't respond.

Jo watched the two men square off, the familiarity of it all frustratingly difficult to pin down. She knew both of them. She had seen them this way before. But her mind simply wouldn't give her any real answers. She stared at them a moment longer before turning and walking to the window, leaning against the edge to look out.

They were on the first floor, in a section she hadn't seen when she'd first arrived. This was the first window she'd seen that actually had a view outside the sanctuary. The other windows all overlooked inner courtyards that seemed to be intended solely to provide the illusion of having an outside.

But here she could see a large circular drive that the auction attendees presumably had used. There were carriages lined up outside, each with two large wheels and a man holding a metal bar that jutted out at one end of the carriage. Human drawn carriages. And it was bright outside, as if it were day. She couldn't see the ceiling of the underground from where she was, but it must be the famed fake blue sky she'd heard about.

The sadness of it all hit her. She would never see the real blue sky again. She would never be free again. She looked back over her shoulder to see Christopher looking at her. Her eyes softened at the concern she saw in his, and she saw the tension leave his body the same moment it left hers.

Adam's eyes moved slowly between them.

"How long will it take you to complete the tier one form?" Adam's voice was cold now, and Christopher's eyes snapped back to his.

"If you make her tier one, you'll have to sell her to someone else." Christopher's voice was quiet, but there was a note of restrained anger underneath.

"I know my job," Adam said, his eyes narrowing. "Now do yours."

"I can protect her. Leave her with me. Tell the matron you changed your mind."

"You think you can control everything," Adam said sharply. "But you can't. And I've seen what happens when the Director in your office is displeased. What happens if your card gets revoked?"

"It won't." Christopher's eyes were furious.

"You don't know that. At least with me, she will be tier one. It's the best protection she can get here."

"Protection," Christopher spat out. "To be forced into bed by some entitled dilettante whose only noteworthy feature is that he's been here so long he has become untouchable. And you would put her under that."

"At least it's only one," Adam said hoarsely, "and she won't get carved up every night and burned all day to get her ready for the next twenty or thirty guys they'll expect her to fuck *every day* in tier five."

"That won't happen." Christopher was trembling in fury. "She will be with me."

"I'm not taking that risk. Fix the fucking papers."

Jo sank down the wall, her knees finally giving out. This was what was in store for her?

Christopher shot Adam a look of pure venom before coming over and kneeling beside her. She looked up at him as he reached up to stroke her cheek.

"Please keep Missy safe," she whispered. Christopher stilled, his eyes burning.

"You want to go with him."

Her brows raised in helpless apology, and she reached up to cover his hand with her own.

"Is there another way?" Her voice was pleading, and she watched his eyes as he struggled with the question, seeing the answer he didn't want to admit. He looked down in frustration, and she squeezed his hand.

"Delay getting sold as long as you can," he said, his voice hoarse as he looked back at her. "I'll fix this."

"And Missy?"

He exhaled and looked away, irritation in his eyes.

"I'll take care of it." He softened again when he looked back at her. "Don't worry."

"What happens to you…if you get caught?" she asked, gripping his hand tightly. He dropped his forehead to hers.

"I won't get caught. Trust me."

"You have about ten seconds before I open that door." Adam's voice was harsh. Christopher glared at him but got to his feet, pulling Jo up with him gently.

Jo looked at Adam, beginning to feel frantic. He was huge. What had she been thinking? She didn't know this man. Not really. Whatever had been in the past felt like an echo now.

Adam stalked over to Christopher's desk, rummaging around until he found whatever he was seeking. Then he marched back to where they were standing, almost slamming the parchment into Christopher's chest before grabbing her arm to pull her a bit roughly to his side.

"Fix the fucking paper."

Christopher held the parchment, his knuckles white, as he stared back at Adam. Then he walked calmly to the desk and sat down.

A few minutes later, Jo had a parchment in her hands and was walking out of the sanctuary, Adam's hand in a tight grip on her arm. Amber climbed into the carriage first, and Jo sent one last look behind her, scanning to find the window she'd looked out. Christopher was watching her, his hands in his pockets, looking as relaxed as ever. Jo couldn't see his eyes. But she knew what was in them, and her own filled with tears.

Then Adam was lifting her into the carriage to sit beside Amber before climbing in to sit across from them. She wanted to shrink from the look in his eyes. Every bit of the humor she had seen in him before had vanished.

She could only see rage.

9

MOON DAY 160

THEY RODE THROUGH THE CITY, the metal wheels jarring the carriage with every bump on the stone street beneath. At least the seats were comfortably upholstered in soft leather. Jo turned to look out the window, grateful to escape Adam's eyes.

"Wow—this is amazing. How big is the city?"

The matron would have approved. They'd already learned about the city in their classes, but Amber was following the handbook on how to talk to men: pretend you don't know the things you know and ask the man instead.

"The population is between eighty and a hundred thousand," he said, adding under his breath: "depending on how you count."

Jo's eyes darted to his. He hesitated a moment, but the steel returned to his eyes quickly so she turned back to the window.

Amber was feigning shock.

"Oh my! How can there be so many people? And everyone fits underground?"

"It's a large area, nearly ten miles across for the main section. I know you already learned about this," Jo thought she detected a wry note to his voice, "but it can't hurt to revisit.

"The city is arranged like a large wheel. In the center of the wheel is City Hall, the courthouse, and other city services. That's where Goldi—" he paused and cleared his throat. "The *Assistant Director*," he said carefully, "reports back to the Director of Intelligence about all potential threats in the city."

Jo forced herself to keep still, but she wanted to crane her neck out the window to see if she could see the city center.

"In a wide band around the center is the market district, and that serves—or is served by—the six districts that branch off of it. Each district is divided by a stone wall, like the spokes of a wheel. We're in the main district right now, which has a mix of various businesses.

"If we had turned left and headed clockwise around the city, we would have gone through the worker's district, where the city owned women are housed." His eyes flicked to Jo. "From there, you enter the manufacturing district, entertainment district, temple district, and finally the Brahmin district, before arriving back here. There are three other locations, but they aren't part of the wheel and can only be accessed through one of the other districts."

Jo watched as they passed a type of stone age office park. It was such an odd blend of ancient looking stonework branded with more modern titles. The Law Offices of Webster and Pomeroy. Dennis John, CPA. City Postal Service.

"We are going to the temple district. There is a university connected to that district, where you will be in a private dorm and have access to the best training in the city."

"But I thought you would be training us?" Amber's surprise was genuine this time.

"I assess your educational needs and design an appropriate curriculum. Once you are ready, I'll introduce you to society and facilitate the placement process. The more bids you get, the better you tend to place, and the more I'm rewarded. So we both win when you do well."

Jo glanced over at him again.

"So you've done well for yourself. Buying and selling women." She said it without inflection, but she saw him grit his teeth.

"It's the world we're in. And you're going to need to keep your opinions about it private. The city has harsh penalties for insurrectionist ideas, and a very broad definition of what they think qualifies as insurrectionist."

He looked prepared for battle, but Jo just stared at him before turning once again to look out the window. The world they were in sucked.

They went under a gated arch with guards on either side of the open gates. Jo knew they closed the gates at the end of every day, barring further traffic between the districts. The guards never left their posts, though, but would lie down just before the wave of sleep hit everyone so they were there the instant the new day began.

Amber gasped. They had just entered the Brahmin district, and the homes around them were gasp worthy, Jo had to admit. No—not homes. Estates. From the intricate stonework to the marble pillars and statues, every aspect denoted luxury with plenty of wide, open space between each estate. Although there was no plant life, great care had been taken to recreate the effect with a mixture of stone color and lights from the sands.

"These are the homes of the men who buy tier two women."

"This isn't even tier one?" Amber couldn't hide the excitement in her voice, but Jo's stomach sank.

"No. The Ancients, who will bid on you, have a separate area that can only be reached through the Brahmin district. I'll take you there eventually."

Jo watched estate after estate pass by as the carriage rolled on. She wished, desperately wished, she could feel the way Amber did. To be able to accept what she couldn't change.

But even if she could...it wouldn't matter. There was no way she could do this. She wasn't qualified to even associate with people who owned homes like these. She almost laughed remembering how she had thought she might be able to get into tier two. And she was supposed to be *above* this?

She stared outside with wide, unblinking eyes before turning her head slowly back to Adam. He was watching her. Waiting for something it seemed. But all she could do was stare back. What had he been thinking to put her in tier one?

"I think you made a mistake," she said at last. He narrowed his eyes.

"One of the first things you should learn here is women don't criticize men. Men decide. Women follow."

She blinked.

"That explains why everything is so fucked up."

A light glinted in his eyes.

"Jo, you aren't in the world you knew, and you need to adapt."

"It's Josephine."

She wanted to take the words back the instant she said them. Silence crackled between them, and Jo watched as a coldness crept into his expression.

"Learn the rules. Obey them. You won't like the consequences if you don't."

Then he turned back to talk to Amber for the remainder of the trip, pointing out landmarks and being a little too charming, it seemed to Jo. She tried to ignore the confusing sting it left.

They passed through the next set of gates and entered the temple district. Occasionally someone in a scratchy looking cloak could be seen kneeling on the sidewalk.

"Ew, what are they wearing?" Amber wrinkled her nose.

"It's made out of hair. It's not actually common for people to walk around this way, I was told. But some Ancient is visiting from another city and holding services at the temple. Evidently people find religion when he's here."

Jo glanced over with wide eyes.

"There are other cities?" They hadn't learned about this.

Adam didn't acknowledge her, though a muscle in his jaw twitched.

"So there are other cities connected to this one?" Amber breathed with a smug glance at Jo. She leaned toward Adam and put a hand to her chest, making sure not to cover her cleavage. Jo clenched her own jaw a bit and turned to stare out the window again.

"No. Not connected. He travels on the surface."

"How does he avoid the sun?" Amber's breathy voice was grating on Jo, but she was glad she was asking questions.

"He doesn't. He seems to like burning. There's actually a hole in the ceiling of the temple and he does some sort of altar call, trying to get people to stand underneath it with him before the sun rises every day. He thinks after some allotted number of burnings, we'll move on to a better place. But he's been here for around a thousand years and no reward yet."

"A thousand?" Amber squeaked, forgetting her seduction practice for the moment. She cleared her voice.

"He's older than the Ancients in this city. Oh, and the temple is where you get taken to burn if you get damaged, so be careful with your bodies."

Amber fell silent, and Jo wondered if the idea of burning was still too traumatic for her.

Burning on purpose. Jo didn't know how he could do it. The pain... She shuddered and looked down at the hand she'd injured. There were of course no scars. She'd burned completely afterwards. But for some reason, that brief contact on her fingertips stood out more vividly in her mind. Perhaps because it was the only time she had been able to witness what happened each time the sun touched them. No matter what she faced in this fucked up society, it still couldn't compare to that.

She looked up to find Adam's eyes on her again, and she quickly turned her attention back to the view outside.

They passed under a large stone archway that marked the entrance of the university. Men with their arms full of parchments were going from building to building. Jo didn't see any women.

In the campus center was a tall tower that extended to the cavern ceiling high above, giving it the appearance of disappearing into the sky. Here the carriage at last came to a stop, and the door beside Jo opened. She started to get out only to find Adam's hand on her arm and his eyes boring into her.

"Could you at least *try* to remember some of the etiquette they taught you."

"Ladies always wait for the gentleman to exit first, Josephine," Amber said, her voice dripping with sweetness. "That way he can help you down."

Jo felt the heat rush to her face and leaned back for Adam to exit.

She might be willing to do what it took to avoid the sun, but that didn't mean she would be able to do it well. She didn't belong here. Even if she'd been paying attention in the etiquette class—which she hadn't, since she'd been trying to get into tier five—it all felt too foreign to her. Too nonsensical. She knew how to get out of a carriage on her own, after all.

"Hurry up!" Amber hissed.

A growing crowd of men was gathering in the distance, craning their necks to see into the interior of the carriage. Adam was standing with his hand outstretched as he waited, but his eyes grew darker with each passing moment. She hurriedly slid her hand into his, trying to stop her heart from racing the moment their skin touched, and jumped out.

Adam's grip tightened on her hand as she tried to pull it away, holding her in place beside him as he rubbed his brow. When he finally looked back at her, his eyes were bright with barely restrained temper.

"If you're trying to convince me to send you back to tier five," he bit out in a low voice, "you should know that's impossible now. They don't give refunds. If you fail to place, the company will cut its losses and auction you off to a collective of men. So maybe you should stop trying to provoke me."

He didn't wait for her reaction but released her to turn back and extend a hand to Amber.

Jo felt sick. If he—someone who seemed to have cared about her in their past—thought she was so bad that it had to be intentional, what hope did she have of convincing anyone else she was tier one quality?

Adam turned back with Amber's arm tucked into his. Jo lowered her eyes and stepped back to allow them to pass so she could follow.

"Jo!"

She jerked her head back up to see Adam glaring at her. She'd made another mistake?

She saw Amber roll her eyes at her as Adam inclined his head toward his free side, holding his arm away from his body for her to slide her arm through. Oh. She awkwardly slid her arm through his, hoping he wouldn't feel her slight tremble.

She must have done it wrong because it only seemed to make him more angry. But he said nothing more to her and led them inside.

————

A few days later, and Jo was sure she had never felt more stupid in her life.

She and Amber each had their own room in a very large, luxurious suite, while Adam was in a separate suite down the hall on a floor they had entirely to themselves, complete with a library, conference room, spa, and fitting room. A clothing design team visited them the first day to take their measurements and personalize their clothing. Evidently it wouldn't do for tier one women to be seen in anything that might be seen on the lower tiers.

The design team was supposed to try to capture the essence of each woman and reflect it in her clothing. They seemed overjoyed to be working with Amber, but when they'd looked at Jo… Well, she probably hadn't helped matters when they'd asked her what type of design she thought would best reflect who she was inside, and she'd answered "a t-shirt and jeans." Adam was snapping everyone's head off by the end of the whole thing, so it hadn't exactly gone well. And she was stuck with a variety of suede dresses for now. At least they were super soft.

Adam had been in assessment mode since they'd arrived, and it had gone about as smoothly as the ride from the Sanctuary. He'd ended up focusing his attention on Amber and setting up her schedule, but today Amber would be away all day at her classes for the first time. So it was Jo's turn.

She felt a little queasy. As insulting as Amber could be, she still served as a buffer and a distraction. Jo didn't want Adam's eyes locked solely on her. She didn't want the full weight of his criticism as she repeatedly failed one expectation after another. And she did not want to ever again feel what she'd felt when she first saw him. She couldn't. She was going to be sold as a glorified sex slave one way or another. Or maybe…Christopher would somehow manage to save her again. Either way, Adam was just the handler here. Nothing more.

She was flipping through a thick book of mythology in the library and had just found a small section on the *Insomnolent*, when she heard a door close and footsteps approaching down the hall. Shit. He was back from escorting Amber to her classes.

She looked down at the page she'd just turned to, hurriedly scanning. The lore talked about men and women able to stay awake while the sun was up. But the stories all cast them as bogeymen, evil people to be feared and captured, their heads cut off and hidden in a dark place never to burn again.

The footsteps grew nearer, and Jo snapped the book closed. She felt pale and weak. Did it really mean she was evil? More evil than the others? She really couldn't believe that. But regardless of why she was able to stay awake—at least for a few minutes—it was clear she needed to keep that information to herself.

She was leaning forward to put the book on the low stone table in front of her when Adam came into view.

He was disturbingly handsome. Frightening even. His large frame filled the doorway as he stood watching her, and she couldn't stop the small shiver that went through her. He was wearing a short sleeved button up suede shirt that draped comfortably across his broad chest and leather pants that laced up the front and didn't drape at all. They didn't leave much to the imagination, and Jo could feel the heat climbing to her face.

Adam stepped into the room, and she could see he was already angry.

"You need to stop acting like a frightened rabbit." His voice was gruff, but he didn't meet her eyes as he spoke, walking past her to the desk across the room. "The Ancients get plenty of that from the lower tier women. You have to convince them you're more valuable." He grabbed a parchment out of one of the desk drawers and lapsed into silence as he looked it over.

She looked frightened? Jo looked down at her hands clenching in her lap. Yes. Frightened. That's probably what this was.

She took a deep breath and looked up. He was still reading. Was he expecting her to answer? Or should she not disturb him while he was reading? Well, if she wasn't supposed to be frightened...

"Maybe it's just your charming personality."

His back immediately tensed, and she clapped her hands over her mouth. That was not what she meant to say. He turned to face her with a calculating look, the parchment low in his hands.

"You aren't likely to find the Ancients very charming either," he said, leaning back on the desk. He ran his eyes down the length of her. "Come here."

Every hair on her body stood on end. She didn't move.

His eyes narrowed.

"You are going to have to learn to obey here," he said softly. "Come here."

Her hands were still over her mouth, so he couldn't see her lips part in response. Shit. Shit shit shit. Every nerve in her body was screaming at her, but she couldn't make any sense of what they were saying.

"Why?" The sound came out muffled, and she lowered her hands.

"Jo, you don't get to ask why. You need to learn this." His voice was low. Guttural. "Now come. Here."

It took her a moment to realize she was shaking her head back and forth, the growing heat in his eyes alerting her. And then he was moving.

She scurried up on the couch an instant before he made it to her, standing on the cushions and flattening herself against the wall.

"This is ridiculous," he ground out, his hand lashing out to grab hers. She jerked her hands up out of his reach. "Goddammit! This isn't a game!"

He grabbed behind her knee with one hand while his other went around her back, yanking her off the couch and into his arms. Her hands went to his shoulders as she fell toward him… and then it was as natural as breathing.

Her body molded around him, her legs sliding around his waist, his hand slipping up her dress to cup the bare skin of her thigh. Her arms folded around his neck until her forehead was pressed against his.

He stood very still, his breathing ragged, one arm around her waist, locking her to him. Her dress had ridden up to the top of her thighs, and she could feel him pressing into her through the leather of his pants.

She couldn't think. He was here.

"Did you do this with Christopher in the desert?" he growled.

Jo's eyes snapped open, and she blinked at the seething resentment in his. She swallowed and put her hands on his shoulders to carefully push herself away, sliding her free leg down his until her toes barely touched the floor. He hadn't let go of her thigh or her waist, and she stared up at him, trembling, her fingers pressing into his shoulders.

Christopher. How could she have forgotten, even for a moment?

Adam's eyes grew darker.

"Answer me."

Guilt threatened to drown her. She couldn't…

"I…" she whispered. She made a small sound. An expression of regret. Of confusion. Of longing. "I couldn't remember anything."

Adam's fingertips bit into her skin.

"You should have known when he touched you," he said hoarsely. "You should have never felt anything."

His words pierced like arrows. She wanted to say it wasn't fair. That she couldn't control her feelings. Her body's responses.

But she couldn't escape the feeling that what he was saying was true. She just didn't know if it was true about Christopher… or Adam.

She looked down, her brow drawn in confusion. Maybe the book was right. Maybe there was something worse about her.

"I'm sorry." She kept her eyes down, waiting for him to release her. He was still for a long time.

At last, he let her leg slip from his grasp, following it down until it fell from his hand completely. Jo closed her eyes and tried to hold steady. He dropped his arm from her waist and stepped back.

"We don't have much time to prepare you. I have three months before I have to take you to meet prospective buyers. The auction takes place a month later with sealed bids that are above my pay grade. If no one bids on you, you won't have a second chance. They'll open it up to corporate buyers who deal in second and third tier stock." His voice was distant. Wooden.

Jo felt a band tightening around her heart. Choking her. She kept her eyes down, afraid her sudden tears would spill over.

"You'd still be much safer than in tier five, but—" He cleared his throat. "But it would be bad. You need to try, Jo. Really try."

She nodded. She couldn't look up. She couldn't tell him she *had* been trying.

He exhaled.

"Go on back to your room. I already know the classes you need. I'll put your schedule together and get you started tomorrow."

She nodded once more and turned to go without looking up.

"Jo. You need to learn how to fake a smile. You need to be able to hide what you feel." His voice was husky, and she looked up at him at last.

His image was blurry, but she could see the pain she felt reflected in his eyes. She curved her mouth upwards, just slightly. And then she was turning, before he could see the tears overflowing.

———

The weeks went by. Adam kept his distance, in every way. He seemed to have put her in every course possible, and Jo could barely remember the morning's class by the end of the day, let alone advance her overall social status to fit into tier one. Adam was growing progressively more frustrated with her, and Jo felt ashamed on a daily basis—and deeply inadequate.

She hadn't heard from Christopher, but she supposed that

wasn't surprising. Tier one women in training were highly isolated. Other than Adam, she had spoken to no one except the fashion team and her private instructors. She was fairly certain they were all gay, which explained why they were permitted to be alone with the women. She didn't know why Adam had so much freedom, but she knew he could be very persuasive. He'd probably just insisted with a twinkle in his eye until he got his own way.

She smiled into space for a moment before Adam's voice snapped her back to attention.

"Jo!"

She jerked upright in her seat and her eyes flew over to the door. She was supposed to be listening to her current instructor who had been droning on about the scientific reasons women needed men to make their decisions for them. She'd had to let her thoughts drift just to be able to keep her temper. Adam was standing in the doorway, glaring at her as usual. He *would* decide to check on her now.

Amber was smirking behind Adam, but she morphed it into a sweet smile as he turned back to her. She was revolting…but she was everything Jo was supposed to be. Adam had used her as an example multiple times. *Watch how Amber does it* or *just copy Amber when you don't know what to do.*

Jo would almost have thought being used by multiple men was the lesser of two evils, but Adam had quickly disabused her of any idea she could be herself if she dropped to a lower tier. He said to imagine having one boss she needed to please versus multiple.

"Women are naturally inferior and must rely on the man's protection. Men are stronger, faster, larger, and less emotional. These traits make them the superior worker. Moreover, as women no longer bear children in society, their only function is to serve as decorative ornamentation and vessels for men's pleasure."

Jo bit down on her tongue. Christopher had been right: the

population was definitely intellectually stunted. She held on for
the remainder of the class, but when the instructor was done she
walked to the door quickly.

"Goddammit, Jo," Adam said under his breath. "How many
times do I have to remind you to move slowly? You can't look like
you're running a race all the time."

Maybe if she weren't always trying to escape the insanity
around her, she'd remember. But his words still cut. There were
just too many natural traits she needed to change. She couldn't
seem to keep them in mind when it was taking all her energy just
to keep silent.

He was taking them on a walk around campus. Amber
seemed to love it, and why wouldn't she? Adam approved of
everything she did, and the men who walked by practically
stumbled over their tongues when they saw her. Whereas they
always looked confused when their eyes happened to fall on Jo.

She knew she wasn't beautiful, but she kind of liked what she
saw in the mirror. Bright, open almond shaped eyes with long
brown lashes. A cute little bow of a mouth. A nose that, well,
perhaps wasn't perfect but seemed well suited for her face. High
cheekbones and smooth eyebrows that she didn't need to wax.

And oh, the waxing. They seemed to have to do it constantly
as their hair grew pretty quickly. Jo's hair had finally come back
to something that felt familiar to her, the reddish brown locks
falling just to her shoulders in soft waves that curled up near her
temples. The stylist in the fashion team had tried various styles
with it, but it always seemed to go back to a fluffy wind blown
sort of look. Jo liked it, but then, she liked t-shirts and jeans. Her
opinions didn't seem to be widely shared here.

They walked outside, the girls' arms threaded through each
of Adam's. Amber kept up conversation with him, pulling him
back to her each time he tried to turn to Jo. It was a mercy. He
was only going to criticize whatever she was doing anyway.

She distracted herself from the pain by counting the number

of men who tripped when they saw Amber. She was in double digits when she saw a pair of boots that didn't falter. Something about them... Her eyes flew up to his face and she froze, her hand slipping from Adam's arm. He turned back to glare at her but stopped when he saw her eyes, following her gaze back up the path.

Christopher was approaching.

10

MOON DAY 220

"WHAT ARE YOU DOING HERE?" Adam demanded.

Christopher stopped a few feet away, staring at Jo. He had let his hair grow out on top, and his soft golden curls tumbled onto his forehead. Her fingers itched to brush them from his brow.

"It's a pleasant place to walk. I try to be here whenever I can."

His voice was quiet. Still. And all her worries over the last few weeks that he might have stopped caring evaporated. Her knees felt weak, and she wanted to throw herself in his arms and hide.

"Then be on your way." Adam was equally quiet, but Jo flinched as if he'd yelled.

The softness left Christopher's eyes as they turned to Adam.

"We need to talk."

Adam's muscles tensed. He stared back at Christopher for a long moment before rubbing his jaw.

"Girls, wait here." He didn't bother looking at either of them, but inclined his head and he and Christopher walked far enough away to keep whatever they said private. Dammit.

Jo kept her eyes locked on Christopher's, trying to figure out what he was saying.

"Do you suppose you were his maid?" Amber mused with a lilt in her voice.

Jo froze. Did Amber know she and Christopher had a past? Did it matter now if people knew?

"I've been thinking maid…possibly some other type of servant. A very bad servant who can't do anything right. His frustration seems deeply rooted."

Jo breathed an inner sigh of relief. Of course. Adam.

Amber continued talking in the singsong tone she used when she had something she wanted Jo to hear but didn't want to lower herself by actually talking *to* Jo.

"I feel so bad for him. He must have felt a jolt of familiarity and it got him all confused for a moment. The poor man. I hope they won't fire him when the Ancients see he's brought them tier five quality. Of course, he has me…" A self-satisfied smile spread across her face as her eyes ran the length of Adam's back.

Jo wrapped her arms around her body. She wasn't supposed to stand this way, but Adam's back was to her for the moment.

She couldn't really argue anything Amber had said. She had no idea how she had known Adam. She clearly wasn't in his league. Maybe he'd been sleeping with the help, and they'd both mistaken the familiarity of the intimacy for something more. Would she have done that? Slept with her boss? She didn't know. It didn't feel like something she would have *wanted* to do at least.

She rubbed her arms, the knot in her stomach tightening, and watched Adam pointing at Christopher, punctuating whatever he was saying with small jabs at his chest. Christopher just stared back with his hands in his pockets, his eyes at first cold but growing more heated with every exchange.

Adam turned and took a step away, tearing a hand through his hair, and Jo's heart plummeted. Was the conversation over? Was Christopher leaving? No. His eyes turned to Jo.

She stared back at him, searching. His expression was dark, a muscle in his jaw flexing. It was the same expression he'd had when he'd told her she was stupid for trusting him. She shook her head. She couldn't stop shaking it, and she saw his brows twitch just a bit, just barely. Just enough.

He was worried.

Then an embittered look settled in, and he turned to speak to Adam once more. Adam didn't respond at first but eventually threw up a hand, not bothering to face him. And Christopher turned and left.

She heard the small sound escape from her throat as she took a step toward his retreating back.

"Back inside. Now." Adam grabbed her arm and turned them both so quickly that Amber released an audible gasp. He ignored her complaints, snapping at her for the first time and shocking her into silence as he marched them both back to the dorm.

"Amber, go to your room," he said, releasing her once they were inside but keeping his hand locked on Jo's upper arm, pulling her down the hall. Jo didn't look back to see if Amber had obeyed.

He pulled her all the way to his room. She barely had time to blink in shock before he'd pushed her through and closed the door behind them.

Adam released her to walk to the middle of the room while Jo leaned back against the door, rubbing her upper arm. He stood with his back to her, one hand on his hip and the other massaging his brow. She could see his muscles rippling beneath the thin leather of his shirt, the cords of his neck thick with tension. Finally he turned to face her, his hand rubbing his jaw as he looked at her with raised brows.

"He can't help you." His voice was blunt. Absolute. "Whatever he told you—whatever you've been holding onto that's had you dragging your feet here—you need to let it go."

Jo leaned back further into the door and clenched her jaw a

bit. She had seen Christopher's face before he left. He wasn't giving up. She knew he wasn't.

Adam narrowed his eyes.

"Ancients are the only ones permitted to purchase exclusive rights to a woman, so even if he were *able* to find the money—which he *can't*—he still couldn't bid on you."

"Just because you can't imagine a way doesn't mean he won't."

"Goddammit, Jo!" he yelled, causing her to jump. "Do you know what he was doing here? Digging for information—anything that might give him a way in. Do you think if anything existed I wouldn't have done it myself?"

"I think…he might recognize opportunities that other people can't see," she insisted, although she could feel the blood draining from her face.

Adam crossed the room swiftly and put his fists against the door on either side of her. His face was a mask of fury, and she shrank back further into the door.

"*It can't be done!* They have been doing this for hundreds of years, and the people who got in power first—the Ancients—aren't just going to let some new arrival share their power."

"Then he'll find some other way!" Tears were beginning to clog her throat, but she refused to back down.

"There is no other way!" He hit the door beside her, and her body jolted involuntarily. "You are a woman," he ground out. "You *will* be in one of the five tiers, and with every step down, it will get worse.

"You can't get a job. The matron's role is the only female role that *looks* like a job, but she is actually a tier three who entertains men in the evenings. The city reimburses the *men* for her time in the sanctuary.

"You can't leave. You have seen the guards—they are everywhere. Heavy stone and metal gates, heavily guarded. The few escapes that occurred happened over a century ago, and they have sealed up every single avenue possible. The *only* person permitted to leave the city is the temple Ancient, and he gets special treatment because he brings news from other parts of the world.

"*You. Can't. Do. Anything.* Do you get that?" He was practically yelling now, and Jo finally dropped her eyes, her body shaking as she tried desperately to hold back her tears.

"It's not about what I can do," she managed to choke out. "Chri—"

"I swear to god if you say his name, I will bend you over my fucking knee," he said hoarsely. "He can't beat the entire goddamn world. And if *he* could, then *I. Fucking. Would!*" He punctuated each final word by slamming his hand on the door, the vibrations siphoning off the little control she had left. She sank to the floor to bury her head in her knees, only to be jerked back up by Adam's hand on her arm.

"We don't have time for you to have a nervous breakdown," he snapped with a small shake. "Stop cowering. These men are not going to want some fragile, frightened little mouse. That's not desirable. That's not interesting. That's not going to save you."

Jo's body was trembling so violently her teeth clicked against one another, and she bit down, struggling to breathe. Adam's fingers dug into her arm as he continued.

"You have to hide your feelings. Smile. Flirt. Be what they want you to be. Show me." He stared at her, his face dark. Waiting.

Jo blinked rapidly.

"Show you…flirting?" Her voice shook, and his voice dropped to a menacing tone.

"Show me you can hide what you feel. Now."

Jo swallowed. Okay. Think of…something else. Anything else. Smile.

Her mouth tilted upwards for an instant. And then her entire face seemed to crack as the tears wouldn't stay back any longer.

She brought her fists to her face, driving her palms into her eyes as her body shook with silent sobs.

She felt Adam's hand fall from her arm as he stepped back. He stood in silence as she struggled to regain control of herself.

"Go on to bed," he said at last, his voice rough. "Tomorrow is your first meeting with the Ancients. They won't be the bidders —they are happy with their current tier ones—but you'll be able to see what they are like and how the women act around them. Just...just study them, Jo. Figure it out. Before it's too late." He sounded weary.

Jo couldn't bear the idea of looking at him, so she kept her head down as she turned to go. She had just opened the heavy door when his voice stopped her.

"Wait." His tone was sharp again. Irritable. "Your friend… Missy? She was assigned to tier four."

Jo's heart jumped. Christopher had at least been able to help her friend. Tier four was still…well, she couldn't think about it. But it was better than being cut up on top of everything else. She closed her eyes and leaned her head against the door for strength. She could take this. Tier two, tier three…or even tier four. If Missy could do it, she could do it.

She straightened her back and walked out, closing the door behind her.

Tomorrow was going to be a big day.

———

The entertainment district was a giant, medieval theme park, replete with public execution style events where people who had run afoul of the law were punished in gruesome ways. Numerous locations hosted various forms of fighting as well as team sports taken to excessively violent conclusions. They passed by circus events advertising insane acrobatic acts performed without nets, and Jo could hear the disappointment of the audience inside the arena when a trick was evidently successful. There were chariot races where men of higher status rode with whips while low status men served as horses. They even had a zoo of sorts, although Adam steered them far from it as they weaved through the maze of people.

People of every type were there—mostly men, although many of the men had brought along a woman. Those with women had gravitated away from the more violent forms of entertainment in the district and congregated instead in the area with plays, book readings, museums, dancing, and more gentle games ranging from chess tournaments to card games and roulette tables.

Adam was taking them to a concert. After showing some type of embossed leather card to the attendant at a heavily guarded side entrance, Adam escorted them through a stone passageway and up a long flight of stairs. At the top was an enormous balcony that overlooked the stage below.

It was the first time Jo had seen an even distribution of men and women since she'd entered the city. Half a dozen men were chatting, some standing, some seated at the small stone tables set up on the platform. And each man had a woman by his side.

"Adam! Join us!" A short, rather pompous looking man held up a goblet, beckoning them over to his table of four. He wore a well tailored suit that covered, to Jo's shock, a somewhat stout middle. This was the first she'd seen anyone show any sign of extra weight. It appeared limited to his midsection, however, as the remainder of his body showed no sign of additional fat.

She was frowning to herself in thought when she felt Adam's hand on her back digging into her. She glanced up, but he just smiled smoothly at the man who had called them over.

"John, I'd like to introduce you to the latest tier one women. This is Amber." He gestured to his right, and John's eyes lit up.

"A pleasure, my dear. You are a true beauty. It will be a very lucky man who wins your bid!" He bowed low over her hand, and Amber put a hand to her cheek.

"You are too kind! I only hope he will be half the man you are!"

Jo sputtered before she could stop herself, but choked when every face at the table turned her way. She could feel Adam's eyes burning into her.

"And who is this…" John's small eyes swept up and down her body derisively.

She looked around the table, avoiding Adam's gaze. Amber was bright red and glaring at her. John sipped his goblet, his eyes narrowed at her over the rim. An exceptionally striking woman with ebony skin and long, elegant limbs, stood beside him, towering over him by at least half a foot, while beside her stood a pale blonde woman of the same height. The two made a stunning picture as they stared coolly down at Jo.

Only the tall, thin man at the end didn't seem to have noticed Jo's blunder. He didn't seem to notice much at all, in fact, as his eyes stared rather blankly in front of him.

"This," Adam bit out with a forced smile, "is Josephine."

John raised a brow.

"A bit too elegant a name for that, I'd say. You know I like you, my boy," John bellowed, clapping Adam on the shoulder, "but I think you may have flubbed this one!"

The dark woman leaned down and whispered something in his ear, and he chortled.

"Quite right! Quite right! Very basic indeed!"

Adam's fingers were digging into her almost painfully, and she struggled for something to say to try to repair the damage.

"I'm so sorry. I was just nervous meeting you for the first time," she said earnestly.

That met with three identical raised brows from John and the two women. Then John shook his head in a feigned shudder and turned to Amber once more with a smile, while the other two women sent knowing looks at one another. Jo didn't dare look up at Adam.

The minutes passed slowly as they waited for the concert to begin. John quite clearly had cut her out of his existence, and the two women didn't bother to hide their disdain when their eyes landed on her. Adam interacted with them all smoothly, and the ladies' eyes warmed each time he gave them his attention.

Jo felt sick. She occasionally tried to interject something, doing her best to try to be a part of their group, but with every attempt she seemed to invite further contempt. She couldn't fit in with these people. She had absolutely no idea how to please them. She tried compliments. She tried questions. She tried just smiling and being friendly. But every single move she made was wrong. Over and over.

Finally the music began and conversation mercifully fell silent as they moved to the seats by the balcony's edge and everyone's attention turned to the stage. The performance consisted of a lead singer and a type of orchestra band with instruments that didn't quite sound the way she expected. She supposed that was because there was no wood. It all began smoothly. Gently. And Jo was finally beginning to relax when it kicked into high gear and everyone below started hooting and yelling.

She looked over the balcony to see hundreds of very wild looking men caught up in the music. It was a stark contrast between their wild abandon and the still, settled attitude of everyone on the balcony. Jo wondered if it was because of the class difference or the age. If these were Ancients on the balcony, they must have seen every concert imaginable by now. Or perhaps they were just pretentious fops who wouldn't lower themselves by acting like the rabble below.

When the intermission arrived, the men and women split off into two groups. Adam directed her and Amber to join the women. As she was about to walk over, with dread in her stomach, he leaned down to hiss in her ear.

"Fix it!"

She faltered for a moment, but he nudged her a bit hard in their direction. She approached slowly.

The women had quickly formed a circle, and when Jo arrived, she couldn't seem to find a space to stand beside anyone. They were all laughing and chatting, and she walked around the group, looking for an opening. She glanced back at Adam to find him staring at her furiously. He gestured for her to *get in there*. She looked back at the group of women, and drew in a deep breath.

"Excuse me…" It came out rather meekly and she wasn't really surprised when no one reacted. "Excuse me!" she tried again, this time a bit more loudly. The women closest to her looked over their shoulders at her, raised their brows, and gave a little laugh before turning back to whisper something to the group. The laughter increased.

Jo wanted to cry. She looked back at Adam again, but even through her blurry gaze, she could see he was practically raging. She turned back to the group and stared at the beautiful backs in front of her. What could she do? Squirm her way in? For what purpose? They weren't going to suddenly accept her even if she did manage to physically push her way in.

She didn't understand their rules. She wasn't good at whatever it was they were good at. If she knew what to do, at least she could attempt something. But she had no idea. And…

And fuck this. Why the hell was she obsessed with their shitty rules? To be able to get some pompous little asshole like John? Was there any way tier two could really be worse than that? She considered the men below. They were wild. Brutal. Maybe like that guy she and Christopher had seen in the desert.

So maybe she'd drop all the way down to tier five. So what? She had burned every single day for over two months in the desert! She knew how to take pain. But she didn't know how to do this.

She clenched her fists beside her and turned to stalk back to

Adam. He was responding to one of the other men when they saw her coming and he turned to follow their gaze.

"I'm done with this bullshit," she said crisply, not bothering to keep her voice low. "I quit."

"Have you lost control of your stock, son?" It was John again, but the others looked to be in agreement with him.

"I am not stock, you bloated, disgusting little man!" Her yell reverberated through the concert hall, and everything suddenly went quiet.

Adam was completely pale and reached for her arm, but she evaded him, moving backwards toward the balcony.

"Jo," he said hoarsely, "come with me right now."

She jumped again when he reached for her, and she grabbed a goblet off one of the tables nearby and threw it at him.

"I am DONE!" she screamed. "I have HAD IT with your STUPID RULES!" She was picking up everything she found to throw, pelting things at him as hard as she possibly could and feeling immensely gratified that she connected every time.

Jo could see Adam was trying to avoid deflecting the items onto any of the ancients or their women, which gave her just enough time to turn and climb over the balcony. The men below were now gathering underneath her, cheering and calling up encouragement while the men on the balcony looked nearly apoplectic.

"You have been training me to be STUPID just like every other shallow, vapid, pointless tier one, with their fake smiles and souls as ugly as the disgusting OLD MEN WHO OWN THEM!"

That drew a huge surge of shouts and cheers, and the men and women on the balcony began to look nervous. Jo was trying to climb down but there was nothing between the balcony and the ground, which was more than twenty feet below. She looked down at the men beneath her. Their arms were all raised, reaching for her, calling for her to drop down.

Adam was now approaching slowly with his hands held up in surrender.

"Jo, for god's sake," his voice cracked. "Just come back over on this side."

Jo could hear the yell of guards in the background and saw two as they appeared at the top of the stairs over Adam's shoulder. She narrowed her eyes, the image in front of her growing blurry.

"Fuck you," she whispered. He lunged for her as she threw herself back, his hands just missing her as she fell through the air, her arms spread wide.

And then twenty sets of hands or more were catching her. Touching her. Ripping at her clothes. Everyone was shouting. Fighting. Her legs were yanked apart as she fought back, biting, punching, and scratching at whatever she came in contact with.

The man between her legs was pulled off only for another to take his place, and she dug her nails into the skin on his back.

"Jo!" he yelled in her ear. "Just stay under me!" Adam was trying to cover her body as completely as he could as all around them, men were trying to rip her out from under him, kicking and beating his body.

She wrapped her legs and arms around him, trying to be a shield, and he yelled furiously in her ear again.

"I said STAY UNDER ME!"

"FUCK YOU!" she yelled back, wrapping herself around him more tightly.

He was still yelling at her when the guards finally made it through the crowd.

11

MOON DAY 221

THE CARRIAGE WHEELS clicked over the stone lane. Jo leaned her battered body against the window, watching the city go by, with Amber silent beside her. Adam sat shirtless across from them with his head buried in his hands, his back and arms scraped and bruised. Jo pulled the leather of his tunic more tightly around her. Her own clothing was in tatters beneath.

She'd been sure the guards were going to take her away, but it seemed there was one benefit of being property. They didn't arrest property. Instead, Adam had been given a ticket for her conduct and would have to appear in court in the next few days.

Jo would have liked to have seen what the Ancients thought of that, but by the time the guards had cleared a path for Jo and Adam, the Ancients had disappeared. Only Amber had remained on the balcony, looking so pale that Jo almost felt sorry for her. She supposed they'd deserted her when the crowd below had descended into anarchy.

Fortunately, guards were everywhere and escorted the three of them back to their carriage. It took a good while for them to handle all the parchment-work required before letting them go.

But even so, the mob still raged inside as the carriage pulled away.

They arrived back at the university, and Adam got out on Amber's side. Jo didn't bother waiting this time and opened her own door to hop out. She saw the carriage operator shoot her a glance out of the corner of his eye as she rounded the carriage, but he otherwise kept his composure. Adam said nothing but reached out for her arm as she went to pass him. His grip was gentle but firm, and Jo decided not to fight it. It had been a long day.

He led them back to their rooms, and Amber went into her suite and closed her door without a word. Jo started to pull away to go to her room as well.

She might as well have tried moving a boulder.

Adam stood unmoving in the hall, staring down at the floor, his hand locked on her arm. And for the first time since they'd gotten free of the men, Jo felt a small tendril of fear creep up her spine.

"It's...late," she said, trying to keep her breathing even.

He didn't answer. After a moment, he started walking toward his room, his grip still a vice on her arm. She stumbled along, periodically trying to slip out of his hand. His grip tightened, but he didn't look over.

Her feet tripped on the grooves in the stone floor as he pulled her into his room. The sound of the door clicking into place as he rested his head against it sent a coldness through her. She stood beside him. He hadn't let go of her arm.

Everything was silent.

Jo started to tremble. She wasn't afraid of being hurt. But she found herself desperately afraid that Adam would be the one to hurt her.

Without shifting his body, he pulled her in front of him, under him, trapping her between him and the door, staring down blankly. Then his eyes slowly shifted to hers. And he leaned down to rest his head next to hers, relaxing his grip on her at last.

"I'm so sorry," he whispered. "I couldn't—" He choked on the words and tried again. "I couldn't…keep losing you."

Jo could barely breathe. Her brows pulled together again and again.

He reached up to cup her cheek, and lifted his head. His eyes were heavy as they moved across her face. Heavy and bleak.

"I didn't want you to be you. You can't be you. You can't." His voice was husky, and the sound rippled through her until she ached. His thumb moved to her bottom lip, brushing back and forth slowly, his eyes soft as he watched.

"Stop," she choked out, putting her hands against his chest.

His skin was warm beneath her touch and he groaned, closing his eyes as he turned his head into her neck and leaned further into her. His tunic slipped off her shoulder, exposing her breast, and she gasped at the shock of his chest against her skin.

His groan was pained this time as he moved his hands behind her back to lift her up to him. She pushed against him in alarm, but he didn't seem to notice, his eyes locked on her breast. And his mouth enveloped her, sucking her into the soft warmth of his lips. A strangled cry left her as her arms cradled his head instinctively.

Then she was pushing at him again, almost in tears as she fought against the fire in her body.

"You have to stop, Adam," she said, the tears thick in her voice.

He slowly let her nipple slip out of his lips, drawing another cry from her, and looked up to face her, his eyes tortured.

"Is that what you really want?"

She stared back at him helplessly, her fingers digging into his shoulders.

"I…" Her body was screaming at her. Screaming and screaming, and she couldn't hear anything else.

He eased his hands down her back, sliding to pull her thighs around his waist as he pressed her into the door, his body hard and thick between her legs. He kept his eyes steady on hers as he stroked the backs of her thighs, pressing into her rhythmically, watching as shivers went through her.

"Baby, why do I know this," he whispered. "And this," he breathed, grinding into her at an angle that had her clinging to him, her body doubling over until her head was pressed against his once again. She could feel his breath warm against her.

"And this," he whispered one last time before his lips met hers, teasing them apart with his tongue until she at last parted them on a sob. And she was lost.

His tongue pushed inside, fully invading her. No more hesitation. No more softness. His hips locked her in place against the door as his hands tore off what remained of her clothing until she was naked around him.

Jo reached between them, her hands swiftly undoing the ties of his pants. He stilled, his lips hovering over hers, as she slipped her hand inside the smooth leather, enveloping him.

God, she'd forgotten how huge he was. She bit his lip lightly, pulling another groan from him as she wrapped both her hands around his shaft, pressing him into her hands and sliding down to the base to feel the length of him. She knew every ridge, every vein. This was Adam.

His hands gripped her thighs painfully. She bit his lip again, harder, as she squeezed him between her palms, and he pushed her into the door so hard she could barely breathe. Jerking her hands away, he bit her back and positioned himself between her legs, stroking back and forth between the wetness of her lips before finally pressing into her.

It stung, and she gripped his hips with her thighs, pushing herself away just enough to provide relief. He pulled her back down and pushed harder, and Jo winced, her fingers clenching his shoulders as she struggled to be still. It hurt but she needed him inside. She needed to feel him again. She needed *him*.

But it was no use. He was too big.

They pulled back slowly, their eyes meeting as realization dawned. She was a virgin.

Jo watched the glazed look of desire disappear from Adam's eyes to be replaced with horror.

He stepped away from her immediately, looking around, a severe line between his brows. He grabbed the cover off his bed and returned to wrap it around her quickly, almost roughly, as she watched him with a raised brow. He seemed to want to look anywhere except at her.

"You should go to bed," he said gruffly. She glanced at the clock. They still had an hour before the sun would put them to sleep.

Her body was on fire. His effort to get inside her had left a dull throb between her legs, and every movement of her body sent sharp pangs coursing through her.

"No."

"Jo…"

She ignored the warning in his tone and walked past him, focusing on making it to the bed before the sensations overwhelmed her thinking. She managed to climb in without making a sound and arranged the cover over her neatly.

"What are you doing?"

She didn't answer but pulled the cover up until only her eyes were peeking out at him. She wasn't moving. He looked away for a long moment before turning back.

"Jo." He was serious now. She dropped the cover back down and frowned back at him. He closed his eyes and rubbed his brow. He tried again without opening them, his fingers pinching the bridge of his nose.

She let her eyes wander down his body as he spoke. How could she have ever forgotten him? Every single line pulled at her memory now, filling her with warmth. With pleasure. No…it was so much more than pleasure. Her eyes felt heavy as she watched him twitch beneath her gaze, his thick length jutting up out of his pants, throbbing in time with the ache inside her.

"Are you listening to me?" Her eyes snapped back up at his outrage to find him glaring at her. She suddenly felt the urge to giggle, but she hid her smile under the cover again and snuggled more deeply into the bed.

"Jo, you can't stay in here," he said hoarsely, coming over to stand beside the bed. She looked up at him.

"So carry me to bed," she challenged, starting to peel back the cover. He grabbed it before she had made much progress, his face pale, and held it in place as he stared down at her.

"It's not like I'm a *real* virgin," she whispered.

Adam groaned and collapsed on top of her, trapping her hands against his chest. He kept the cover between them and pressed his lips on her forehead, unmoving, before finally pulling back.

"They check, Jo. When women are sold. They check."

She hesitated before responding.

"Well…couldn't you just…take me to the temple? Before you tried selling me? Everything would get put back…"

"Do you really think I'd *burn* you so we could fuck?" He was back to sounding outraged.

She frowned.

"I think *I* should be the one to decide how much pain to take."

He stared down at her.

"That's dumb," he said flatly.

She narrowed her eyes at him.

"But you're fine with actually selling me. Letting someone else fuck me. Never touching me again."

"Don't," his voice was hoarse.

"Why not? It's the truth."

"The truth?" He took her face between his hands, stroking his thumbs against her cheeks as his eyes grew dark. "The truth is I want to kill anyone who touches you. I want to cut them into pieces so small they can't come back. To bury them in some hole so deep that no one will ever find them.

"But if I did, it wouldn't save you. I have been here for months, and before you arrived, I spent all my free time trying to figure out how the fuck to get out. I've read everything I can find, talked to everyone, scouted every area." His expression was grim. "But the control here is absolute.

"Selling you to an Ancient was the only way I could think of to make things better for you here. I just...I was so angry, I couldn't see straight," he muttered, avoiding her eyes.

Jo bit down on her lip.

"Because I kept messing up?"

His gaze snapped back to hers.

"You know that's not it."

She groaned.

"I'm sorry. I am. But how can you blame me when...when I couldn't remember anything?"

His eyes blazed down at her.

"Because I never forgot you."

She blinked up at him, frowning.

"You told Christopher you just remembered some images—"

"Do you really think I'd tell him?" he cut her off furiously. "We were friends, but if he doesn't remember me, then I'm nothing more than a pawn to him, like anyone else. They don't trust people with too many memories here, and I'm not going to hand him a weapon to use against me."

Jo felt the heat rising up the back of her neck.

"What do you remember?" she breathed, her eyes wide.

He exhaled.

"Not everything. But..." His expression grew wary. "Enough."

She hit his chest, scowling at him. He groaned and buried his face in her neck.

"I remember how violent you were," he sighed. She mock punched him again, and he cuddled her closer to him. He lay unmoving and silent, his lashes occasionally brushing her skin. When he spoke, it was in a whisper.

"I remember you fixing my computer. A lot. I remember starting to mess it up on purpose."

Jo's heart started hammering. She hadn't been his maid.

"I remember how you filled out your jeans." His hand ran down her body to reach behind her, pulling her into him as he kissed her neck. She barely stopped herself from moaning and pushed at him to go on. He sighed against her skin.

"I remember your eyes when you'd get an idea in your head. I was never sure when I was going to need to grab you before you did something crazy."

She frowned and felt him smile against her.

"I remember you trying to break up with me every five minutes," he said irritably, "always so sure things weren't going to work out."

"I'm sure it wasn't because you were *mean* to me."

He leaned up to glare at her.

"I fucking adored you!"

"You said I was a frightened rabbit that no one would find desirable."

"That's not what I said—"

"It's close enough," she interrupted but dropped her eyes quickly, not wanting to think too much about it.

"Jo…" His voice was husky again and he stroked her cheek. "I wanted to hold you so badly it hurt. I knew I was scaring you. I just…I fucking hated you being afraid of me. You were never afraid of me."

She stared at his chest. Was that true?

"You were ashamed of me," she whispered.

He gripped her face, forcing her eyes back to his.

"*Never.*"

She tried to turn away again but he wouldn't allow it.

"Do you have any idea how fucking proud I was of you today?"

She stilled.

"You were mad at me for not saying the right things."

He groaned and leaned his forehead against hers.

"No, baby…no. I was scared. And so angry that this is what was required to save you. Letting them think they could even approach your level. That they were *above* it. For fuck's sake, look at Amber. You can't actually think I'd want you to be like *that*."

She stared up at him.

"I was trying." Her voice sounded so very small. "You thought I wasn't trying. But I was. I'm just not able to do the things you all can do. I'm just…I can't really do much," she whispered as he stared down at her in choked horror.

"Jo…" his voice was scratchy. Raw. "Jo, those things I said were bullshit. When you jumped out of the carriage, I wanted you jumping into my arms. Every time you ran, I wanted you running to me the way you used to. I was just…I was so busy trying to make you stop being you—to stop reminding me of everything I couldn't have anymore—that I didn't realize…"

His eyes were wide as he shook his head.

"Jesus. I didn't know I was hurting you. Or that I made you think…*you* were the one not good enough. I was trying to make you *worse*. A lot worse. To completely change you from being everything I…"

Pained warmth filled his eyes.

"Although I was also…trying to punish you. I'm sorry. Not hurt you. I never wanted you to be hurt. But…I did want to be harsh. Rough. To yell at you for looking at him the way you did," he whispered, and she dropped her eyes.

"We were alone in the desert for weeks," she said softly,

closing her eyes as she felt tension filling his body. "We didn't even know there was anyone else on the planet. It was… frightening. And…Christopher protected me," she whispered, looking back at him.

Adam's eyes shifted back and forth between anger and remorse. Until he at last groaned and dropped his forehead to hers.

"Fuck. I'm sorry. It wasn't fair. It just…it fucking hurt."

Jo felt the tightness in her chest begin to relax at last.

"I don't want you to be hurt," she whispered. His lips were so close to hers. "Why can't I stay in here?"

He groaned again and pressed into her.

"Because Amber is a viper, and I'm still on probation with this job. And after today…"

"Did I get you in trouble?" she asked in a small voice.

"No, honey. I did. But we need to be very careful now. I should just have to pay a fine but until I know more, we need to be extra careful."

She hesitated.

"I can sneak back in the morning. Before Amber can even move."

Adam grew still.

"What are you saying."

She bit her lip.

"I'm not affected by the sun as much as everyone else, I guess. I can't stay awake long when it's up, but I can get right up as soon as it sets."

He was quiet for a moment. When he spoke, his voice was harsh.

"Don't ever speak about it again. Ever. Don't say anything and don't do anything that could ever make anyone suspect."

He stood up and swept her into his arms, carrying her to the door so quickly she was out of breath by the time he deposited her on her feet. He grabbed her clothes off the floor and yanked the cover away, dressing her with a grim expression. She shivered each time his hands touched her, but his eyes stayed dark.

"Get back to your room. And make sure you don't let Amber think anything has changed between us. Maybe I can still fix this." His voice was back to normal. Stern. Commanding.

Jo's vision blurred, and Adam's eyes jerked to her face. He reached for her immediately, resting his forehead on hers.

"No, baby, no," he whispered. "I need you to pretend. Please. Please pretend. I can't—" His voice sounded strangled. "If they know I love you, they'll take you from me sooner. Please, please pretend." A shudder went through him as he wiped away her tears. Then he looked over his shoulder at the clock.

"We're out of time."

She pulled back and wiped her eyes, looking up one last time as he opened the door. He just told her he loved her. She could put up with a few stupid rules a while longer. To stay with him a while longer. Just a little longer.

She gave him a brief nod and walked out. The door didn't close behind her until she'd made it back to her room. She managed to undress and crawl into bed seconds before the exhaustion hit, and she collapsed onto her pillow.

She didn't want to think anymore. To feel. To remember. Memories of Adam's touch. His scent. The sense of rightness she felt in his arms.

But most of all, she didn't want to think about a pair of piercing blue eyes in the desert and what she was supposed to feel about them.

———

Jo didn't see Adam much over the next few days. When he wasn't at the courthouse, he seemed to be in one meeting after another, though never on campus. He always returned looking pale and would spend most of his time in the library.

Jo followed his lead and left him alone, focusing instead on paying attention in her classes and making sure she looked miserable around Amber. It didn't take much. She *was* miserable.

"It's such a waste of good material," Amber sighed. "It's not like they'll auction you *now*."

They were being fitted for their meeting with potential buyers, less than a month away now.

"I'm happy to leave those repulsive freaks all for you, Amber."

The tailors looked at Jo with some alarm, and she wondered if she should hold her tongue. Adam had asked her to pretend, and she *meant* to behave. But every now and then…

"*Those* weren't the ones who will be bidding," Amber said.

Jo rolled her eyes.

"And anyway, they weren't freaks. They just didn't like *you*."

"Then I'm sure you'll be very happy every time your buyer decides to rut you like a pig."

Amber blanched.

"They have class. They wouldn't do it that way."

This time it was Amber the tailors looked at, and she fidgeted inside her pinned dress.

"Careful, miss! If the pins cut you, they may want you to go to the temple!"

Jo hadn't thought Amber could get any more white. She stood perfectly still and quiet for the remainder of the fitting.

But after a few minutes, Jo wished she hadn't shut her down. Her insults were annoying, but they'd lost their sting after that night with Adam. And she needed the distraction.

That night… She hadn't been able to escape it. How could she live with these feelings? Knowing she would be sold to someone else? Sold to many someones in all likelihood. And each day that passed was one day closer to losing him. Again.

She frowned. Again? She tested the thought. It felt true. But he'd said he couldn't lose *her* again. Had he left her or had she left him? She reached up to rub her head, and the tailor cautioned her worriedly. Nothing made sense. Until she was in his arms. Then everything made sense. Except…

She closed her eyes. She couldn't think about Christopher. She just couldn't. He was as far from her as Adam soon would be. What did it matter? There was no sense feeling guilty when she was going to be separated from both of them soon enough.

The door to their dorm slammed. Jo looked at the open doorway of the fitting room in time to see Adam stalk by. He didn't look over. Another door slammed and everything was silent for a moment. Then loud thuds reverberated through the hall, over and over.

Jo and Amber looked at each other. For all her snobbery, Jo suspected she was just as nervous about the consequences of Jo's little rebellion. After all, despite their seeming acceptance of Amber, the Ancients had abandoned her at the first sign of trouble. And neither of them knew how it would all play out. At the end of the day, they were both at the mercy of the men.

Amber curled her lip and turned away. So much for the moment of sisterhood. She heard Adam's door open down the hall and his footsteps approaching.

"I need to speak with you." His voice was short. Clipped. But he stood casually, his hands in his pockets. "Get dressed and meet me in the library."

Jo nodded. He didn't bother instructing the tailors before turning to walk out, but they had already begun unpinning her dress. She put her short suede dress back on once they finished and hurried down the hall, her stomach in knots.

"Close the door." He was standing at the window, looking out, his hands still in his pockets.

She closed the door behind her gently and leaned against it. Okay. They were alone now.

He didn't turn around.

Jo gripped her hands together before forcing them back to

her sides. It couldn't be that bad. What could they do to her worse than tier five? Worse than burning? She squared her shoulders and walked forward.

"Stop." He turned his head to the side as he spoke the word harshly.

She froze, her brow drawing together. No one could see or hear them right now. This room was the most private on the floor. Maybe because he was at the window?

"Stop giving me orders when we're alone," she frowned.

The sound he made in response was low and guttural. He pulled his hand from his pocket to brace himself on the wall, leaning forward with his head down. She could see blood on his knuckles.

"Adam…" She stepped forward the last few steps and slid her arms around his waist. His entire body felt like iron. She leaned her head against his back and squeezed tightly. "What happened?"

He stood very still, but his heart pounded beneath her cheek. She tugged at him.

"We should move away from the window," she whispered.

His head rose to look out before he stepped back out of sight, pulling her into his arms. He leaned back against the wall and buried his face in her neck.

His strength engulfed her, and she snuggled in as close as possible, finally able to breathe again. Safe. She knew it couldn't last though.

"Tell me."

He squeezed her so tightly she couldn't breathe for a moment.

"Okay, you're scaring me—and also suffocating me," she managed to rasp out. He quickly released her and looked down, worry filling his eyes. "Adam, I'm teasing. It's not like we need to breathe."

Her smile only seemed to make him feel worse, and he

slumped back against the wall as he stared at her, his hands falling to his sides. She frowned.

"You don't have to let go *completely*."

He just stared at her, his eyes weary.

"The lower classes have been rioting. They've been a powder keg waiting to go off for a long time, and…what happened at the concert lit a match. Now the Ancients can't go beyond the Brahmin district without a mob forming. And they want someone to pay."

Jo stared at him.

"You mean they want me to pay."

He slid down the wall to sit with his arms on his knees and leaned his head back, closing his eyes. She sat down as well, facing him, her arms wrapped around her knees.

"The judge ruled that because it was a public rebellion that created civil unrest, the punishment must also be public. And severe. They wanted to make an example of you. So no one else follows in your footsteps."

Well that didn't sound good.

"Okay…so…do they have something worse than tier five or burning?"

Adam opened his eyes, frustration warring with pain.

"Do you know what caning is?"

"Beating with a stick?" Painful, but compared to burning? Please. She could take it.

"They use a metal rod here with specific dimensions based on the man who beats her." His eyes were bleak. "The length of his arm and the width of his thumb."

"In three days, they will take you to the center of the city common, strip your clothes away, tie you to a post, and…give you a hundred strokes."

A hundred… She swallowed. No, she could take that. It's not like it would last all day. It still wasn't even close to burning. She could take the pain. But public humiliation...that was going to be harder.

"Fifty strokes from behind," his voice was barely audible, "and fifty from the front."

Jo blinked. So she would be completely exposed. Would they hit her breasts? She suppressed a shudder.

Adam closed his eyes. His voice was barely a gruff whisper now.

"They expect men to keep the women they own under control. When they fail, they pay a fine to the city...usually."

He faded off. Jo's heart began racing. He couldn't be in trouble, too. Not like this. She reached for his chest, her eyes full of worry, and he opened his again at last.

"But the judge has decided that if the loss of control is too severe, it has to be publicly rectified."

Jo's brow pulled together. How? What did that mean?

"I'm the one who has to hit you."

She stared at him a long moment.

"Tell them no," she said flatly.

His eyes glistened.

"I could," he said, his voice hoarse. "But it would only make it worse. They'll think you have too much power, and they'll increase the penalty for you. And someone else will do it."

Jo looked down and pressed her palms into her brow, rubbing hard. Okay. Okay—she could take this.

"Well...at least...you won't hit as hard, right?" she looked up, but what little hope she had faded at the anguish in his eyes.

"Right." The sound was tortured.

"Why do I get the feeling that's not exactly true?" she whispered.

He buried his hands in his hair and dropped his head between his knees.

"If they think I'm holding back, it won't stop at a hundred.

They'll make me keep going or replace me with someone else. And then we're back to square one." He looked up again, desperation in his eyes. "But if you scream—hard. Beg me to stop. Maybe I can make it look real without actually hurting you."

She looked at him with steady eyes.

They would be in the middle of a park. People everywhere. Close to them. It would be very easy for them to see everything. To see any hint of restraint. Adam had already realized this.

She closed her eyes.

"Baby, I'm sorry—I am so sorry." He grabbed her, his arms tight around her now. She felt so cold. "If I hadn't been pushing you so hard—criticizing you instead of supporting you. If I hadn't been so fucking jealous."

She leaned against him weakly.

"I don't want it to last longer than a hundred. Just do it right the first time. Just...get it over with. Don't give them any reason to doubt it. Promise me?"

Adam closed his eyes.

"Forgive me, Jo. Please forgive me." A shudder went through him as she reached up to stroke his back.

"You have to promise..."

She felt him nod against her.

"I promise," he choked out.

She relaxed into him, her hands gliding across his muscles. He was so strong.

"Do you think...I'll have to burn after? Will it damage me?"

Adam stilled.

"No. I won't hit your bones, and I'll make sure the edge doesn't clip you. At least I can spare you some pain," he said bitterly.

She sighed. That was something at least. Although if she did end up having to burn, they wouldn't need to worry about keeping her body undamaged in other ways.

She pulled back to look at him.

"Now that you know what to expect...can you stop avoiding me? I don't want every moment of my life to be miserable."

He stared down at her, sheltered in his arms. His eyes were heavy, and he brought his hand up to her cheek, caressing her skin...her lips. Then his mouth descended on hers, and they didn't speak again for a long while.

12

MOON DAY 230

Jo sat silent in the carriage as it neared the park, the air around her heavy on her skin, burying her under its weight. Adam sat beside her, equally silent, his hand crushing hers in its grip. She didn't pull away. The small pain kept her grounded, preparing her for what was to come.

They rode alone for once. Adam had instructed Amber to remain in the dorm, much to Jo's relief. She feared she might have clawed her face off if she'd had to deal with even a single smirk. And at least she had these few last minutes of comfort.

But the park arrived too soon. Guards covered the area, standing shoulder to shoulder in a path from the carriage to the park center, before fanning out in a wide circle. Some of the ancients she'd met stood inside the circle beside court officials. And outside the circle must have been hundreds of men, mostly from the lower classes, judging by their clothing. They strained to see into the center, where an ornate stone pillar stood on a circular platform.

The carriage came to a stop with a sickening thud.

"Don't forget," she whispered. "Quickly. You have to do it quickly."

She felt a shudder go through him but he gave a short nod, his expression dark. Then he was climbing out and reaching in to pull her out behind him. And they walked up the path side by side, no longer touching.

No one made a sound. The guards stood as still as ever, but even the men behind them grew silent as Adam and Jo approached.

Jo kept her head down while her eyes scanned the crowd, searching for Christopher. He had to have heard what was happening. It seemed to be the talk of the city. Public punishment had not been used on a female in over a hundred years, and it had never been used on women in tier one. But then, no tier one woman had ever behaved as she had.

She dropped her eyes to the ground again. He wasn't there. If he had been, she was sure he would have made certain she could see him. He hadn't come.

Her eyes were wet as they came to a stop in front of the judge. John, the Ancient, stood at his side, his expression full of self-righteous disappointment as he looked at Adam. He did not bother to so much as glance in her direction.

Get it together. She couldn't fall apart now. They might be able to hurt her body, but that didn't mean they'd won. She just had to get through the next few minutes. She could do this. She had burned more than most of them had. She could take pain.

John leaned in to the judge to say something in his ear before standing upright once more, his nose high in the air. Well, as high as he could manage. The judge nodded and stepped onto the platform. He turned to face the crowd.

"We have long maintained that men cannot be held responsible for the irrationality of the female. As such, we have had a long tradition of allowing men to punish their females in private. Unfortunately, the magnitude of the foolishness of this woman, her wanton disrespect, and her sheer ingratitude demand a more public display of accountability."

Jo could feel the heat from Adam's body rising along with her own. If the judge didn't stop talking soon, she feared she would make things even worse for herself. And for Adam.

"Her corporate handler is here today to teach her submission. The rod has been chosen according to his measurements."

Here the judge nodded toward a man on the side who came forward to present Adam with an iron rod around three and a half feet long and the width of his thumb, as promised. Jo's courage drained from her. She loved Adam's hands. She loved how strong they were. Large and strong.

She began shaking.

The judge stepped down and gestured for Adam to proceed. And suddenly it was just the two of them standing there in the light of the fake day. Everything was quiet.

Adam stared down at the rod in his hands, unmoving. The seconds ticked by. He just stood there, his body as rigid as the iron in his hands.

"Adam," she whispered, keeping her head down to hide her lips. He didn't react.

Shit. Okay. She had to do this. Taking a deep breath, her lashes closed. She could do this.

A small ripple of sound traveled through the crowd as she began stripping off her clothing. Adam turned his head to her in a daze.

Jo made a small sound of frustration. He needed to snap out of this.

Her eyes widened at him expectantly for a brief moment before she stepped up on the platform. A length of rope was on the ground beside the pillar, but she couldn't very well tie herself up. Fifty strokes on each side. Should she get the front over with first? A shudder went through her. No. She stepped forward and wrapped her arms around the pillar.

She clung to it gratefully as Adam walked over. Her blood had drained from her skin, and she could barely support her own weight. He reached for the rope, leaning the rod against the pillar, and began binding her wrists together. Gently. Too gently.

"Tighter," she whispered. She didn't know if she would be able to stop herself from throwing her hands behind her to protect herself from the pain once the hitting began.

Adam looked as pale as she felt, but he tightened the rope. He kept his eyes down after he finished and picked up the rod again. This was it. Her knees gave out as his footsteps moved behind her, and she clenched the pillar to hold herself up.

The cold stone sucked the heat from her skin. The air suffocated her in its stillness. All was quiet.

Adam placed the cold metal against the swell of her bottom. She would not cry. She could do this. She pressed her face into the stone, digging in painfully and squeezing her eyes shut.

The rod pulled back.

The torture of waiting for it to strike pulled a small sound from her, and she pressed her lips together, fighting to be silent, her body trembling too violently for her to hide it any longer.

She heard the sound of metal falling on stone and jerked her head around to see Adam staring at the Ancients, fury in his eyes.

"The Ancients have told you to be grateful," he shouted. "To do your jobs and you will be rewarded with a few minutes with tier five women every few months." The Ancients and officials seemed to have been immobilized with shock, but the crowd buzzed instantly.

"Meanwhile they enjoy exclusive access to tier one women, something you will never be permitted to enjoy!"

What was he doing? He'd barely managed to prevent them from raping her at the concert. Was he hoping they'd stampede the guards and he'd somehow be able to get her free? Where could they go? He'd said there was no way out of the city.

The officials snapped out of their stupor and directed a guard to stop him, but the crowd pressed forward, yelling. The Ancients looked around nervously while Adam picked up the rod again, holding it in warning toward the guard as he continued yelling at the crowd.

"But every man who works hard deserves the right to save his money and buy the exclusive rights to a woman if that's what he wants! It's time for change!"

The crowd cheered while the officials and Ancients pulled closer to the center, toward Jo and Adam, shouting at more guards to control Adam.

"Are we really going to accept a violation of a man's right to punish a woman as he sees fit, just because she is emotional? Has any man found a woman who isn't?"

Laughter erupted along with further jeers toward the officials and ancients. Adam held the crowd, but he was losing his battle against the guards. There were too many. Thankfully, they seemed intent only on subduing him rather than cutting him.

He struggled powerfully but they managed to force him to the ground at last, binding his mouth with a leather strip to prevent him from inciting the crowd further.

He looked up at Jo, helpless grief in his eyes. She sagged against the pillar. Whatever this cost her, she was glad he couldn't do it. Her eyes softened. She could breathe again. For the moment.

The judge stepped up on the platform, the agitation thick in his voice as he tried to calm the crowd.

"Men! Men! This man has clearly been bewitched! We have all seen this happen. It is truly tragic and a great loss to our city!"

Adam closed his eyes, the color in his cheeks disappearing completely. Jo frowned in confusion. What did that mean?

"This must not go unanswered a moment longer!" The judge nodded toward a guard Adam's size. The guard quickly marched toward them and picked up the rod. Adam's eyes flew open.

The judge and the Ancients backed away from the platform

again. The crowd was still agitated but their agitation seemed laced with excitement. Whatever Adam had said, they wanted to see Jo hit.

Adam began struggling again in earnest, but the guards were prepared and kept him locked in place.

Jo turned back to the post. Okay. This was it. She released all the breath from her lungs and resisted taking another breath. When he hit her, she wouldn't have the air inside to scream. She wouldn't give them the satisfaction.

She heard the iron whistling through the air the moment before it hit her back.

Nothing could have prepared her for the pain. She gasped, pulling the air into her lungs helplessly just as it landed a second time.

She screamed, crying. Screaming. There was no way she could have controlled it.

She arched her back into the pillar, desperately and pointlessly trying to get farther away from the pain. It struck again, the edge catching her skin this time and cutting through her flesh.

She was sobbing. She barely noticed the buzz growing in the crowd. The march of guards approaching. The shouts around her.

Then she was being untied as she drew gasping breaths and fell weakly into two familiar arms that trembled as they pulled her against him. While another voice, not familiar, spoke from nearby to the crowd.

She looked up to see a pair of cold blue eyes, burning in icy fury, underneath angelic golden curls.

———

Christopher pulled Jo's head into his neck carefully, cradling it in his hand, while his other hand slid low down her back to cup her from behind, sheltering her as much as possible from the eyes all around.

She clung to him as a tall, slender man climbed on the platform, holding his hands out toward the crowd. To her surprise, the entire park went almost perfectly silent.

"Folks...folks...This is an incredible time for our city. An incredible time. Jobs are booming, incomes are soaring, and we have completely rebuilt the awesome power of the city guard. Let's give a big hand to our guard, we love you guys!"

Jo stiffened as she turned her eyes back to Adam, still trapped on the ground beside her. The guards were looking at one another in confusion while the crowd contributed some halfhearted claps.

"You have done your jobs here admirably, and I commend you for it! But for now you may stand down."

He turned back to the crowd as the guards stepped away somewhat cautiously from Adam. Jo sagged with relief.

Adam pushed himself to his feet, tearing the gag from his mouth, his large chest heaving. He shot a heated glance at the guards and then Christopher before rubbing his jaw fiercely and looking away for a moment. When he looked back, his movements were calm, and he reached down for Jo's dress before stepping behind her. He bent his head to her ear as she leaned against Christopher's chest.

"Honey, can you raise your arms?" The low rumble of his voice didn't carry beyond the three of them.

"*It pains me to inform you that a respected official, someone we all put our trust in to uphold the law, has conspired to commit extortion!*"

She nodded, beginning to reach up, only to gasp at a sharp pain in her lower shoulder.

Christopher glared furiously at Adam.

"She shouldn't be moving," he said in a harsh whisper.

Jo felt Adam's frustrated rage behind her, and she reached

back, searching for his hand. She vaguely registered the judge protesting his innocence in the background.

"She shouldn't be naked in the middle of a mob!" Adam hissed back, capturing Jo's hand in his and lacing their fingers together.

"And whose fault is that," Christopher snapped.

Adam clenched his hands in response, and Jo groaned.

"*We know the great Ancients have no need to pay for the law they themselves created, but he thought he could win favor by subverting the natural order.*"

"Not you, Jo—"

"Sorry, baby—"

Their whispers overlapped as they stroked her head, neck, shoulder...

Jo opened one eye. Okay, this was getting weird.

The judge was yelling now. Jo turned her attention gratefully to his voice, her face brushing against Christopher's hand. He let it fall to cup her cheek, and Adam's hand tightened on her hip. His broad form shielded her back from view, but Christopher didn't move his hand from behind her. Jo tried to ignore the heat flowing a little too strongly through her body.

"You son of a bitch!" The judge was being led away by the guards. "This is a set-up! You've had it out for me since I denied you that license! Let me go!" He fought against his restraints as the speaker shook his head dolefully.

"Help me! You have to tell them! Tell them I was only following your orders!" the judge pleaded, calling out to the Ancients in desperation.

The speaker looked at the Ancients, a small smile curving his lips. He waited.

One of the Ancients Jo didn't recognize stepped forward.

"He speaks nonsense. As you said, we created the law. What cause do we have to bribe officials duly appointed by your office, Director?"

The director gave a short bow.

"I had every confidence this was the case," he boomed, but his smirk lingered. The crowd shuffled restlessly. *We should all have the right* and *time for a change* began floating around. Adam went completely still. Those were his words.

The director seemed oblivious to the growing chants while the Ancients looked around in unease. Jo felt Christopher shift, and she looked up to see him exchange a glance with Adam.

"Can you work with this?" Adam's voice was low, his eyes unusually shrewd.

Christopher paused for a long moment before turning back toward the director, his eyes narrowing.

"I can."

———

Jo groaned.

"I'm sorry, baby," Adam said between light kisses on her back, his voice husky. She was lying naked on her stomach in his bed as he lay clothed beside her, smoothing some type of salve on her cut.

"Will it scar? Will I have to burn?" She didn't like the weepy tone in her voice, but it had been a long day.

"No," he murmured, his strong hands rubbing the ointment in carefully. "No more pain."

The judge's ruling had been vacated. They'd ordered Adam to pay a fine on behalf of the company, which technically owned her, and told him to punish Jo as he saw fit. And while Adam still wasn't certain what would happen with his job, for now they seemed to be safe.

Christopher had departed with the Director, passing her back to Adam without any outward hesitation after the director's speech concluded. But Jo had felt the sudden tension in his body the moment before he moved to release her, and she'd hadn't been able to keep herself from clinging to him just an instant too long. His eyes told her he'd noticed.

She couldn't even begin to sort out her feelings. Her emotions swirled inside her along with all the questions she couldn't answer. Things she didn't know how to ask Adam. Who had Christopher been to her?

Adam had said Christopher had been his friend—worked with him. And she and Adam… She sighed. They *had* to have been together, as preposterous as that seemed on the surface. He was beyond gorgeous, sexy as hell, and dominated every room he entered. But she could think of no other explanation for the level of comfort they felt with each other—for the familiarity they had with one another's bodies.

It couldn't have been just sex. He'd said he loved her, and it was too obvious by now even for *her* to doubt. And although it had taken her some time to figure out, she knew what it was she felt when she was with him: happy. Just…happy. In a deep way that bubbled up from inside and spilled out into laughter or teasing or even a strange anger that made her want to jump on him rather than get away.

It was his voice she had remembered in the desert. And the idea of ever being without him again…

But then there was Christopher. And the question she had been dreading asking herself. The question she did not want to believe. Did not want to think herself capable of.

Had she cheated?

"Adam…" She hesitated. She didn't want to talk about this. But it was long overdue.

He kissed her shoulder and dropped his head beside hers, his hand warm on her lower back. Lower. She closed her eyes and tried to concentrate.

"Can you tell me what you remember about…me… and…Christopher?"

He stilled, and she opened her eyes. The lazy softness was retreating as a hard glint replaced it.

"I'm sorry," she breathed, a faint cry in her tone. "But...I need to understand."

"And you think *I* understand?" he said, gritting his teeth together.

She reached her hand up to stroke his cheek, her eyes pleading.

"Just anything. Anything at all."

The fire grew in his eyes, and Jo thought he might just tell her to go to her room. He pulled away with a low growl, sitting up beside her with his arm resting on his knee. But after a moment, he put his hand on her head, stroking her hair softly if a bit grudgingly, his fingertips rubbing her neck.

"Honestly," he sighed, "I didn't even think he liked you. He got angry every time I remember him seeing you, even before we were together."

That certainly fit with how Christopher had been when they first woke up in the desert. But even then, she had felt... something. Was it just her? Had she just secretly pined for him?

Please don't let that have been her. She didn't want that to be her.

"I don't know who I was," she whispered. "But I'm scared I wouldn't like her."

Adam dropped down beside her again, glaring at her as usual.

"*I* like her!" He buried his fingers in her hair, pulling on it a little too hard. Tears sprang to her eyes, whether from the pain or his words she wasn't sure. He leaned in, his lips hovering over her own. His tone was gruff when he spoke again. "I like *you.*"

And then she did cry. He ignored her tears, biting her lip before plunging his tongue into her. She whimpered as he rolled onto his back and pulled her body on top of him, careful not to touch her wounds, keeping their lips connected with his hand still buried in her hair.

Heat flowed through her in waves. She moaned into him, and he pushed a knee between her legs, forcing them apart. His hand slid between her thighs from behind, and she gasped as he stroked her. She couldn't breathe. She couldn't move. Her fingers dug into his shoulders, and he groaned into her, pushing more deeply into her mouth as he began moving his finger back and forth.

She pushed herself up with a gasp.

"Stop!"

Adam didn't stop but leaned up to pull her chest to his mouth. She pushed at him harder as he sucked a nipple in between his lips, his finger continuing to drive her closer to the edge.

"Adam! I'm serious—stop!"

He pulled back, his eyes heated.

"Why?" he demanded. "You want him?"

She looked down at him helplessly.

"No…" she whispered. Then… "I don't know!"

She started to bring her hands up to hold her head, the flash of pain in his eyes cutting her heart, but the pain in her shoulder stopped her. She gripped his shoulders again with a cry.

"I don't know who I am. Or who I was! I don't know anything. My head is spinning and my body hurts and I don't know anything and…and…"

Adam's eyes raged at her in fury and pain, his hand still between her legs. He was so hard beneath her, beneath the suede of his pants, that her body refused to listen to her. She pressed down into him, just barely, her wetness causing the material to cling to him even more tightly.

"I'm so sorry. I'm trying to do the right thing," she whispered, her head falling forward onto his, her fingers flexing on his shoulders.

Tension rippled through his body as he held her, and she stayed very still, struggling not to press against him again.

"Tell me why you want me to stop. Tell me exactly," he said, his voice low.

She closed her eyes.

"Because…I shouldn't be letting you comfort me. Letting you make me feel the way you do. Not when I…" her voice faltered. She took a deep breath. "Not when I can't be loyal.

"And I'm so sorry," she said, her voice breaking as she pulled back to look at him. "I don't know what happened. I don't know what's wrong with me! But I'm so afraid of why I was sent here. Of what it must mean. Of what I might have done," she finished hoarsely.

Adam was still for a while. Finally he sighed and laid back on the bed, pulling her down with him and tucking her head into his neck. His fingers slipped from her body slowly as his hand came to rest at the base of her spine, pressing her down into him. He groaned before sighing again.

"You just can't be easy, can you," he said dryly. She frowned against his skin, but he kissed her forehead before she thought of anything to say.

He stroked her back for a while.

"You didn't cheat on me, Jo."

She didn't move.

"Well…it's not like you'd know," she said quietly.

He snorted.

"Baby, I know you. And you didn't cheat."

She frowned again. She wasn't so sure.

"Then why would I have been sent here?"

"Who knows. Why was I?"

Her frown deepened.

"Maybe *you* cheated!"

He chuckled at her outrage, his chest shaking until she hit

him with the side of her fist. He pulled her close when she started to get up.

"Stay, Jo. I never cheated. You never cheated. And I don't know why people are sent here, but I'm pretty sure it isn't for cheating."

She calmed in his arms, considering this. The people here seemed to be more prone to violence if anything. But...her? She didn't feel violent, even if Adam teased her about it. Adam was big and forceful, but he couldn't even bring himself to hit her once.

And Christopher? Well, she'd seen Christopher gouge a man's eyes, so she supposed he was capable of it. Still, between the three of them, what could they possibly have done?

She groaned and turned further into Adam's neck.

"Do I have to go back to my room tonight?"

He stroked her hair as he relaxed under her, one arm beneath his head.

"No. If Amber tells someone, I'll just say it was necessary to tend to your wounds."

She sighed. She was still very wet and in this weird world climate, what was wet seemed to stay wet for hours. She whimpered.

"Regretting stopping me?"

"No!" Yes. God, yes.

He chuckled again, and she wanted to punch him. Maybe she *was* violent.

"What was it you meant earlier? You asked..." she hesitated to say his name. "You asked if he could work with this? What did you mean?"

Adam's hand stilled on her hair. When he finally spoke, his tone was cautious.

"The director made a power grab today. I can only assume Christopher pushed it somehow. And now there's more heat in the populace that the director can draw on to take even more power. Blondie is good at manipulating systems."

Jo raised a brow at his pet name for Christopher, but didn't interrupt.

"So..." he sighed, long and loud. "Maybe he can do something about you being sold after all. But I helped!" He looked down to glare at her, and she looked up to let him. And a smile spread across her face until she was beaming up at him.

Adam believed he could do it. He really believed it. And if Adam believed it, it had to be true.

Christopher would find a way.

13

MOON DAY 250

Jo TWISTED AND TURNED, trying to see her back in the mirror as she pulled the skin on her side, stretching it to see as much as possible. A small whimper escaped her. She held the pose for a moment before flopping down on the floor, her back to the mirror. Tears stung her eyes, and her chin jutted forward a bit.

It was definitely a scar. A big, long, ugly red gash that stretched from her right shoulder blade down to her left hip.

She pulled her knees to her chest and rested her chin on her forearms, sniffling. She was allowed to feel sorry for herself. Just for a moment. No one could see her.

Adam was off with Amber, helping her be more of her beautiful, wonderful self, she was sure. While Jo sat in her room with nothing to do but worry.

Okay, that wasn't exactly true. There were books in the library. Musical instruments, not that she knew how to play anything. Art supplies if she wanted to paint or draw. Cards to play solitaire.

But she just wanted to sit here and pout. She should be allowed to pout.

She whimpered again and looked over her shoulder at the mirror again. Yep. Still there. It wasn't going anywhere…not unless she burned.

She was so tired of pain. Over and over she'd told herself she could take it. That she was strong. But it was all so exhausting.

The door to the dorm thudded.

"Jo?" Adam was calling for her.

She stared at the closed door across her room, pushing her lip out further. Okay, maybe she was being a baby. But she wasn't ready to move.

Her door opened, and Adam paused in the doorway as she stared up at him. His eyes glinted.

"What are you doing?" he murmured, his eyes scanning her naked form.

"You said it wouldn't scar." The petulance in her voice was childish. She knew that.

He hesitated, raising a brow and biting the inside of his cheek before moving to approach her.

She watched him cross the room, fully embracing her sulk. He knelt beside her and reached out to smooth her hair from her brow. She didn't pull back, but she did shift her eyes away. His hand went to her back, his fingertips gently gliding down her scar.

"I'm so sorry," he whispered, and her eyes snapped back to his in alarm.

"Don't you dare! I'm allowed to feel sorry for myself without you feeling guilty!"

He raised his brows helplessly, his lips parted. Then he sighed and sat back, pulling her on his lap. She curled up with her head in his neck as he wrapped his arms around her, one hand flat against the part of her scar that tended to itch the most, rubbing gently. She groaned. Or maybe it was a whine.

"I'm just being a baby," she sighed, snuggling into him more. "Did you see Christopher today?"

Adam tensed, and she smacked his chest lightly.

"You know why I'm asking!"

He grunted.

"That doesn't mean I like it," he muttered, pulling her closer. "No, I still haven't heard from him."

Jo bit her lip.

"Will it matter that I have a scar when we meet the buyers?" It was only five days away.

Adam kissed her head. The kiss went on a little long. Jo frowned, pulling back to look at him.

"You're stalling."

He eyed her warily.

"Adam, just *tell* me what I'm facing!"

He rubbed his brow, frustration in his eyes.

"They inspect the women fully at that point," he admitted on a sigh. "But—" he continued when she paled, "I'm not letting you burn regardless. I'll sell it as a mark of…their power, or something. They're not exactly my biggest fans right now, so maybe they'll see it as a peace offering." His eyes grew pensive.

She yelped when he turned her over face down in his lap, pressing her body down toward the floor when she tried to rise.

"What are you doing?"

"Sh…I want to think about how to do it." His hands moved across her back slowly, soothing her. She melted into him with a groan. "Mmm…I'll have them make a dress with a cutout here," he trailed his fingertips in a line beside the scar, "and here." He outlined the other side of the scar before his hand drifted lower, slipping over the curve of her backside and down her thighs.

She shifted, the hardening bulge beneath her growing painful.

"I don't think you should cut it that low," she murmured, her body getting lost in sensation.

He ignored her, sliding his hand back up her inner thigh until his thumb reached the wet warmth between. She shivered. She should stop him. At least she thought she should. Should she? She whimpered.

"You're not supposed to do this," she half whispered, half moaned.

"Hush..." His voice was husky. "I'm just planning your dress."

She would have chuckled, but his thumb began slipping into her and it was all she could do to breathe.

The bells outside their dorm jingled, and Jo raised her head.

Adam made a sound of frustration.

"Do. Not. Move," he growled, gripping her body and pressing her down into him for a brief moment before shifting her off his lap. "Stay," he whispered, stroking her body as the bells jingled again.

He groaned as he stood and adjusted himself. She put her head on her arms and closed her eyes, smiling happily.

The bells jingled again.

A low sound came from Adam's throat as he turned and stomped off, taking a moment to close her door behind him.

She grinned and flipped over on her back. It didn't hurt so much now. She stretched her arms up above her head, squeezing her eyes shut and arching her back, as the sounds of male voices drifted to her. Her eyes flew open.

She jumped up and grabbed the quickest dress she had, a short brown stretchy shift that clung to her like some sort leather spandex hybrid. She flung open her door just in time to see the door to the conference room closing. Her feet were still bare, but she raced down the hall and pushed the door open.

Adam was a couple paces away and turned back in surprise. And annoyance.

Christopher was leaning casually against the conference table, his hands in his pockets. He didn't move, but his eyes burned as they met hers.

"Jo, you can't be in here," Adam warned.

She turned to him.

"Why."

He ran a hand through his hair and rubbed his jaw, his eyes bright.

"Because you don't need to hear everything."

She raised her brows, her lips parting with a half laugh.

"Like hell I don't."

He glared at her.

"He's right, Jo." Christopher's voice was low and steady. Adam waved his hand toward him.

"See?"

Jo looked at the two of them, her hands clenching and unclenching at her sides.

"So I can be bought and sold like livestock, stripped and beaten publicly, I can listen to *you*," she pointed at Adam, her voice beginning to tremble with anger, "point out all my deficiencies for weeks—"

"I was just trying—" Adam began hoarsely, but she cut him off, turning toward Christopher.

"—and *you*," her eyes felt like fire, "tell me over and over in the desert how annoying I was—"

Christopher's eyes had grown hesitant, but he didn't try to speak.

"—but I don't need to hear everything?" Her voice had risen in volume and she clapped her hands over her face, squeezing her eyes closed while she tried to regain control.

She lowered her hands carefully, speaking in a hushed voice.

"Maybe there is nothing I can actually do in this stupid world, but I at least should be able to know what the situation is. Do you have any idea what it is like to be at the mercy of *everyone* and not even be able to know what's going on?" Her voice was hoarse as she finished.

Christopher's eyes glistened and he started to stand, but Adam grabbed her, wrapping her in his arms tightly and holding her face to his neck.

"I'm sorry." His voice was gruff as he leaned down to whisper in her ear. "You're right. It was stupid. I'm sorry." He rubbed her arms vigorously, the heat of his body seeping into her, slowly calming the rapid beating of her heart. His hand went to her scar, rubbing the leather over the line carefully, and she trembled and leaned into him more.

Adam rested his cheek against the top of her head for a moment before exhaling and looking toward Christopher.

"Well?"

Jo turned her head.

Christopher still reclined against the table, his hands in his pockets. His eyes held hers as he began speaking.

"The riots have continued. I've been told they haven't witnessed this type of pressure on the Ancients since the voting system was implemented over two hundred years ago. The director has been in his position for the last hundred years, and he resents the barriers the Ancients keep around him. So tomorrow, he plans to issue an executive order: the auction for tier one women is to be open to all bidders, regardless of position."

Jo felt Adam's heart hammer against her chest, and she hugged him close, feeling breathless.

"Large collectives and companies won't be permitted to participate, but individuals in smaller groups will be allowed to pool their resources."

His eyes shifted to Adam.

"How much do you have?"

Adam's body was so rigid, she might as well have been tied to the pillar again. She looked up to see his eyes blazing.

"Not enough," he bit out. "But you already knew that. Your office has access to our accounting."

Christopher was calm.

"I don't have enough either," he said quietly.

They stared at each other, the muscle along Adam's jaw flexing.

Jo looked back and forth between them.

"So...I just...basically I'm tier two then?" Disappointment threatened to choke her. "If someone—or...someones, I guess —wants me?"

Adam didn't look down, but his arms tightened around her.

"No," he said in a rough voice, glowering at Christopher. He stood staring, shaking his head slowly, until the words seemed torn from him, the sound harsh and grating in the silence.

"I am not sharing her with you."

———

Jo didn't want to go to this stupid function.

She wore a long black dress for the occasion and, as promised, it had a rather daring cutout in the back that exposed her scar in its entirety. Little strips of fabric held it together as it followed the scar from her shoulder to her hip, where it turned into a long slit in the skirt. She had to be careful to take small steps, or she would end up exposing a little too much.

Her hair had been piled on the top of her head, with a few delicate strands escaping, while her body had been stripped of hair everywhere else. They'd started to add a ton of makeup, but Adam had caught sight of it and snapped at them to keep her look natural before marching off.

Adam was in a bad mood, one that had lasted since Christopher's visit. At least, it seemed that way. She barely caught sight of him anymore as he looked for ways to obtain as much funding as possible before the auction next month. The bidding would all be private, and if they ended up not making the highest offer, they would lose—both her *and* the money. Adam had explained the auctions were a little different than what she'd thought. The winning bidder would get the girl, but everyone would lose their bids. And the company would rake in the profits.

Well, at least he had to hold still for a while tonight. He had to escort her and Amber. A very unhappy Amber.

Poor Amber. Life had not gone the way she'd planned. All her preening herself on her tier one status only to discover she could now be sold to men who normally bought tier two or even tier three women. And perhaps worst of all, the Ancients had decided to boycott tier one sales for the foreseeable future, believing the city needed them and their resources more than they needed the people of the city. So tonight, they weren't even going to meet the Ancients.

They were going to a ball for The People.

It would be heavily guarded, but every man who made the necessary down payment on his bid could attend. They could talk to and dance with Jo and Amber to their heart's content, and at the end of the night, Amber and Jo would be inspected in front of them all fully.

Well, at least Jo had already been naked in front of them all. She hoped that would help her get through it.

"Let's go." Adam's voice cracked like a whip, and Amber jumped beside her. They had been waiting as instructed by the door while he'd been gathering the necessary paperwork, and he now stood holding the door open, impatience etched into every muscle of his beautifully muscled body.

She sighed, letting her eyes run down him. God, he looked so good. His shoulders nearly spanned the width of the door as he stood in front of it, his strong arms crossing as she stared. Her eyes traveled lower, absorbing the thick muscles of his thighs as he stood straight and tall, his feet shoulder width apart. She let her gaze drift to the growing center of his body…

She hadn't realized she was just standing there, staring at him, until he cleared his throat. She blinked and looked around.

Amber had already gone on ahead. Her eyes met his to see his brow cocked in amusement.

"I'd like to be able to walk tonight without holding a jacket," he said dryly.

Jo pressed her lips together, fighting the grin that had already climbed to her eyes. She ought to be embarrassed. Shy. But somehow, he made all that disappear, and all she wanted to do was close the door and tell him he didn't need to stop anymore.

Except…she groaned internally and stepped toward the doorway. Nothing had changed. And there was this insane ball to get through tonight, where she was going to be touched and ogled by a room full of who knew how many men.

Adam's arm caught her waist as she passed, pulling her back into him, a hand coming up to cup her breast. She shivered as his lips touched her neck.

"You look beautiful," he whispered, his thumb teasing her nipple through the dress. The hand on her waist slid down to the slit at her hip, slipping under to move between her thighs. They both groaned as his fingertips touched her, and he pressed her back into him, his hard length grinding into her almost painfully.

She smacked his hand.

"I'm going to be wet all night!" she whispered.

"And I'm going to be watching other men touch you all night," he whispered back.

"And do you want me wet while they do?"

His fingers dug into her and she gasped.

"I want you thinking of me," he said, his voice rough.

They heard footsteps and straightened just as Amber came into view. She hesitated when she saw them and stood back, fidgeting with her dress.

Adam grabbed his jacket off the chair nearby, carrying it in front of him as he turned around. He put a hand on Jo's back, his thumb almost absently stroking her scar as usual, and led her out, closing the door behind them.

It was a very long night.

When the dancing began, she tried not to visibly cringe each time a man touched her on her back. They all seemed fascinated with her scar, but their hands on her skin made her ill. *Adam* touched her there. Not these men. Her body was screaming it, but she couldn't afford to anger anyone else. And dance after dance went by, each one with a different man, each one running his hand along the raised ridge on her back. It was inflamed and raw by the night's end.

And the body inspection finale sucked.

Jo and Amber didn't say a word after. They just waited until they could leave and climbed in the carriage. Calm. In control. Because it was the only thing they could control.

At least it was over now and they were back at the dorm. Over the next month, whoever wanted to buy them would submit their payment to the company, and at the month's end, the winning bid would be announced. And that would be that.

She was lying on her stomach in bed, her scar throbbing while she waited for the sleep to hit, when her door opened.

"What are you doing," she whispered, her eyes wide as Adam entered.

He closed the door quietly and walked over, his feet bare.

"I couldn't think of a reason to send you to my room," he said, pulling his shirt off and crawling into bed with her.

She blinked rapidly, her thoughts scattering.

"I have news." His voice rumbled deeply, trying to get her attention. But she really couldn't be bothered right now. She reached her hand out to stroke the dark hair that ran from his navel in a thin line down to…

Adam grabbed her wrist.

"Jo—are you listening to me?"

"Why would you take off your shirt if you wanted me to listen to you," she murmured, struggling to stretch her fingertips out to touch the bulge growing in his pants.

He exhaled with a grunt and pressed her hand against his cock.

"Okay, listen now?"

"Not yet," she whispered, her eyes heavy. She squeezed and ran her hand down the length of him, drawing a groan from his lips before he moved her hand away again.

"Jo, I'm under contract." He stared at her, his eyes bright, as he lay on his side beside her.

She blinked.

"Yay?"

He released a sharp breath.

"The company board let me know tonight. It seems that because of your revolt, and everything that came of it, they will be earning far more than they were able to earn with just the Ancients."

She raised a bored brow.

"I'm so happy for them."

Adam grabbed her head and kissed her hard before pulling back, his excitement still unabated.

"It means I'm safe. And so long as we get the winning bid, that means you're safe. They can't get rid of me. Ever. As long as I don't break the law."

The corners of her mouth began turning up. She had no idea why this was such a big deal. Did he love this job? But he was so adorable when he was excited. In a masculine, completely fuckable way.

But something was nagging at her mind. Something the judge had said.

She frowned.

"What do you mean by *get rid of*? I remember the judge saying it would be a great loss to the city. What did that mean?"

"That I'm irreplaceable, of course," he murmured, moving in to kiss her and pulling her hand back to touch him.

She wouldn't let him.

"Okay, now you're trying to distract me," she frowned.

He looked hurt, and her eyes narrowed.

"I am telling you good news and you first ignore me and now don't believe me," he complained, undoing his pants quickly.

Her body flowed in response.

"I thought we couldn't," she whispered as he pulled himself out, the rigid thickness hard against his stomach.

"I won't put it in," he said, his voice gruff as he moved between her legs, careful to hold himself up off her scar. He rubbed the large head against her, moving it up and down between her lips. She moaned.

"Thirty more days, baby. Then," he leaned down to whisper in her ear, "I'm taking your virginity."

And he proceeded to get as close to doing that as possible until the sun put them to sleep.

———

The next thirty days were torture. Adam had thrown caution to the wind, sneaking into Jo's room after Amber had gone to bed and back out before she opened her door in the morning. But not before making sure Jo's morning was just as agonizing as her night.

"Promise me…"

He said this every morning. Every fucking morning.

Her legs were wrapped around him, pressing up into the hard length of his shaft as he rubbed back and forth, pushing her to the edge. God, she wanted to cum so badly.

"I hate you," she groaned, wrapping her body around him more tightly. Her fingers tangled in his hair, keeping his head in her neck as she clung to him.

"It's going to hurt when I go in," he groaned into her. "I want your body ready for me. Don't cum until then. Promise."

Jo kicked him with the back of her heels and whimpered.

"I've waited this whole time. It's not like I'm going to fall at the finish line," she said peevishly.

He pressed against her one last time and kissed her hard before hopping to his feet to get dressed. She wanted to throw something at him. *He* hadn't been waiting.

She flopped over on her stomach after he left the room, the urge to touch herself close to overwhelming her. But they really were at the finish line. Today was the day.

Her stomach was in knots. Adam seemed so sure things were going to go their way, but Jo couldn't stop the sick feeling that had taken root inside her. This wasn't a good place. And good things didn't tend to happen in bad places. How would she bear it if they lost? Her only hope was that everyone would want Amber instead and that if they did happen to bid on Jo, they would bid low, not expecting her to fetch a high price.

Adam and Christopher had pooled everything they had and had taken out every loan possible for her bid. But even so, they had only been here a few months. How much could they possibly come up with compared to men who had been here decades, let alone centuries?

She got up to dress. *There's no sense worrying about it now.* In a few hours, she and Amber would be taken to company headquarters where all the bidders would be gathered. The winning bids would be announced…and their new owners would take them away. She could be taken away from Adam immediately.

Stop it!

She pulled herself back to the moment and finished tying up the laces of her leather pants. She'd chosen the most ridiculously difficult outfit to get on and off. Just in case. The dark brown pants rode low on her hips and laced all the way down the sides. They had to be untied at the ankles and loosened progressively up the leg in order to remove them.

The matching cropped bodice wouldn't be so difficult to

remove, as it laced up a very short front, exposing both her midriff and cleavage. But she was a bit more concerned about someone getting into her pants.

Adam's eyes glinted when she walked into the library after the fashion team had come and gone. They hadn't approved of her clothing choice, but Jo told them Adam had okayed it. Amber hadn't seemed to even notice as she numbly followed whatever instructions the team gave her, but she'd managed to sneer at Jo when Jo asked quietly if she was okay. Jo still couldn't help feeling bad for her.

"Ready?" Adam's eyes swept her body. They were warm. Possessive. He really believed she was about to be his.

She nodded, a small shiver running through her. The heat in his eyes grew, but he just put his hand on her back and escorted them to the carriage, his knuckles caressing the line of her scar as they walked. He was barely trying to hide at all.

The carriage took them back to the main district, where the corporate headquarters were located. The men from the ball filled the large room...along with two more.

"My dear, it's lovely to see you—lovely!" The Director beamed at her as he approached. "But where is this scar the people have been talking about? You should display it always! A reminder of the common man's fight against his oppressors! But no matter, no matter—all in due time," he chortled.

Christopher stood beside him casually, his expression unreadable.

"We have a great battle yet to be fought for the people. You will find my position keeps me very busy, but there will be many functions for you to attend with me where you will be greatly celebrated! But of course I'm getting ahead of myself. The results have yet to be read!" He winked at Christopher.

Adam had turned to stone beside her. His hand was still on her back, and she focused on the heat, her entire body suddenly cold.

"Ah, my dear, I didn't notice you—my apologies!" The Director turned to Amber who stood looking as sickly as Jo felt.

"Ladies, there you are! Follow me, please." A man wearing a company name tag gestured for her and Amber to go to the stage at the front of the room. They looked up at Adam.

He looked dazed.

"Come on, come on," the man rushed them. Jo felt Adam's hand fall away from her skin slowly, and she looked back to see him staring at Christopher, his eyes still somewhat blank. But the director's eyes were following her, so she turned back around before her expression gave away her growing horror.

The room grew silent but for the occasional whisper as Jo and Amber stepped on stage. Many men were huddled together in groups, some as large as six, leaning toward one another nervously.

Her face felt hot. The silence swirled around her.

The man who had led them to the front held up a parchment with a wax seal. The room went completely quiet as he opened it.

"Tier One Amber—please step forward!"

Jo's stomach sank and she felt relieved all at once. She wanted to get this over with. She wanted to never hear what she feared was coming.

"The winning bid for Amber was made by…Albert the shoe-smith, William the tanner—" shouts and cheers from a group of five men interrupted him as they yelled and whistled their victory, jumping up and down and giving one another high fives while most of the remaining audience looked sick with disappointment. Most. But not all.

Far too many faces still looked at the stage expectantly after Amber was escorted off by her new owners. She appeared ready to cry, but most of her men were too busy congratulating one another to notice. One had, though, and Jo watched as he offered her his jacket, his expression concerned…and she looked repulsed. He put it back on awkwardly.

The man on stage hushed them as he held up a second parchment. The room once again went quiet as he broke the seal. His eyes widened as he read it, and he looked up a bit nervously.

"Tier One Josephine—please step forward!"

Jo focused on her feet. On not falling. She couldn't bring herself to raise her head. The man cleared his throat.

"The winning bid for Josephine was made by the office of the director of intelligence—"

Groans and gasps from around the room accompanied the news, and Jo wanted to cry.

"—and our own company handler—"

The air rushed from her lungs and her knees gave out as the speaker called them forward. She fell on all fours, the tears choking her, only to be pulled to her feet almost immediately and crushed in Adam's arms. She gripped him back until she thought she would break, her breath coming out in shuddering gasps. Her nails were digging into him and she worried she was damaging his body, but she couldn't get close enough. Couldn't hold on tight enough.

She forced her eyes open and looked over Adam's shoulder, searching for Christopher. He stood beside the director, his eyes dark as they met hers. She shifted her gaze to his left.

The director's eyes were on Christopher. And he wasn't smiling anymore.

14

MOON DAY 285

"YOU KNOW I only agreed to that so they wouldn't question the bid," Adam ground out. "She stays with me."

They were in a private conference room, awaiting the final paperwork transferring ownership from the company to Adam and Christopher. Adam sat with Jo on his lap—he hadn't let go since he'd grabbed her from the stage—while Christopher sat across from them.

"No."

Christopher's calm rebuttal only enraged him further.

"She doesn't belong to you!"

"I own half the contract."

Adam looked ready to throw something, and Jo thought it might be time to intercede.

"Why can't we all just stay in the same place?"

"No." They answered in unison without even glancing her direction. She put her hands over her face with a groan as they continued.

"You can visit," Adam said.

Christopher narrowed his eyes.

"We can divide the time in weeks. But you've had her for over four months. She leaves with me today. You can pick her up next week."

"Like hell." Adam's voice was hoarse.

Jo stared at them between her fingers.

"You know, as much as I appreciate what you've both done for me," she said dropping her hands and slowly looking back and forth between the two of them. "I'm not a child."

Christopher looked at her, and she felt the heat rising to her face remembering the last time she had said that to him. And what he'd done right before.

"What do you want to do." His voice was soft, but his eyes demanded an answer.

Jo blinked. Shit. What did she want? She wanted to crawl under the table. How could she possibly say what she really wanted? She didn't even know herself.

That wasn't exactly true though. She knew some things she wanted. They just all seemed to be in conflict.

She looked at Adam hesitantly.

"Am I even allowed to stay with you in the dorm? Isn't that just for girls the company owns?"

"No new tier ones are ready yet, so it's fine."

"Yes, but what about when they are?" Jo pressed him. "Will I be allowed to stay?"

"I'll figure it out then." He was glaring at *her* now. She raised her brows at him helplessly. The truth was, she wanted to go with Adam. And she wanted to go with Christopher.

What she wanted wasn't very helpful.

She looked back at Christopher.

"Honestly?" she hesitated again. No one was likely to like her response, but at least it was true. "I want you both where I can see you... see you are okay." She bit the inside of her cheek, waiting for their reactions.

"Well, you can't," Adam snapped.

She looked at him, her patience dwindling.

"Why?"

He looked up at her perched on his lap and cocked his jaw.

"Because."

Jo had to press her lips together to not laugh. He could be such a child. She combed her fingers through the hair at the base of his neck.

"Adam," she began with a sigh. "You said you worked together. That you were friends."

His glare increased, and she groaned and leaned down to drop her forehead against his. He tilted his head up at the last moment, capturing her lips instead and biting her bottom lip softly. Her heart hammered in her chest as she pulled back. She couldn't turn around now.

"We know each other," she continued a bit shakily. "Shouldn't we…band together? Look out for each other?" She considered the look she'd seen in the director's eyes earlier when he was looking at Christopher. It scared her.

Adam didn't seem to be listening. His eyes were more cocky now as they stared at Christopher. Challenging. Oh god. She swallowed and turned to face Christopher again.

He sat leaning back in his chair, watching them, his face impassive.

"Do you have space?" she asked tentatively.

She could feel Adam's outrage, but she squeezed his leg below the table. His body tensed, but he held his tongue.

"I do," Christopher said, his voice soft.

"So can't we all stay there?"

"Jo—" Adam began heatedly. She dug her nails into his leg, still watching Christopher, and Adam all but growled at her. She ignored him.

Christopher stared at her unsmiling, his eyes dark as he considered her words. The silence stretched between them. No one seemed to be breathing.

He gave a small nod.

Relief poured through her and her eyes stayed locked with his even as Adam lifted her to slide out of the chair so he could pace back and forth.

"I'm not staying at his place!" he thundered, his hand tearing through his hair.

"You *are*," she said, turning in the seat to glare at him. "You have been telling me what to do for months. But I'm telling you now! I'm…I'm worried. And I am not going to be able to…relax if I don't know you're both okay," she finished, a tremor creeping into her voice. Okay. Bravery over.

She turned back around and sat on her hands, trying to control her shaking. Her eyes lifted hesitantly back to Christopher's while Adam stormed back and forth behind her. Heat flooded her body.

His eyes had lost their coolness. They burned into her, searing her with the memory of every moment they had touched in the desert. Face down in the sand as he pushed into her from behind. On her knees as he throbbed beneath her lips. Her back against the wall as she convulsed over him, his beautiful lips between her thighs.

She took a shuddering breath. What was she getting herself into?

Adam was still silently raging as the company representative brought back their parchment-work. As they left the building. As they rode side by side in the carriage while Christopher sat across from them, his eyes locked on Jo's, and Adam's hand held her possessively high on her inner thigh.

Then they were stepping out in front of a charming townhome in the temple district. Jo eyed the stonework as they walked inside. It had an Old World feel to it, which of course made sense—this *was* an old world. The entrance opened up into a nicely appointed living room, with a couch that looked inviting, a soft rug of some material she couldn't place, and comfortable leather chairs. The walls twinkled with bits of glowing sand, reminding her of their time in the desert. She smiled. She couldn't believe she was nostalgic about the desert...

Adam shot Christopher a murderous look.

"I thought you put everything in the bid," he seethed. "*I* did."

Christopher eyed him calmly.

"I made sure we outbid everyone."

"How?" he demanded. "Can they take her back if you get caught?"

"Not without implicating themselves."

"And if they get in trouble some other way? What's to stop them from unloading all their sins along with yours?"

"I took care of it." Christopher's voice was growing testy.

Jo looked up at them worriedly as they glared at each other.

"They could take me away again?"

They looked down at her, their expressions shifting quickly.

"No, Jo—"

"No, baby—"

She frowned at them.

"I know you don't want me to be scared, but I would like the truth, please."

Adam glanced sharply at Christopher.

Christopher's eyes were somber.

"I swear to you that if I'm caught, they can't take you back." His voice was quiet. "I didn't take any risks with that."

Adam stared at him a moment before nodding, but Jo's anxiety didn't go away.

"What would that mean for you? If you're caught?"

Adam had never given her a straight answer about his risks, and she'd been too busy being lost in his touch to follow up as she should have. She frowned. Had he been distracting her on purpose?

The men exchanged a glance above her, and she narrowed her eyes.

"Okay, one of you needs to tell me. Clearly there is something you know that I don't."

Their eyes became guarded, and she stepped back to look at them both, her temper growing.

Christopher released a breath.

"Life imprisonment," he said bluntly.

She blinked. Life? But they never died. So they just got locked up forever?

She looked at them horrified. That's what they had been risking for her? Eternity?

She gave a small cry and wrapped her arms around Christopher's waist, squeezing tightly. She looked up at Adam, her eyes tortured.

Adam rubbed the side of his mouth, but he didn't say anything. His eyes shifted to Christopher's again, narrowing as Christopher's arms went around her and his head dropped to hide in her neck.

Then she closed her eyes and didn't open them again until her shaking had stopped.

———

"You can play with her later."

Adam stood with his muscular arms crossed, leaning back against the open door of her room—their room as he'd claimed it—waiting impatiently for Christopher to exit.

Christopher's jaw clenched, but he didn't acknowledge him. He just continued setting up the chess pieces on the board as Jo sat across from him, biting her lip. She sucked at chess. But she'd seen a light in his eyes when he was showing her the things he'd bought for her, and she didn't have the heart to tell him. Well, he'd find out soon enough. Her stomach sank at the thought of disappointing him.

Adam snorted in disgust, coming over to drag a chair over

beside Jo. He stretched his legs out and crossed his arms, dominating the space, as he stared at Christopher.

Jo glanced at him. What would they both think of her when she couldn't do this?

She blinked rapidly at the board, moisture obscuring her vision, and Christopher frowned.

"You know how to play?"

She hesitated. She could pretend she didn't. Then maybe she could blame how bad she was on being new. But she couldn't bear the idea of lying to them.

She sighed and nodded.

He leaned back. When she didn't move, he inclined his head.

"White goes first."

Oh. Right.

She stared at the board. Let's see…the pawns moved two on their first move…but maybe that would be too obvious…so she should only move one space…so…this one?

She glanced up after moving. Christopher looked at her, his expression unreadable. He leaned forward and moved a pawn up two spaces.

She bit her lip again. Maybe moving up one space was dumb. She moved the pawn beside her first one up two spaces and looked up again. Christopher stared at her for a long moment. She saw Adam glance at the board out of the corner of her eye and then glance at her, biting the inside of his cheek.

Christopher blinked and moved another piece. She kept trying to follow, not having any idea what he was building towards, or how to counter it. It took her about fifteen moves, and them each losing pieces, before she realized.

"You're not playing for real," she said quietly.

She could see them both look at her, but she kept her eyes on the board, her vision blurring.

"Baby, I've played with him a hundred times. He always kills me." Adam's arms went around her, hugging her close. "And that was *after* I'd looked up all the fastest checkmates possible."

Christopher's expression was dark as he stared at her, his eyes glistening.

"I'm sorry," she said, swallowing the tears back. She was being a baby. "I just don't have the brain for this."

Adam rubbed her arm vigorously and shot a black look at Christopher.

"Are you ready to leave yet?" he demanded.

Christopher stared at her a few moments longer before getting up abruptly and walking out, closing the door behind him. She felt her face cracking as she looked down, and Adam made an inarticulate sound and pulled her into his lap. He held her face in his neck as he rubbed her back hard, avoiding her scar.

"I'm stupid," she whispered.

He froze and pulled back, his expression stern.

"You are *not*. I told you he always beats me, too. Am I stupid?"

"Yes, you're stupid, too. Just like me."

He snorted, pulling her close again and biting her neck gently. She wrapped her arms around him with a small smile.

"He's smart, but he's also an idiot," Adam mumbled against her skin as he picked her up and carried her to the bed. Her heart began racing.

He laid her down carefully, his eyes no longer playful.

"What did you wrap yourself up in," he murmured, his hands untying the leather strip holding her bodice together. She shivered as her breasts fell out into the cool air. His eyes grew heavy as he looked down at her, but he remained standing, cupping her breast in his hand as his thumb teased her nipple in slow, smooth circles. Sharp pangs of need shot through her, and she tugged on him, trying to pull his body close. He ignored her, his eyes devouring her body.

His gaze swept down, and he slid his hand to her ankle, loosening the cords inch by inch up her leg, his breathing growing more shallow as he neared her hip. He leaned down to take her breast, sucking her nipple into the warmth of his mouth as his hand reached out to her other leg, loosening the ties the same way until he was able to drag the material over her hips. He pulled her up just enough to remove her bodice completely and stood back up, his eyes dark with desire as he stared down at her naked body.

She leaned up on her elbows as his hand tugged at the leather constraining him, her eyes growing heavy as he freed himself. She pushed herself low in the bed in a smooth movement, noting his sharp intake of breath as she wrapped her fingers around him, the warmth of her breath sending shudders through his body. He buried his hand in her hair as she leaned forward to trace the tip of her tongue along the contours of the thick head before slowly sucking him inside her.

They both groaned. He was enormous, his head barely able to push inside her wide open mouth. She held his hip, stopping him from forcing himself deeper, as he tried to push her mouth down farther. He groaned again and pulled her off, quickly pulling off his clothes and scooping her up in his arms to lay her head back at the top of the bed. He spread her thighs apart and settled between them, positioning his head against her wet entrance, and looked down into her eyes.

"Ready?" he whispered, his voice husky.

She clenched his back but nodded, wrapping her legs around him. And he began to push.

It stung. He pressed harder, and she bit down on her lip, the pain warring with the pleasure.

He groaned and pushed himself up to look at where their bodies were trying to connect. He stroked the head up and down against her slit, slipping easily through her wet folds, and repositioned himself. This time it went in more, and she gasped and started to push him away.

He pulled her hands away and pushed harder. The pain increased, and her thighs pulled together involuntarily as she shoved both hands against his stomach.

He grabbed her wrists, leaning back down on her body and trapping her hands above her head.

"I'm sorry, baby," he said hoarsely, pushing harder. She could feel her body starting to tear, and she released a small cry, burying her face in his neck as he forced himself inside her. Inch by inch he slipped in, drawing whimpers of pain from her along with stabbing pangs of need. He laced his fingers through hers, his body tense with restraint, as he shoved himself in the last few inches, sending a jolt through her.

"That's it," he choked, throbbing inside. He lay still, his breathing ragged, and Jo trembled underneath him. It hurt. She wanted him to take it out. And she wanted him to push even deeper. She bit his neck softly, tugging on her hand, biting down harder when he didn't release her immediately.

He shuddered and moved his hands down her body to cup her from behind, pulling her up to him more fully as she moved a hand between their bodies, the tip of her finger slipping between her lips. His hands gripped her painfully as she began moving her finger in slow circles, her other arm wrapping around his shoulders to hold him to her. And he began moving.

Jo was torn between crying and moaning, and she dug her nails into his skin as he increased the pace, rocking into her over and over, his breath warm against her neck.

"Baby, I need you to cum now." His voice was strained, and she gripped him harder.

"Wait," she whispered, her fingers moving faster. A tortured moan came from Adam's throat, but he continued thrusting in steady strokes.

The pain was excruciating. Exquisite. Every movement

driving all her focus, all her sensation to her core and gathering in a giant crescendo until she gasped, her body locking as it exploded in harsh shards that spread outward, shooting tendrils of deep pleasure through her.

Adam gripped her with a guttural cry, no longer making any effort to be gentle, and rammed into her again and again as he shuddered deep inside her.

They lay together, breathing heavily, tremors running through their bodies. Every twitch continued to send stabs of pleasure through her. Of pain.

Jo pulled her hand from between them and put it against his chest, pushing.

"Ow," she said.

He half groaned, half laughed into her neck but only pushed more deeply into her. She whimpered.

"You're killing me," she said with a moan, her body shuddering around him.

He sighed and pressed in one moment more before withdrawing. She gasped in relief and reached down between them to hold herself, moaning in pain.

His lips touched her forehead.

"Hang on. I'll get something to stop the blood."

She looked down as he got up, noting the redness on his cock and between her thighs. She groaned.

She heard the sounds of him searching through the room, but he couldn't seem to find anything. In retrospect, she really should have known. If her eyes hadn't been closed—if she hadn't been so focused on the pain—she might have been able to stop him.

But they were, she was, and so she couldn't. And he'd opened the door before she could react, practically strutting out, naked and bloody.

"Adam—" her choked sounds died as she heard him calling for Christopher, asking where he could find a towel.

———

Christopher wouldn't even look at her now.

Of course, since she wanted to disappear into the floor every time she saw him, that wasn't necessarily a bad thing.

But Adam…

"Jo, talk to me," he pleaded.

"Go away." She stared down at the book in front of her.

He exhaled in exasperation, dropping his head against her leg.

She had been sitting on the couch, her legs bent as she leaned her side against the back, trying to read. Christopher was at work.

Adam had been kneeling in the floor, stroking her shoulder, her leg, and peppering her with kisses while she tried to ignore him. But his patience was wearing thin after two days.

"How long are you going to punish me?" he asked, irritation creeping into his tone.

"This isn't punishment. I just don't have any desire to talk to you," she said, keeping her own tone even.

"Well you can't just ignore me!" He grabbed her book and threw it over his shoulder, glaring at her when she looked up in fury.

"You want me to talk to you? Fine!" Her voice shook. "How about this? You used something personal between us—something special, something that should have been *ours*—just to score *ego* points!" She hit his chest as he tried pulling her into his arms, but he ignored her. "Or to…to mark your territory!"

She hit him harder when he wouldn't let her go, but he just wrapped an arm around her and pulled her to the edge of the couch, yanking her legs apart until he was between them, her dress riding up to her thighs.

"So fine! You got the points and you pissed on your territory!

Now leave me alone." She tried shoving him off of her, but he pushed her back into the couch, kissing her neck.

"Goddammit, Adam, get off of me!"

"No." His voice was muffled, and she felt him harden between her legs. She was still sore, but it didn't stop her body from responding.

She beat her fists into his back, but when he didn't budge, she released a short huff and hit him one last time, rather lightly, and then stared mutinously to the side. But she kept her arms around him.

"Are you done?" he murmured into her neck. She didn't answer.

He leaned back to look at her, keeping her lower body locked to him, and she crossed her arms in front of her, still looking away. He scratched his brow.

"I'm sorry."

"No, you're not," she shot back, looking at him briefly before looking away once more.

He exhaled sharply.

"You're right. I'm not." He captured her wrists before she could push at him again. "And you can be as mad as you want, but if I had been the one fucking another woman here for months before you, you wouldn't even have looked at me again. So I think letting him know you are mine is pretty fucking small, all things considered."

"I didn't...we never—we didn't have sex," she mumbled, avoiding his eyes. But she couldn't really argue his point.

But was she his? Wasn't that really why she was so angry? Because she didn't want Christopher thinking that? Shit. She swallowed and covered her face with her hands. She was a horrible person.

"Adam," she began, her tone husky behind her hands. "I think we need to talk..."

She felt his muscles tense between her thighs.

"Did you just tell me we need to talk after I've spent the past two goddamn days trying to talk to you?"

She groaned and peeked out. Maybe she hadn't been as right as she'd thought.

"I know," she whispered. "It's not fair. But I can't be what—"

"I don't want to hear it," he snapped.

"And I don't want to say it!" she cried, dropping her hands. "God, I don't want to think it. I don't want to *feel* it. But…I *can't* be whatever it is I was before! Or what you thought I was!"

He started to get up and this time she grabbed him, wrapping her legs around him tightly as her arms went around his neck. He froze.

"You can let go now," he ground out.

"Just listen to me," she whispered against his neck. "I don't love you any less. I may not exactly remember things that happened or who we were, but these feelings I have for you… they are old. Deep. They're in my soul."

"You don't love me less. You just love him more."

She pulled back, stunned.

"No! That's not what I meant at all!"

He wouldn't meet her eyes and glared down at the couch. She raised her brows helplessly, her lips parting as she stroked his cheek.

"Baby," she whispered. "You're my world. I feel it. I do. When I was in the desert, I felt the loss. I couldn't remember, but I felt it. And when I saw you…" Her eyes grew soft as his glistened, and she slowly brushed her fingers through the hair at his temple. "The darkness finally went away. I don't think I can escape the darkness without you."

He looked back at her at last, his eyes wet. Tears stung her own in response.

She swallowed. She didn't want to say the next part.

"But something happened in the desert." Her voice was

hoarse. "And it changed me somehow. And I am so fucking sorry."

Their eyes were both brimming now, and Adam leaned his forehead into hers in helpless surrender, his hands moving up to cup her face. It was more than she could take, and her face broke at last as she brought her palms up to cover her eyes.

"Don't," he choked, pulling them away. "Just stay with me. Stay with me," he whispered, his lips touching hers, his thumbs stroking her tears away.

She shook her head, hopeless.

"How can I?" she whispered.

He pulled back, frustration returning to his eyes.

"What's the alternative? You decide not to be with me at all?" He put his fists on either side of her on the couch again. "What am I going to do—find someone else? Look around! Women aren't exactly available anymore!"

His broad form towered over her as he stared down at her with hard eyes.

"Is that what you want? To not be with me at all?"

She blinked, her lips slightly apart.

"No!"

"Then can we stop this stupid conversation!" he exploded, his eyes raging into hers.

She groaned in frustration. And he turned his face away for a moment, his jaw clenching, before looking back.

"I'll stop trying to…score points. Okay? Happy now?"

When she hesitated, he blew up again.

"For fuck's sake, what do you want! To fuck him? Am I supposed to give you my approval?"

She looked around helplessly and grabbed a nearby pillow to cover her face. She locked her arms over it, clasping her head, and heard him grunt.

He was silent a long time. Finally he exhaled.

"You really didn't sleep with him?"

She waited a beat and responded from behind the pillow.

"I would have. He wouldn't."

"Dammit, Jo," he rasped, pain lacing his words, "could you be a little less honest sometimes!"

She dropped the pillow, her eyes tortured, and flung her arms around him tightly. He crushed her to him, rocking them both, pressing into her.

"I'm sorry," she breathed, squeezing her eyes shut.

He shuddered and stroked her back, his hand sliding gently along her scar.

"Can you give me time?" he whispered thickly. "Don't do anything with him yet. Let me...get used to the idea."

She wanted to tell him that's not what she meant. That Christopher hadn't even wanted to touch her before, so it's not as if anything would happen now.

But instead she turned her lips to his neck, the guilt overwhelming her, and nodded into him.

"I promise."

He relaxed in her arms, and she rubbed his back a while longer before letting her hands drift down his body.

"Sit on the couch for me, Adam," she whispered, tugging at his pants. He stilled for a moment before tearing them off to do as she said.

She might not always be right. But she knew how to apologize very sweetly.

15

MOON DAY 305

CHRISTOPHER STILL WASN'T TALKING to her.

She would catch him watching her on occasion, but he always looked away as soon as their eyes met. Usually he retreated to his room after getting home from work and stayed there until he had to leave again.

They had taken over his house, and Jo hated it. She knew how private he was, and Adam invaded his space constantly. Made it his own. Jo had tried enticing Adam back to the bedroom as much as possible to give Christopher a break, but Christopher's eyes would be even darker the next time she saw him so she stopped. Of course that just meant Adam started taking her more often in places Christopher would see, and that hadn't exactly helped either.

Her idea about looking out for each other really wasn't going that well.

She heard the front door and looked up from her book. Adam was back at work, and neither of them were due home for hours.

Christopher paused as he walked in, and her heart skipped.

He stood unmoving, his eyes sharp on hers, before his lashes swept down as he turned aside to put his things away. Jo took a breath again.

He had a place for everything and was always careful to put things where he'd designated. Adam was the opposite, throwing his things wherever they landed, too busy with whatever he wanted in the moment to be concerned about order. Jo was constantly picking up after him, trying to reduce the chaos, but inevitably she'd miss even things of her own only to find Christopher quietly putting them away.

His footsteps didn't falter as they moved across the room to the bookcase before turning to the chair beside where she sat curled up on the couch. He sat down and began reading without a word, so she dropped her eyes to her book again and stared down blindly.

Five minutes later, she had yet to turn the page, and she snuck a peek at him. He was staring at her.

"I'm sorry."

Jo blinked and frowned.

"Why would you be sorry? You've done...everything to help me." Her voice grew thick with emotion, and she dropped her eyes for a moment before looking back up.

The line between his brow had deepened.

"I chose the wrong game."

Her lips parted, and she could only stare. Then she released a small laugh.

"I don't think it would have mattered. I would never be able to compete with you."

He looked away, his expression troubled. Too troubled.

"Christopher, I just—I didn't want to disappoint you," she said on a sigh. His gaze flew back to hers.

"You didn't."

A small smile touched her lips as her brow lifted.

"Adam showed me what I did later. You had me on my

second move. You were very sweet to try to make me feel like I wasn't an idiot, but it actually feels a lot worse knowing you were sitting there playing with me like...like I was a kid you needed to coddle."

His brow cleared.

"I was just trying to spend more time with you," he said quietly. "I wanted to make it last as long as possible."

Her eyes froze on his. Oh.

Christopher watched her, unmoving, his eyes falling to her lips when they parted beneath his gaze. Her body tightened, and she struggled to breathe. To be still. To not throw herself at him. His lids were heavy when he looked up once more.

"Are you safe?" she whispered. "From—from the director," she stammered at the look in his eyes.

He stared quietly a moment longer.

"Yes."

"Would you lie to me?"

He hesitated and turned away, the line returning to his brow. When he faced her again, there was caution in his eyes.

"I don't want you to worry."

She exhaled sharply.

"So you are in trouble."

"I can handle it, Jo." His voice was soft. Could he? Alone? She swallowed.

"Is there anything I can do?"

He locked his gaze on her for a long moment.

"Yes. Spend time with me." His eyes swept over her as he stood, putting his book aside and holding out his hand.

"I have something else to show you."

Heat spread through her body as she placed her hand in his and he pulled her to her feet. And suddenly he was too close. Too warm. She looked up...and lost herself in the soft blue pools, their depths darkening as she stared.

He looked so young and so old, as if he carried the weight of the world in those eyes. Her hand reached out unconsciously to brush her fingertips along his temple, and he stared unmoving as she stroked his hair. Her hand stilled. What must he think of her?

"Are you angry with me?" she whispered.

The line between his brow returned. He stared down at her in silence for so long Jo thought he might not respond.

"You...like the way he is." Confusion laced his tone. Frustration.

"I remember him. Or, I remember feelings I had. I didn't remember before...in the desert," she answered, swallowing at his expression. He waited, and she dropped her eyes, her hand falling from his hair.

"Yes," she whispered. "I like how he is." More than like.

A heaviness settled in her blood as she stood, quiet and still, watching the rise and fall of his chest. Would he push her away now? Did he regret everything he'd done to help her? Her breathing grew shallow as she tightened her grip on his hand. *Stay*.

"I don't know what you want," he said, the frustration clear in his voice now.

Jo raised her face to his once more.

"I don't know what you want, either," she said softly, watching the storm behind his eyes build with each word. He held her gaze and reached up to brush her cheek softly with his knuckles.

"And if you knew what I wanted," he whispered, his thumb tracing her lower lip. "What would you do?"

Heat pulled at her, dragging her into him, and her eyes grew heavy.

"Show me."

His thumb continued moving across her lips as he stared at her intently. They were alone now. No burning waiting for them if they didn't find shelter. No random men stumbling into their world. No rules preventing them from being close. Nothing to stop them.

He leaned down until his lips were poised just above hers, and her breath caught. His thumb still stroked her lip as he watched her. Then he moved it aside and his lips brushed hers, his touch so very light.

Her lashes fluttered closed at last as his hand crept around her waist, pulling her to him gently. And then the tip of his tongue touched hers, and she was lost.

They both groaned, a helpless, aching sound that came from deep within, as they melted into one another. Christopher's tongue pushed inside her, slipping into her slowly, steadily, sending sharp pangs shooting through her. She wrapped her arms around him, burying a hand in his curls, her body hugging his every line.

She needed more.

She sensed the shift in him a moment before she felt it. His hand around her waist began gripping just a bit too tightly. The hand he'd buried in her hair pulled just a little too hard. She opened her eyes to see him watching her through thin slits, his tongue still deep inside her, as his hand slid down the center of her back, pressing into every hollow. He continued until he reached the hem of her dress, pulling it up as he watched her.

She gasped the moment his fingers touched her, stroking her softly, moving smoothly through the wet folds before sliding his finger back up higher to lubricate the smaller entrance to her body. She blinked rapidly and her hands went to his shoulders, but he held her head, his tongue still moving deep inside her mouth, as he watched her through narrowed eyes.

She jumped slightly as his finger pushed inside her, catching her breath and tensing as he slid into her, holding her still. He trapped her against him, his hand in her hair, his tongue in her mouth, and his finger behind her slipping in until the rest of his hand cupped her. She trembled, the sensations confusing, different...scary.

His eyes slowly opened, awareness seeming to return, and his brow pulled together multiple times as he slowly withdrew from her body. He let her skirt fall back down as he moved his hand back to her waist, relaxing his grip in her hair and dropping his forehead to hers, his body trembling.

Her heart was beating out of control. Why was she reacting so strongly? She wasn't a child—an innocent. So why couldn't she just relax?

Christopher pulled her closer, dropping his head into her neck as his arms wrapped around her tightly. She wrapped hers around his neck again, gripping hard as their bodies shook. She pressed him to her more tightly, and he turned to press his lips to her neck.

It took a while before they could breathe normally again. Christopher pulled back a bit, avoiding her eyes. She looked up at him, stopping him as he tried to step away. He turned worried eyes to hers.

She stroked his hair for a moment, her eyes roaming over his face. When she met his again, she smiled. Just a small smile. But a real one.

His brows pulled together in tender disbelief. And he leaned down to press his lips to hers once more before pulling back with a sigh.

"Come on. I think you'll like this one better than chess."

He threaded his fingers through hers and pulled her along with him, looking down at her by his shoulder as she wrapped her other arm around his and looked up with a smile growing in her eyes. She felt it bubble up into a charmed quiet laugh as she saw an answering smile in his.

And then he was pulling her through the house to show her another game, this one based on luck. They were still playing when Adam got home from work.

———

Jo fidgeted with her dress, what little there was of it, tugging at the hem before pulling back up at the strapless bodice. Adam's body shook with silent laughter as he sat across from her, his arms crossed and his eyes squeezed shut while he held his hand on his brow. She kicked him lightly and he opened his eyes, tears leaking from them. He wiped them away, still laughing, as she glared at him.

"You told me to wear this!"

"I didn't tell you to keep pulling it down so your tits spill out," he said, trying to suppress his laughter. "Not that I'm complaining."

Christopher sat beside her, his eyes calm as she glanced at him nervously.

"You look beautiful," he said quietly.

Adam stopped laughing as a smile spread across her face. He snorted and stared out the window for the remainder of the ride.

They were headed to Adam's corporate Christmas party.

The last two months had been pleasant. Christopher seemed to have decided not to pursue anything physical with her, and while a part of her still wanted him to, it was also comforting to know that Adam wouldn't have that hurt to deal with. And she didn't have to worry about her own anxiety over the change she felt in Christopher at those times. Although being close to him without touching would probably always be painful.

Still, they had found a comfortable equilibrium, it seemed to Jo, where Christopher would step in when she got too frustrated or flustered with Adam. And while Adam wasn't always very thrilled with that, he had accepted Christopher's presence around her, no longer trying to drag her away when she and Christopher were playing a game, or reading side by side, or just talking. Adam might flop his head in her lap and glare up at her, but he was quick to let her soothe him.

But she wasn't going to soothe him now. She hated social functions, and he had just made her more nervous.

They arrived and Adam climbed out, turning around to lift her down and put her at his side farthest away from Christopher. He put her arm under his, giving her a brief glance to make sure she wasn't planning on pulling away. She flattened her mouth at him, rolling her eyes when he crossed his arms, keeping her hand locked inside.

Christopher stepped down and raised a brow at him. But he didn't say anything and they went inside.

They were in the same ballroom where Jo had been presented prior to the auction—and where her body had been publicly examined. She tensed and Adam looked down. When he saw where her eyes were focused he exhaled and took her hand from his arm to put his behind her, rubbing her scar absently.

"Yeah, I don't like it either," he said. "We only need to stay a couple hours. You okay?" She nodded, crossing her arms and leaning into him as he hugged her close. She really should have thought her outfit through more.

Christopher stepped beside her, standing with his hands in his pockets as he surveyed the room. She looked over at him, wondering what he saw. Were people really pawns to him as Adam had said? She caught a small smile lurking at the corner of his mouth a moment before he turned to her.

"What do you think about when you look around?" she asked.

Adam looked down at her and then over at Christopher. She felt him exhale, but he didn't pull her away.

"Well," Christopher nodded toward an area of the room. "When I look over there, I think there is more room to stand and it's out of the way, so fewer people will bother us."

Adam raised a brow.

"Well that's one thing the two of you have in common," he said under his breath.

Jo looked up at him.

"What do you mean?"

He looked down at her and rubbed his jaw.

"I mean you're both socially dysfunctional," he said, his look daring her to contradict him.

She snorted. Christopher was unruffled.

"Oh really? Well, Mr. Sensitive, why don't you show us how it's done?"

"You don't have to be sensitive. Just charming. Watch and learn." He kissed her quickly on the mouth as she rolled her eyes at him. And then he proceeded to show them.

An hour later, and she was ready to go back to the desert. How did people spend so much time asking the same boring questions to person after person and hearing the same boring answers each time?

True to his word though, Adam showed them, moving with ease through the crowd with the most charming and likable version of himself. Which was pretty charming. Except when he turned to them.

"You two are useless," he ground out with a smile and a wave to someone across the room. "Go over and hide in your corner. I'll come get you when we can leave."

Christopher didn't wait for Jo to agree, but quickly grabbed her hand and pulled her with him, ignoring anyone who tried to speak to them. She had her hand over her face by the time they stopped, slightly mortified at how rude they'd been. Between Adam and Christopher...was a wide, wide gulf. Perhaps that's what had made them friends.

A server walked by carrying drinks.

"What are they drinking? And why?" she asked. She never became thirsty. She assumed no one else did either.

"Different types of flavored water. Because they are bored," Christopher said.

"Should we try some?"

"No."

She looked over at him, surprised.

"Why not? I'm bored. You're bored."

He looked at her.

"I'm not bored now," he said softly, looking at her.

Skepticism was in her eyes.

"Well, I want to try some." She started to hold her hand up, but he quickly grabbed it, surprising her again.

She exhaled.

"Okay, is there poison in it? Does it turn you into a monster?"

He frowned at her.

"It makes you fat."

She stared at him a moment before sputtering with laughter.

"You're worried I'll get fat?" She was still chuckling as she raised her hand again. This time she was ready for him and ducked to the side when he reached for her.

"Okay, that's it," she said. "*What*. And *don't* tell me it's about being fat." She held up her hand as he'd started to speak. His brows pulled together, and he looked away.

"Do you remember the short Ancient at your...the day the judge was taken away?" he asked.

John? With the fat gut?

"Yes..." And he'd been drinking when she met him. "So you're saying I'll look like that?"

"Yes!" he was adamant.

She didn't buy it for a second.

"What about all these people drinking?" she gestured around. "They don't look fat."

He hesitated.

"Yet," he answered.

She narrowed her eyes at him and evaded his hand as she raised hers for the third time. This time she caught the server's eye, and he headed over. Christopher's jaw clenched, and she watched him with bemused eyes.

The server arrived and held the tray out for them to choose.

"We changed our minds." Christopher dismissed him.

Jo looked at him with exasperation.

"Can you tell me what's in this?" she asked the server.

Christopher paled.

"Jo—"

"Only the best, miss. Nothing from the lower class."

"What do you mean?"

"From the same resources as your gown, miss."

Jo looked down. Her leather dress came from the same resources? Christopher tried sending him off again, but she put her hand out and grabbed the man's jacket.

"Wait. Be more explicit," she said, enunciating carefully.

"We only use the finest refined liquids - the upper class are separately harvested. Like your dress, miss. Only the finest skins."

He pulled away, his sleeve falling from her fingers.

"Jo..."

Refined liquids. Skins.

A line cut into her brow painfully as she looked around. At the carefully tailored suits. The flowing gowns. All made of leather.

She barely noticed as Christopher put his arm around her, pulling her quickly out of the room and down a hall to open the first door they came to. Some sort of small broom closet. A lovely broom closet. Well lit. With objects of metal. And leather.

Her eyes fell to her dress as Christopher closed the door behind them.

Leather.

She looked up dazed to see him staring at her, a harassed look in his eyes.

"Where does the leather come from?"

"Jo—"

"Christopher, for once just stop hiding things," she said hoarsely, grabbing his shirt and clinging tightly. "Please!"

His brows raised helplessly, and he dragged a hand through

his hair. Her hands tightened on his shirt as he stared at her, and he sighed with a nod.

"They don't have resources on this planet, Jo. No plants. No animals. Only rock—and humans."

———

No animals. She'd just assumed there were creatures somewhere. She'd just assumed…

Her eyes fell to her short black dress.

No animals. She blinked.

And grabbed the dress and yanked it down her body, tearing at the zipper, ripping the material until it fell to her ankles around her shoes. Her leather shoes. She tore at the straps, her fingers shaking in her haste, scarcely aware of the shudders going through her as she yanked and pulled until every bit of dead flesh was off her.

She kicked it away from her with her bare feet, stepping back into the metal shelving. Her hands reached behind her to grip it as her eyes finally moved from the pile on the floor.

Christopher stood frozen in place in front of her, his body rigid beneath his clothes—his leather clothes. She released a small cry and grabbed the front of his shirt, struggling to get the buttons undone, ripping it apart when she couldn't do it fast enough. Waves of revulsion went through her with every touch and she pulled and ripped, ignoring his choked sounds and attempts to grab her hands. Her hands went to the waistband of his pants, untying, struggling with him as he tried to stop her.

"Take them off—get them off!" her voice was hoarse. Horrified. He finally stopped fighting her.

"I'll do it," he choked out, his hands shaking as he quickly removed them, revealing his hardness underneath. Jo grabbed their clothing and shoes and cracked the door open slightly to shove them out before pulling the door closed again.

She pressed herself against the shelving once more, trembling, and looked at Christopher in front of her.

He leaned with his hands above her, his knuckles white as he clung to the cool metal, his eyes squeezed closed. Their bodies were so close she could feel every shuddering breath he took.

The door jerked open beside her, and they looked over.

"What the fuck."

Adam stared in shock an instant before anger began building in his eyes. He reached down furiously for her dress, but his eyes widened when Jo ducked under Christopher's arm and kicked the clothes away. When he moved to shield her naked body in the hall, she cried out at the feel of his shirt, grabbing it and struggling to tear it off of him. He made a strangled sound and pushed her back into the small room, closing the door behind them.

"Are you crazy?" His voice was hoarse. "Do you want everyone seeing you!"

She wasn't listening. The room had just become even smaller, and she was trapped inside with…

She tore at his clothes more strongly, finally ripping through, Adam's shocked curses barely registering.

"She knows." Christopher's voice sounded strained. In pain.

Adam stilled as she ripped at his clothing.

"Fuck." He quickly tore his remaining clothes off, rubbing his brow as Jo pulled him away from the door to shove the clothes out and close it again. She stood shaking, her body just touching Adam's. Christopher had collapsed against the wall behind her, and she could feel the heat from his body flowing into her.

Chaos swirled in her mind. She turned and reached her hands out to grab each of them by their arms, digging her nails into them when they resisted and pulling hard until they stumbled to stand side by side in front of her. She hunched over with her head hanging, gripping them to stay upright, as she trembled. She spoke without looking up.

"Who." Her voice was quiet. Dark.

She felt them shift, but when they didn't respond, she raised her head, digging her fingers into their arms as they stood looking down at her with a mixture of alarm and—

"*Who* are they using?"

Her eyes moved back and forth between them, but they avoided her gaze.

"Adam," she whispered, looking up at him. His eyes met hers reluctantly. "The judge said it would be a loss. That what you'd done... What would they have done to you?"

He shook his head and took a breath. Only to release it and rub his jaw in frustration.

"I have a contract now. I told you—they can't get me so long as I don't break the law."

Her lips parted as she stared up at him, her eyes helpless pools of horror.

She dropped their arms and grabbed them each by the waist before they could move, wrapping an arm around them and hugging them to her as tightly as she could, overriding their strangled resistance. Her body shook as she pressed her forehead against their shoulders where they stood side by side. She turned her face toward Adam, still leaning her head against them both.

"Baby," she whispered, "it was only pain…I could have taken physical pain…" she raised blurred eyes to him, her face breaking. "But I could *never* take losing you to…to…"

Adam stared down at her in pained frustration.

"Jo…" He glanced at where her naked body pressed against Christopher, the line between his brow twitching. Then he exhaled with a grunt. "Ah, fuck it."

He wrapped an arm around her tightly and pressed her face to his chest, rubbing her back and kissing her head. Christopher tried to step back and her arm tightened furiously.

"Don't you dare!" She glared at him, pulling back in Adam's arms, her arms holding tight to them both. "Don't…" she was shaking her head back and forth, her face breaking. "Is this the trouble you're in, Christopher? Is this what you've been risking?"

Adam glanced over as Christopher struggled to answer. His eyes were turbulent as he stared at Jo.

"I'm handling it," he managed at last, his voice strained.

A breath of disbelief escaped her.

"What were you thinking," she whispered, her head shaking back and forth. He looked away, glaring.

She pulled him even harder towards her, pressing her face against him.

"Jo, you need to let go," he bit out harshly, his hand grabbing her upper arm.

"I won't. I WON'T!" she cried, fury taking over. She shook her head back and forth against his skin, repeating it softly, over and over. "I won't...I won't..."

His heart hammered beneath her cheek. The warmth of his skin flowed through her. Her eyes were closed and she breathed him in as she held him close, brushing her cheek, her lips, against his chest.

She stopped speaking, her mouth open against his skin. He shuddered as her tongue reached out, tasting him, and her arms tightened on both of them, her palms flattening against their backs, pressing them to her.

Adam tried to pull away, and she turned to him, standing on her toes and pressing her body against him as hard as she could, her mouth against his neck. He froze as she sucked gently, his hands behind his back on her wrist, his hardness pushing into her stomach between them. She pushed herself up higher on her toes, dragging her breasts across his chest, biting and sucking his skin softly until her cheek was against his.

His chest expanded against her, shaking with every breath, as she turned her face to his. Her eyes opened, and she looked up with heavy lids to find his head bent low, his lips a breath away, his brow pulling together repeatedly. He let her wrist slip from his fingers, his breathing growing more shallow, as she touched her lips to his.

He groaned and grabbed her head between his hands, sinking his tongue into her deeply as his thumbs stroked her cheeks. She held onto Christopher, her hand gliding down his back, as Adam ravaged her mouth. She heard Christopher's sharp intake of breath as she cupped his body from behind, her fingers splaying wide on his skin. She moaned into Adam's mouth, her arm coming up to wrap around his neck and tangle her fingers in his hair, while her other hand pressed Christopher to her, his rigid length hard against her hip.

Christopher's grip on her arm tightened as she pressed him into her body. She tore her lips away from Adam, keeping her fingers locked in his hair, and turned back to Christopher. Adam pressed his face into her neck and plunged a finger inside her.

She gasped, dropping her head forward against Christopher's chest. When she looked up, his eyes on her were hard. Burning. His fingers bit into her flesh, and she trembled against him.

"Are you sure this is what you want."

Her heart pounded at the warning in his voice. She shivered, her eyes wide. And nodded.

He stared at her for a long moment, throbbing against her, before he relaxed his grip.

"Turn around."

16

MOON DAY 360

TURN AROUND.

Jo shivered as she stared up into Christopher's eyes. She suddenly found herself rooted in place. His eyes chilled her. Burned her.

Adam's touch stilled. His breath felt warm on her neck as he slowly withdrew. As he put his hands on her waist…and turned her towards him.

His eyes were heavy. Consumed. And far beyond her reach.

A small sound escaped from deep in her throat as she tried pulling back. She gasped as Christopher pressed his body against her, running his knuckles up her sides as he leaned his head into her neck, sucking gently. His hands moved to cup her breasts as Adam watched, pulling her lower body back to him.

"Maybe…maybe I wasn't…thinking clearly," she whispered.

Adam's eyes grew darker as Christopher pinched her nipples just a little too hard. She jumped and brought her hands up to grasp his wrists, her movements grinding her slightly against Adam's shaft. His brow pulled together and his lips parted as he shifted, lifting her thighs around him and positioning his head at her entrance. She swallowed.

He had been inside her more times than she could count. Christopher had caught them multiple times. This wasn't so very different. There was no reason to be afraid.

But her body trembled as Adam pushed into her slowly, filling her, stretching her painfully even now. His eyes never left her breasts as he began moving in and out, tightening his grip on her hips.

Christopher's hands slipped from her grasp, pushing her forward with one while his other...oh god. She jerked toward Adam as she felt the head of Christopher's cock rubbing her, lubricating her. Adam groaned and grabbed her hair, pulling her mouth to his and pushing his tongue into her as he pushed her down on his own cock more fully. Then he stilled, buried deep inside her, his tongue unmoving, and watched her through narrowed lids as Christopher began pushing.

Panic shot through her, and she clawed at Adam's shoulders, trying to climb his body, but he held her in place, pulsing and hot inside her. His fingers tangled more deeply in her hair, holding her still, as she tried jerking her head to the side to free her mouth. She whimpered against him, pushing at him, the pressure growing more intense until Christopher suddenly pushed past her barrier and both men groaned.

She cried out in a sharp sound of pain against Adam's lips, frantically trying to escape the sensation as Christopher continued sliding inside her slowly. So slowly. Adam held her down on his cock, his mouth locked on hers, until Christopher had buried himself inside her completely.

She couldn't breathe. Her thighs were shaking, and her body burned. Ached. Tears stung her eyes as tendrils of pain and pleasure pierced her core. She pushed toward Adam with a small moan, trying to escape, driving him more deeply inside. He groaned again and pulled his mouth off hers to bury his head on the other side of her neck, each of them sucking and biting as her small cries filled the room.

And they began moving.

Jo gasped as they rocked into her, over and over. She wrapped her arms tightly around Adam as they met each other's rhythm, burning her with sensation until she couldn't think—couldn't move.

Christopher pulled her back just enough to slide his fingers between her legs, sending a jolt through her body the moment he touched her center. She moaned on a whimper, her head falling forward on Adam's neck. Her arms clung to him, her nails digging into his back, and he pushed into her faster.

Christopher met his pace, his touch driving Jo closer and closer until every part of her body was on fire. She couldn't get away. She couldn't get close enough. A kaleidoscope of feelings pierced her and she was lost, pushed over an edge she hadn't known existed, pain and pleasure consuming her until nothing remained.

Adam muffled his hoarse cry against her skin and shoved her hips down against him as he erupted inside her a moment before Christopher...Christopher, whose fingers bit into the flesh between her legs as he plunged inside her deeply, groaning her name.

Their shuddering breaths were the only sound in the room. No one spoke. No one moved. Until voices approached in the hall.

———

The ride home passed in silence.

Jo sat curled against the corner of the carriage with her face turned toward the window and a hand at her brow, guarding her eyes. Christopher sat beside her, a large space between them, while Adam faced them, his arms folded over his chest. Every now and then he would rub his jaw, but he never spoke.

Their clothing was in tatters. There had been no real choice but to put it back on or parade naked through the party.

The carriage stopped at last, and they alighted in silence. Jo kept her head down while waiting for the door to be unlocked and walked straight to her room once inside, never raising her eyes. She ripped her clothes off immediately, throwing them in the trash, only to hear her door open again behind her. She froze. When she didn't hear it close again, she looked over her shoulder.

Adam stood in the doorway, his large form more imposing to her than before. She turned back around and squeezed her eyes closed tightly as he walked up behind her. The swish of clothing whisked by her ear a moment before arms went around her, and she jumped. His naked body pressed against hers as he leaned down to press his lips to her shoulder, trying to look at her face. She turned her head the other way, ignoring his loud exhale.

"You know, you're the one who started it," he began, but she put her hands over her ears. She felt him exhale again before grabbing her wrists and forcing her hands down in front of her.

"What are you going to do. Hide in here naked the rest of eternity?"

"Yes."

He dropped his lips to her neck with a grunt. He didn't move, and she felt him breathing against her. The minutes passed, and Jo's eyes shifted to the side as she bit her lip. He'd been silent a long time. Too long. She looked over her shoulder at last to see an unusually serious expression on his face. Uh oh.

She was just about to try to run when he scooped her up in his arms.

"What are you doing?" the panic in her voice was real as he carried her back out of the room.

"We're figuring this out tonight."

There was no time to scramble out of his arms, even if she'd been able. He was at Christopher's door.

"Hey, Goldilocks," he called while Jo hid her face in his neck and curled into a tight ball. "We need to talk."

Jo heard the door open behind her, and she clenched her arms around Adam even harder as he strode into the room and turned around. He exhaled slowly.

"You broke it. Fix it." Jo jerked her head up. He was staring at Christopher.

Christopher's expression revealed nothing as he stared back. He still wore his pants but had removed his shirt, and Jo's stomach clenched at the sight of his muscles rippling when he moved at last to close the door.

He turned back around and leaned back, putting his hands in his pockets. His pale blonde curls spilled onto his forehead as he studied Adam with a somber expression. Then his eyes shifted to Jo.

Her arms tightened around Adam's neck, and he looked down at her. She was grateful to have an excuse to look away from Christopher. Adam sighed yet again, his eyes rueful. Then he carried her to the bed, plopping her down and lying on top of her as she yelped at the touch of the cover on her back.

"I know, baby. I had to get used to it, too. But you can't sleep on the floor forever or walk around naked everywhere. As much as I would like that." He looked down at her breasts.

She was arching her back, her shoulders cringing into her neck.

"I can sleep on the floor—I can sleep on the floor!" she gasped, thrashing around. Adam just stared down at her, propping himself up on his elbow as he waited.

"You done?" he asked once she'd finally stilled. The sound that escaped her sounded suspiciously like a whine, so she forced herself to remain silent. But she couldn't stop the shudders that went through her.

He waited until they had passed before speaking again.

"It's not like they're dead."

"That doesn't help," she groaned. But she gave in at last, her eyes searching his face. "I don't know what I would have done if they'd taken you," she whispered.

He stroked her hair. Her cheek.

"Christopher!" Jo jumped when Adam didn't bother looking away before he barked his name. He looked over his shoulder, impatience etched in every muscle.

Christopher still stood by the door. His jaw clenched and his brows pulled together at Adam's voice, but he walked towards the bed, hesitating a moment beside it before pulling at the strap on his pants. Jo squeezed her eyes closed again, jumping slightly when the bed moved. Adam rolled to one side of her, and she felt Christopher's naked body press against her. Her hands flew to cover her face as she lay between them, the heat of their bodies flowing over hers.

The silence stretched in the room.

She gasped as Adam's hand covered her breast, and her eyes flew open as she grabbed his wrist. His brow raised. He wasn't going to let her hide from this any longer. She reluctantly turned her eyes to Christopher.

He was staring down intently.

"I won't hurt you, Jo."

Some of the bands of tension inside her loosened a bit. She stared up at him, wariness filling her eyes.

"That's not what—" Oh, how could she explain? She wasn't afraid exactly. She just…never knew what he was thinking. What he thought of her. What he felt…

What he remembered.

"Will you tell me now? What you remember?"

He hesitated before answering.

"It's just a moment. You were in front of a mirror. And I…" He hesitated once more before leaning down to rest his forehead against hers, a small shudder going through him. "I remember what I wanted to do to you. And that you were...nervous," he whispered.

Jo saw Adam frown out of the corner of her eye, but he didn't say anything.

"What was it you wanted to do?" Her breath caught on the question. Feeling nervous was something she had felt quite a lot with him.

Christopher leaned back up, his eyes running down her body.

"You should know by now."

Jo's hands came back up to cover her face with a small whimper at the reminder. Adam pinched her nipple, and she glared at him as she clasped her hands over her breasts instead. The warmth of him nuzzling her neck sent tingles through her that she tried to ignore.

"I don't want to make you nervous, Jo," Christopher whispered, pulling her eyes back to his. "Let me try again."

His knuckles brushed over her skin and up her body, his fingers gently sliding under hers to cup her breast. Her heart pounded against their joined hands as she stared into his eyes.

Adam's hand was stroking her inner thigh as his lips sucked on her neck softly. She shivered. They were both so much bigger than she was. Physical size. But also smarter. Braver. Better at every single thing society demanded. She was nothing by comparison. Swallowed up. How could she ever be enough for even one of them?

But this was the world they lived in now. And they couldn't just go find someone better. Someone who actually deserved them. So she had to at least try to be what they needed.

Because she needed them.

Heat flowed through her, and she shivered...and nodded.

Their hands were soft on her waist as they turned her to face Adam—and they were both extra gentle this time.

———

Jo opened her eyes slowly as Adam brushed his thumb against her brow. He was on his stomach, his eyes still closed, and she reached out to stroke his back. He couldn't move fully yet, but he'd be up soon.

She felt Christopher's breath against her skin behind her as he touched his lips to her shoulder, and she shivered.

Four days of sleeping together, and she still couldn't just turn and face him. What did he think of her? What did he think about everything? He was so quiet. Her flashes of bravery could never sustain themselves, and it was so much easier to just cling to Adam. She never had to guess with Adam. Whatever he wanted, he tried to take.

Would Christopher be forever hidden from her? *He will if you keep being a ninny. Turn around.*

She cringed at her own thoughts but took a deep breath and turned.

Christopher didn't try to stop her, but she couldn't read his expression. Had she displeased him? His hand was on her hip as he stared at her. Unmoving.

She should be able to kiss him now, right? She hadn't tried yet, and he hadn't kissed her lips since the day they'd been alone together. He and Adam seem to have some unspoken agreement about who got to do what with her. But no one had asked her.

She bit her bottom lip before leaning forward, watching his brows pull together ever so slightly as she pressed her lips to his. Her lashes fluttered closed as she sank into him.

Christopher moved his lips to her cheek, kissing her softly but quickly before turning to get up. He kept his back to her as he dressed, and she pulled her knees to her chest, gripping them hard.

"Merry Christmas." Adam's deep voice sent vibrations

through the bed, and she turned back to him gratefully as he pulled her into his arms.

"Merry Christmas!" She threw her arms around his neck, her eyes lighting up. "What type of human remains did you get for me?"

"Funny," he murmured against her mouth, holding her head as he kissed her deeply. She sighed into him, all her stress melting away. She froze when she felt him get hard.

"No no no no no," she smacked at him, trying to get up. "I'm sore, and I need a break!"

"Baby—"

"Don't!" She flattened her hand over his mouth, and he raised pleading brows at her.

"But it's Christmas." His words were muffled, and she couldn't help laughing at the plaintive tone. He was just a big child.

She hit him lightly a few more times as she disentangled herself from his arms, still laughing, and he finally groaned and sat up with her. Her eyes swept the room.

Christopher was gone.

Her gaze went back to Adam.

"What do you think about all of this?" she whispered.

"About what?"

"You know…" she swirled her hand around them. "This. All of…us."

He bit the inside of his cheek as he looked at her.

"It didn't end up bothering me as much as I thought it would," he murmured, his eyes starting to wander down her body. She grabbed his hair to hold his head up. "Ow!"

"I'm serious," she whispered.

"So am I," he whispered back. "And why are we whispering?"

Her fingers fidgeted with his hair and she looked down. Adam stilled.

"What do you think about it?"

She stared at her hand, playing with her nails. She didn't know how to answer. She knew they cared about her. But sometimes it felt…scary. Overwhelming. She didn't know how she was supposed to act.

And she hated the distance Christopher kept between them. Even now, after everything…

She crawled into Adam's lap and curled up, sighing in relief when he just held her close. However he felt about them all having sex together, she didn't think he'd be quite so keen on hearing how much the barrier Christopher put up bothered her. How much she felt it.

She was smacking his hands away again when they heard the bell outside the door. Her eyes flew to Adam's, her heart hammering in her chest. He shrugged.

Jo jumped up to get dressed as she heard the front door open, her worry growing at the silence immediately afterwards. She was rushing to the bedroom door while lacing her top when Christopher stepped into the doorway, and she stopped short, exhaling.

"I have a present for you," he said. He hesitated a moment before stepping to the side. And a rather tall girl with excited eyes stepped into view.

"Missy!" The breath left Jo's lungs in a rush as the two girls flung their arms around each other, holding each other too tightly to breathe. They were laughing and crying, and their bodies shook as they held on, rocking back and forth.

Jo saw Adam through her tears as he walked by, pulling his shirt over his head and sending Christopher a withering look. But Christopher just kept staring at Jo, a half smile on his lips. She closed her eyes and hugged Missy even harder.

When they finally released each other, they gulped for air, laughing as they tried filling their lungs enough to talk again.

"Oh my god," Missy gasped first. "I heard about what you

did at the concert! I am so pissed I wasn't there to see it! Did the caning hurt much?"

"A little," Jo laughed. "But what has been going on with you? All I knew was that you got into tier four!"

"No, girl—I'm tier three now! That stunt you pulled made all the boys crazy. Suddenly having a mouth that talks back became a good thing and I got bought by a football team. A fucking football team." She fanned her eyes, trying to stop laughing.

Jo paused with her mouth open and Missy leaned over and pushed her chin up.

"It's not bad. I mean, if you're into being a glorified sex slave, that is." She looked around. Adam and Christopher weren't in the room anymore, and the door was closed.

Missy turned back to her, her eyes bright.

"Actually, I kind of love it now. My boys are a rowdy bunch, but they like it when I put them in their place! And believe me— it's a full time job!"

Jo laughed in helpless awe. And relief.

"I am so glad it isn't all misery! I was so worried about you. I couldn't tell you before that I knew Christopher—I trusted you, but it wasn't just my secret. I've been wanting to apologize to you ever since."

Missy waved her hand.

"Oh, pfft. I figured that out after I saw the way he was looking at you. Jesus, I've never seen a man need anything the way he needs you."

Jo stared at her. Then her brows raised in comprehension.

"Ohhh, you mean Adam."

"Uh, no. The big guy? Yeah, he clearly adores you, but it's not like the other one."

Jo frowned at her.

"What do you mean?"

"What do you mean what do I mean?" she laughed, shaking her head at her. "How can you not see this?"

They heard the bell at the door and a swarm of voices. Jo started to stand in a panic.

"Sounds like my boys got tired of waiting," Missy said, a thread of pride in her tone. Jo looked at her in surprise, her pulse calming.

"They came with you?"

"It's Christmas! You think they'd let me wander off without them? Pfft. Come on—I'll introduce you!" She grabbed Jo's hand and pulled her to the door.

Jo wanted to hold her back and make her explain what she'd meant about Christopher, but it was clear Missy was too eager to have her meet everyone. Or maybe just too eager to get back to them.

A shout went out as they rounded the corner and too many men for Jo to count came barreling toward Missy, lifting her up in hug after hug as they passed her around. The front door was open and the line of men extended through it. Jo could see Adam above the crowd, his arms crossed as he rubbed his brow. She looked around until she spotted Christopher standing near the door, watching her.

Her breath caught in her chest. He had let this chaos into his home. Into his well ordered, well planned life. The chaos of her. Of her friend. Of Adam.

For her.

His eyes were uncertain as he stared at her, and her own filled with tears while a smile tugged at her lips. She stepped toward him just as another group arrived. Only they didn't bother with the bell.

Jo could only watch in horror as the guards surrounded Christopher.

———

Christopher stood still as the guards encircled him. Very still. His eyes were locked on the guard in front of him who was reading from a parchment.

"Your employment with the office of the director of city intelligence has been terminated. Your citizenship is hereby revoked. You are now the property of the city." The guard folded the parchment as two guards grabbed Christopher's arms and chained them behind his back.

He didn't struggle. He just continued staring in front of him, his eyes darkening until the guard took a step back. He didn't react. He didn't look around.

Jo was fighting to get through the crowd of men and had just made it to the guards when a strong hand grabbed her.

"Let me go!" She jerked her arm away, but he held tight, pulling her back into his arms.

"Just wait, baby," he ground out in hushed tones. "We're not letting this happen. But the guards aren't the ones who make the call. Just wait."

She trembled as he wrapped his arms around her tightly.

"I can't see," she whispered, emotion choking her.

He lifted her until her eyes were at his level. Her arms wrapped around his neck, her body continuing to shake, as she turned her head back toward Christopher.

He had turned his head at last, and her breath caught in her throat as they locked eyes. She had seen that look on him before. In the desert.

He hated her.

Tears filled her eyes, and she brushed them away furiously, needing to see him. But they were leading him away.

He didn't look back again.

She turned back to Adam, desperation in her eyes, and he gripped her hard as he set her back on her feet.

"Let's go," he breathed, his jaw clenching as he stared at the retreating backs of the guards.

Jo nodded furiously. She had no idea where they were going, but this was something. They could do something.

The crowd of men made low murmurs of condolences as they exited the house, setting Jo's teeth on edge. Missy gripped her hands tightly before she left, opening her mouth to speak but closing it again with helpless sympathy in her eyes.

"He's going to be fine," Jo bit out.

Missy nodded, her eyes wide, but her eyes were wet. She hugged her quickly, strongly, and then they were gone.

"Where are we going?" Jo looked up at Adam as he pulled her down the street in a rapid pace. They hadn't bothered with the carriage.

"The Director's. He lives in this district as well."

"Can we run?"

Adam glanced down at her and nodded.

A few minutes later, they stood banging on a large iron door.

"Open up!" Adam yelled. A few doors opened nearby, but he ignored them. "Open up or I start talking!"

The door opened at last, and a timid looking girl came into view.

"The director says he's not receiving visitors tod—"

Adam shoved the door open and marched inside as the girl shrank back against the wall. Jo reached out to touch her arm for an instant, her eyes apologetic, as she flew by to follow Adam.

"Where are you, you piece of shit?" he yelled, looking around the rather luxuriously appointed main room.

A door creaked down the hall seconds before the tall lanky form came into view.

"Now Cindy," he said to the girl, his voice dripping with disappointment. "Didn't I say I wasn't to be disturbed?" The girl shrank back into the wall even further, her body beginning to shake.

"Don't you blame her, you coward," Adam raged, approaching him. The director raised his hand.

"Now now. You don't want to do anything illegal."

Adam stopped short, tension in every line of his body.

"True," he said, his eyes bright. "Like manufacturing evidence against a judge, for example."

"Cindy, return to the tier five house immediately," the director snapped, turning a narrow gaze back to Adam as Cindy rushed out the door, closing it behind her.

The director walked across the room to pour himself a drink. Jo wanted to ram the goblet down his throat. Her fists clenched at her side.

"I suppose it isn't surprising that he told you," the director mused, swirling at his drink in his hand as he stared down at it. "Clever as always. Well, almost always."

He smiled as he turned back to Adam.

"You need to undo this," Adam said. "Or I start talking."

The director chuckled.

"No, no. I don't think you will. You will be silent. Christopher will be silent. And I…well, I suppose I will have to allow you to keep your girl, won't I?"

Adam stilled.

"Oh, I see. Did he fail to explain the implications? Let me help you." He walked over to a plush chair and sat down, stretching his long legs out in front of him and crossing them at the ankle. "You see, if this business with the judge were to come out, I'm afraid his sentence would be overturned. This would, of course, reinstate his rulings. And the punishment would proceed as he had intended.

"And not only this, but if anything were to happen to me, I'm afraid the Ancients would use this to undo the positive changes I have made in the city, changes that have allowed you to claim what you so clearly want." He nodded toward Jo. "No, I don't think you will say anything."

Jo stared at the director, a cold fury building in her.

"He might not. But I will." She didn't actually know what

they were talking about specifically, but it was clear that it was the threat to her that was being used to control both men.

The director blinked, his body tensing for a moment. Then he sighed.

"No, my dear, you will be silent as well. What will you gain if you speak? It does Christopher no good at all. He assisted me. He will still be sent to resources, along with me."

Jo paled.

"You would have your revenge, to be sure, but at what cost? Once again, if I am taken away, the Ancients regain their power. Will you lose both men? After all they have done for you, do they mean so little to you?"

Jo threw herself at him, avoiding Adam's hands as he tried to stop her. But she collapsed at the director's feet.

"Please…" Tears choked her. "Please. Tell me what I can do. Anything. I will do anything you ask. Forever. Just please please please release him."

The director stared down at her, a slight smile on his face.

"But what use are you to me now? None at all. The tide of public sentiment in your favor has already turned to other interests. I could have kept it alive with you by my side, and who knows how much farther I could have gone in my fight against the old oppressors. But now…"

He reached out to stroke a thumb along her jaw.

"Now you are nothing."

Adam pulled her back to her feet and pushed her behind him, the muscles in his back rigid and hard.

"Don't touch her."

The director grinned.

"Do you know, I believe I will do you both a favor. I will allow you a final visit. Fortunately for you, it's Christmas and I am feeling magnanimous. And most Resource Allocation personnel have the day off, so my dear former assistant won't be added to their supplies until tomorrow."

Jo's body shook so hard her teeth clicked against one another. She bit down, holding onto Adam's back. This couldn't be it. There had to be something they could do. Christopher would know though. He could tell them.

The tension slowly seeped out of her. They could go see him. He would know what to do.

The director stood and crossed the room. He shuffled around in a drawer and leaned down to write something on a parchment before walking back to them.

"Just show this to the guards. They will let you in."

Adam didn't move and Jo reached for the parchment herself. She wanted to get out of there. To find out what they could do from Christopher.

"And to be clear, if anything ever happens to me at all, I will have no incentive to remain silent about the judge myself. And if I lose power, my initiatives can be undone. So I suggest the two of you become my most loyal, ardent supporters."

Jo pushed at Adam, feeling his fury. Ignore the director. Get to Christopher. She at last got Adam to start toward the door, her grip tight on the parchment in her hands.

"Oh, and one more thing…"

They paused with the door open. Adam didn't turn around, but Jo looked back.

"Do give Christopher my regards. And let him know I understand his decision to steal from me. I really thought he had me for the longest time. Until I finally realized something."

The director gave Jo a slow smile, and her stomach turned over.

"You had already taken his power away. He would never turn me in if it meant hurting you. Thank you, my dear. If not for you, I could never have eliminated him."

Jo's breath escaped on a cry as Adam grabbed her and pulled them both past the door, slamming it behind him.

17

MOON DAY 364

They ran through the city using the most direct route possible—through the market district, through the factory district—until they stood in front of the doors to the prison. The guards waved them through after viewing the parchment and opened the large doors.

Jo reached for Adam's hand as they stared into a wide tunnel, and he laced his fingers with hers before walking through. It stretched on and on before opening into a small courtyard surrounded by a giant wall of stone. A tower stood in the center with a single door and two guards on either side.

Jo and Adam glance at each other before moving forward.

"Someone was brought here this morning. We have permission to visit him." Adam handed the parchment to one of the guards.

He scanned it and nodded toward the door.

"You may proceed. The jailor inside will lead you to his cell."

The guards didn't open this door for them, so Adam opened it and they walked inside. It was a small room with a single desk in the center toward the back. A man sat behind the desk, his leather armor similar to the guards but in black rather than brown.

He examined their parchment without expression and took a key ring off his belt to unlock a door on the side of the room. They followed him down a short hall with empty cells until they reached the last one. The guard used his key ring again to open the door.

"You have ten minutes."

Ten? That wasn't long enough—not nearly long enough!

But the guard was already walking back up the hall. At least they were being given privacy. Jo turned her head to the inside of the cell and understood why.

Christopher was sitting against the wall with an iron collar around his neck, attached to the stone behind him on a short chain. His wrists were secured similarly on either side of him, preventing him from bringing his hands closer to his body. He stood as they entered, the chain lengths just long enough for him to stand near the wall.

She darted toward him but stopped when he flinched back.

"What do we do?" she whispered, her eyes searching his face.

"There is nothing to do." His voice was as empty as his eyes. "It's done."

Adam exhaled in a huff. His voice was low but furious.

"That's bullshit. You don't get to just give up now. We're still on the outside. We can help. Just take some fucking help for once."

Christopher looked at him.

"There's nothing you can do. I made a mistake." A touch of bitterness crept into his tone, and Jo felt it cutting into her. She was the mistake.

"There must be some way," she began, her voice hoarse. "I'm not smart enough to see it. But you are. Just…please…just tell us." The tears choked her, and she stopped speaking.

Christopher's face grew darker as she spoke, refusing to look at her. She couldn't blame him. If it weren't for her, he would be free. Comfortable. Safe.

"Maybe if we gave back what you stole—the director said he understood."

His eyes finally flashed to hers, furious.

"Why would you speak to him? Stay out of it, Jo!"

"Now don't go yelling at her for it—I took us there," Adam said roughly.

"You keep her away from him." Christopher's voice was acid, his eyes narrow slits on Adam. "Far away. Forever."

Adam tore his hand through his hair, restless under Christopher's gaze. But he nodded.

Christopher slumped against the wall, his head down.

"I stole evidence he was using to blackmail the company executive responsible for choosing the winning bid. And I gave it back to the guy. It's not something that can be returned. Now go. I'm tired. And I don't want to be bothered anymore."

"Please…" she whispered, horrified yet again. It was her fault again. "Please, Christopher…I can't—this can't happen. Help us. Please. Something. Anything."

She stepped closer, and he turned his face into his arm, squeezing his eyes closed.

"Get her out of here, Adam!" His voice was hoarse, but he was yelling. Christopher was yelling.

Jo shook her head, reaching for him, and he cringed back further from her touch.

"Now! Get her out now!" He sounded frantic, and Adam grabbed her, pulling her away as she struggled.

"No! No, you can't just give up! You can't! Dammit, Christopher, you look at me!" She was screaming at him as Adam carried her from the room. "You look at me this minute!"

But he didn't. He kept his face buried in his arm, and he never looked at her. And Adam crushed her to his chest as he walked up the hall. She beat on his back, sobbing, trying to get him to let her down.

"I know, baby. I know. But you're just making it harder for him."

No. No, it couldn't end this way. It couldn't. It *couldn't*.

She turned in tears to the jailor as he walked by them to close the door to the cell.

"Can we come back tomorrow morning?"

"He goes to resources tomorrow morning."

"What time? We can come before!"

The guard locked the cell and started back towards them.

"No time for that. The night shift switches a half hour after the sleep ends, and that's when they take him."

A half hour. Her heart hammered against Adam as he held her tightly to him.

"Maybe I could make it in time if I ran. Will you still be here?"

The jailor ushered them through to the main room of the tower, turning to lock the door behind him.

"Not sure how long it takes you, but it takes us fifteen minutes before we can move again. After that, we're busy getting things shifted, so we won't have time for you. Sorry. You had your visit. Afraid that's all there is."

He finally glanced at her with a touch of sympathy, but it only lasted a moment before he turned back to his desk.

Fifteen minutes.

She trembled in Adam's arms as he carried her back outside. *Two guards at the door.* Back through the tunnel. *Two guards at the gate.*

He didn't put her down and she didn't ask him to. He was walking slowly. She needed him to walk slowly. Back through the factory district. *Maybe an hour.* Back through the market district. *Maybe an hour and a half.*

She saw the temple.

"Adam, stop. Stop!"

He followed her gaze. A service was about to begin. He hesitated.

"You want to…pray?"

"I…want to never again wear skin," she forced out, her voice cracking. "Please…please just…let me get one of the hair robes. Please."

She looked up at him as he lowered her, his eyes wary. She shivered.

"At least for a little while. Please. I can't bear it." She didn't have to fake the tears that fell.

He hugged her tight.

"Okay, baby. Okay."

They walked to the temple but didn't go inside. Robes were available at the door. No charge.

Jo grabbed two.

"Maybe you'll want to wear one, too," she mumbled, avoiding his eyes.

He exhaled but didn't say anything and put the robes over his arm to carry them. They held hands the rest of the way home.

That night they made love desperately, the pain coming through in every touch. Jo pushed Adam over underneath her, riding him until he bit into her and cried out as he came. Then she did it again, her own body shattering over him in waves as he rose up to meet her, forcing himself deep inside.

She lay on his chest, trembling, never wanting the moment to end. Never wanting the morning to come.

Finally, she looked at the clock…and sat up, dropping her eyes down to his, the grief almost overwhelming her. She pushed her hips down, needing him to be as deeply inside her as possible. Needing to remember this forever.

"Adam," she whispered. His own eyes were tortured as he looked up at her.

"We'll get him out. Some day. We just...we'll figure out a way."

She stroked his hair away from his face. He was always so much bigger than life. So sure he could have whatever he wanted if he just kept pushing. And she knew he would work tirelessly to try to free Christopher. For as long as it took. Year after year... while Christopher was being cut to pieces and burned over and over again. While people paraded the streets in his skin. While the director drank from his blood. Her voice was husky as she continued.

"I want you to know I wanted to stay with you forever. That I love you more than I could ever, ever tell you." Her voice broke, and she stared down at him through the tears. He grabbed her arms and half sat up, glaring into her eyes.

"Whatever you are thinking, stop. Do you think I would let you say anything? I will lock you in this room permanently if I have to." His voice was as rough as his hands. "And it won't do him any good. It won't save him."

Her tears spilled over as she nodded.

"I know," she whispered. She looked back over at the clock.

"Why do you keep looking at the clock?"

She waited. Counting the seconds. Finally she turned back to him, her voice thick with grief...and acceptance.

"Because I don't want you to have time to tie me up and stop me."

His brow drew together for just an instant before recognition lit his eyes. He threw his arm toward the nightstand, reaching for the clothes they had tossed on it. She knew what he was after. Strips of leather to tie her.

But he was too late. She caught his head as the sleep hit him, carefully lowering him back to the bed as she fought off the weight trying to drag her down with him.

She had a lot to do tonight.

————

Jo bit her arm hard as she roamed the room, trying to focus. It took her far too long to tie Adam up, but she needed to make sure no one could blame him for anything. He had to be safe. So she'd searched the house until she found some rope and secured him tightly to the bed. The leather would have been too easy for him to break.

She found a knapsack and filled it with the two robes, biting herself again and again to focus. To stay on her feet. Did she need anything else? *Go.*

Her feet stumbled toward the front door, the knapsack on her naked back. She hadn't bothered dressing. The door was heavy. Very heavy. But she pushed hard for a long time. Until she bit herself hard enough to realize she needed to pull it toward her.

She clung to it as she almost fell outside. Everything swirled around her, but she knew which way to go. The long walk home had provided ample time to memorize the path. Commit the image to her mind. She followed it now.

Past the temple that rose to the ceiling high above. To the gates separating the temple district from the market district. She struggled to open them. Locked. She looked down at the guards on either side of the gate, and fell over as she bent to search for a key. *Stay up. Stay awake.* Her hand touched a small metal rod and she pulled on it. A key. Yes.

She shoved herself to her feet again, the urge to lie down pulling her back over. The pain cleared her mind as she bit into her flesh once again, and she unlocked the gates. She was through.

Through the market district and the gate to the factory district with two guards as well. Again, she unlocked the gates. All the way to the large stone doors to the prison.

She knew what she had to do. They would have to walk out

this door in the morning, and the guards might be awake by then. She didn't want to do this. But she had to.

She drew one of the guard's swords from his scabbard. The world spun around her, and she grabbed the blade, gasping as it cut into her fingers. Dumb. She needed her hands, and she couldn't afford to leave a trail of blood everywhere.

She bit down hard on her lip, enough to stay focused. Enough to lift the sword. It swung down, cutting the first guard's neck halfway. Blood spurted everywhere.

Not enough. They might be able to move around if their heads were attached. She bit her lip harder and struck again, this time severing it completely, and turned to the second guard. Her strike was clean on the first blow.

The sword fell from her hand as she dropped to her knees, fumbling for keys. Shit. She should have searched for those first. Blood was everywhere. Hadn't she been worried about that a moment ago? She couldn't remember.

She found the key and unlocked the doors. They were heavy. She tried pulling. Still heavy. She bit herself again and remembered they opened inward. She just needed to push hard. They finally began moving, and she was through.

Through the tunnel. Into the courtyard. The two guards by the doors. She couldn't risk them waking.

"Sorry," she mumbled over them. But she made sure they wouldn't be able to move either.

Shit. She forgot to get the key first. Again.

She fumbled around in the blood but couldn't find one. Wait. The guards hadn't opened this door. She stood and pushed on the door, and it opened easily.

Inside. The jailor. Where was he? She looked around the room. Nowhere.

She checked the door to the cells. Unlocked! She stumbled through, relief rushing through her. Almost there. Wait. Where were the keys?

She was about to turn around when she caught sight of the jailor. He had lain down near Christopher's cell. To watch him? Or to give him some sense of support?

He was the last. The only guard who had shown at least a spark of decency. And she wanted to just tie him up. But she could barely think. And she didn't see any rope. She drew his sword. He would be fine. He would have to burn and that would be awful...but he would be okay.

Wait! The keys!

She remembered first this time. She grabbed the key ring and opened Christopher's cell before turning back to the guard.

Had to be done.

"I'm so sorry," she whispered, struggling to stay upright. She couldn't seem to raise it. She bit her lip. Harder. No use. It was too much. Her thoughts were fading. What was she doing? Oh. Head.

She put the sword to his neck, slicing back and forth as blood sprayed around them. Had to be done.

The sword fell from her hands as she turned back to the cell. Christopher was slumped over in a seated position on the wall, the metal collar biting into him. She reached for him and slipped in the blood that had pooled at her feet, falling to her knees. No. Had to stay up. She crawled her way to him, struggling to stay awake, but her knees slipped in the blood and she fell on her stomach just before she reached him.

Shit. The keys. They were still in the door.

Her arms pushed at the floor beneath her. No use. Bite. Bite harder. No use. Christopher. Her hand reached for him, her bloody fingers barely touching his leg.

And then the darkness overtook her, and she slept.

———

"Jo..."

Her eyes flew open at Christopher's choked voice. She pushed herself up in a panic. Blood surrounded her. Wet blood. Scrambling to her feet, she reached for the knapsack, jerking it off her back and holding it away from her to examine it. She exhaled. Just a few spots. The robes should be good.

She carefully walked to the side of the room and set it down where it would be safe until they had cleaned up enough to put them on.

Keys. Where were they? Door.

Moving quickly, she grabbed the key ring and tiptoed back to kneel beside Christopher, trying to avoid making more of a mess. She searched through the keys, not sure which to use, only half registering Christopher's eyes as they moved across her face.

"Jo," he whispered. She glanced up.

His eyes were as soft as she had ever seen them. But full of pain.

She ignored him. They didn't have much time. She tried the first key. No. The second.

Her fingers fumbled through them as Christopher rested his head against hers, moving it slowly across her skin.

Why weren't any of these working? She must have gone too quickly. She went back to the first key.

"Jo…" His voice was scratchy. "The guards don't have this key."

She froze.

"Where is it?" she whispered, raising her eyes to his.

They roamed her face, drinking her in.

"It's kept with resources. They'll bring it when they come for me."

She stared at him. No. She shook her head.

"No. No no no no no…" she looked back at the keys, fumbling with each of them in the lock again desperately.

He turned his head, pressing his lips to her hand as she tried, again and again.

"Jo..." His voice was husky. Shaking. "Kiss me goodbye. Please. I want that memory with me. I need it…"

She looked up slowly. The tenderness in his eyes weakened her muscles and the keys fell from her fingers. She stared at him, unblinking. Unmoving.

He leaned into her but the collar stopped him.

"I can't reach you." He choked out. "Come closer. Please…" His voice faded as he looked at her, helpless tears in his eyes.

She stared at him a moment longer. And got up and walked away.

The guard's sword was lying beside his body, and she leaned down to pick it up before turning to face Christopher once again. The devastation in his eyes was quickly replaced by confusion.

"No." Her voice was firm.

Recognition dawned, and his head dropped onto his arm as he stared at her with tortured eyes.

"It can't cut through the chains," he said hoarsely.

"I'm aware of that." She walked over. "I'm going to need you to lean over."

He blinked. Twice. He raised his head again and his eyes widened almost imperceptibly—an instant before narrowing. When he spoke, his voice was as firm as hers.

"Jo, you need to get out of here. If they catch you—"

"They won't catch me if we hurry!"

"Hurry where?" He was angry now. "Where will you go?"

"I don't know! I'm figuring it out!" she cried.

"You need to listen to reason!"

"I am," she said, furious. "Just not *your* reasons."

"This isn't logical—"

"It is!" She dropped the sword and fell to her knees, grabbing his face with both her hands. "How could it be logical for me to do nothing while they take you away to torture you—*forever*? How could it be logical for me to protect my body when my mind and my heart will be there with you every single day? When I would never have another moment of peace. Of joy. Of anything that wasn't crushing agony? *How could that possibly be logical?*"

She was yelling and crying in his face, and he turned his mouth to her palm.

"Don't cry. I'm sorry. Don't cry." He repeated it again and again, kissing her over and over. "But I can't bear an eternity of this unless I know you are safe."

She jerked away.

"We don't have time to argue!" She grabbed the sword and faced him, her eyes raging. "I am doing this, whether you like it or not! And if you want to give me the best chance of not getting caught, then please...please just...help me." She ended on a whisper, her eyes pleading with him.

A myriad of expressions ran across his face, each fighting for dominance. Frustration. Worry. Hope. And something softer— something she had only just seen moments before.

The moment seemed to go on and on, but only seconds passed before his expression cleared. His lips set. And he gave her a brief nod, his eyes bright.

"Okay." His voice was steady. Firm. "Get us out of here." He leaned his head forward, waiting.

Jo took a shuddering breath as she moved into position, placing the sword against his neck with trembling hands. *Calm down.* She could do this. She had to do this. She raised it above her head and closed her eyes, making sure she was steady. She had to be very steady. Her eyes opened. And she brought her arms down.

The sword sliced through the air and through his neck cleanly.

18

MOON DAY 365

Jo BURST out into the courtyard, leaping over the bodies of the guards, with the knapsack slung over her shoulder and Christopher's head in her arms. She couldn't think about how much pain he was in—if she didn't get out of there, it would all have been for nothing. And he would experience it again and again.

So she ran, flying through the tunnel, her mind working furiously. What now? Where should she go? The factory district would be swarming with guards as soon as the bodies were discovered. But if she ran for any of the gates leading to the other districts, the guards were sure to be awake by the time she got there and stop her. And that would be that.

She had the robes. She could hide under one and try exiting the district. But no one lived in the factory district. It would be horribly suspicious. And even if she made it through, as soon as the bodies were found, they would be on the lookout for someone in a robe.

So her options were to hang out in a guard infested district, go ahead and get caught now, or blow her only cover completely.

These weren't great options.

Jo ducked into a somewhat dark alley lined with human hides and looked behind her. A trail of blood followed her path. Time to fix that.

She pulled the robes out of the knapsack, laying them aside to keep them from getting any blood on them. Christopher had stopped bleeding for the most part, so she put him in the sack, swaying on her feet a bit as her stomach churned. *Stop it, Jo.* This was no time get sick.

Blood covered her body, so she grabbed some of the nearby skin and wiped off as fast as she could. She had a trail leading right to her. Time to go.

She looped her arms through the bag, holding it in front of her, before putting on a robe. It itched, but it hid her well. If she hunched over a bit, as she'd seen so many of the temple people do as they walked, it worked perfectly to hide him.

She looked at the second robe. If she left it here, it seemed likely they would then be looking for someone walking the pilgrimage path, and that was the last thing she needed. Could she wear it on top of her current robe? She tried it. Yes. Very difficult to move, but this was a disguise—she didn't intend to try running away in it. Still, if she needed to, that would prove extra challenging. But at least the extra bulk made her look more like a man.

She scurried back out of the alley, moving as quickly as possible beneath the heavy robes. The area was still clear, so she ran as fast as the robes allowed, trying to get far away from the trail of blood. She headed toward the gates leading to the tier five house and the lower class men. It was a busy, boisterous area with plenty of temple devotees coming and going, so she might have a better chance of blending in until she could figure out what to do.

"You opening today?"

Jo ducked into another alley, her heart hammering. The

guards at the gate were letting someone through.

"Yeah. I drew the short straw. Some fancy schmuck got himself fired yesterday, and I gotta go unlock him and get him processed."

"Damn. On Christmas? That's cold."

Jo had never heard the guards being chatty. But no one was around yet and this must be a familiar morning routine. One that was too short.

The gates opened, and Jo heard the sound of the man walking away. Toward the prison.

Her heart pounded so hard she could see the robe vibrating. No. No no no. It was too soon. She had to get out of here.

"Oh shit, here they come."

Jo flattened herself against the wall, desperate to risk a peek. But she didn't dare.

"Think any of them will burn this time?"

"Ha. I'll make the same bet I always make: if anyone burns with him, I'll eat my hat."

"That's gross, man."

They both laughed quietly before going completely silent. The thud of footsteps approached. Many footsteps.

She ducked further into the alley but froze as she caught sight of the cause.

Multiple hooded figures were walking in a procession, their heads down low. Her pulse raced. Could she join them? Would the guards see her come out of the alley? Would the group?

Her pulse raced as she crept near the alley entrance. She had to go for it. Any moment, the area would be on high alert.

She waited until the last person had passed and then walked quickly behind them, keeping her head down. Please please please don't let anyone have seen her. She didn't dare look behind her to check.

They marched in slow procession—far too slow—to the opposite side of the district and the gates leading to the entertainment district. This was a longer route to the temple, but she had heard the market district didn't like people being reminded what all their products were based on. So the pilgrims weren't allowed to walk their route through it.

They were at the gates. Walking through! Jo's legs trembled. What if she fell? *Keep it together!*

She heard a shrill whistle in the distance.

"Close the gates! No one goes in or out!"

Footsteps running.

No—she wasn't through yet!

"What about the hair suits?" one of the guards called out.

Muffled sounds.

"Get them out of here and lock the gates behind them! Then get over here—we need all available guards!"

Relief almost buckled her knees. Christopher had been right. The population really was intellectually stunted.

The gates closed behind her, and she entered the entertainment district.

What now? What was her plan? She didn't have one other than to hide as long as possible.

That's a bad plan, Jo. Because they will *catch you eventually.*

So what could she do? The exit to the desert was on the opposite side of the city completely. And if she kept following the pilgrims, she was going to end up right back in the temple district, and who knew how long Adam's ropes would hold? She needed to stay as far from him as possible. It couldn't look like he had any part in this.

She needed a way out. Christopher seemed to think there weren't any ways out that she would be able to use. So how could she possibly find a way he had missed? He was a strategist. He worked with systems, manipulating moving parts in order to achieve some goal. She could never hope to see the things he saw and use them the way he could. But...he never would have used her to save himself. That was his limitation.

What skills did she have that she could use? She was an *Insomnolent*. But that skill had likely run its course unless…could she somehow make it until the sun came up again? Her heart skipped a beat. She could hide out in the temple. All day. Would the guards ever think to search it? Would they even dare? Superstition ran deep here, as well as awe for the Ancient who led the services and who knew this world better than anyone.

Her pulse raced, this time with excitement. This was a plan. This was a plan that could work! And hopefully being in the temple would hide her from Adam as well.

She smiled under her robes, for the first time feeling a measure of hope. And followed the procession to the temple.

———

They were among the first to walk inside.

Jo tried to look around without uncovering her face. She didn't know if she'd gotten all the blood off, but she knew her lower lip was swollen and torn from all the biting she'd done during the sleep. Plus, she didn't know if women were even permitted in here. They certainly would't be if unaccompanied. So she kept her head down and just scanned her eyes around the little bit she could see.

The temple interior stretched out in an enormous open semicircle around a marbled center dome with a large hole in the ceiling. Jo had difficulty seeing over the people in front of her but caught glimpses of a kneeling figure crouched low in the center. A long platform extended behind him, many feet above the ground and much smaller than the one she'd been on at the concert. That must be for the Ancients.

The group she was with blended with another as they made their way to the front. That was good. It would put her close to the center of the temple, as far from the exits—and the guards—as possible.

The people in front of her stopped and got to their knees, keeping enough space in front of them to bow. Jo frowned as she lowered herself to her knees as well. She had Christopher in her lap. She didn't want to add to his pain by crushing him. But she couldn't afford to be conspicuous.

She bowed low but put a hand inside her cloak, trying to protect him as much as possible, and peeked out. They weren't getting back up. Great. How long would they need to stay this way?

The kneeling figure in the center finally rose, and she ducked her head again as he walked to the side to put on a robe.

"Welcome everyone." His voice rang out through the great room, warm and pleasant, with a surprising note of good cheer. The people around her sat back up, and she joined them, keeping her face hidden beneath her robes. "Do we have anyone new here today? My name is Peter and as I'm sure you've heard, I've been around a while. I'm here to answer any questions I can."

Jo cowered a bit lower, her eyes shifting from side to side as random hands were raised. She sat very still as Peter's eyes scanned the room. Were they lingering on her? She breathed a sigh of relief as he called on someone a ways behind her.

"Are we in Hell?"

A few people in the room groaned and Peter quieted them.

"Now, every single one of us has had this question. And maybe some still have it after hearing my answer. Because I'm afraid I don't know." This met with sighs of disappointment, and he held up his hand. "I know, I know. You want firm answers, and I wish I could give them."

Jo was interested in this, very interested, but she had things to do. She looked around the room, keeping her head down, trying to figure out what she could do once the sleep hit.

"But I do have some theories based on the things I've seen. And no, I don't believe this is Hell."

Peter should be burning in the center of the temple once everyone was asleep, if the tales she heard were true. And based on his appearance this morning, with his unblemished naked body and short hair, she believed the tales.

"I have a few memories from our past, and one is this: every doctrine of Hell I recall strictly tied fire to punishment. But there was another place of fire that was thought to be purifying. A place where you could achieve atonement. That is what I believe this place to be."

She could possibly burn Christopher beside him and maybe pull him out quickly so he wouldn't need to burn long. She would need to use something to grab him because she remembered what had happened to her hand last time when the sun caught it. The light needed to hit the brain to regenerate the body.

"But you've burned a lot, right? How much do we have to suffer before we get out?"

Peter rubbed his brow as Jo's eyes scanned the area for something to use to pull Christopher out of the sun.

"I don't know. I do know that it gets easier. I don't find it very painful anymore. Perhaps when the pain goes away completely, then it is enough."

But if she burned Christopher tonight, she would need to drag his body around with her as she tried to get them out. She released a small breath of frustration, and Peter looked over at her.

She dropped her head immediately, her heart thundering. Had he heard her? How? The people around her hadn't twitched. She kept her head down, her heart beating hard against her chest, until Peter continued calling on people to answer their questions.

She released her breath slowly, quietly, and peeked up again. Okay, he wasn't staring her way anymore. She looked up further, indecision returning as she stared at the tunnel through the ceiling. Should she burn him or not?

She froze. Tunnel. Tunnel tunnel tunnel. Her heart raced, and she dug her fingers into her knees as she stared hard at the little she could see of its interior. The edges inside were jagged with pieces of stone jutting out intermittently. Did it go all the way up like that? Was there anything blocking the top? A grate of any sort? She needed to see!

Peter looked over at her, and she yanked her head down with a silent cry of frustration. Had he seen her face as she was staring up at the ceiling?

"What do you know about the *Insomnolent?*"

Jo went cold inside.

Peter didn't answer immediately, but she didn't dare look up again.

"That's what this city calls the ones who can resist the sleep?" His tone was cautious.

"Yeah," said a voice from the back of the room. "The guards blocked off the usual path because someone walked in the sleep last night!"

Whispers flew around the room.

Peter was silent a long time. When he spoke at last, his voice was somber. Almost sad.

"I knew a man once who could do that. He was…unusually kind."

Jo's eyes darted up in surprise, but she lowered them again quickly.

"The city he lived in had him drawn and quartered and buried him deep in the ground. That was centuries ago. I haven't been able to convince them to free him. People are afraid of them, but I don't believe there is any reason to fear."

"No reason?" Another voice from the back. "I heard she cut off the guards' heads!"

Gasps around the room.

"She?" Peter's voice sounded shocked, and his eyes went back to her again. Jo started to panic. Had he seen her face?

Why did he keep looking at her! The director's office had probably been called in as soon as the guards were discovered. It wouldn't have taken him long to figure out she was the one to break in.

Jo heard *devil* and *succubus* flying around the room, and she pulled her arms inside her robes. If she was going to have to run, she wouldn't be able to do it in these. She reached up to the neck, ready to push the cloaks apart and dart out from under them.

Peter turned back to the man who had just spoken.

"Where were these guards?"

The man didn't know, and murmurs went around the room until someone in front of her spoke.

"I bet they were in the prison." The men around her nodded. "We came through the factory district, and the guards at both gates were fine. But they must have just discovered something while we were there because they locked the gates behind us."

The blood drained from her face. There was no mistaking it now. His eyes were locked on her. Her grip tightened on the edges of her robes.

He finally turned and walked to the side, a fist to his lips and a deep line between his brow.

He stood silent and still. At last he turned again.

"Wasn't someone supposed to be added to your...resources today?"

The room grew restless.

Noise. People talking over each other. Finally someone called out excitedly.

"I know who it was! It was one of the guys who bought that tier one with the scar!"

Peter stilled.

"The girl beaten in the park."

"Yes! Holy shit—do you think it was her? I was at the concert the day she told those ancient schmucks just what she thought!"

Peter glanced up behind him, and the room went completely

quiet as all eyes followed his to look at the platform that stretched overhead. Empty.

A collective sigh of relief went around the room.

"Present company excluded!" someone else called out, and humor touched his eyes for a moment.

"I'm an even more ancient schmuck, I'm afraid. But be careful." His eyes became serious again. "They don't attend often, but they sneak up the stairs quietly sometimes."

Jo glanced toward the platform and noticed a doorway at the very end. She couldn't see the stairs from where she was—maybe the Ancients entered from the outside so they wouldn't have to worry about mingling with peasants.

Peter didn't look at her again but instead engaged with the people in the room. They talked on about her for a bit longer before branching out into other topics.

Had he figured out it was her? She saw intelligence in his eyes. Different from Christopher's piercing sight but shrewd nonetheless. But there was more there. She saw...kindness. He didn't wear human skin. He burned every day. He had spoken well of an *Insomnolent* and seemed to look out for the welfare of the men attending. Maybe she really would be safe in the temple until the sleep hit again!

She relaxed her grip on the robes and dropped her hands to stroke Christopher's head under her cloak, hoping it might offer him at least a little comfort. *Just a few more hours.* Well, a lot of hours. The days were really long. She settled more comfortably on her knees for the long day of waiting.

Once the questions ended, Peter began his sermon. Except it wasn't a sermon. He told story after story from his experiences on the planet—about the area, the other cities, what everything was like, what the people were like. He didn't lecture. He just told stories. Funny stories. Sad stories. Tales that made you want to rush out and rescue someone who had been wronged or cheer for someone who had done something brave.

Jo found herself utterly lost as the hours flew by. She could have listened forever. A thousand years of tales seen through the eyes of someone wise enough to appreciate them. This is what the Ancients should have been. This is what a person could follow to the end of time. Strength. Compassion. Courage. Everything she wanted to be. And failed at so much.

Tears stung her eyes. She couldn't fail this time.

She looked back at the tunnel in the ceiling. If it really were possible to climb out that way, how could they reach it? Multiple metal chandeliers surrounded the entrance. If they could reach those in the morning, they could climb up the chains and grab the inside of the tunnel. The jagged edges were just deep enough for their fingertips to latch onto. She was strong in this world. Her grip would hold. She knew it would. And once they got high enough to get a hold with their feet, it would be easy to make it the rest of the way. To get out of this place forever.

Would Peter be able to move immediately in the morning? Would he try to stop them? She couldn't believe that he would at this point. Not after listening to him all day.

So her only dilemma was how to make it to the chandeliers. And that was quite a dilemma. She couldn't think of a ladder she'd seen that was this tall. Could they put together a makeshift ladder quickly? Or...maybe they could throw a rope up! Probably not from the ground. It was too high above them. But maybe...from the Ancient's platform?

She studied it, beginning to get excited. That could work! They would just need something to latch on or a long enough rope to maybe have Christopher pull her up with one end and then she could tie the other to the chandelier! She could get the rope tonight after pulling Christopher out of the fire. It would only take them a couple minutes in the morning to get into the tunnel. They would have time.

Adam. They would have time. She could get Adam! Maybe they could run and drag him together. It might scratch up his back, but they could probably get there and back in five minutes if they ran immediately when they woke up. And by the time she fastened the rope, Adam would be able to move again—they could all get out!

Although if there were a grate at the top of the tunnel... No. There wasn't! The red moon must be high in the sky now because it cast a large red circle on the ground beneath the tunnel. A clean, clear circle without any shadows!

She bit her lip to stop herself from laughing and crying with relief but promptly flinched from the pain. Oops. Swollen lip. She sighed with a smile instead, and settled into Peter's latest tale. There was no grate. And she knew just where to find a long enough rope.

She ignored the little niggling doubt clawing at her mind about whether Adam would want to go with them...would be willing to burn every day... She swallowed. No. He had to go. He *had* to. She had found a way for all of them, and he was just going to have to take it. Besides, Peter said it got less painful in time. They could do it.

A commotion behind her made her want to turn around, but she resisted. She was at the finish line. She would not risk exposing herself now. She kept her eyes on Peter.

He continued speaking, but his eyes had grown sharp as he looked toward the back. Alert. He glanced at her but kept telling his latest tale. Her pulse raced. What was happening?

"I see the guards have decided to join us today." Peter's voice was friendly as it rang out. The blood drained from Jo's face. "We are always happy to welcome the hardworking men of the city."

Murmurs and grumbles went through the crowd.

"Perhaps someone would like to join me for once? Begin the process of atonement—I promise it does get easier. I'd like everyone to bow their heads for a moment, and if anyone feels the call, please join me in the circle."

He gestured toward the fading red glow—the moon must be

setting—with a smile. But his eyes locked on hers. Serious. Urgent.

She heard the jostling around her getting closer.

She swallowed and got to her feet, ignoring the startled sounds around her as she quickly stepped between the men in front of her. She kept her cloaks tight around her and her head deep within their folds as she moved past the front line of figures seated perhaps ten feet away from the red circle on the floor.

Peter welcomed her with happy surprise in his voice but a warning in his eyes. She stood in the circle and started to turn, but his voice stopped her.

"Kneel in prayer, my son." He said the words loudly. "We wear our robes until just before the cleansing fires burn away our sins."

"There are about twenty guards that have filled the room and more are still coming in, removing people's hoods." His voice was low beside her as he turned his back on the crowd. "I'll try to keep them from coming up here for as long as possible, but if you have a plan, now would be the time to make it happen."

Jo sank to her knees under the disappearing red glow as her strength gave out. The commotion in the crowd behind her continued to grow. Tears choked her. She had been so close. She'd only needed a few hours more. She'd had a plan. A good plan. It would have worked.

But the one ability she had that might have saved them was useless now.

———

Jo fought against the panic overtaking her. She had no time for that. *Think!* There must be another way! She could hear the room behind her filling with more and more guards. The longer she waited, the more difficult it would become. It might already be too late.

No. She refused to think that way. There was a way out. Her body could move so fast here. And while everyone else could as well, she would be naked. Unencumbered. While the people had robes on and the guards had armor. Could she outmaneuver them? Where could she run though? The only way out was high above her. And she had no rope and no time to use one even if one were available.

She stared at the empty platform in front of her. Her heart skipped a beat. She could move fast here. Yes. And she could *jump*. She could jump a very long way.

Her eyes lifted to the iron chandelier closest to the platform. How far away was it? Would that even be possible? Her heart hammered against her chest painfully. It had to be possible. It just had to. But she would need to be going as fast as she possibly could off that platform to have any hope of reaching the chandelier. And then she would need to hang on. Because the momentum was going to try to jerk her body right back off. Hard.

How could she get to the platform?

Then she saw it. The banner hanging on the wall.

She could see guards beginning to close in on the sides of the domed area. It wouldn't be long now before they dominated the space completely—and she wouldn't be able to run anywhere for long.

Peter was standing in front of her, facing the crowd as he spoke, and she lifted her eyes to his. She needed him to move. Her arms crept beneath her robes and removed the satchel as she sat upright, repositioning it on her back and making sure it was carefully secured. She must look like a hunchback now. Odd. Suspicious. She needed him to move *now*.

His eyes fell to her at last and she inclined her head to the side.

He blinked. And walked away, his speech never faltering.

Jo watched the guards in her view out of the corner of her

eyes. Waiting. *Just turn away.* She just needed a moment where they weren't watching. Just enough to give her a chance.

Because once she moved, all hell was going to break loose.

Here we go.

She crouched low…and bolted out of her position at the same moment she threw off her cloak, her bruised, bloody body flying toward the wall. Even Peter stumbled back from her, his surprise seemingly genuine, as shouts erupted all around. She could see the guards turn and begin to run towards her, stumbling over the people around them.

Then the banner was in her hands and she was climbing faster than she ever imagined she could. Faster. *Go.*

She reached the edge of the platform and pulled herself up, her muscles straining with everything in her as she vaulted over the edge…and ran toward the door.

Guards were coming up the stairs. She could hear them. She had to reach that door. She needed every single bit of space to get a running start or she would never make it.

The guards were at the top of the stairs. About to reach the open doorway. She pushed herself forward, the tears stinging her eyes. She had to get there first!

She made it seconds before they did and grabbed the wall, the jolt reverberating through her bones as she jerked herself to a halt and turned in one movement, using her grip on the wall around the door to propel her back down the platform with all the strength she possessed just as their hands reached for her.

But they were in armor. And she was faster. And she ran, the end of the platform approaching all too soon. Not enough power. Not enough speed. *No.* It was enough. *It was everything she had.* **It. Was. Enough.**

Faster. There was nothing else. Fly over the stones. Don't slip. Focus on the chandelier. Closer and closer. Hit the ground perfectly. She couldn't afford a mistake. There was no time to think. No time to count steps. There was no time.

The end of the platform was right in front of her, and the chandelier seemed a thousand miles away. Impossible. Why did she think this was possible?

Because nothing else was acceptable.

Her foot hit the last tile to shove herself with her final thrust from the low railing and then she was flying through the air, her hands outstretched, her body a spear, her eye never leaving the chandelier. She would only get one chance. One chance to hold on to everything. This was it. This was forever.

Her fingers touched metal and she closed them around it with all her might as her momentum whipped her forward so hard she thought her shoulders might have been dislocated. But she held on.

Ignore the pain. *Climb!*

Her hands flew, one above the other, as a sword flew by her.

The violent sway of the chandelier must have confused their aim or she would have been pierced. No one missed where they aimed in this place.

A scream sounded out. The sword must have hit somewhere.

She stretched her hands out to the tunnel edge, her stomach plummeting. It was farther than she'd realized. She swung the chandelier. Harder. Reaching...she had it!

She let the fixture slip from her grasp as she clung to the rock, the world dropping out from under her. Hold on. Her shoulder screamed at her but she swung her body just enough to reach another jagged piece with her other hand. Her cut hand. Ignore the pain. Climb!

Back and forth, faster, faster. One piece after another, a bit higher. A bit more! A sword sliced her leg. Another scream below. Up up up!

And she was inside the hole, her feet helping now. The tunnel was too long! She was too far down! The guards wouldn't miss her now if they stood directly beneath. She wasn't swaying anymore. She couldn't.

No crying. Go! Just go!

But she was crying. Desperate tears choked her as she grabbed for every ledge, every moment expecting to be impaled. To be unable to go on.

A sword flew by her. It missed. Another. Blood spilled from her arm but she could still climb.

Shouts below her. The clang of metal. It went on and on as she climbed.

The edge was right above her. She was so close! Please please please let her make this!

And then her fingers met the surface and she was pulling herself out, pulling her body over and away from any more risk of falling. She felt her back. Christopher was safe.

Her heart shook her body, and she risked a small peek over the edge—nothing that would risk her falling back in.

Peter had done what he could. And it was quite a lot. Multiple bodies of guards surrounded him. She pressed the back of her hand to her lips, the tears breaking hard now.

Suddenly the remaining guards seemed to lose interest, and he relaxed. And looked up.

"They're coming for you from the city entrance," he shouted. "Head that way—" he pointed, "and just keep going straight."

She looked down in teary eyed gratitude, a small smile touching her lips. He nodded. And she turned, flying as fast as her feet would take her in the direction he'd indicated.

She couldn't see. Tears blocked her vision but she kept going. Away from the city. Away from Adam. She hadn't been able to get him. She hadn't been enough.

She ran and ran and ran until she heard shouts behind her. She didn't look. She just ran. Until she saw glowing sand again. Until the dark sand was far behind her. Until the sun had almost cleared the horizon. And for the first time since she'd been in this awful place, she was desperately happy to see it.

And the flames tore through her body.

19

MOON DAY 366

"You did it," Christopher whispered above her the moment the sun went down.

She was stretched out on her stomach, her hands above her, and his fingers curled into hers as he kissed the back of her neck, her shoulder, her back, his free hand running down her skin. Warm. Whole.

She turned over with a cry, capturing his face between her hands. His eyes were wet and his lips slightly parted as he stared down at her.

Tears streamed down her cheeks as she pulled him to her, hiding her face in his neck and wrapping herself around him. He groaned into her, his body hardening, as he kissed her neck, her cheek...

He leaned up above her, shaking, his eyes on her lips...before lowering his head slowly.

Jo's breath caught in her throat as his lips touched hers, and her lashes started to flutter closed before flying back open.

"Stop!" She grabbed his shoulders and pushed him off.

Confusion filled his eyes, but he turned his head to follow her gaze as she sat up looking around franticly.

The guards were lying on the ground perhaps a mile away.

She and Christopher stood immediately.

"Come on." He was steady again as he pulled her away. In control once more.

"Wait!" He stopped short at her cry, his eyes on hers.

Peter had told her which way to go. If the guards hadn't followed, she never would have been able to figure out the direction she'd been going once the sun had burned her. But now she knew!

"We need to go this way," she breathed, tugging on him as one of the guards began moving. He squeezed her hand—and followed.

They raced across the sands. Jo ran as fast as she could, and Christopher kept pace beside her. They didn't look back. The guards wouldn't be wearing any armor now. Jo's legs were long but shorter than the men's—and less muscled. She would be slower.

Why were they following her if they had to burn? Would they be punished if they returned without them? Turned into resources? The guards had always been particularly obedient. How long would they chase them?

The moon rose high in the sky, and Jo began to hear the sounds of feet hitting the sand in the distance, above the sound of their own. Still following. What could they do? She glanced at Christopher, and the concern in his eyes only made her fear increase.

They raced on and on until the moon had set once more. The sounds grew. Louder.

Jo's brow pulled together. That didn't sound like feet. And it didn't sound…behind her. Was that dark sand?

They flew forward as the sound grew until the roaring was

unmistakable. Until the darkness approaching could no longer be denied.

A giant wall of sand was barreling towards them.

Jo stopped, her breath coming in shallow gasps as her hand reached for Christopher's, their fingers lacing together. Had Peter known about this? They glanced behind them. The guards had gained on them but were still half a mile away. They must have seen the storm because it looked like most of them were turning back! Most...but not all.

They looked at each other, and the helplessness Jo felt was reflected in Christopher's eyes. The roaring grew louder. The wall was almost upon them.

"Hold on to me!" he yelled, pulling her close and crushing her to him as he laid them on the ground, his body on top of hers. "Wrap your legs around me and *do not let go!*"

Their bodies were already shaking before the ground began shaking beneath them. Jo gripped him as tightly as she could, her arms around his neck and legs around his waist as the sands began flying around them. They buried their faces in each others' necks.

Their hearts pounded together as the winds grew stronger, the sand beginning to rip at their skin. Stronger. It lashed at them, over and over, cutting ever more deeply.

And still the storm grew.

Jo's breath left her as the wind pulled them up for just a moment. Again. No! It would pull them apart!

She gripped him harder just as another gust captured them... and this time carried them into the swirling vortex, spinning them and grinding away at their flesh until Jo feared she would no longer have the muscle to hold him.

Hold on. She had to hold on.

Every part of her was being torn apart. But Christopher's arms around her remained. And she held on.

On and on it went, shredding them before finally throwing them back to the ground, breaking them—but not apart.

They lay silent until the sun hit once more, and they burned together.

———

Jo awoke on Christopher's chest in the glowing sand, and she sat up quickly, straddling him. Her eyes scanned the horizon, her body twisting around, making sure. Relief made her limp, and she placed her hands on his chest to hold herself up. No guards!

But what was that? Her eyes narrowed on the large, dark area that loomed in the distance. Was that a mountain?

She turned her gaze back to Christopher, about to mention it, and her breath caught in her throat.

His eyes roamed her body…soft…pained. He leaned up, his hands slipping warmly up her thighs, and captured her nipple between his lips, sucking softly and pressing her down into him.

She moaned as her head fell forward, sliding her hands up his chest and moving her hips against him.

His tongue trailed up to her collarbone, up her neck, his lips brushing softly across her skin. The warmth of his breath sent shivers through her, and a small sound escaped her throat.

Sliding his hands up to cup her face gently, he pulled her forehead to his.

"You saved me, Jo," he whispered, his thumbs stroking her cheeks. "You came for me. And you saved me. I didn't think there was any chance…"

He lifted her head and ran tortured eyes over her face. She swallowed, unable to look away.

"I can't remember much, but I know I've been alone a long time. Maybe always. And I know I never wanted to depend on anyone else. For anything. But I…"

His thumb stroked her lower lip, his eyes torn between watching and looking in her eyes. "I need you." His voice was hoarse. Strained. "I can't remember ever needing anything. But I need you."

"I need your smile." He moved his thumb and kissed her lips lightly. "Your laughter."

"I need your courage." He pressed his lips to hers again. Longer. "Your strength," he whispered against them.

His tongue crept between her lips, just touching hers. She couldn't move. She couldn't breathe.

"I need your softness..." His lips moved on hers as he murmured the words, his tongue teasing hers, and she moaned, leaning into him.

"I need your heart, Jo...I need it." His voice grew hoarse again, and he touched his lips to hers as he whispered his next words. "Because you have mine."

Jo looked into his eyes, her own breaking, and she brought her hand up to his cheek, stroking him as she took a shuddering breath.

"I've been trying to get close to you for so long," she whispered. He moved his hands to her back and pulled her closer, his lips capturing hers. She pulled back again, threading her fingers in his curls and resting her forehead on his. "I was so scared...anything could have gone wrong. Everything was going wrong."

Tears choked her, and she closed her eyes, threading her fingers more deeply into his hair as she brushed her skin back and forth on his, feeling him.

"Kiss me, Jo," he whispered, a slight tremor going through him. "I don't want to be apart from you anymore. Never again. Kiss me..."

She opened her eyes. He was looking up at her, suffering. Desperate. She blinked, her breath catching. And then she leaned down, pressing her lips against his fully as they sank into each other, their groans blending as their tongues reached for one another at last.

Christopher brought a hand up to cup the back of her head, exploring her mouth as he rocked up into her, pressing her hips against his. Her arms wrapped around his neck, deepening the kiss, needing to be closer. Needing him to be part of her.

She reached between them and lifted herself up slightly on her knees. His moan was almost a cry as she wrapped her hand around him, positioning herself…and slowly lowered her body.

He pulled her lips back to his, sucking her tongue deeply into his mouth, his brows drawn together as she slid down. The stinging between her legs drew a whimper from her, and he grabbed her hips, holding her in place and breathing into her, breathing her in.

"Don't stop," she whispered against his lips. His moan was pained but he relaxed his grip and she slid down more fully, the pressure pulling a gasp from her as her barrier stretched. He gripped her again, and she groaned…and pushed herself down on him, driving him into her. Breaking her. And burying him deep inside as they both cried out.

She shuddered over him, and he wrapped an arm around her hips, rocking her back and forth softly, locking them together. He held her head to him, his tongue deep in her mouth.

They barely moved, their hips grinding in to one another, trying to get closer. Clinging. Pressing into each other. They weren't close enough. They could never be close enough. Rocking over and over, the pressure building, until it was too much and Jo gasped against him, her body shattering and pulling her over as he drove up into her with a final thrust, shuddering beneath her violently.

They trembled together in the sand, their lips just touching, sharing the same air. Jo opened her eyes to find Christopher watching. Taking her in.

And then their eyes closed once more as they sank into each other again and again.

———

Jo lay on Christopher's chest, her knees on either side of him as he stroked her back, one arm behind his head.

"Was it horribly painful the whole time?" she asked in a small voice.

His knuckles skimmed her shoulder.

"No. I pulled my thoughts away and really didn't notice anything. What happened?"

She groaned but kissed his chest, grateful he had such mental control.

"God, that question is too big...I promise I will tell you. But...later."

He hugged her to him, and she sighed.

The red moon glowed above as Christopher continued stroking her back.

"He'll think I just left him there," she whispered. "That I didn't even try. But I did. I tried so hard," she choked. "I wanted to save us all."

He kissed her forehead.

"We'll go back for him, Jo. What you did was impossible. No time to plan. No help. But now we have all the time we need. We'll figure it out."

She leaned up, hope beginning to blossom.

"How will we figure out where it is?"

He smiled up at her, his eyes crinkling.

"I have no idea. But we will."

She stared down at him, a bit breathless.

"We will."

It was a promise.

"Oh!" Her eyes brightened, and she sat up suddenly, drawing a groan from him. He was still inside her. "There's a mountain!"

She looked down to find his eyes roaming over her body as he hardened again.

"Are you listening?" she laughed, trying to lift herself off of him.

He moved quickly, wrapping his arm around her and flipping her beneath him, keeping them together.

"Yes," he whispered, moving to kiss her. "A mountain."

"A mountain *here*! Or," she looked around and waved her hand toward the area she had seen it. She couldn't see it lying down. "There!"

"Later," he murmured, taking a nipple between his lips and pulling a frustrated moan from her.

Then she wrapped her legs around him, and it was quite a bit later before they got to their feet.

They brushed the sand off as they stood, smiling at each other happily. She shouldn't be this happy. He caught her hand, kissing the back as they set off toward the dark mass in the distance.

A strange rushing sound began to grow as they walked. Jo hadn't heard anything like it during their time in that world, so she didn't recognize it at first. Then her eyes widened, and she looked over at Christopher.

He was looking toward the sound with bright, unguarded curiosity. She hadn't seen that look before. It mesmerized her.

"I thought you wanted to see the mountain?" He turned to her as she stopped, his eyes still bright but with something else.

"I do," she breathed, looking up at him as he wrapped his arms around her. "But I want to see this, too."

Her heart skipped as they stared at each other.

"You trust me," she breathed.

He nodded, his eyes growing serious.

"I do."

She continued staring.

"I thought I was the one who needed to trust you."

Pain flashed in his eyes, and he hesitated. But she pressed her lips to his softly before he could speak.

"I do trust you," she whispered. "And that doesn't make me stupid."

Her eyes were vulnerable as she looked up at him, and he groaned as he dropped his head to hers.

"No," he said, his voice hoarse. "It makes me stupid. For not being worthy of it."

She frowned at him.

"Would you hurt me?"

His eyes darkened.

"*Never*."

She searched his face.

"But you still think I'm wrong to trust you?"

He groaned helplessly.

"You're not wrong. You're beautiful. And good. And...I've learned from you, Jo," he whispered, looking into her eyes. His hand stroked her cheek tenderly. "I'm not the same as I was."

He kissed her lips, his touch soft.

"I would do anything for you. Forever." He looked down at her, his voice husky. "You can trust me."

A smile stretched across her face.

"Okay."

And she leaned up to kiss him until the sadness left his eyes again and he was pulling her down into the sand.

"Wait! We have to go investigate before the sun comes up!"

She pulled at him as he groaned again and ran a hand through his curls. She smiled in delight as they scattered over his brow.

"Have I ever told you how much I love your hair?"

He kissed the back of her hand, and raised his brow a bit at her. But he let her pull him forward until they reached the mountain and found the source of the rushing sound.

It wasn't really a mountain. It was more like a giant stone hill…with a waterfall.

They looked at each other before kneeling down to look at the pool that had formed.

"Acid?" she asked, but more to stave off the sheer force of the optimism that had engulfed her. Everything felt beautiful and perfect right now.

Christopher reached in before she could stop him. And splashed her.

"Not acid."

He grinned at her as her lips parted and hopped in before she could retaliate, pulling her with him.

Her arms went around his shoulders as her breath left her lungs from the shock of the sensation. It wasn't cold. But they hadn't seen liquid in any significant quantity since they'd arrived. Bathing consisted of nothing more than wiping off anything that had happened to get on their skin. There was no decay, so nothing ever got dirty in any real way.

The water went up to their waists, to their chests, as Christopher pulled her in deeper, closer to the fall. She supposed they were both being a bit insane. Anything could be in the water. They hadn't even checked. But she didn't believe it was dangerous any more than he did.

Wrapping her body around him, she let him walk them both to the fall. A light glow seemed to be coming from behind it, and they looked at each other.

"Ready?" He looked so young, and her heart turned over. She nodded happily. And he walked them underneath the falling water.

They both blinked and stared in silence once they emerged on the other side, their arms wrapped around each other tightly.

Surrounding them on every side in the small cavern, over every surface above the water, grew glowing plants.

They looked at each other for just a moment before Christopher lifted her with an arm beneath her legs and pushed through the water. Then he finally got a little cautious again and pushed her behind him as he looked down at one of the plants.

She tried peeking around his shoulder, but he held her back.

"Will you let me see?" She pinched him lightly, but he grabbed her hands, locking her in position, and wrapped them around his waist.

"Hush. This could be dangerous."

"Holding me like *this* could be dangerous," she said, lowering her hands between his legs, and he laughed as he turned, pulling her close.

If they hadn't been so wrapped up in each other, they wouldn't have taken so long to notice the dark form under the waterfall, watching them.

———

Jo froze, her stomach turning over, at the sight of the large figure standing in the water, the fall above cascading over his head and scattering droplets all around. Then she was moving so quickly the water shoved her back, fighting to make it through until she could throw her arms around him, crushing his large form with her small one.

He didn't move but stood wooden in her arms.

She looked up, relaxing her grip slightly.

"Adam?" she whispered.

He stared down at her, his eyes blank.

She stroked his cheek.

"Baby, what's wrong?" she asked, searching his face, his body, her brow drawn together. A tremor crept into her voice when he didn't respond. "Adam? Talk to me."

He blinked.

She pulled his arms, trying to move him further into the cavern and out from under the fall, but he wouldn't budge.

He just kept staring down at her.

"You always leave me."

Toneless. Empty.

Her stomach flipped again, and she shook her head, her eyes wide.

"No...I wanted to get you," she breathed. "But the guards kept coming."

He just kept staring.

"I know," he said. Flat. "I was with them."

She blinked, and her lips parted.

"You were...helping them?"

Anger flickered in his eyes. The first sign of life.

"No. I convinced the director it would be in his best interest if I disappeared on the surface, looking for you with the guards. They turned around at the storm. I didn't." His words lashed at her, and she swallowed.

"We didn't know that was you," she whispered.

"We." Fury filled his eyes.

Her breath caught. For a moment. Then she narrowed her eyes, beginning to burn with her own anger, and stepped back.

"Did you think I would leave him to be butchered?"

"I think you wouldn't leave him at all," he hissed.

"And why should I!" she yelled out. She was done feeling guilty. "I don't remember what you do! How do I even know you knew what I felt! Maybe *he's* the one I really loved!"

Whatever spark had flared in Adam's eyes before went out now, and she held the back of her hand to her mouth.

"I didn't mean that," she whispered, wrapping herself around him again. "I'm sorry. I didn't mean that."

"You did." He sounded tired. "Maybe you're right. I thought I knew you. Maybe I didn't."

No no no. This was wrong. Something was terribly wrong. Her eyes glistened as she tilted her head back to look at him, and she noticed the light behind them.

"Adam, come inside," she tugged at him, her voice scratchy.

"It's a little too crowded in here."

"The sun, Adam—it's coming up."

"So let it. Go back to playing together." A bitter note crept into his voice. "I'll see myself out."

He started to turn, and she wrapped her arms around him.

"Stop being so stubborn! We were coming back for you!"

"Yes, I could see you were very concerned," he snapped, undoing her hands.

"She's telling you the truth."

Adam froze at Christopher's quiet voice. He stopped pulling Jo's hands apart and turned slowly, his eyes narrowing.

"And what about you, Christopher. Have you been telling the truth?"

Christopher frowned.

"As much as I know."

"I doubt it. You always hold something back. Always."

"I've told Jo everything," he said softly. "Everything I know that matters."

Adam laughed, a humorless sound.

"It's the things you think don't matter that worry me."

Christopher's brow pulled together, but Jo was tugging on Adam more strongly now.

"Adam, the sun—please come inside. Please."

He turned back to her, pulling her hands apart once more and trying to push her away from him. She managed to duck under his arm and wrap hers around him yet again.

"This is stupid! You don't need to burn because you're angry with me!"

"It's not your concern," he bit out, struggling to undo her hands again.

"Christopher!" she called over her shoulder, a note of panic entering her voice as the light grew brighter.

He was beside her in an instant, pulling Adam hard enough to bring him through the fall completely. Adam shoved him away and turned back to trying to free himself from Jo's grasp. Christopher glanced at the light behind the waterfall and moved back in to grab Jo's waist.

"It's too late, Jo. If he wants to burn, let him. We need to get out of the water."

"No," she ground out, her legs going around Adam as she plastered herself to him. "I'm not moving."

Christopher hesitated, his arm still wrapped around her waist, while Adam furiously tried peeling her off of him. The light was growing.

Christopher glanced up once more before making a sound of frustration and wrapping his arms around Jo to hold Adam to her.

Jo looked up to see Adam glaring above her head.

"What the fuck are you doing."

"She says stay. You stay."

"Get her out of the pool, blondie," Adam said, gritting his teeth.

"If you don't want her boiling, then move yourself."

They glared at each other as Jo's heart pounded harder and harder. It was so light out now.

"I'm not letting go of you, Adam," she whispered up at him, her eyes wide.

He looked down at her, wounded fury carving his features in harsh lines.

Finally he looked away, dropping his hands.

"Fine. I'll get out."

When they didn't release him, he glared back at Christopher.

"I'm not going to dive for the exit! She'd just dive with me," he muttered, looking away again.

Christopher looked down at Jo, and she nodded, swallowing. She was pretty sure he wasn't faking.

Christopher relaxed his grip first and was just about to drop his hands, just about to step away, when the sunlight hit the water.

The current shot through them, rooting them where they stood, jolting them again and again, over and over, as wave after wave of memory crashed down on them. Colliding. Merging.

Hour after hour without end. A relentless storm dashing them against the rocks, breaking them into pieces only to suck them back into the tide and do it again and again.

And when the sun set at last, they fell apart, their bodies doubled over, gasping for air…before their faces lifted to look at one another. One in shock. One in horror. And one in cold, deadly hate.

20

ADAM

Stupid computer.

Adam clicked the return key furiously, trying to login, before standing up and walking away with his hands on his head. Fuck. He punched a key on the phone on his desk.

"David, send IT in here, will you? Thanks."

He exhaled and grabbed a ball off his bookshelf, tossing it up a few times before glancing over to Christopher's adjoining office. Still out. What the fuck was he up to today. Always late delivering his status report. Deliberately. If he'd wanted to be the CEO, he should have just said so when they put the company together instead of pissing Adam off every week trying to get information from him. Always playing everything so close to his vest.

Adam had been the one to insist on adjoining offices. They were located at the end of the hall upstairs, which meant they never had to worry about employees passing by their suite unless they called them in. But it also meant Adam got bored. He liked marching into Christopher's office and making random demands, seeing if he could get a rise out of him. It was good for blondie. He took things far too seriously. And was annoyingly calm.

A quiet knock sounded at the door and he frowned. Who the fuck knocked like that. Either bang on the goddamn door like you want in or go away. Probably a woman. A little mousy woman who was going to jump every time he barked at her and then HR would be lecturing him on some bullshit about equality. And lawsuits.

Fuck. He was probably going to have to be charming again.

He opened the door with a smooth smile just as the girl raised her fist again. She yanked it to her chest immediately.

Yep. Mousy as fuck.

"I'm here for your computer. To fix it."

Jesus, even her voice was small. She was staring up at him with wide blue-green eyes fringed in brown lashes. They would have looked huge on her face if she'd been wearing any makeup, but her skin was bare.

He stepped aside, forcing himself to smile until she passed. He left the door half open—HR wouldn't get him on this—and turned to follow her to his desk, his eyes drifting down her body. Jeans and a t-shirt. Nicely filled out at least. Everyday was casual Friday for IT. Not that he cared. He just wished they could manage to fix his computer for longer than a few days.

The girl stopped beside his computer and looked up at him. He raised a brow. Was she waiting for permission?

"Is it okay if I sit here while I work on it?"

Holy shit. She was. He crossed his arms and rubbed his forehead, nodding. She bit her lip slightly, hesitation in her eyes, and his cock twitched. He frowned.

A whisper of air floated to him as she sat down quickly and turned to the computer. Clean. No perfume. But somehow heady.

Adam rubbed the back of his neck as he walked to the other side of the room. He must be in a mood. But he turned back to study her more carefully while she worked.

She wasn't bad. Her long brown hair was pulled back in a

pony tail high on her head, making her look about twelve. Or twenty. But she had to have her Bachelors to be working in that role, so she was at least twenty two. How long had she been there? Why hadn't he seen her before?

"Where's the guy who normally fixes my computer?" he demanded. Her wide eyes flew to his and her lips parted. Shit. He forgot to be charming.

"He's out today. And everyone else was busy. So…sorry," she finished quietly, returning to her task.

He frowned again.

"How old are you?" Fuck charm. If HR was going to get on him again, he might as well do as he pleased.

She eyed him nervously.

"Twenty-nine."

His frown deepened. Not too much younger than he was. She could have been an undergrad when he and Christopher were getting their graduate degrees and working out the details of their then-to-be investment firm.

Her eyes were wary as she continued doing whatever she was doing on the computer, glancing at him on occasion as he stared at her. He probably couldn't get away with fucking her. She'd either get her feelings hurt or start thinking she could show up to work late and the next thing he knew, he'd have to offer some ridiculous severance package to get rid of her.

He sighed and started to turn away, but she suddenly pressed her lips together as she stared at the screen. And looked at him. It was so brief he almost missed it as she was back to her normal expression immediately. But he'd seen it.

She was laughing at him.

He narrowed his eyes and walked over to look at his computer.

"What?"

She glanced up, her eyes wide still. Innocent. But the corner of her mouth looked suspiciously tilted. He narrowed his gaze further and leaned back against his desk, facing her with his arms crossed.

She couldn't contain it anymore and her head dropped as she brought her fist up to her mouth. A small sound escaped her.

"How often do you have this problem?" she asked, keeping her head low while managing to peek up at him.

"Every few days. It's annoying. It would be nice if someone in your department could manage to fix it for longer than that."

She giggled. She fucking giggled.

"Well...it might help if you...maybe...bought a separate computer to use for...certain things."

She was pressing her lips together again as her eyes stared up at him in helpless merriment.

Shit. He was definitely going to fuck her.

He bit the inside of his cheek as he looked at her, his brows slightly raised, and she turned immediately back to the computer. Her fingers whisked out a few more keystrokes before she stood.

He frowned, and her eyes looked worried again. He didn't want her to go yet.

"Well...you shouldn't have any more problems logging in. For a few days."

He raised an amused brow at her, and she clamped her lips together again. Then she nodded and headed toward the door.

Fuck. What could he say that wouldn't get him in trouble?

"And just so you know," she swung back at the door, her hand on the door handle and her body slightly hidden between the door and the wall. "I won't say anything. I mean, I wouldn't spread rumors or anything."

He opened his mouth, but he couldn't think of anything to say except *what time do you get off work*. And that was too full of problems. Besides, Christopher had finally shown up. With his cappuccino or latte or whatever the fuck it was. He'd have to figure out this thing with the girl later.

One moment she was standing with her hand on the door,

and in the next, she'd slung it wide as she moved rapidly to exit. Spilling Christopher's drink all over him as he came through the doorway.

Adam caught Christopher's shock and her look of horror as she reached out for his arm with one hand and slipped the other in the gap between the buttons of his shirt to try pulling it away from his body, evidently hoping to stop it from burning him. She might as well have been his mother, apologizing over and over, soothing, touching him instinctively. Protectively.

Adam collapsed against his desk, his hand over his eyes, tears coming from their sides as his body shook in laughter at Christopher's silent outrage. He was glaring down in fury at the girl who seemed completely oblivious, her entire focus on trying to make sure he was unharmed. Until she finally looked up.

Adam didn't think he could laugh any harder. But when she jerked both her hands back to her chest in tight little fists, her expression horrified, it was all he could do to draw a breath to call out a question before she ran down the hall.

"Wait! Your name! What is it?" He was practically wheezing as he leaned out of the door. The girl swallowed nervously as she looked back and forth between him and Christopher, staring down the hall at her, his eyes burning.

"Josephine. Or...Jo." She shrugged, her eyes heavy with worry.

Then she scurried away before he could point out employees normally should give their last names as well. But how many Josephines could there be in IT? There couldn't be more than one like that.

He turned back to Christopher, grinning as he watched him stalk toward the restroom to clean up.

God, his cheeks hurt. And his cock.

This girl was going to get him into so much trouble.

———

"No, send the girl who was here before. Jo. Or Josephine. Does she go by Jo?"

Adam fiddled with his computer after he hung up the phone. It wasn't actually messed up this time. He'd tried, but clearly it would only stop working when he needed to accomplish something else.

He probably could have just looked at porn again, since that seemed to work well. But he had his eye on something else now, and he didn't want any distractions.

He unplugged it under the desk as Jo stepped into the open doorway.

Her face was pale. She wore her hair down today, tucking it behind her ears as it fell in loose waves almost to her waist. Jesus. He wanted that spread out around him.

He moved quickly so she could sit down, grabbing a chair nearby and pulling it over to sit beside her. To watch and learn, of course. She eyed him warily as she sat down, and his body responded immediately. What was it about her? Timid girls did not normally turn him on.

She fiddled with a couple things. And then went very still.

When her eyes turned to his, he blinked rapidly. They were a little too aware.

She reached under the desk and plugged in the computer before sitting back up to turn it on. Waiting.

He held his fist to his lips, watching her, but she didn't look over.

When the screen came up, she typed in a few keystrokes. A few more. And groaned, dropping her head forward into her hands. She turned towards him, opening her fingers just enough to see him.

"Did you do this on purpose?" Her voice was muffled.

Shit. Should he confess? He cocked his jaw.

"And if I did?"

She groaned harder until it turned into a whimper before

turning back to the screen, still staring between her fingers.

"Do you have any idea what you did? Do you know how many files you might have messed up?"

His gaze swept her body. God, she was cute.

"How many?" Uh oh. Too husky. He cleared his throat.

Her hands fell, and she sent him a sharp look.

"A lot!"

His cock definitely jumped that time. He pressed his knuckles against his lips harder as she glared at him.

"You can fix it though, right?"

"There are other people in the department with more expertise in this area. You should probably call them."

He almost snorted.

"No. Only you. You already know my secrets, and I don't want anyone else nosing around. Who knows what they might find?"

He tried to look innocent, but based on her narrowed gaze, he didn't think he'd succeeded.

But she got to work.

———

A few hours later, he thought she might be ready to quit. Other than a few calls he had to take, he'd been sitting beside her, looking over her shoulder and asking random questions. Why are you doing that? Is that an important file? What's your favorite food? What does file system corrupt mean? Are you single?

"Do you *want* me to fix this?" she finally asked in exasperation.

He tried looking contrite, but it didn't last long.

"Go out with me." Fuck it. He sucked at subtlety.

She turned horrified eyes to him, and he frowned at her. Not exactly flattering.

"*Why?*" She sounded as if it were the most ridiculous idea

she'd ever heard, and his frown deepened.

Because I want to fuck you.

Charm. Come on.

"Because you're a beautiful, intelligent woman."

She snorted and turned back to the computer. Dismissing him.

He cocked his jaw in irritation.

"Fine. Because I want to fuck you," he said, his eyes bright, taking some satisfaction in watching how quickly her eyes snapped back to his.

She blinked rapidly. But she didn't look away.

And he was suddenly painfully hard.

"What happens when you don't like me anymore?"

Her straightforwardness took him by surprise.

He stared at her, reassessing.

"We can talk to HR. Make sure there's no risk to your job."

She stared at him, and it seemed minutes stretched by. He needed to adjust himself, but he didn't want to move.

"Okay." And she turned back to the computer.

His lips parted. And he quickly moved his hand between his legs, shifting until he had some degree of comfort back. He saw her eyes glance down at him, but she didn't say anything. She just went back to typing.

It took him a few minutes more to realize that he had no idea what to do next.

He hesitated. And tried something new.

"I have no idea what to do next."

She looked over. Startled. And broke into a smile.

"Me neither."

He stared back at her, finding himself the one charmed for once.

Was it too soon to try something? He hesitated before slowly leaning forward. Watching her. She didn't move away so he reached cautiously for her chin and tilted it towards him. Waiting.

Giving her every chance to move. She just stared at him as he held her in his hand, her breathing shallow.

His lips hovered over hers for a moment as they looked at each other, before he captured them beneath his, still holding her gaze. He coaxed her lips apart, slipping just the tip of his tongue between them, hardening painfully as she met every touch, her eyes never leaving him.

Then she moaned, and he abandoned all restraint.

He buried a hand in her hair and pulled her body up in his arms as he stood, pressing her hips into his as he pushed his tongue deep inside her. Her arms wrapped around his neck, and she leaned her body into him fully. It wasn't enough.

He moved both hands to her waist quickly, sliding them under her shirt to unclasp her bra. Her eyes opened wide and he slowed, watching her, as he slid a hand under her bra and enveloped her breast with his palm. They paused with their tongues touching as his thumb caressed her nipple, their eyes locked on one another.

God, he wanted her. Now.

He was unbuttoning the top button of his pants when something slammed in Christopher's office. He tore his mouth from Jo's to see Christopher seated at his desk, glaring at him through the long glass wall between their offices. Shit. He was so quiet in there, Adam forgot about him sometimes.

He looked down at Jo and could have cried from the pain between his legs. It didn't look like he was going to find relief anytime soon. She had refastened her bra and sat back down, her face a deep shade of red.

Next time, he'd have to remember to close the blinds.

———

"Well, where is she? No, it's fine. Don't send anyone."

Adam pinched the bridge of his nose.

It had been almost three months since he and Jo had started having sex, and it had been working out really nicely for him. He didn't have to take her out but could just buy takeout and work late from the office. She'd fall asleep on his couch sometimes while he was on the phone, and he'd fuck her awake later. He'd gotten her prior consent first, of course.

He knew she'd be here waiting for him when he got back from a trip. He never had to worry about a jealous girlfriend being upset that he'd had dinner with women he needed to network with in the evenings.

She was always available when things got stressful at work and he needed a release. He didn't have to wait. She came every time he called.

She was the perfect fuck toy.

Until today.

He texted her again. Had she turned off read receipts?

She couldn't be mad about his latest trip. He'd explained the pics. It's not like he'd been sleeping with the woman. He hadn't even watched porn since he met Jo. Why the hell would she think he'd want some blonde bimbo one of his contacts had brought along, who seemed to feel the need to drape herself all over him each time she saw him? He couldn't think about anyone but Jo. He told her that yesterday. Well, something like that. How much more convenient it was being with her than being in any of the relationships he'd had the past few years.

So where the hell was she?

He got up and walked to open the blinds on the wall he shared with Christopher. Having them closed just pissed him off now.

He pulled the cord, absently looking through the glass, and froze. What the hell was she doing in there? He marched over to the door and shoved it open to find Jo at Christopher's desk, looking more pale than usual, as Christopher leaned against the wall, watching her.

They both jerked their heads toward him as he strode into the room.

"Where the hell have you been?"

Jo stared up at him, her hands shaking slightly.

"You're not the only one who uses our IT services," Christopher said frowning.

Adam scowled at him.

"Is there some reason you couldn't find someone else?"

Christopher narrowed his eyes.

"Is there some reason I should?"

"I got the account for us."

"And I will make all our money with it. What does that have to do with the IT girl."

"Jo, get in my office," he snapped, his eyes on Christopher. "Now."

Christopher looked over at her.

She swallowed.

"I have to finish this first."

Adam turned to walk toward her and scooped her out of her seat, ignoring her protests.

"No you don't."

He carried her through their shared doorway and closed it a little too hard behind him, yanking the cord again to close the blinds.

"Let me down, Adam." Her voice was quiet.

"You need to fucking talk to me." He glared down at her. "I've been trying to reach you all day. Don't even try to tell me you've been in there the whole time."

"Put me down. Now." He blinked at the venom in her tone. Wait. Was she really angry?

He set her down slowly, his eyes wary now as he watched her.

And she marched straight for his door.

He blocked her quickly.

"Wait—wait, Jo." He put his hands out, hoping to calm her, but she jerked back. Shit. She was mad. What had he done?

"What did I do, baby?"

"Don't call me that!" she snapped, her eyes flying to his.

Fuck. He needed to fix this.

"Please, Jo…just talk to me. Tell me what's going on."

She gripped her hands tightly at her sides, her body rigid, before taking a deep breath and flattening her palms against her thighs.

"I'm done. That's all. It was fun. Thanks for the sex. But I actually do have feelings. And…" Her eyes glistened, and she looked away. "And I don't want to do this anymore."

Shit. Shit shit shit.

He swallowed.

"Then…let's do something else." His voice shook, and he cleared it.

Her eyes kept filling with tears.

Fuck. What was he supposed to do?

"Jo, I…" He felt like the world was dropping out from under him. "I feel like the world is dropping out underneath me right now," he said hoarsely.

Her eyes jerked back to his in surprise. Then her brow pulled together.

"You told me I was convenient."

His lips parted. Closed. Parted again.

"I just meant…it was easy being with you."

"Well I'm tired of being easy!" she yelled, tears in her voice. She clenched her jaw and looked down a moment before lifting her eyes once more to glare at him.

"And the truth is, I *hate* being nothing more than a blow up doll for you to pull out and use whenever it's *convenient* for you! I *hate* having to listen to the shitty comments people make when I walk in or out of the room because I'm sleeping with the boss."

She drew in a shuddering breath but cut him off as he started to speak.

"And I *hate* being with someone who goes out with other women and can't even manage to tell someone to get the fuck off him when they are hanging all over him! And that's assuming you're not lying! You can do whatever you want, but you can't do it with me!"

Adam felt every word like a physical punch to his gut.

"I'm sorry," he breathed. "I've been…maybe…a little selfish."

She looked ready to explode.

"Okay okay! I've been very selfish! I'm sorry. Just…yell at me, Jo. But…don't go. Don't go…" He stepped closer with each word. Slowly. Carefully.

Her tears looked ready to spill over as his hands touched her arms at last, sliding around to pull her to his chest. And then she was crying against him, and he was stroking her back.

"I'm sorry," he whispered. "My dad always said my mom let me and my brother have our way too much. But he could never bear to go against her, so…I probably got a little spoiled."

"Probably!" her muffled outrage against his chest made him bite his tongue, trying not to laugh. He held her more tightly.

"I like you, Jo. I like being around you. Fucking or not. And I don't like sharing you. So I haven't wanted to take you around anyone else. I just wanted to keep you for me."

He sighed down into her hair.

"Come with me. I have another trip in a few days. Come with me."

She stilled.

"I have a job here."

"It's over the weekend. Come with me."

She groaned against him, shaking her head.

He kissed her cheek. Her neck.

"Come with me," he whispered. Teasing her skin. Coaxing her. "Say yes, Jo." His lips paused over hers, waiting for her answer. "Say yes, baby."

She groaned once more, a helpless sound. And nodded.

And then he was the one groaning as he captured her lips at last and spent the next little while trying to make things up to her.

————

"Well, you have to attend. It's the Christmas party. And you can't hide from every social engagement we have."

Adam was in Christopher's office, his arms crossed as he stared him down.

"It's a waste of time." Christopher leaned against his desk, his hands in his pockets. "I have better things to do."

"Morale is not a waste of time."

"And you think my presence will increase morale."

"It would if you could stop being a condescending prick for one goddamn night!"

Christopher stared at him, unfazed.

Adam rubbed his brow.

"Look, I have…other reasons I want you there."

When Christopher just stared at him, he sighed.

"Hang on."

Adam walked back to his office quickly and unlocked his desk drawer. He hesitated for just a second before he grabbed the box and walked slowly back to Christopher's office, biting his cheek.

He walked over to lean on the desk beside Christopher and held out the box.

"What's this."

"Well fucking look at it, goldilocks, and you'll know."

Christopher stared down at the blue box, a muscle flexing in his jaw. He finally held his hand out and Adam all but slammed it in.

"Would it kill you to show a little bit of interest?"

Christopher said nothing but opened the box slowly, taking out the smaller black suede ring box inside. He opened it.

"Well?" Adam could hear the nervousness in his own voice. "What do you think?"

Christopher was silent a long time, and Adam clasped his arms across his chest.

"I'm sure she'll love it. Six months sleeping with the boss, and she'll never have to work again."

Adam snatched the box from his hand.

"She's not like that," he ground out furiously, stalking back to his office to put it away. But he paused in the doorway and turned around.

"You know, when you wanted to tank our investment in that start-up, I didn't say shit, did I? Because I could see it was important to you for some reason. I didn't ask why. I just fucking supported you."

Christopher's eyes burned as he looked away.

"So maybe you could try returning the favor. Because Jo is important to *me*."

He waited. Christopher could be as selfish as Adam, but he'd always come through for him when it counted.

"Fine. I'll be there."

He didn't look at Adam but turned to sit at his desk.

Adam exhaled. He supposed that was the best he was going to get.

He looked down at the box in his hand. He wished Christopher had given him a real answer. His brother was no help at all. Too strung out all the time. And he'd argued so much with his parents about them bailing his brother out of all his problems all the time that they really didn't talk to him much anymore.

Christopher was the closest thing he had to family. Their strengths balanced each other out, something Christopher had noticed when he approached him with his business plan in school. He might piss Adam off a good deal, but Adam had a tendency to get pissed anytime he didn't get his own way.

Christopher seemed immune to his raging, so Adam never had to worry about being himself. Christopher could take it.

"You're still here."

Christopher's voice was tinged with irritation, and Adam gave him a brief glance before turning and closing the door.

———

"Are you ready yet?"

Adam leaned against the door to the bathroom in his office suite and almost fell in when Jo jerked it open, exasperation in her eyes.

"Does this look ready to you!"

Her shirt was off, and her jeans were unbuttoned and unzipped. She still wore a single sock, but her shoes were both missing. And she only had one of the earrings in that he'd given her for her birthday.

On any other night he would have pushed her back through the door and helped her delay getting ready for at least ten minutes.

But tonight he was nervous as fuck.

He frowned.

"What the hell have you been doing for the last fifteen minutes?"

She glared at him.

"My hair is *curled*."

He took a closer look. Oh, yeah, the ends were curled. But they hung down so low, he'd hardly seen them. She was a good bit shorter.

He started to say as much, but a tiny voice warned him that might not be the smartest idea.

"Can you get out of here and stop bothering me?" She smacked at him with the brush he hadn't seen her holding, and he grabbed it from her, jerking her to him.

"If you promise to hurry. The party's going to be over before you ever make it downstairs."

"It hasn't even started! Half the company is still working!"

"Yeah but the other half is already mingling!" he glared at her. Then he kissed her hard until she melted into him, and whacked her ass with the brush.

"Ow," she muttered against his lips. She sighed as she pushed herself away, snatching the brush back out of his hands. "I need at least half an hour, so go away!"

He groaned as she slammed the door in his face, and he banged his head against it.

"Go away!" Her muffled cry came through the door, and he glared through it. "And stop glaring at me!"

He snorted, but finally turned to go. Shit. What was he going to do for half an hour? He looked across the suite and saw Christopher still working in his office. Yeah, probably not the smartest choice to go bothering him, either.

He sighed and went downstairs to mingle for a while, trying not to think about the box in his pocket.

———

"Jo? It's been thirty minutes! Are you ready?"

He heard muffled sounds but she didn't answer immediately. What was she doing now?

"I'm...almost ready."

He frowned. She sounded a little choked. Was she crying? He knew she hated socializing.

"Baby, you don't have to worry about anyone else. Just me. Just hang on me." She didn't answer. He jiggled the handle.

"I'm almost ready! I'll be down soon! Just wait for me downstairs!" She sounded a bit panicked, and his frown deepened. Then recognition hit. Bathroom. Got it.

"Okay, okay—I'm going! Just...I'll be downstairs," he sighed.

And he turned to go, his eyes darting toward Christopher's office. He wasn't in there anymore. Had he missed him downstairs? Time to go drag him out from wherever he was hiding. Christopher could handle one damn night for the sake of his only friend.

———

Twenty minutes later and Adam was ready to go tear down the door. Dressed or not, he was dragging her downstairs. And it didn't help his mood that Christopher seemed to have completely ditched him.

"There you are!" Adam glared at the figure walking down the hall, away from their office suites. "Jesus, you look like death warmed over," he said as he got closer.

Christopher didn't even pause but breezed past him, his face stony.

"Seriously?" he called out to his retreating back. "You better not fucking leave!"

What a fucking night already.

He finally made it down the hall and went to bang on the bathroom door.

"Jo! For fuck's sake! Will you get out here?"

He heard her footsteps, slow and soft. And finally the door opened.

She peeked out with wide eyes, her face as pale as he'd ever seen it.

"Shit. Are you sick?" He stared at her for a moment, the ring in his pocket screaming at him.

"Sorry," she whispered.

He groaned looking at her. He *had* to propose at the Christmas party. It was all planned out. He couldn't just wait and ask tomorrow morning when she felt better. Was it nerves from the party? Food poisoning from something earlier?

"Come on. We'll move slowly and get you some ginger-ale or something."

She nodded, still wide eyed, and stepped out. Her long legs stretched out beautifully under the short blue dress, and he reached down to run his hand up her thigh.

She froze.

"Sorry—I know you're sick. But you look beautiful," he whispered, kissing her head.

She nodded again.

Dammit. She must really feel terrible. Should he wait?

No. He'd had this planned for the last fucking month and besides. Marriage was supposed to be in sickness and in health. Why not the proposal?

He pulled her downstairs with him, trying to maneuver her carefully, until everything was in position. He saw a splash of golden curls out of the corner of his eye and turned, his eyes lighting up at the sight of Christopher. Maybe the night wasn't the train wreck he'd feared.

Then he was on his knee in front of Jo. In front of Christopher. In front of everyone. And the music he'd chosen started on his cue as he opened the black box. One of Jo's favorite songs. An early one they'd danced to together. He'd wanted to dance to it tonight, but that might be pushing it now.

He held up the ring, still a little terrified.

"Will you marry me, Jo?"

She stared down at him, so pale he feared she might fall over. Don't get sick now, baby. Just say yes first. Then we can go home.

Her eyes were huge. She just stood there in silence. Everyone was silent.

Lifting her head slowly, she looked behind him. And she was shaking her head. Back and forth. Back and forth.

Her eyes fell to his again, and a coldness seeped into him.

"I'm sorry," she whispered. "I can't."

And she walked out of the room.

21

CHRISTOPHER

CHRISTOPHER COMBED his golden curls carefully in front of the mirror, his little five year old hands precise and efficient. His mother was sad again, but there was a certain way she liked his curls that always made her smile.

"Christopher!" His father's voice shot through the room, and Christopher jumped as he turned around. "Didn't I tell you to keep your toys off the stairs? Are you trying to kill your mother?"

Christopher paled. He thought he'd put everything away. He hurried to the stairs, his eyes scanning each wooden step, searching for what he'd missed while his father stood at the top. When he didn't see anything, he walked downstairs, looking at each step more closely. He finally found it on the seventh step.

He'd taken a board game upstairs to play with his mother and a little piece must have slipped out when he brought it back down. He shouldn't have tried carrying more than one box at a time. He was too little. No wonder something had slipped.

He picked it up and took it downstairs, his father following behind. He pulled a chair over to the closet where the games were kept and put the piece away before dragging the chair back, making sure it was positioned properly.

"If you can't be responsible, you won't be allowed to play. Understood?" His father stared down at him, his eyes cold. Christopher nodded.

His father looked at him a moment longer before walking down the marble hall to turn on the tv.

Christopher hurried back upstairs and knocked on the door at the end of the hall. Nothing. He tried again a little louder, still keeping it low enough so his father wouldn't hear. He wasn't supposed to disturb his mother. Still nothing.

He reached into his pocket for the little piece of metal he carried, and pushed it into the door handle until it unlocked.

"Mommy?" he whispered. He didn't see her in bed, so he crept inside and closed the door. He tiptoed over the carpet carefully. He could hear the tv below.

The bathroom door was closed.

"Mommy?" He tried to sneak in as often as he could. She always looked happy to see him. But his father was usually around, and he didn't like Christopher bothering her.

He tried the bathroom door and it wasn't locked. He pushed it open.

"Christopher!" His mother's voice sounded a bit slurred, but he raced forward with a smile as she held out an arm. She was in the tub, bubbles covering her. An open medicine bottle sat on the edge. She patted his head. "So cute."

Christopher stared at the bottle.

"Are you sick, Mommy?" He peered inside. It was empty.

"Not anymore, sweetie…not anymore…" She patted his head again. "Stay with me…"

He smiled, nodding. And he stayed. His mother fell asleep, and he knew that was dangerous in a bath. He would watch over her and make sure she didn't drown.

And the bathwater grew cold, as cold as her skin when he held her cheeks as she started to slip beneath the water.

He was still holding her when his father finally came back upstairs.

———

Christopher stood on the steps of the boarding school as the headmaster introduced himself. Behind him, he heard his father's car door slam and the crunch of the tires pulling away over the pavement. Christopher didn't look back. He was eight years old now, old enough to be on his own. That's what his father said.

A group of older boys came out of the building, talking loudly. One of the bigger ones winked at Christopher, and Christopher gave him a little smile. The boy looked back as they walked by.

Christopher paid close attention to learning the rules that week, even rules that weren't written down. He already knew it wasn't okay to cry. That failure was a bad word. He was lucky his father had taught him so many of the rules already.

"Hey, you're that kid I saw on the steps last week!" The tall, athletic boy with bright green eyes grinned down at Christopher as they left the dining hall. The weekend wasn't quite as crowded as many of the boys had passes to visit their families or go on trips to other places. "You headed to study?"

Christopher nodded. Boys on the premises had an hour of compulsory study time after dinner.

"I know a really good place to study. Want to see it?"

Christopher smiled up at the boy and nodded again. He liked the library where he normally went, but they weren't required to use any particular location. And this boy was the only one who had been really nice to him. Some of the other bigger boys were really rough.

Christopher had already been hit a few times, and he had a few bruises in places the teachers wouldn't see. But he hadn't told anyone. Another boy told, and Christopher heard him getting taught a lesson after lights went out that night. Christopher wouldn't tell. He would figure out how to defend himself on his own.

"Here it is." The boy pulled a key out of his pocket. "One of the teachers used to bring me here all the time, and now he lets me use it whenever I want when he's off campus."

The boy opened the door to a small study, and Christopher went inside curiously. It didn't look like such a great place to study. There was only one desk with one chair. Where were they going to sit?

The boy closed the door behind them and locked it before guiding Christopher over to the desk.

"What's your name?" he asked, looking down as he sat in the heavy chair at the desk.

"Christopher."

The bigger boy's eyes crinkled, and he tousled Christopher's hair.

"Aw, cute name! Here, you can sit on my lap, and I'll read you a book."

Christopher frowned. That wasn't really studying.

"Have the big boys been picking on you?"

His eyes were so warm that Christopher felt his own stinging, and he blinked furiously. No, he wasn't a crybaby. He just nodded briefly.

"Can I see? Don't worry. I promise not to tell."

Christopher hesitated, but the boy was the only one who seemed to care. He nodded again and pulled his shirt up.

"Ohhh...poor kid!" The boy's voice was soft as he reached out, stroking the bruises on Christopher's ribs. Christopher blinked. He didn't want to back away because the boy was being so nice. But it felt weird.

"That used to happen to me, too. Want to see a scar?"

Christopher nodded, and the boy began unbuttoning his pants. He frowned and started to step back, but the boy grabbed his wrist.

"It's okay. Don't worry. No one can see in here. Or hear, really. No one comes down this way much on the weekends."

He smiled at Christopher again, but this time there was something else in his eyes.

Christopher tried pulling away more strongly, his own eyes beginning to panic.

"Shhh," the boy soothed, pulling him close. "You don't need to be afraid. I'm not going to hurt you."

But he did hurt him. Every weekend for the next year until the boy graduated.

By the time the next year arrived, Christopher no longer smiled.

Weakness was failure. Softness was weakness.

He would never be soft again.

————

Christopher grabbed his latte from the cafe downstairs. It was a little too early to head up. Adam would still be too comfortable. Too in control. Christopher preferred to keep him on the edge for their meetings as he was easier to manage. And it was somewhat amusing.

He walked slowly, giving his drink time to cool, and looked around at their company.

All was going as planned. Adam brought in the investors, while Christopher handled the investing. Their partnership worked perfectly so long as Adam stuck to his role. But occasionally he got a little too interested in what was going on behind the scenes. And Christopher didn't like explaining himself.

At least Adam hadn't pushed back about the start-up fiasco.

He hadn't meant for Adam to find out, but he was around when the opportunity had presented itself, so it couldn't be helped. Christopher hadn't expected Adam to back off so easily though. But he was relieved.

Because Christopher would never tell anyone about the green eyed boy whose fortune from daddy was rather small these days. Christopher had made a few strategically bad investments over the years in order to make that happen. A few more moves, and he would eliminate the boy's fortune completely. And then he'd destroy what remained of him.

Adam didn't need to know any of that. He just needed to keep being Adam and bringing in the capital for Christopher to use. Besides, Christopher had made a much larger fortune for the two of them, so Adam had no cause to complain.

He checked his phone. That was probably enough time.

Come over later.

He frowned as the text came through. He just saw her three days ago. Did he want her again yet? He sipped his latte as he headed toward Adam's office. He hoped she wasn't growing attached. He'd found even hard, ruthless women had a tendency to soften over time. It was annoying.

Christopher could see Adam leaning against his desk as he approached his office, his eyes flicking to Christopher irritably. Christopher frowned. Not irritably enough. Maybe he should have waited longer.

He walked through the door and caught the briefest glimpse of a pair of blue green eyes widening up at him as soft breasts suddenly plastered into his chest. It was only instinct that caused him to tilt his cup toward himself rather than her, and hot liquid drenched his stomach.

He might have jumped back. He might have walked away to clean up immediately. But her hands were suddenly everywhere, sliding into his shirt and pulling the burning fabric away, stroking his arm, his back, his side, as she apologized softly over and over, her eyes glistening as they roamed his body. Trying to make sure he was okay. Trying to protect him from damage.

His heart hammered in his chest as her soft hands stroked him. He glared down at her. No one touched him. *No one.* But she didn't look up, and she didn't stop. And he couldn't step away.

Her eyes lifted at last. Soft. Open. Kind. Until she looked into his eyes—and hers widened in horror as she jerked her hands away to her chest and scurried back.

He tried to control the shuddering breaths shaking his chest, ignoring the confusion in his body as he focused on her instead. On burning his eyes into her. On making sure she would never step foot near him again. Ever.

She was smart enough to run.

Christopher watched her disappearing down the hall, furious when his pulse raced, urging him to go after her. But Adam stepped in front of him, leaning out of the doorway and calling out to the girl. Christopher watched her over Adam's shoulder as she turned back around.

"Josephine. Or...Jo." Her voice was small. Afraid.

Good.

He turned and stormed to the restroom to clean up. He would go visit Deanna tonight after all.

———

She was on the phone when he walked in, but he didn't pause. Her eyes grew wide with excitement as he pushed her over on her desk, not making a sound, as she continued her conversation.

"Their merger didn't go through. The SEC got involved, and now we have an opportunity," she was saying.

Christopher grabbed the lotion out of her drawer, lubricating himself so he wouldn't tear, before dragging her pants down and positioning his head against her. She grabbed the edge of her desk as he forced himself deep inside, not giving her time to adjust, and she coughed to cover her gasp.

He drove into her over and over before pausing and pulling out only to slide back in slowly. He didn't want her getting used to this. He wanted her to feel every moment. To hurt her. Punish her.

She dropped her phone on the floor, her call over, and began moaning. Loudly. He hated it.

He put his hand around her throat to keep her quiet, and she rubbed herself furiously. She would try to cum before he did, but he didn't want her enjoying this today.

He grabbed her wrists and twisted them behind her back before returning his hand to her throat as he began thrusting. Over and over. *A pair of blue-green eyes staring up at him, warm and wet. Soft hands stroking his body. His skin. The crush of soft breasts against his chest.*

He drove into her in a final thrust as he spilled out all his frustration and anger. His grip relaxed on her throat.

"Dammit, I wanted to see you so *I* could cum!"

Christopher didn't say anything as he stepped back, pulling out of her. He went to the restroom to clean up as she finished herself off on her desk.

He didn't bother saying goodbye before he walked out.

He was still frustrated. It wasn't satisfying.

She wasn't the one he wanted to punish.

———

Christopher sat in darkness, staring at the personnel file on his laptop. The lights of the city surrounded him as he relaxed in his high rise condo.

Bachelors in computer science from a state school in the midwest. Above average GPA but nothing stellar. No extracurricular activities. Kept her first job out of college for five years before making a move across the country and working for them.

He clicked on her medical file again. Yes. Her move coincided with the first of many visits to a specialist in the city. Chronic insomnia.

He looked at the attached doctor's note. *Patient complains of frequent and disruptive nightmares since childhood, resulting in a learned resistance to sleep.*

Christopher frowned. Why was she having nightmares?

He looked for the list of medications, his pulse rate increasing for a moment. None. His heart beat slowed, and he leaned back, pulling up her social media pages. Mostly memes. Some gaming posts. Music—highly eclectic selection. Occasional selfie. Candid shots almost never.

He stopped on one of the few. She was staring at the camera with the same warmth he'd seen in her eyes before, but with a smile in her eyes this time. A deep, happy smile. She loved the photographer.

Christopher stared at the picture, his eyes narrowing. Then he blinked and his brow cleared as he read her caption: *taken by my little niece with her birthday present from me.* He looked back at her face. It was so unguarded. Open. Soft.

Weak.

He snapped the laptop shut.

———

He was going over their investment portfolio when movement in Adam's office caught his eye.

Josephine.

His pulse raced, and he glared down at his screen.

She moved away from the door towards Adam's desk, and he looked back up. She had her hair down today. Like in some of her pictures. It flowed down her back in random waves.

She sat down as Adam grabbed a chair and pulled it next to her. Christopher frowned. She wasn't Adam's type. He preferred aggressive women. She was too gentle for him. Why was he looking at her like that?

She dropped her face in her hands and peeked out between her fingers, and his pulse picked up again. He glared back down at his screen. But his eyes drifted back again to see her hands fall once more. She looked irritated. Good.

He dropped his eyes back to his work. He should close the blinds. Whatever she was doing was irrelevant to him. She was nothing.

So there's no need to close the blinds.

He left them open, and his eyes drifted up over the next few hours, watching her work. Watching Adam lean in close to her. Watching them look at each other. Watching them talk. Watching Adam lean forward and touch her face…

Christopher dropped all pretense of working, his eyes locked on them. She wasn't backing away. She should be backing away. Adam was too aggressive. Too demanding. She would break under him. But she was leaning in, and Adam grabbed her, pulling her to her feet.

Christopher's body hardened painfully. She should be pushing him away. Hiding. Not letting him…

Christopher grabbed his desk drawer and slammed it hard into the desk as Adam's hand went to unbutton his pants, his lips still locked on hers. He looked up.

Back off, Adam.

She looked over her shoulder, her eyes soft. Her mouth slightly swollen. Adam's hand on her breast beneath her shirt. And he hated her.

Her eyes widened and she jerked her head back to the computer on the desk as she dropped back in the chair and reached her hands around her back.

Christopher forced his eyes back to his own computer, the

blood under his skin burning him. He hadn't been back to see Deanna. So his body was just on edge. That was all this was.

But he didn't go that night either. Or the next.

And Adam started closing the blinds more and more often.

————

"Send Josephine."

Christopher stood by his office window, his eyes dark as he stared at his computer. Waiting.

Adam's blinds had been closed for weeks now, but he wasn't back in his office yet. It was time.

"Hello?" She stood in the doorway, peeking in, and he waited until her eyes found him. Her startled jump was small but he caught it. He inclined his head toward the computer, and she came in nervously.

He moved to close the door after she'd sat down, and she looked up, her eyes huge in her small pale face. She lowered them again almost immediately and got to work. It was going to take her a while. He'd made sure of it.

She looked tired. He wondered if she still had nightmares.

Where did she sleep at night? Did she stay with Adam? Could she sleep when she was with him?

Her hands were shaking. He was making her nervous. Good.

"Did you sleep with your boss at your previous job?"

Her head shot up, and the remaining blood left her face.

He just stared at her.

"I..." She didn't seem to know what to say. He wondered if she had. Not that he should be asking an employee this type of question. But she wouldn't go running to HR. Or Adam. She was too soft. Too weak.

He could feel his anger simmering beneath the surface, but he forced his voice to remain calm.

"I read your performance reviews. You have a history of sleeping at work."

"It was only twice! Sleeping, I mean." She looked a bit frantic. "That hasn't happened since I've been here."

Her eyes glistened, and his anger grew.

"Of course not," he said smoothly. "You've been too busy with other things."

Her hands clenched on the keyboard, and her eyes flew back to the screen, deleting the keystrokes.

"I...meet service levels for...help desk tickets." Her voice shook a bit.

"I'm sure you do." Acid laced his tone. "You've serviced Adam quite a bit. Perhaps we should change your job title. How does *whore* sound."

She flinched in shock, her eyes flying to his before looking back at her screen.

"It's not like that," she choked.

Wounded. Fragile. Helpless.

He clenched his fists in his pockets.

She continued struggling to work as he stared at her, his anger growing with each passing minute. With each whisper of a feeling buried deep inside him. *I'm sorry. I didn't mean it.*

He *did* mean it. He glared down at her. She was nothing.

But he didn't speak again.

They heard Adam's door open out in the hall, and the girl's eyes flew up toward his office. Hopeful. Longing.

"Have you fixed my computer yet?" Christopher snapped.

Her eyes jerked back down.

"Sorry." The tremor in her voice infuriated him. The minutes ticked by as she clicked away on the keyboard.

"Where the hell have you been?"

Christopher's eyes flashed to Adam as he stormed in. He was too enraged. He cared too much. He needed to be reminded what she was—how insignificant she was.

But minutes later, Christopher's eyes were burning as he listened to their argument through the glass partition. To her yelling. Her tears. And then her softer cries.

And his own rage grew.

————

Christopher stared down at the ring. He couldn't breathe.

It had been six months. Six horrible months.

He kept expecting Adam to tire of her. To go back to the type of women he used to be with. Or to push her too far. For her to have enough of his yelling. Of his stubborn insistence that he get whatever he wanted. He expected them both to realize she would never fit into his world. She didn't belong.

Adam was waiting for a response. Maybe there was still a chance.

"I'm sure she'll love it. Six months sleeping with the boss, and she'll never have to work again."

"She's not like that." He grabbed the ring back, furious, and started to go back to his office.

I know what she's like, he seethed inside. But he'd hoped Adam had some doubts. Evidently not.

"You know, when you wanted to tank our investment in that start-up, I didn't say shit, did I?"

Christopher tensed. Why was he bringing that up?

"Because I could see it was important to you for some reason. I didn't ask why. I just fucking supported you."

Confusion shot through him, fueling his anger, and he turned away. They were business partners. Why was he talking about support?

"So maybe you could try returning the favor. Because Jo is important to *me*."

Frustration poured through him. Was he supposed to care what was important to Adam? But his gut twisted inside.

"Fine. I'll be there."

He walked to the other side of his desk and sat down to stare at his computer, a muscle twitching in his jaw. She shouldn't be important to him. She wasn't important. She wasn't *anything*.

Adam was still in the doorway. What more did he want from him?

"You're still here." Go away.

He thought he saw a flash of hurt in Adam's eyes and glared harder as he turned and left. She wasn't good for him. She was making him weak. And if he married her, it would only get worse.

They needed to be free of her.

———

Christopher wanted to get a few more things accomplished before having to go down to the party, but Adam's pacing in the other room was distracting. Adam had opened their blinds earlier. Probably to try to rush him, as he kept sending him impatient glances through the glass.

Christopher would have closed his own blinds, but then he wouldn't have been able to keep an eye on *her*. She didn't seem to realize they were open.

The bathroom door in Adam's suite flew open, and Christopher caught his breath. She was half naked, her breasts spilling out of her bra. The breasts he'd felt against his chest. He adjusted himself under his desk, furious at his body's response. But he couldn't tear his eyes away.

Her jeans were unbuttoned and unzipped. They would be so easy to slide off her hips. To turn her around and slide a hand down between her legs while he took himself out…

He forced his eyes back to his computer as Adam grabbed her. Christopher gripped himself hard beneath his desk, trying to regain control. Tighter.

He needed this to end.

She filled his dreams. His nightmares.

He had searched through every single file they had on her, through every piece of information he could find online, over and over. An endless search, trying to find some way to get rid of her. Something to convince Adam she wasn't worth his time.

Her laughter surrounded him nearly every day, taunting him from behind the closed blinds before turning into soft moans.

He couldn't even think of another woman long enough to work up any interest. He couldn't go back to the comfortable situation he'd had with Deanna.

She was ruining his life.

Adam's office door closed, and his footsteps retreated down the hall.

Christopher looked up at the closed door across their suites. He couldn't even think anymore. Because of her. Because she had touched him. She should never have touched him.

He got up and walked to the door between the offices, yanking it open and striding through the room to knock on the door. Hard.

"Are you kidding me? I am not opening that door for thirty minutes! Go away!"

Her laughter infuriated him. Her lightness. Her happiness.

He reached above the door for the thin strip of metal that hid above the frame and popped open the lock.

She froze holding her lipstick to her lips, looking at him in the mirror as he walked inside.

And closed the door behind him.

22

JO

Jo STARED at Christopher in the mirror and slowly lowered her lipstick.

"Wh—what are you doing?" She heard the catch in her voice.

He didn't answer. Or move.

He just stared, his eyes dark. Poisonous.

She swallowed and turned slowly to look at him, reaching behind her to grip the sink for support.

"Adam will be back soon—" her whisper broke, and he moved across the small room too fast for her to scream. Too fast for her to understand she needed to scream.

He grabbed her arm and yanked her to him, whipping her body around so that he was behind her as his hand covered her mouth. She reached up to tear it away but he held it tightly to her, his other arm strong around her waist, lifting her slightly as his knee went between her legs and he pushed her to the ground.

She tried screaming through her nose, but he covered that as well until she couldn't breathe. Tears choked her as she dragged her nails down his wrist.

He grabbed both of her hands and shoved them down under

her stomach, locking them between her and the floor. She gasped, dragging the air into her lungs to scream, but he covered her mouth again immediately as he pressed her into the ground with the full length of his body. Then he stilled, his chest pounding against her as hard as her own.

She trembled beneath him, the sound of his breathing ragged in her ear.

"I don't want to hurt you," he whispered.

A small sound came from her throat. A half sob. But she didn't try screaming again.

He released his grip on her mouth slightly. Enough for her to try to talk.

"Please let me up." Her voice was shaking. "I won't say anything. Please."

She could feel him hard against her, his rigid shaft digging into her.

His thumb stroked her cheek, and she forced herself not to cry out. To be still. He would let her go. Any moment now, he would release her.

His hand moved at her waist, and she tensed. He stilled again, his knuckles hot against her bare skin. She felt his lips brush her cheek, and she couldn't stop the whimper that escaped her. His fingers slowly covered her mouth again as her eyes grew wide, his hand pulling down on her jeans. She started struggling, but he had her trapped.

"Shhh…I'm not going to hurt you…"

She tried screaming through her nose again but he blocked her again, waiting, and releasing just when she was desperate for air. All the while tugging at her jeans, shifting them lower and lower on her hips.

She started crying, deep sobs shaking her body, and he kissed her cheek softly. Gently. Dragging her panties down with her jeans until she was completely exposed.

"Don't cry." His voice was husky against her skin as he undid his pants. She gasped under his hand as she felt the hot length against her flesh, and he groaned.

He shifted his body to put his hand between them, and she jerked away as much as possible, trying everything she could to throw him off, yelling and yelling into his hand as he cut off her air over and over, all the while working to position himself.

"I know," he groaned into her. "I know you don't want this…shhh…"

She sobbed into his hand as he trapped her into position at last, his head against her soft, wet folds. Wet from Adam. Wet because she wanted Adam. Always.

He rubbed back and forth, stopping her each time she tried to scream. Each time she tried to move. Over and over, again and again. Stroking her. Pressing in so very lightly.

And then moving up.

Her eyes widened in horror as he repeated the movement. Dipping into her before moving higher…and finally starting to push at the tight pink ring that even Adam had never penetrated.

She renewed her kicking, fighting him with every bit of strength she had.

He kept soothing her as he stopped her. Kissing her softly. Until she collapsed in helpless tears beneath him.

"I'll be gentle. Just relax…" he murmured thickly.

He pushed harder, and she tensed her body as tightly as she could, fighting to keep him out.

He made a sound of frustration.

"I don't want to hurt you! I don't want this to hurt you," he whispered.

And kissed her cheek again. Her shoulder. Her neck. Always soft. Always tender. And he kept pushing. Carefully. Slowly.

She held herself rigid. She wouldn't break. She wouldn't let him in.

Then he moved his hand around to slip beneath her, keeping

his tip pressed hard against her, and slid his fingers between her folds until he found her hard nub. And pinched.

She gasped, the shock causing her body to jerk—to release its hold for just one moment.

And he slipped inside.

She cried out into his hand as he groaned, pushing his full length into her until he was buried completely. He stopped moving, hushing her again as her body went into helpless spasms at the invasion. Soothing her. Kissing her gently.

"It's okay. Shhh. That's the hardest part. I'll go slow."

Her cry was hopeless. Defeated. He kissed her again and moved his hand up to stroke her hair.

And he began moving in long, slow strokes. Pulling out almost completely only to slide back in. He gripped her hair, his lips against her cheek, his hand still covering her mouth.

"Good girl...just be still..."

She cried harder, and he pressed his lips on her cheek tenderly, sinking into her again and again.

They heard the office door open, and they both froze.

"Jo? It's been thirty minutes! Are you ready?"

Christopher leaned into her ear quickly.

"Call out to him," he hissed. "Let him see me buried inside you. I wonder if he'll ever be able to look at you the same way. Knowing what you let me do to you."

Jo made a strangled sound as Christopher released her mouth. He watched her through narrowed eyes as he flexed inside her.

She felt her face collapsing into tears again. Would Adam forgive her? Would he believe her? That she had tried to stop him? And even if he believed her...would he still be able to want her?

She choked back her tears.

"I'm...almost ready."

Christopher relaxed against her, releasing a moaning breath in her ear.

"Baby, you don't have to worry about anyone else. Just me. Just hang on me."

His words almost broke her. She couldn't stop the tears.

Christopher's fingers began biting into her.

The handle jiggled, and Jo panicked. He couldn't see her now! Not after she'd just pretended everything was okay!

"I'm almost ready! I'll be down soon! Just wait for me downstairs!"

Please go away, Adam. Please please please don't see me this way.

"Okay, okay—I'm going! Just…I'll be downstairs."

Jo collapsed in a broken sob as his footsteps retreated. Christopher let go of her mouth completely and grabbed her hair, more firmly this time.

"Have you let Adam do this to you?" he snapped, pushing into her hard.

She tensed with a cry of pain, and he slowed again, his fingers relaxing in her hair as he kissed her.

"What would he think of you," he whispered between kisses. "Letting me inside you this way."

He kissed the back of her neck softly, her ear, her cheek, her silent sobs shaking their bodies as he stroked in and out of her.

"Do you think he will be able to love you after this? After you're broken?"

Jo let exhaustion replace her tears. Waiting. Just waiting for it to be over.

Christopher stilled again, his heart beating hard against her.

He reached underneath her, his finger searching for the hard nub once more.

She tried to pull away. It was painful. Sensitive.

His touch softened. Light. Delicate.

She stopped fighting. Just let him do as he liked. She just wanted it to be over.

He was stroking her softly. Carefully.

Expertly.

Her eyes flew open. She began struggling again, but he subdued her.

"Shh…this can be over whenever you are ready…all you need to do is cum…"

Jo's eyes widened in horror, and she fought harder. He groaned against her, but didn't move inside her. He just kept stroking. Learning her.

"If you don't want it to end, don't cum. I like it, too," he whispered, "so just stay like this…"

She cried out, trying to get away from his hand, but he wouldn't release her. And he began moving inside her once more. Testing. Watching her.

She could feel it building, and she fought harder, more terrified of the sensation than anything else he had done.

He moaned, finding the rhythm she feared the most, driving her closer and closer, the burning in her body unbearable.

"Please cum—please please please just end this," she sobbed, desperate for him to stop.

He groaned and kept going, watching her constantly. Adjusting every time she thought she might be able to avoid it. To escape it. Until there was nothing she could do to stop it and she was cumming, the harshness of it unlike anything she had ever felt. He grabbed her and drove into her in a few final hard thrusts until he cried out, the sound as pained as her own.

They lay on the hard floor, shaking together violently.

———

Christopher pulled out of her slowly, pausing each time she tensed, their bodies still trembling. Jo closed her eyes tightly as he finally withdrew and felt him raise his body above her, his hands beside her shoulders. She didn't move.

He slowly got to his feet and stood over her. Still and silent.

She didn't look up. She didn't open her eyes. She didn't move.

Finally he stepped back. It seemed to take far too long before he turned and walked to the door. He paused again.

Go away. Just go away.

The door opened and he walked out, closing it behind him quietly.

She jerked up, flying to the door to lock it before backing away, her breath coming in shuddering gasps. She couldn't get enough air. She couldn't stop shaking. Her stomach churned and she ran to the toilet just in time, vomiting until she fell weakly against the wall. She closed her eyes. He was still inside her. Her hand flew to her mouth. She needed to clean up.

A few minutes later, she walked weakly back to the sink and looked at herself in the mirror. Her eyes widened in alarm. Adam would be back any moment!

She tore off her clothes, never wanting to see them again, and turned on the water, trying to wash every part of herself that she could. Hurry hurry hurry.

She scrubbed her face, wiping hard everywhere he'd kissed her, and dried off quickly. Her eyes were red so she grabbed the eye drops out of her purse, hoping they would work by the time he returned.

She ran a brush through her hair, dabbed on some mascara, and added a touch of lipstick. No blush. She didn't have any. Too pale. No time.

She slipped into her little blue dress and silver heels. No bra or panties.

Her eyes fell to the clothes on the floor. She didn't want to touch them. But she didn't want Adam to see them.

She grabbed them, swaying slightly at the feel, and quickly carried them to the trash, stuffing them down and putting paper on top.

The bang on the bathroom door made her jump.

"Jo! For fuck's sake! Will you get out here?"

Her body started shaking again. Calm down. She took a deep breath. Exhaled. Then carefully walked to the door and opened it.

Adam stared down at her. Huge. Bigger than life. Always.

"Shit. Are you sick?"

She knew she looked terrible. And he'd been waiting for her for so long.

"Sorry," she whispered, and he groaned.

"Come on. We'll move slowly and get you some ginger-ale or something."

She nodded, stepping out, and he reached down to run his hand up her thigh.

Her body panicked, and she froze.

"Sorry—I know you're sick. But you look beautiful," he whispered, kissing her head.

She nodded again, her mind in chaos. Adam's touch had terrified her. Adam. She wasn't broken. Christopher was wrong. She couldn't be—Adam was her heart. She was not afraid of him.

But every touch sent a jolt of fear through her body as he pulled her downstairs and through the crowd. Through the crowd…in front of Christopher.

His eyes locked on her, a dark storm swirling inside them. And the storm whipped through her, ripping her apart.

She dropped her eyes blankly as Adam got on his knee in front of her. What was happening? She vaguely sensed there was music in the background. Everything seemed still. Silent.

"Will you marry me, Jo?"

She could barely hear him. Marry. He was holding a ring.

Broken.

Her eyes lifted slowly, locking with Christopher's as they burned into her.

Broken.

She shook her head, over and over.

Her eyes fell again to Adam's. So strong. So perfectly him. Quick to laugh. Quick to yell. Quick to hold her.

She had never been worthy of him. She knew that. But he always made her forget that when he was around.

And now she wasn't even what little she had been before.

She could barely find the energy to speak, and her words came out in a quiet whisper.

"I'm sorry. I can't."

Everything felt so far away as she turned and left the room.

———

Jo went back to her apartment. She hadn't seen it much in the last few months. She lay in bed, her eyes open, staring blindly in front of her, until her body could no longer stay awake.

She got up the next morning. Christmas Eve. She showered. Ate. And she sat down.

She didn't look at her phone. She just sat quietly until it was time to eat. Then sleep.

Christmas day. Adam never knocked on her door. She didn't expect him to. There was nothing here for him anymore.

Monday morning. She still had a job. She still had rent to pay. She still had to keep going.

———

Everything seemed dark when she walked into the building. Everyone seemed to be wearing black.

She heard whispers drift through the air.

How can she show her face here.

She can't really think she'd going to keep working here now, does she?

What a waste—if only they had never hired her.

Jo couldn't disagree. No one met her eyes, yet everyone seemed to be staring.

She had a contract. But maybe Adam would prefer for her to just leave. She hadn't heard from him. She had finally checked her phone, but there were no messages. He must have written her off completely.

She still had things in his office. She could just leave them. Just leave.

But would another company hire her? Would they give her a recommendation?

Adam deserved better. But she needed to ask him if he would release her. They never had bothered to talk to HR.

She walked toward his office, whispers all around her.

Her body locked. The air around her choked her.

Christopher was in his office. His blinds open. And he was staring at her.

He walked slowly to the door. Hesitant. And opened it.

She forced herself not to back away. She was there to see Adam. She looked toward his office. It was still dark. He wasn't in yet.

A few employees were talking in low voices a ways behind her. Christopher's eyes lifted to them for a moment before he looked back at Jo. He tilted his head toward his office door.

Her brow pulled together. She could barely breathe. The murmurs seemed to grow louder.

She swallowed. She couldn't keep making a scene. There were people around. Nothing could happen.

She stepped forward, feeling cold. Sick.

Christopher stared down at her as she approached, and she stopped a few feet away. She couldn't make herself walk by him. She couldn't.

His brow pulled together slightly, and he stepped back. She took a small step forward. But again, she couldn't make herself move further.

He exhaled, the line deepening, and turned to walk to his desk and sit down.

Some of the tension left her, and she stepped into the room. But she left the door open.

He turned to his computer, frustration in his voice when he spoke.

"What do you want?"

He had no right to ask her that. He had no right to know anything. She wanted to talk to Adam. She wanted...

Her stomach suddenly clenched as she realized they weren't together anymore. No. She couldn't think about that.

"I have some things in Adam's office."

He glanced up at her, his jaw clenching.

"Fine." He got up, and she stumbled back. He stilled, his eyes growing darker, before walking to the door between their offices and opening it. "Go ahead."

When she didn't move, he stepped back from the door and looked away from her.

She walked as far from him as possible and went inside. She'd just wait here until Adam arrived. There was no sense trying to work.

Christopher didn't close the door, and she looked behind her.

"You can close it. I'll just wait here."

His brow drew together for a long moment. Then his lips parted slightly as it cleared.

"You don't know." His voice was low. Scratchy.

She frowned.

"Know what?"

He stared at her a moment before walking in and closing the door behind him. Her eyes widened in alarm, and she scrambled back towards Adam's desk, grabbing a pair of scissors.

Christopher paused, looking ill. But he just reached for the lights, turning them on.

"You should sit down."

She frowned again, and her brows pulled together uncomfortably. She rubbed the line between them.

"I don't need to sit down."

He hesitated.

"Please sit down," he whispered.

She rubbed her brow more furiously.

"You have no right to ask me to do anything. You have no right. You have no right." Her voice started to crack, and she stopped speaking. But she couldn't stop rubbing her brow.

His eyes glistened, and he cleared his throat.

"After you left…" He paused with his lips parted.

She stared at him, her hand on her brow.

"He…was upset," he whispered.

She wouldn't cry. Not in front of him. She wouldn't.

"He stayed late. Drinking. I tried to stop him, I swear." His voice was hoarse, and Jo blinked. "Everyone tried to stop him. But you know how he was. You could never talk him out of anything." Anger crept into his voice. Frustration.

Jo blinked again. She could only stare.

Christopher ran a hand through his hair before looking at her with tortured eyes.

She shook her head.

"Where is he? Where did he go?"

Christopher made a small sound and took a step toward her. She cringed back, and he stopped, frustrated.

"He was going too fast. I don't know how he even made it as far as he did. He could barely stand up," he said roughly.

She shook her head. She couldn't stop shaking it back and forth.

"Where is he?" Her voice was so small. So very small.

He looked at her helplessly.

"He crossed the median. It was a head on collision. No one survived."

Jo stopped shaking her head.

She stopped everything.

There was nothing. Nothing at all.

Christopher took a step toward her. She didn't react. He walked toward her slowly, carefully.

"You don't need to worry. You have this job as long as you want it," he said, his eyes hesitant.

"I can have my job…"

He swallowed.

"Or…if you don't want it…I…I'll make sure you have a generous severance package. If you want to leave." His voice was hoarse.

She stared at him blankly.

"You think…" she whispered. "You think I care about money…"

She stared up at him with wide eyes. Pale. So pale. As if all the blood had left her. She couldn't even hear anything now. There was a train somewhere. It was getting so loud.

She saw Christopher mouth something. She tried to tell him to speak up. But she couldn't speak. And it was getting hard to see him. The lights were dimming.

He reached out to grab her as her knees buckled, and everything zapped back into focus and all she could see was red. She hadn't even realized she was still holding the scissors until she had buried them in his neck.

And there was red everywhere. Flowing out of him as she pulled them back out, his hands clasped to the wound as he fell to his knees with wide eyes. Red. A pool of red.

She looked down at her hands. Glistening. Bright. The color of Christmas.

She swayed and dropped to her knees as his blood continued to flow. It was all over. Everything was over.

Her eyes locked on the scissors. Slender. Pointed. Delicate.

She only vaguely registered Christopher's cry as he pulled his hand from his wound to stop her. Too late. She fell over slowly, mesmerized by the spray of color in front of her. It hadn't even hurt. She couldn't feel anything.

Christopher's hand was on her neck, pressing down on the wound. She couldn't even try to stop him. She was too tired. Finally. She could sleep.

And she closed her eyes and knew nothing.

23

MOON DAY 368

Jo raised her head slowly, the weight of the memories dragging her down. Three lifetimes, weaving in and out, each struggling to take hold. Her mind fought to take it all in, to sift through the chaos and find what belonged to her. To remember who she was. Who she had been. And who she had become.

Slowly, the storm settled; the pieces fell into place, each finding their rightful home, while she made a new home inside to lock away the memories that weren't hers. Adam.

And Christopher.

She sucked the air into her lungs, suddenly unable to breathe. Gasping. Drowning in the air itself.

Christopher.

She raised her eyes in shock. He was staring at her. Horrified. He hadn't remembered. He had known how he felt when he stared at her in the mirror. But he hadn't remembered what he'd done.

What he'd done.

A wave of feeling hit her, choking her, and she turned away as dry heaves racked her body. A hand touched her, triggering a new round of convulsions. She shoved it away, clawing her way to the bank to collapse onto the moss covered rock until the violent sensations had passed. Her eyes closed tightly as tremors continued cycling through her body. Each time she thought it was over, a new shudder would overtake her. So she lay still and silent as it ended. Waiting.

Maybe he's the one I really loved.

An involuntary sound escaped her. More than a cry. She couldn't. She couldn't face him. He had never done anything to deserve any of this. And she had failed him.

She was sobbing silently against the rock when she felt a large hand soft on her back, following the line where her scar used to be, and she shook her head back and forth, the sounds escaping her now, deep and harsh.

"Baby—" his voice was choked. Crying. "Baby, don't cry. Oh, fuck, please don't cry. I'm sorry. God I'm sorry. I was so fucking stupid. So fucking blind. Please please forgive me." The words were strangled. Raw.

Her brow pulled together as she raised her head, trying to control the sobs shaking her body, and looked at him in tortured confusion.

"How can you not hate me?" Her face broke as she cried quietly, looking up at him with wide eyes as her chest shook with each breath.

The sound he made came from deep inside, and he reached slowly for her face. She didn't flinch, but she couldn't look at him. She couldn't. The tears fell and fell as she squeezed her eyes closed.

"Fuck, Jo," he rasped. "You haven't done one damn thing wrong. Jesus. The shit you've been through...I should have known. I fucking knew you. That was my goddamn job. To protect you. And I...talked to you...through the door...while—" He made a strangled sound.

"I was so focused on myself. So fucking self absorbed. You

were right in front of me. Everything was right in front of me...
and all I could see was what I wanted."

He stroked her cheek with his thumb, smoothing away her
tears.

"Honey, look at me," he said softly, cupping her face between
his hands. Her lashes fluttered open, the tears spilling out, as he
looked into her eyes, his own brimming. "The things you
thought...they weren't true," he whispered.

"I could always believe what you told me. I knew that maybe
from the first day we met. It was part of you. I never, ever would
have doubted you. *Ever*."

He kissed her forehead before drawing back to look her in the
eye once more.

"And I never, never would have seen you as less for something
someone did to you. It could never make you anything less than
what you are."

"Beautiful." He kissed her forehead again.

"Intelligent." He kissed her eyes gently as her breath caught.

"So fucking brave you scare the shit out of me." He kissed her
lips. Light. Careful. He rested his forehead on hers, his voice
hoarse as he continued.

"And so goddamn sexy just being you that the idea I could
have ever stopped wanting you..." He shook his head against
hers, stroking her cheeks. "Baby...it's just impossible."

Jo was shaking. As if she were cold. Her body vibrating
violently.

Adam slowly pulled her close, and she could feel his own
body trembling as he wrapped his arms around her, his warmth
surrounding her.

"You died." Her teeth were chattering. She couldn't stop.

"I'm sorry," he choked out, holding her more tightly and
tucking her head into his neck. "More selfishness. My own pain. I
didn't even stop to consider what you were feeling. Stupid."

He drew a shuddering breath before continuing.

"But baby...you can't hurt yourself. You can't." His voice broke, and he held her head, pressing his lips against her forehead.

She clung to him.

"And not good enough...for fuck's sake, Jo." He pulled back to look at her in amazement. "I already knew how rare you were —and how fucking lucky I was. But now after seeing everything...baby..." He shook his head, his eyes roaming her face as he whispered. "Baby, I'm in awe of you."

She shivered, staring up with wide eyes as his worshiped her.

"*Nothing* can break you. You are the smallest, sweetest girl... spunky as fuck...the cutest little kitten..." She pushed him lightly, and he smiled. But his eyes were serious. "And you will fucking tear Hell apart for the people you love."

His eyes darkened for a moment as his head began to turn to look behind him, but he pulled his gaze back to her quickly, warm again.

"You're so small," he whispered, touching her face lightly. "So beautifully soft... Vulnerable... Warm... And too many people have tried to destroy that. Too many...so many, Jo..." His voice was hoarse again. "I see them all in your memories. I see the scars, baby."

She stared up at him helplessly.

"Nothing can break you, Jo. But I swear, for the rest of eternity, I will stand in between you and anything that dares to try. I know you don't need it. But you fucking deserve it."

Her tears kept falling as she stood shaking her head back and forth.

"I would have said yes," she whispered, her face breaking with his as he rested his head on hers.

"Fuck..." He brushed her tears away as she reached up to smooth his away as well.

Jo shivered, and Adam wrapped his arms around her tightly, tucking her head into his neck again.

"I don't know what I'm supposed to do now." Her voice was barely a breath of air, and he stilled.

"I have a few things to say to him, but if you need me to be silent," he took a shuddering breath, trying to control the rage underneath. "I will."

Jo felt his lips soft on her head as he held her to him, the strength of his arms a wall keeping her safe. Sheltering her. This was home.

"I think...I'd rather you speak," she whispered. "If you don't mind."

"Are you sure?"

She nodded, and he crushed her to him for a long moment. Nothing could hurt her here.

She felt him shift, and she looked up to see him looking over his shoulder. A shiver went through her, and his arms tightened, his hand cupping her head protectively. But his eyes stayed locked where they were.

She had seen Adam angry before. Raging. A thundering storm that billowed and shook everything in its path.

But she had never seen the cold, deadly fury in his eyes that he had now.

————

"CHRISTOPHER!"

Adam's voice lashed out like a whip as he unleashed his fury, and Jo jumped. He rubbed her softly but didn't look down.

She pressed her face against his chest, trembling. He wasn't yelling *at* her. He was yelling *for* her. Her head turned to look at Christopher at last.

He was standing where he'd been, his head down low, and his body was shaking.

"Face me, you coward," Adam snarled.

Christopher's golden curls quivered softly as he stood

unmoving for a long moment. Then he slowly raised his face to Adam's. Pale. Sick.

Broken.

Adam stared at him, his body vibrating with rage.

"Your father was a piece of shit. And all those lessons he taught you? Absolute bullshit. You were a good kid, Christopher. A good kid. All those things your dad blamed you for. They were not your fault."

Christopher's face broke, and he dropped his head again.

"DON'T YOU FUCKING LOOK AWAY FROM ME!"

Christopher jumped along with Jo, and he jerked his head back up. Adam squeezed Jo but didn't take his eyes off Christopher.

"Your mother..." Adam gritted his teeth as the tears fell helplessly from Christopher's eyes. "She was sick. You didn't kill your mother, Christopher. She took those pills. She knew her son was right down the fucking hall. And she let you watch her die. She left you there alone to deal with your father. To hold her as she slipped away so she wouldn't have to be alone. It was *not your fault.*"

The tears fell freely from Christopher's eyes as he took deep shuddering breaths. But he didn't look away from Adam.

"And that sick fuck at your school who hurt you." Adam's voice grated out as Christopher's eyes begged him to stop through the tears. "He turned kindness into a weapon. He pretended to have something that he didn't really have. To win the trust of a sweet little kid who the whole fucking system failed. A kid who should have been protected. IT WAS NOT YOUR FAULT, CHRISTOPHER."

Adam was trembling, his face a dark and terrible storm as Christopher sobbed.

"But what you did to Jo..." His voice was low. Ugly.

Christopher shook, his eyes locked on Adam.

"*That was your fault,*" he hissed. "Hating her for being what you needed. What you never had. What you couldn't have. Hurting her—" His voice broke, and he squeezed her tightly, his body shaking as hard as Christopher's.

"You knew how it felt. You knew how it hurt. The shame. Humiliation. And you did it to *her*." He ended in a harsh whisper, his eyes incredulous. Furious.

Christopher looked ready to fall, but he stayed on his feet, struggling to breathe.

"The moment you touched her, you became exactly what that boy was," he ground out hoarsely. "That boy you spent your life trying to destroy. Taking his fortune from him bit by bit. Interfering in every possible way to cause him damage. Punishing him for what he did. But not enough. Not nearly enough. He deserved much worse. He deserved so much worse."

He choked back his tears, hugging Jo close.

"Tell me, Christopher. *What do you deserve now.*"

The sound of the waterfall filled the cavern. Jo clung to Adam as his shaking finally calmed and he waited. Waited in a cold fury, never once looking away from Christopher.

Jo watched him, his golden curls bright in the light of the cavern, as she sifted through his memories.

Shame. Weakness. Everything he had tried to hide in his entire life, exposed fully to both of them. Everything he thought he'd failed at. Every flaw. Every hidden desire. He had fought against softness for so long, so afraid to be weak. To be hurt. Afraid it would destroy him.

And it had. Not the way he'd feared. But it had.

If he had never felt for her, he would never have set all this in motion. He would have never turned into that boy. Never been stabbed. Never wound up in a burning desert, finding himself drawn to the softness of the girl who woke beside him. A girl he could only remember he'd wanted to hurt. A girl he'd tried so hard not to hurt time and again as she threw herself at him.

He would never have chosen to burn with her when her hand

was damaged. To risk everything to save her from being beaten. From being made into a prostitute. He would never have been captured and endured everything he had to endure in order to escape.

She really had destroyed his life.

Jo saw it in his eyes. She knew what he was going to do before he did it. Her heart screamed at him to stop. To make a different choice. But she could see it.

He dropped his head at last, never once looking at her, and turned toward the fall. He hesitated only a moment at the edge, and hope surged inside her that he might turn. That he might say something. Anything.

But he walked out.

———

Jo turned to Adam, struggling to breathe. She couldn't breathe.

He was rubbing her back as she dragged the air into her lungs. It didn't matter that she knew her body didn't need to breathe. It wouldn't stop. On and on as Adam crushed her to him.

"He...didn't even...say...he was sorry," she gasped. "He didn't...say...anything."

Her body shook and shook, and he gripped her hard before starting to pull away.

"I'll drag him back here—"

"No!" She looked up at his face with wide eyes, her hands clinging to him, and shook her head. "If he can't do it on his own...I don't want it."

His hand cupped her head against his neck as he pulled her back to him.

"I'm sorry, baby," he whispered. "He's fucked up. He can't see anything straight. I'm so sorry he hurt you."

She clung to him more tightly, so grateful for his strength. For his heart.

Where would Christopher go? Maybe he'd find another city. He'd learn the system there. And without her, he'd be fine. Safe.

Jo's breathing finally calmed. Everything felt calm. Empty.

"Can we get out of the water?" she whispered.

Adam kissed her head and put his hands on her waist, boosting her out of the pool onto the moss covered stone. Deeply covered. The moss was quite thick and soft, sparkling similar to the sand but with lights that felt alive. Adam climbed up beside her and pulled them both to their feet, holding her close while the water dripped off them to be absorbed quickly by the moss beneath their feet.

She should be happy alone with Adam—the way she'd been before. When bliss had bubbled up inside her each time she saw him, spilling out into her world and coloring her life in a way she'd never known.

But her life was over now. The color gone. And all she could do was lean against his chest and try not to think about the hollow in her own.

"I really was coming after you."

"I saw," he said gruffly. "And I saw what you were planning in the temple. I had just been so terrified I'd lost you forever in the storm."

"I know," she whispered. "I can see it."

Adam's desperate struggles to free himself from the ropes she'd tied him with. His terror when he'd learned what she'd done. How he'd searched the city for her and seen the guards running from the temple after her escape. His immediate visit to the director, demanding to be added to the guard going to the surface…demands punctuated by a significant amount of force.

He was the guard she'd seen getting up first, and he'd chased after them, certain that he would catch up. That the three of them would be able to stop the guards. To escape. Even as he watched the wall of sand tear over their bodies, it hadn't occurred to him to run away. He'd just plowed into it, searching for them, as the sand tore at him until it ripped him from the ground.

When it threw him back down, when he woke after the sun's rays had ravaged his flesh once more, he was alone. Again. With only a rock jutting up far in the distance, pulling him with his last spark of hope. When he caught sight of them just before they had gone under the fall, desperate relief nearly drove him to his knees.

Only to find her laughing up at Christopher as if she didn't have a care in the world, the two of them completely lost in one another. She hadn't known she could look that way. Beautiful. Radiant. And so deeply in love, it cut her now to see. As it cut him then.

"You deserved so much better, Adam. So much more. Your life—it was so big. I'm so sorry I—"

Her head snapped back as he grabbed her arms and jerked her to face him, his face furious.

"Don't you fucking dare. Don't you dare add one more voice in your head, telling you that you're responsible for anyone else being a piece of shit." He gave her a brief shake, his fingers digging into her arms, and tears stung her eyes.

She stared up at him helplessly.

"What if...I can't stop loving him?" she whispered.

His brow pulled together, his eyes a violent storm raging at her. But he averted his gaze.

"I don't want to say the wrong thing. After what you've been through."

A sound escaped her, and she hit his chest, a spark of feeling flaring in the emptiness inside.

"And I don't want what he did to change *you*! If you have something to say to me, fucking say it."

He glared down at her, his grip tightening again.

"Fine," he bit out. "Then if you can't stop, I'll shove my cock in you so hard every fucking day you won't be able to think about anything else."

A torrent of heat rushed through her, a fire blazing and chasing the darkness away. The flames crackled between them as the light in his eyes licked over her, and her eyes were bright on his when she answered.

"I can't stop."

Silence engulfed them, the sounds of the fall suddenly far away.

"I mean it, Jo," he said, his voice almost menacing. "I'm trying not to be selfish."

The heat pooled between her legs.

"That's never really been your strong suit," she whispered.

His eyes instantly darkened, and every hair on her body stood on end. If ever she'd had reason to fear him, she would have run now. Instead, she swayed toward him as he reached up slowly to slide his fingers in her hair, grabbing the short locks hard enough to hurt and pulling her head close to his. His chest heaved as he leaned down, his lips hovering above hers.

"I knew you would be trouble for me the day I met you. But I had no fucking idea how much."

"And if you'd known?" she breathed.

"I'd have fucked you a lot harder." And he ground her lips into his in a punishing kiss.

Heat poured through her body, and she yanked her arm from his hand to bury her fingers in his hair, pressing him to her harder. His groan verged on a growl as he plucked her from the ground and wrapped her legs around him before falling on top of her, his cock a thick iron rod throbbing between them.

He moved it between her legs quickly and pushed hard, the pain drawing an involuntary cry from her.

"Fucking Christ." His voice was hoarse with outrage as he

leaned up to look between their legs. The water had done more than restore their memories.

"Is it too difficult for you," she breathed as she pulled him back down. His eyes pierced her as he fell on top of her again, grabbing her hair once more as he positioned himself.

Her breath caught as he gripped her hair painfully, his eyes sharp on hers, until the head of his cock pushed just far enough inside her not to slip. Then his hand moved as he shoved his arm under her hips...and shoved himself deep inside, capturing her cry of pain with his lips.

The brutal pleasure filled her, driving into her, dragging cry after cry from deep inside her throat as he thrust into her mercilessly, his lips never leaving hers. His arm at her waist reached lower, his hand looking for the spot Christopher had always taken, until he had it and plunged a finger inside, forcing her mouth to stay on his as she cried out again, clinging to him.

She was crying. Moaning. Lost to everything but the burning in her body as Adam filled every part of her. Her hand reached between them, and he lifted just enough for her to slip a finger inside her soft, wet petals, rubbing in small circles as he forced her body to take every inch of him.

He drove her to the edge. Claiming her. Possessing her. Filling her so completely there was no room for anything else. No room for grief. No room for anything but him.

Light shards pierced her eyes as her body clenched helplessly, wave after wave of pleasure shattering her, the spasms so strong his own cry was laced with pain as he forced himself inside the final few thrusts, burying his cock, his finger, and his tongue as deeply in her body as possible as he erupted inside her.

The earthy scent of crushed moss surrounded them as they lay locked together, their bodies shaking while tremor after tremor rippled through them.

"Fuck." Adam's voice was hoarse against her lips, and she

groaned. And whimpered. "I'm not fucking moving so don't even try."

She chuckled, her lips feeling his, gasping as he flexed inside her. Then he groaned as well and dropped his head in her neck.

They lay that way a long time, with Jo stroking his hair, his back, her body shuddering in small spasms each time he shifted, drawing more groans from him until he was fully hard once more.

The pain was excruciating when he began moving again, and she clung to it, letting him take her away again and again until they were both raw.

Adam pulled out of her at last, every move causing their bodies to twitch in pain until he withdrew completely and the mix of blood and semen spilled out onto the moss, disappearing into it immediately without a trace. They looked at each other.

"That's a bit disturbing," Adam murmured, pulling her into his arms and climbing back into the water. They both gasped as it hit their wounded flesh. But the sting went away quickly, and they relaxed into one another.

Jo sighed as Adam moved them slowly through the water, a calm embracing her that no longer felt empty. Pain lurked behind it still, but right now...right now she held Adam in her arms as he held her. So right now was beautiful.

His body went rigid, and her eyes flew up to his only to jerk toward the fall.

Christopher had returned.

24

CHRISTOPHER STARED AT HER, his eyes open and raw, and her heart pounded wildly.

"I don't know what I can say. What I can do. But I would do anything, Jo…anything…to take back what I did." His voice was scratchy but earnest. "And I will do anything you ask of me. Anything you need. I'll go back to the city. I'll burn in the desert for all time. Anything. I'll never forgive myself. I swear it. I'll pay."

"Good," Adam's harsh tone shot out over the sound of the fall. "Start walking now."

Christopher looked at Adam, his eyes beseeching.

"I just need to be sure that's what she needs," he said hoarsely.

Jo stared across the water, the maelstrom of emotions inside her confusing her thoughts.

Please don't go. Never go.

Adam spun her around toward the shallow area of the pool that just went to Jo's hips, setting her down on the edge before turning back around. She reached for him as he began walking away, and he jerked his eyes back to hers.

"I'm ready to talk to him," she whispered.

His brow pulled together, and he clenched his jaw. She didn't think he was in the mood to let her anymore.

"Please, Adam." Her voice was for his ears only. "Everything is fucked up. And I don't know what I'm supposed to feel. I don't even know what I feel at all. Except that I can't bear him being gone."

Fury filled his face. An impotent rage he couldn't release— that she wouldn't let him release.

"I know I'm not the only one he hurt," she whispered, stroking him softly, and he glared at the ground beside her. "But I *am* the one he raped."

His eyes shot back to hers at her blunt statement, hesitation in them now. Would he let her have this decision? Could he ever accept her choosing to keep him? Was that truly what she wanted? She didn't know, but she needed the chance to find out.

Adam exhaled at last and nodded, reluctant resignation in his eyes. He sat down beside her, their legs side by side in the shallow water, and turned a sharp gaze back on Christopher. His hand dropped to her leg protectively. Possessively.

It warmed her.

She lifted her eyes to Christopher once again. He stood unmoving. Submissive. Awaiting her verdict.

She hated it.

"Stop." The harsh note of her voice carried across the water, and he looked at her uncertainly. Her frown deepened. "How would torturing yourself for eternity help anything? After everything I did to stop it?"

His eyes grew desperate.

"I...I don't know what to do. I have no right to ask what you want. I don't know what...you need." He ended in a whisper.

She kept staring, a burning growing inside her.

"Then go away," she choked on the words.

He buried his hands in his hair, his eyes tormented.

Her lashes swept down, shutting him out. She couldn't give him a manual for this. She didn't even know what she needed herself.

The rush of the fall in the cavern filled her ears, and Jo focused on the sound. Focused on Adam's hand gripping her leg. On the scent of the soft earth beneath her.

She could see beneath her lashes as Christopher approached her slowly. Carefully. Until he stood a few feet in front of her, and a sliver of panic began to creep in.

"Jo..." Christopher whispered, stepping closer but stopping when Adam's hand shot out to shove him back.

"Let me go, Adam," Christopher exhaled shakily.

"Like hell," he said, outrage straining his voice as he pushed against him.

Jo's heart rammed against her chest, beating the breath from her lungs. Christopher couldn't think she would let him touch her now! But her body begged her to let him. Her thoughts warred with one another, the vortex winding her tighter and tighter until she feared she might snap at the slightest touch.

"Adam..." Her voice was so small. But he heard it. "I need to figure this out myself. Please."

She could feel the tension roiling through him, but he dropped his hand.

Christopher stepped closer. Closer. He stood only inches from her legs, the heat from his body rolling over her in waves, and a tremor coursed through her.

Her eyes raised to his slowly, every moment painful as she took in his body. His beautiful body that he'd used to protect her time and time again. And once to hurt her.

"You wanted to break me," she whispered, and tears filled his eyes as he looked back at her. He nodded, his face breaking slightly.

"If I'd known, Jo…your life…even as I was then, I never, never would have wanted that."

"But you knew I…you knew how small I was. I was nothing. Why would you want to destroy even the little bit I was?"

He did break then, and panic engulfed her as he stepped in between her legs to grab her face. Her hands flew to his wrists, and she could feel Adam's barely restrained fury. But Christopher held her close, stroking her cheeks and kissing her tears as her body trembled violently.

"I'm sorry! I know—I know my touch scares you now. That it hurts you. I'm sorry. I'm so sorry, Jo. But you were never small. Never." He was crying harder than she was now, his lips soft against her skin as he kissed her tears away.

She trembled. Aching. Hurting.

"I was broken," he whispered. "Twisted. I needed you. And I was desperate to stop it. Desperate to have you. Desperate. And lost. I needed to make you small. Because I was small. I needed to make you weak. Because I was weak. And I needed to hurt you, so I could allow myself to be soft."

His hands cupped her cheeks softly. Stroking them with his thumbs.

"I wanted you so badly in the desert. Every time you reached for me, I wanted you. Every time you looked at me, I wanted you. But I knew something was wrong. That there was something wrong with me. And I kept hurting you," his voice grew hoarse again. "Trying to save you from something I thought would hurt you more."

A shudder went through her as he kissed her gently.

"But I wasn't protecting you. I was protecting myself. Hiding. Afraid. Adam was right. I was a coward. And it took me so long…too long… Even when you came to see me in the prison. I was afraid to let you see. Afraid to let myself admit what I felt. Even then."

He kissed her again, longer, holding on firmly when she gave a small cry.

"I'm so sorry. I'm so sorry for everything. You didn't deserve it. You never deserved any of that."

Adam said nothing could break her. But she felt herself shattering, the aching inside tearing her apart. Christopher rested his head on hers, and she breathed him in.

"I stole something from you. From both of you. And I know...I can't give it back. Because..." he stopped, swallowing.

Jo opened her eyes, staring at his lips as he spoke, her need unfurling with every word.

"Because I know you love me," he said, his voice hoarse. "I know a part of you belongs to me now. A part I never should have had."

Tears filled her eyes yet again, spilling over, and he kissed her cheeks softly, his tongue tasting her.

"I'm sorry," he whispered. "That I took it. That I tried to poison what you both had. But," he took a deep breath, his voice thick with emotion, "I can't be sorry that I have it now. And if I could give it back...I don't think I would."

His lips touched hers, capturing her shaky breaths. Soft.

"I know this hurts...and I'm so sorry. But I know you need this. Because you need me."

Her face broke at last, the tears overwhelming her, and he pulled her head into his neck, carefully wrapping his arms around her. A small cry escaped her at the feel of his chest on hers, the coolness from the water growing hot as their skin merged. His breath grew ragged as her nipples tightened between them, and he pressed his lips to her cheek for a long moment as his body responded.

"I love you, Jo," he whispered against her skin, his hand cupping her head close. "And I'll never hurt you again. Never."

He drew a deep, shuddering breath, his body hard now

between her thighs, and the heat of him seeped into her sensitive flesh, burning her with memories.

"I can wait outside the cave as long as you need. Maybe burning is good. Maybe that's what I'm supposed to do. I didn't stop being paralyzed until I chose to burn with you. I won't leave again. I'll wait forever. Until you're ready to see me."

Jo leaned against him, her body limp, a soul deep exhaustion flowing through her, crushing her heart. There was only one answer she could give.

"No."

―――――

Christopher's body clenched, and Jo leaned back, raising soft hands to his face as his eyes struggled with horrified acceptance.

"Christopher..." she sighed, her tone gently admonishing. "No burning. No more pain."

His gaze locked on her for a moment before a small cry escaped him and he dropped to his knees in the water, burying his face in her lap and gripping her waist tightly. She stroked his hair as shudder after shudder went through him.

"You and I had too much pain too early in life," she whispered, combing her fingers through his hair at his small sob. "No more. Stay with me. But no more pain."

Her eyes lifted to Adam's. Fury. Resentment. She sighed again. What a mess this was. But she reached her hand out to stroke his arm, the arm he was using to keep his hand on her thigh, his grip painful beneath Christopher's chest.

"Adam..."

"This is bullshit," he ground out.

She nodded.

"I know. It's not fair. But...*I'm* demanding something this time. This. You have every right not to forgive him, but you have to accept that I have."

Christopher moaned into her, clenching her harder, and she tangled her fingers more deeply in his curls.

"Forgive him all you want—but he's not staying," he said furiously.

"He is." Her tone was flat. Absolute. "And you're staying, too. Because I can't bear losing either of you."

He glared at her, but she knew she'd already won. She drew a deep breath.

"We have an eternity to figure this out. But we can't do that if he disappears. And I need him here. And I need you. So let *me* be selfish this time."

Her eyes were soft as she stroked his arm, soothing, trying to calm the beast inside. The light from the fall pulled her eyes away, and she sighed again.

"Come on. I don't want to see what happens if we stay in the water with our memories already back."

Christopher raised his head and glanced over his shoulder, and Adam used the opportunity to wrap his arm around her waist and pull her to him. He pushed back out of the water, dragging them across the scattered soft plants that grew in patches on the moss and pulling her down beside him, drawing her leg over his and pressing her into his chest. Christopher followed them, hesitation in his eyes until Jo leaned up to pull him down behind her, ignoring Adam's outrage.

She knew it wasn't fair. He really did deserve better. But she would find a way to make it up to him. To make him accept this again.

Christopher curled up carefully against her back, still hard, and she couldn't stop herself from tensing when they shifted and it touched between her thighs. He pulled back immediately, but she grabbed his arm, pulling him close once more. No. She was not going to let their past ruin everything they had worked so hard for here. No more pain. She'd had enough pain. They all had.

Their bodies curled around her, the way they'd just started figuring out before everything had gone so wrong.

"Do you think the guards are still chasing us?" she murmured.

Adam exhaled.

"Probably. Unless they decided to go look for another city. If they go back empty handed, they'll be sent to Resources. But they ran away from the storm, so I don't know how they would find this place. I didn't see anyone on the horizon when I walked here."

They must have been on opposite sides of the cavern since she hadn't seen Adam either. Between them, they would have been able to see the entire plain.

"I wonder if Peter knew what he was sending us into," she mused. "We never saw even the smallest breeze when we were in the desert before."

Her breath caught and she turned her face into Adam's chest as Christopher kissed her shoulder, his lips warm and soft on her skin, sending a sharp ache between her thighs.

Adam tensed immediately, and she wanted to moan and cry at the same time. This would take time.

But the light was growing so there was nothing to worry about for now.

It was only her instinct, born from years and years of fighting off sleep, that kept her from sinking into the oblivion immediately as the sun came up. If she'd only been asleep, everything would have been okay. They would have all drifted off together, and everything would have been okay.

But she held on just long enough as the lethargy dragged her down...to see the moss beneath them sucking them into the earth.

Terror shot through her, lighting her mind better than the sharpest pain, and her arms grabbed Christopher and Adam as they sank, shoving her knees against the chilling, tangled web beneath them and pulling up as it sucked them down. The lights wrapped around them, piercing them, and she screamed, trying desperately to wake Adam, to wake Christopher, until the earth dragged them all below the surface and she could scream no more.

They were drowning, pulled deeper and deeper as she clung to them with every last piece of her soul, rage pouring through her, keeping her awake. Whatever this was, it would not have them. *It would not.* Everything exploded around her, but she held on, gripping, clenching…their bodies were gone but she clung to them, everything that they were, that she was—she could still feel.

Heat seared her as darkness passed by, a hard, ugly obtrusion, and she grabbed it, holding on to the souls she loved as she fought against the light ripping at them, trying to tear them away. Flames sliced through her, the familiar burn clawing at her grip on the darkness, slashing and shredding until at last it had them, tearing them furiously away leaving only the smallest piece of her behind.

She was beyond terror, her only thought to hold on to Christopher. To hold on to Adam. Everything she had done…it couldn't all end now. So she held on and on and on, until blinding light engulfed her, ripping her from them at last and shattering her into pieces.

———

Jo stared at Christopher in the mirror, her lipstick shaking above the soft pink bow of her lips. Her long brown hair tumbled around her small body in waves, the curled ends wrapping around her full breasts as she leaned forward, her eyes locked on the reflection of the piercing blue eyes behind her.

Silence surrounded them. Stillness. Christopher's golden blonde curls fell in disarray on his forehead, the sharp lines of his features cut in beautiful precision and softened only by melting, tender lips and a growing worry in his eyes.

"Jo?" His tentative whisper sent the air rushing back into her lungs, and she dropped the lipstick into the sink, and turned to capture him in her arms as he ran to her.

"You're okay? You're okay!" She was practically shouting as she ran her hands over him, terrified tears choking her.

His arms pressed her to him hard, holding her until her lungs cried out and she tried to draw a breath....only to gasp desperately for air and hit his back. He released her quickly, and she doubled over, sucking the air into her lungs until the oxygen began to clear her head.

"Where are we?" she gasped as Christopher held her waist, stroking her back.

The door shook with a loud thud a moment before Adam crashed through, his wild mane of black brown hair a chaos above dark, fierce eyes and the dark shadow covering his jaw. The thick muscles of his arms and chest strained against his jacket as he towered in the doorway, his chest heaving. Her heart took her to the floor as relief filled every part of her, and she tumbled to her hands and knees.

His gaze turned to Christopher, rage blinding him, and her eyes widened in horror.

"Wait!" she reached for his leg just as he stepped close enough to grab, his fist flying before she could stop him. Christopher didn't defend himself, and the dull thud sent a splatter of blood to her cheek.

She stood quickly, getting between them and grabbing Christopher before looking back over her shoulder at Adam.

"Adam, wait! It's not like before!"

Adam's chest heaved, his body locked in fury, and Christopher tried pushing her aside. She wrapped her arms around him more tightly.

"Enough!" she shouted as Adam reached for him again.

He looked down at her furiously, and she quickly turned and wrapped her arms around him instead.

"Enough, Adam...enough," she whispered, peppering his chest and neck with kisses. Relief filled her again, a soul deep relief that made her want to melt into him, and her kisses grew longer. A small moan escaped her as she pressed her body into his, and her lashes lifted to his face.

She froze.

The door behind him was open. His office. But she could barely see it because of all the people crowding the doorway, trying to see in.

———

Were they real? They looked real. As did their expressions. Uncertainty. Titillated excitement. Giggling curiosity. Horrified judgment. And underlying it all, each time their eyes fell on her, utter contempt.

Christopher stepped beside her, putting his hand on her waist protectively as he wiped the blood from his lip. Adam bit down on his anger long enough to look over his shoulder, and she felt his breath catch.

"Should we...call someone?" One of the employees asked, looking at Adam.

Were they in a dream? A shared dream?

Panic hit her. Was this really Christopher and Adam?

"Are you real?" She whispered up at Adam. He looked down at her blankly. "That's not very reassuring," she said softly, but a tremor crept into her voice.

"I think it's real, Jo."

She looked over to see Christopher staring at the blood he'd wiped from his lip. It was drying quickly on his hand.

"How do you know it's not a dream?" she whispered.

A small glint lit his eyes when they lifted to hers.

"Because I would have had a much better dream. And this isn't a nightmare."

"Maybe not for you," she whispered, her eyes moving back to the door.

"No, everything is fine," Adam had recovered his voice, which boomed out above their whispers. "Go back to the party. And...everyone take Monday off."

The people in the doorway looked at each other.

"Unless you don't like working here," he added. That did it, and they all hurried away until no one was left near the office suite.

Jo looked around at last. If she were in a nightmare, this would have been exactly where she would have gone. A shiver went through her, the air cool on her skin, and her eyes fell to her body. She was still in her bra, her jeans undone and open.

Her eyes flew to Christopher's to see his locked on her, warm and worried. This was different. It wasn't what it was before. This wasn't how he'd looked at her in here before.

A shaky breath escaped her, and he dropped his head to hers for a moment, stroking her cheek before leaning in to lick gently. She blinked. Oh. His blood had gotten on her.

She pulled back and brought her hand up to hold his face, frowning at his lip.

"Are you okay?"

"Are you seriously going to fucking pamper him right now?"

She jumped at Adam's voice behind her and jerked back around to him, reality beginning to set in. Reality. Were they really back in the world? Could this possibly be real?

Adam was yanking off his jacket, and the air suddenly choked her.

If this really was the real world again, if they had really been sent back, he didn't need to stay with her now. Women would fall over themselves for him here. Neither of them needed to stay with her. They could have their lives back. And they'd had such good lives before her.

"Fucking bullshit..." Adam was biting out curses as he struggled with his jacket, and her stomach clenched. "Fine. Keep Christopher as your...whatever. Do whatever the fuck you want with him."

Pain hit so deeply in her chest she couldn't breathe. She couldn't see. Adam's image in front of her blurred until he threw the jacket on the ground.

Then he was down on the ground in front of her, shoving a small box into her hands.

"But fucking marry me, Jo."

The world tilted, and they both grabbed her, Christopher behind her and Adam's hands on her hips.

She blinked rapidly, the tears falling and clearing her vision. Her heart raced as she looked down at Adam's gorgeous brown eyes staring up at her in a mixture of alarm, love, and temper. He wanted to do this...now?

Of course he did. This was Adam. He always reached for whatever he wanted when he wanted it. Her pulse raced.

"Let me see," she whispered, a bit breathlessly. She'd never gotten to really look at it with her own eyes.

Adam sat back and pulled her down into his lap, handing her the ring and wrapping his arms around her. Christopher hesitated before sitting down as well.

The solitaire was huge. Far too big. It would draw too much attention. It would look too ridiculous on her. She wore t-shirts and jeans. She didn't want people staring at her, and they would stare if she wore this.

She slipped it on, leaning her head against Adam's shoulder. He had chosen it because it was huge. Because it was monstrously expensive. Because it told the world she belonged to him and no one could ever take her away. If this were a dream, it was a good one.

She smiled, her eyes dewy and as sparkly as the diamond in front of her as she raised them to his.

"Okay."

His brows raised with a small laugh, his lips parting in a smile of his own. Had he thought she would say no again? And then he pressed her to him, groaning into her as he captured her mouth. She wrapped an arm around his neck, holding him tightly, as her hand crept to the side.

She breathed a sigh into Adam's mouth as Christopher's fingers laced through hers, and Adam lifted his lips long enough to glance over. His jaw clenched and she leaned up, kissing the sharp line until he turned back to plunge his tongue inside her.

"You better not be a fucking virgin again," he muttered, and she laughed with a groan as his hand started dragging her jeans off her hips.

Every breath she took filled her with Adam's scent. It was different here. Full of life. Larger than life. She remembered this scent. Her lashes fluttered open, her eyes watching him under heavy lids, and her heart jumped when his lashes lifted sightly to watch her as well. This was real. The light hadn't been trying to hurt them. It had tried to help them.

They had a second chance to do things right, and they knew so much now. They knew something about how the system worked. Christopher was good with systems. They would figure out what they needed to do. Between the three of them, and everything they had seen and done...they would figure this out.

A few minutes later, she wasn't worried about figuring anything out at all. All she could do was thank god she wasn't a virgin.

THOUGHTS

I know many find this story enraging, but please understand I am not advocating going light on rapists in the real world. This is a fantasy environment where the rapist had to literally go through Hell to earn some type of redemption.

I love redemption stories and wanted to show characters who went through true horror—the stakes were high to forgive. For Jo, the greatest horror was in discovering what she had endured at the hands of someone she had come to love. For Adam, it was discovering what had been happening right on the other side of the door *to* someone he loved. And for Christopher, the horror was discovering that *he* had done it, after finally learning to truly love.

Which horror is worse?

THANK YOU!

Fair reviews help so much, so please consider leaving one here, and thank you for your support!

https://Amazon.com/review/create-review?&asin=
B09CZFHYK3

To get exclusive content and the latest updates, please sign up for my newsletter below. I take your privacy and time very seriously and will only send the most important announcements.

https://www.lexietalionis.com/subscribe

BEHIND-THE-SCENES
LETHE BACKGROUND

Lethe origin

One of the earliest uses of the term *Lethe* in reference to the underworld occurred in Book X, section 621a, of Plato's *The Republic*, authored around 375 BC.

Plato refers to *tes Lethes pedion* or *the plain of Oblivion,* a "place of terrible and stifling heat [...] bare of trees and all plants."

While in later literature Lethe became associated with the "river of Forgetfulness" that ran through the plain, in the beginning it referred to the land itself.

The following has light spoilers about the world; do not read if you prefer to figure things out for yourself.

———

World building

Using the original meaning, I built an underworld that borrowed from various myths and religions. I wanted to suggest that every corner of the globe had obtained a piece of the truth, and over the years the stories took on different forms as people misheard, misconstrued, misremembered, or deliberately falsified. My world of Lethe is therefore not Greek or Hebrew or any other culture's mythology but an amalgamation of all.

Dante's Seventh Circle of Hell is for souls that have committed acts of brutality. I considered what would happen if the laws of the universe worked similar to our own penal systems, with Lethe operating as the maximum security unit. However, not all acts of violence are equal...and I'll say no more about that for now.

The male to female ratio in this world was modeled on the violent offender ratio in reality. My 10:1 ratio isn't precise, but it's close. For example, one U.S. Department of Justice report shows women account for about 14% of violent offenders. But 10 to 1 is more easily conceptualized, and this is fiction, so I rounded! Sorry to the men...

One final note of interest: Lethe refers not only to the moon they were on but to the entire small universe in which the moon resides. Everything within this universe has a function, and Jo, Christopher, and Adam have only been exposed to one of those functions...thus far.

Dreams of Lethe is the sequel in the trilogy and will reveal more, but Peter already exposed one important aspect when he conjectured that they were in a type of purgatory. They have not yet seen true Hell.

The nightmare has only just begun.

———

Personal Background

This story began in my mind back in 2012. I was going through a very rough patch as a single mother with sole custody in a highly competitive PhD program under a mountain of debt...and just as I reached the dissertation stage, my mother was in an accident where her husband was killed and she suffered brain damage. I had to take care of everything.

I could never tell all that entailed, so I'll just say it was a nightmare. To cope, I began building another world in my head with four characters who would weave in and out of various iterations of the tale I kept creating over the years.

And at the end of 2020, I decided to write one of the iterations down.

I know people see different things in this story. Some only see the sex and think it's porn. Others think it's some type of rape fantasy or rape apologist tale. But I see it as an expression of the pain I was in - darkness that you can't always defeat or escape but that you get to choose how to face. There is a fun fantasy element in it to me, but I regard the love as the fantasy. The support. The transformation of something hurtful—of some*one* hurtful—into the very thing that brings the greatest comfort.

It's not reality, at least not mine. But in this fantasy realm, it exists. And I hope some of you find the strange comfort in it that I have.

SNEAK PEEK

Unfated Mates

a fated/rejected mates trope twist series on Kindle, Kindle Unlimited, and in paperback

Nat climbed off the bus, turning her hooded face at the last moment to block the incoming snowball. Her head snapped a bit to the side from the force before the icy globe slid down the worn fabric of her jacket to plop back in the snow.

"Haha—yeah, hide your face, Medusa!" The boys jeered at her as the bus driver closed the door and rolled away. The only other girl who got off at her stop chastised the boys for being mean, but she was giggling as she walked with them to their homes.

Nat adjusted her backpack and trudged along in the opposite direction, tensing when a couple more snowballs hit her. One of the boys must have added a rock, because it stung even through the hood of her jacket. Thankfully she'd been able to find the puffy type this year—seventh grade had been so much worse. She hadn't been quite big enough yet to earn enough money for anything beyond school lunch, and everything had soaked through. And the rocks had left bruises.

She wanted to rub the back of her head, but she wouldn't give them the satisfaction of knowing they'd hurt her. For so long she'd dreamed that maybe when she grew up, she'd be pretty and they wouldn't pick on her anymore. But it didn't look like that was how it would turn out. Her body had gotten so much bigger this past year, blowing up in places that had always been flat before. She was suddenly taller than most the other girls, almost 5'6 now. Big and lurching. As good as being bigger was for working, she knew she was grotesque.

Frizzy long brown hair, always going everywhere. An ugly mouth with lips far too big for her face. Boring almond shaped brown eyes and a nose she hated. And horrible clothing that never fit her properly and someone else had already worn out. At least she was thin, so the *fat Nat* nickname they'd tried using never really caught on. There were some benefits to her mother constantly forgetting to buy food.

Her feet slowed as she neared the end of the lane where their trailer was parked, held up on cement blocks. Their neighbors had normal houses—she was the only kid at school who lived in a trailer. But it was better than the trailer park they'd been at when social services took her away. Safer. Except for when her mother's latest boyfriend-supplier showed up. Like today.

Nat came to a halt and stared at his truck in their drive. If her mother were awake, it would be fine. But if she'd already taken her pills…

Her eyes turned toward the woods far behind the trailer. It was cold today but not the worst it had been, and Missouri had plenty of hills and trees to block the wind, especially if she were deep inside the woods. She didn't need to think further and snuck around her neighbor's house, just in case *he* was looking out the window, before racing toward the line of trees.

The snow crunched beneath her sneakers and found its way

into her socks, numbing her toes by the time she made it to the trees. She glanced behind her. No one seemed to be stirring from the trailer. Should she just hang out at the perimeter? Coyotes roamed the hills out here, and every now and then someone's dog got dragged off, although she hadn't heard of anyone having a problem with them this year.

A screen door slammed far behind her, and her eyes flew back to the trailer in a panic.

"Natty…"

Her stomach lurched, and she abandoned all thoughts of coyotes as her feet raced through the woods, desperate to put as much space between her and the smiling man calling her name.

———

Ten minutes later and she stopped, putting a hand on her knee and one on her side, her icy fingers digging into her as she dragged the painfully cold air into her lungs. Her PE teacher was always getting on to her for being lazy in class, but Nat didn't know how other kids managed to run the track so easily. She ran out of breath so quickly, and her side always hurt.

Better keep going.

She stood up to start forward once more, still holding her side and wheezing while she walked over the fallen pine needles. The snow wasn't too deep in here. The trees had caught most of it, so at least her feet weren't getting any more wet than they already had. She tried stepping in the areas without snow, but she couldn't completely avoid leaving tracks.

The scent of the pine finally began to feel pleasant to her lungs again, and she sighed as she walked. He wouldn't really chase her all the way in here, would he? The forest around her was silent except for the occasional bird or squirrel and the sounds of her feet crunching the snow and bits of forest floor below.

Perhaps another thirty minutes passed before she stepped into a clearing, and her breath caught at the beauty. The trees grew in a circle around a space ten or twelve feet wide, their branches leaning over and creating a canopy that kept out most of the snow. Pine needles filled the area, producing the driest spot she was likely to find.

Dropping her backpack beside her, she sat down to pull off her shoes and socks. Was it cold enough out to get frostbite? Her toes were going to hurt either way once she could feel them again. She unzipped her jacket and pushed the hood off her head, gently feeling where she'd been hit. A groan escaped her, turning quickly into a whine. Life sucked sometimes.

At least flexibility wasn't a problem for her. She pulled her feet up on her legs, keeping them off the forest floor, and leaned forward to warm them against her midsection as she tried pulling the coat around her. It wasn't the most comfortable position in the world, but warmth seeped through to her feet, so it was worth it.

Leaning forward across her legs, she stretched her arms up above her. There was some yoga name for this position, but she couldn't remember what it was. Her memory was terrible. She held the position as long as she could before leaning back up with a groan.

Her body froze halfway through the movement.

In the distance, a bird cried out. The wind whistled through the trees in soft whispers, and the sharp, sweet smell of pine filled the air. Nothing else stirred.

And at the edge of the clearing, only five feet in front of her, a pair of amber eyes watched her above a long black muzzle and snarling white fangs.

The blood pounded in her ears, the air around her vibrating with each beat of her heart. Stay still. Don't panic. Think.

She knew almost nothing about animals, but this didn't look like a coyote to her. A deep, ebony black coat covered it from head to toe—or paw. Huge paws and terrifying jaws that looked large enough to bite off her entire head. Its ears stood straight up as a low growl began rumbling in its throat.

Nat's entire body jolted inside at the sound, but she forced herself to be still. Tears stung her eyes, but she tried not to blink. Tried not to break the stare. Afraid it would be the trigger that made it attack her.

So she stayed very still, half bowed, her vision blurring until the tears wouldn't be contained and they spilled down her cheeks. What could she do? Everything she could think of seemed wrong. She didn't know animals. Or even people, really. Not enough to prevent them from attacking her. But if this was it, if this was her death, she had to at least try something.

"Hi," she whispered.

The wolf's head perked up, and it stopped snarling. Hope sprang inside her. Maybe if she kept talking calmly…

"I'm Nat." Her heart raced, and she struggled with each breath. But it wasn't coming after her. "I didn't mean to come into your space. I was just trying to get away from…" She didn't want to say it even to herself. "A bad man," she whispered at last.

The wolf growled, and her stomach clenched, tears springing to her eyes once more. Why did she think she could talk to an animal? Her body ached from the position she was in, but she would hold it until the last moment. It was the only thing she could do.

Keeping her gaze locked on his, she struggled to control her fear. Her tears. But she didn't speak, and the wolf grew silent once more. They stared for what felt like hours but couldn't have been more than a few minutes.

Eventually the wolf lowered its head…and stepped forward into the clearing.

Panic shot through her, but once again she held herself still. She wasn't able to control her trembling, though, and her bare hands shook on the ground in front of her.

The wolf approached slowly, its eyes never leaving hers, until it stood directly in front of her, its head low and so close she could feel the warmth of its breath flowing across her cheeks. When it leaned in close to sniff her, she closed her eyes at last, biting back a whimper of fear. The wolf pulled back, but she couldn't make herself open them again. Was this what they did before they ate? Checked their food?

Tears choked her. She didn't know why she cared so much about dying. It's not like she had such a great life. But maybe one day, if she just kept going, she would be alone. Free.

When it didn't attack her after what seemed a very long time, she opened her eyes and her breath caught. It hadn't moved. Her heart raced when it leaned in once more to her face. Would it rip her skin off? Did they do that to the face? Or was it trying to reach her throat?

The warmth of its tongue lapping her cheek gently nearly made her collapse. Was it tasting her?

"I'm sorry I don't have any food." She couldn't control the tremor in her voice. "But please don't eat me."

The wolf whined, a small, short sound, but continued licking her cheeks. What did that mean? It wasn't biting her. Maybe… maybe it might not kill her.

She began leaning up slowly, very, very slowly, but it didn't stop licking her. Her heart hammered in her chest as she exposed her throat. Calm down. Animals could smell fear, right?

It whined again, and she jumped when a cold nose touched her neck as it lapped at her skin.

"Are you…really not going to eat me?" she whispered.

It rubbed its head against her, and her hands came up instinctively before she could stop herself. They both froze the moment her fingers touched its fur, and she stopped breathing, every muscle in her body locked in place as warm air flowed across her neck. Any moment now it would sink its teeth into her skin. Any moment.

Instead, it began licking her again.

She remained still, so afraid of being stupid. It couldn't actually like her, could it? It was a wild animal. And she was...her.

But the licking didn't stop.

Taking a shaky breath, she tentatively began petting the deep black fur. Warmth flowed into her fingers each time they slid through the thick coat, and amazed relief began thawing her rigid muscles. It really wasn't going to hurt her!

Eventually she decided to risk leaning her head against its body. When it didn't pull away, she sank her fingers deep into its fur with a sigh.

Her brow furrowed immediately. The coat was very thick but underneath, its body felt far too thin. She pulled back to eye the wolf more carefully, petting it gently. Petting *him*, based on what was hanging from his body, she realized. Heat rushed to her face as she suddenly felt unaccountably rude for having looked. But at least she could stop thinking of him as an *it*.

"When was the last time you ate?" she murmured. He whined again, and she stroked his fur. "I can bring you food, but I don't know what wolves eat. Maybe I can find something about it at school tomorrow. They have a computer in the library."

He growled, and she snatched her hands back. What had she done wrong? But he whimpered and licked her.

It took her a while before she risked petting him again.

"What am I going to do," she sighed. "I can't leave you to starve out here."

He growled again, but this time she only jumped a little. Then frowned.

"Are you growling because I'm talking?" He kept licking her. Stupid. Wolves can't understand people. She sighed again.

"I wish I could stay here with you." She looked up at the darkening sky. "But I better get back now. The creep should be gone, and I still need to figure out where *I'm* going to find food if he cleared the cabinets out again."

The wolf stepped back, his eyes bright on hers, and she wanted to cry. This was the most special thing that had ever happened to her. The only special thing really. How many people could say they had pet a wolf? She couldn't tell anyone though, not that they'd believe her. She didn't want a hunting posse coming in here.

"You be careful, okay? And thank you for not eating me."

The wolf growled again, but it didn't seem like an actual threat. She wiped her wet eyes and started putting her damp socks back on while he stood beside her, watching. The warmth of his body flowed into her in waves, and she wanted to stretch the moment out longer. But it was late, and the long walk back would just be colder the longer she delayed.

The wolf didn't move when she climbed to her feet, and she blinked in surprise to find his eyes nearly at her level. He really was huge.

"Can I hug you goodbye?" she whispered, so unsure of how to indicate her question to an animal. She hoped her body language and voice inflection somehow managed to do it.

Evidently it worked because he stepped in to rub his face against her chest, and she wrapped her arms around his neck, leaning in with a sigh. This moment needed to last in her mind forever.

Wetness filled her eyes again as she pulled back, but she turned away to start walking—only to stop again when he followed her to the edge of the clearing.

"Well...bye." A hesitant smile touched her lips before she set off through the trees, but when she felt the heat of his breath flowing over her neck a minute later, she stopped once more. "You shouldn't follow me, you know. Someone might see you and they'll send hunters in here after you."

He growled and pushed her forward with his head. She

continued walking but started to worry the longer he followed her.

"I wish I could make you understand me. It's dangerous for you. They go after even little coyotes—I can't imagine what they would do if anyone saw a wolf."

He just butted her again, and she kept going, trying to think of how to get him to go away. She wouldn't dare risk yelling or throwing something at him. Maybe he just wanted to make sure she got out of his territory.

She walked on, periodically stopping and trying to get him to turn around, but he never did. Eventually they reached the edge of the wood, and Nat paused.

"That's where I live." She pointed toward the trailer. "So you can stay here." She held her hands up, hoping it was some universal sign of *stay*. He hit the ground in front of her with his paws, and she sighed. She didn't understand him any better than he understood her.

He bit down on her backpack, holding her in place when she tried walking out, and she groaned.

"I have no idea what you want. I can't stay here. I'm human. I'll freeze."

He whined.

"I can bring you food…"

He growled.

"But I have to go! I don't want to. The guy I was running from is gone, and I need to see if he left any food for me to eat or go try to find some."

The wolf whined, licking her again, and she put her arms around him once more. Maybe she'd see him again. Maybe he'd stay in the area. But her stomach sank. If he did, he was sure to get killed by one of the crazy yahoos out here waving their guns around in the woods.

"Please, please be careful," she whispered. "These people aren't all the nicest people in the world."

But he finally let her step out into the clearing, watching while she walked away. Her vision blurred, and she turned to face the trailer once more, her shoulders sagging as the weight of everything waiting for her came back.

When she at last made it to her door, she looked back at the woods. His dark coat was barely visible against the dark backdrop of the trees, but he was still watching her. Watching over her? She scoffed at herself as she went inside.

Don't be ridiculous. He probably just wanted food after all.

ABOUT THE AUTHOR

Lexie Talionis is the pen name of a formerly very bored professor with a PhD in business who published in academic journals and developed a curious case of narcolepsy at the mere mention of having to read yet another academic paper.

But she will stay up all night slaving over heart-wrenching scenes of love, dreaming of the day readers will share in the trauma...and a few laughs along the way to the happy ending she promises to always deliver.

Thank you for sharing in my crazy daydream. :)

https://linktr.ee/LexieTalionis